Watch Me Burn
Watched in Darkness Book 2
V.E. Huntley

Watch Me Burn (Watched In Darkness (Book 2) is a work of fiction. The story, all names, characters, and incidents portrayed in this production are fictitious. No identification with actual persons (living or deceased), places, buildings, and products is intended or should be inferred.

Published in the United States by V.E. Huntley

The Cataloging-in-Publication Data is on file at the Library of Congress

Paperback ISBN 979-8-9933217-0-7

Ebook ISBN 979-8-9907982-9-8

Book Design by V.E. Huntley

Book Cover Design by C. David Photography & Design

First Edition 2025

To all my dark masked stalker-loving girlies out there who read Watch Me Break and thought, "Yes, this level of obsession is completely reasonable..."

If Damien had you reconsidering your stance on healthy boundaries and side-eyeing your hardware store's zip-tie section with newfound interest...

Then buckle up, my lovelies.

Because this one is going to leave you breathless, flushed, in need of a cold shower and possibly a priest.

Exactly how we like it.

Content/Trigger Warnings

This is not a full list, just the most triggering.

Please visit my website (https://vehuntley.com/) for the entire list of TWs.

This story contains the following dark themes, situations, and kinks that may be triggering for some readers: stalking, spying, primal play, fear play, breath play, obsessive behaviors, bondage, graphic violence, explicit sexual situations, pregnancy loss, animal neglect and cruelty (off page), medical treatment of abused/injured animals (NO on page animal abuse), a bullet grazes an animal but it is not badly injured.

If any of these (or the additional TWs listed on my website) are potential triggers for you, please do not read. I won't be offended.

Your mental health matters—do what's best for you.

Despite the content/triggers and dark elements in this series, it is a story full of love, laughter, desire, passion, found family and loyalty. At its core, it's a love story about two people destined for each other.

So, for those who still want to take this ride with me, enjoy.

Some secrets are worth keeping, even the deadly ones.

Chapter One

Luna

"I can't believe I let you talk me into this. Again."

Maren huffs beside me as we make our way over the last foothill behind the sanctuary. Shadow and Ghost run around us, roughhousing. Shadow's gray coat gleams in the morning light while Ghost's silver-white fur catches the sun. At least they like hiking with me.

The house comes into view first, followed by the main sanctuary building, then the barn, and the wolf enclosure at the edge. The sight never fails to take my breath away. I still have to pinch myself sometimes to believe it's real. That this beautiful place is mine.

In less than five years, I've built the property my grandfather left me into a haven for injured animals, where I can treat and heal the creatures I love so much. I channeled the heartbreak of losing him into something positive, meaningful, and worthy of his memory.

"Stop your complaining. Breathe the Colorado mountain air, look at the scenery. Soak it up before winter locks everything down."

"Winter's already fucking us up the ass."

She kicks at a clump of dead grass jutting through the thin layer of snow. We had a decent storm three nights ago and another dusting last night, but daytime temperatures keep melting it back to bare patches. By now, we should be knee-deep in powder. Instead, it's early November, and we can count the actual storms on one hand. The drought that started three years ago has become the new normal.

I adjust the small pack on my shoulders. I never hike these mountains without a stash of provisions, including bear spray, a taser, and an emergency first aid kit. These hills are too dangerous to be unprepared.

"You love winter as much as I do."

Maren makes a disgusted sound in her throat. "You're the only person on the planet I'd let get me up at the ass crack of dawn to traipse through the snowy, muddy foothills around your property." She takes a swig from her water bottle. "And the only reason I did is because you ignored all my texts last night about how dinner with Mr. Billionaire Sexy Pants went."

"Can you stop calling him that? I don't care how much money he has."

"But it never hurts when a man has more money than God." Her eyes narrow as she studies my face. "We've been hiking for almost an hour, and you're still dodging the subject. What's wrong? Tongue tired from putting it to work? Bet you're wishing you'd taken those handcuffs I offered, right?"

I've tried to put dinner and Damien's kiss out of my mind all morning, but the hike has given me too much time to think. That's why I wanted Maren to come with me. Her nonstop chatter was supposed to be my mental lifeline so I could avoid thinking about it, but in all honesty, my mind has been more on my wolf than on Damien.

He left me wrecked last night. Every step emphasizes the aches he left behind. Yet more than the soreness, it's his tenderness I keep replaying, the unexpected gentleness, a side of him I never thought I'd experience, that has left me raw.

All I've ever wanted is the weight of him, the connection that comes from having another person's naked body pressed against your own, that goes beyond slick skin and gasping breath. The part of sex that elevates it beyond the physical aspects and turns it into something sacred.

Almost everything we've had, everything we've done, has always been primal. Need and heat dragging us together in the dark. But somewhere along the way,

I've come to crave more than just rough possession and his hips driving into mine with an urgent, punishing rhythm.

My wolf left me sated, as always, my body bearing his marks both inside and out. One round instead of our usual three or four, yet I'm more exhausted than ever today. And this fatigue isn't so much in my body as in my mind, because something changed last night.

Something shifted. For the first time, it felt like more than fucking. It felt like he wanted more from me than just our mutual orgasms. My skin still tingles where his body grazed mine with the lightest touch, like a brand I can't escape. It's all I've wanted for so long.

That and his kiss.

If only he'd kissed me, everything would have been perfect. I want to taste him, the salt of him, the brush of his tongue, the moment when desire and tenderness collide. He could have left his mask on. As much as I yearn to unmask him, I'd trade the secret of his face for that single taste of his mouth claiming mine. Instead, he left me with the soft ghost of his body hovering above mine, like a promise dangling just out of reach.

Now I'm caught between hope and fear. Hope that last night meant he's capable of tenderness, that maybe, just maybe, we might be able to have more. And fear that I'm reading too much into a single moment of softness, because once I felt that shift from pure hunger to something deeper, I couldn't pretend it didn't happen.

Shadow bounds up to me, pressing his nose against my free hand, and I scratch behind his ears. Ghost hangs back, still cautious despite months of patient rehabilitation. He's come so far from the broken hybrid I first met, even so much as putting himself between me and Caleb last night. But wariness still lives in every line of his body. He's getting better, trusting me enough to stay close, but he still watches everything with cautious, hesitant intelligence.

"Hello? Earth to Luna."

Maren taps her foot against a patch of snow, waiting. My thoughts have wandered again, pulled into the quiet space where my mind goes more often now.

"What?"

"How was dinner with your rich-as-fuck hottie neighbor?"

I ignore her latest money comment. She doesn't care about his bank account. She just likes getting a rise out of me.

"It was nice."

"Nice?" Her voice goes up. "No. You are not using the word 'nice' right now. I want details. And there better be some dirty ones in return for getting my ass out of bed this fucking early."

My fingers touch my lips, where the memory of Damien's kiss lingers. The fierce possession of it had given way to a soft declaration of his desire that weakens my knees even now. Then I touch my throat. The fresh fingerprint bruises beneath my turtleneck still throb, where my wolf's hands gripped me as he punished me and made me his once again.

Two men. Two different kinds of desire. Two different ways of making me feel wanted.

"Hey." Maren snaps her fingers in front of my face. "That dreamy look tells me it was definitely more than 'nice.'"

"He's complex." I twist the cap on my water bottle, tightening and loosening it. "There are layers to him I wasn't expecting."

"Good layers or ogre onion layers?"

"Interesting layers."

That moment in my kitchen comes flooding back. The way Damien moved when he grabbed Caleb, the icy menace in his voice when he threatened him. So similar to that day with Mr. Pearson at Elk Fest, like glimpsing a predator beneath his polished surface.

"So, did it end in a tangle of sweaty limbs and sticky bodily fluids? Please say yes, please say yes."

I step around a fallen log. "No. We didn't have sex."

"That sucks." Her face falls, then she studies my expression, and her mouth quirks up. "But you've got that just-got-laid glow. Are you lying to me, Luna Marie? Did you get some billionaire dick last night and don't want to share?"

"We didn't have sex, Maren." I pause, heat creeping up my neck. "He kissed me, but that's it."

She lets out a little squeal and grabs my arms. "That man has a mouth that looks like it should come with a warning label. Does he know how to kiss?"

"Yeah, he does."

Jesus, does he know how to kiss.

"I fucking knew it. So, come on, spill. How was it? Scale of one to 'holy shit, I need to change my panties.'"

I roll my eyes and sigh. "You're the only woman I know who measures everything by how wet it makes her panties."

She shrugs. "That's how I judge the world. So?"

"It was... intense."

"Intense like 'I want to climb him like a tree' or intense like 'he's trying to eat me alive'?"

"Both. But in a good way."

"I'm so fucking jealous. So, are you going to see him again?"

"I don't know." I avoid her gaze, instead choosing to watch Ghost sniff at something in the underbrush as we slow our pace a little. "I mean, I like him, but I have so much going on right now, and I'm not sure I'm ready for a relationship."

Maren pauses in her stride to give me a pointed look. "Lu, I'm not asking if you're going to marry him, for Christ's sake. But how about a little fun? It's been over a year since you broke up with shithead Caleb. And Damien is fucking hot. What more do you need?"

I can't believe Caleb had the gall to show up here last night. Then there's the way he went from his smarmy attempt at being remorseful to grabbing and threatening me. Not that I expected any less after the way our relationship ended.

"It's complicated."

"Everything's complicated when you overthink it." Maren huffs as she steps over a puddle. "Which you usually do. But sometimes you just have to say, 'Fuck it,' and... fuck it."

If she only knew how much I fuck these days. How every night for almost two months, I've been claimed by a man whose face I've never seen, whose name I don't know, and whose touch sets me on fire in ways I never imagined were possible.

A man who's also a serial killer.

That's way too much truth for a morning hike. Caleb seems like a safer topic.

"Speaking of complicated. Guess who decided to make an appearance last night?"

"Who?"

"Caleb." My boot connects with a loose rock, sending it skittering ahead of us. "Showed up right before Damien arrived."

Maren stumbles mid-step and grabs my arm to steady herself. "What the actual fuck? What did he want?"

"The usual." We trudge across the low foothill that leads to the backyard. "Claimed he's changed, been in therapy, wanted to apologize in person. He even brought flowers because apparently that's what passes for accountability these days."

"And you told him to fuck right the hell off, right?"

"I tried. I heard him out. Let him in the door like I shouldn't have."

"Are you fucking serious?"

"I know."

"Restraining orders don't work if you let the assholes in your house."

"I said I know, Maren." She opens her mouth, then closes it when I glare at her. "Anyway, after I shut him down, that angry, violent side reared its ugly head, and he got grabby."

"Shit! Did he hurt you?"

"No, he didn't get a chance. Shadow lunged at him, and then Damien showed up." I can't suppress the small smile that curves my lips at the memory, even though something about it still doesn't feel quite right. "You should have seen it, Mar. He took one look at the situation and threw Caleb out. Grabbed him by the throat. I've never seen Caleb back down so fast."

"Good. Fucker. I can't believe he tried to put his hands on you again."

"Yeah, but I'm not surprised. I never should've let him in the house."

"Damn right, you shouldn't have. But I've gotta say I'm liking Mr. Sexy Silver Fox Superhero even more now."

A smile tugs at my mouth. Maren's collection of absurd nicknames for Damien seems to multiply by the day, each one more elaborate than the last.

"The way Damien handled him was pretty impressive."

But did I mean "impressive" in a positive or negative way? I shiver as I think about how he grabbed Caleb's neck and shoved him against the wall with little effort.

"Sexy and protective? Girl, you better lock that down before some other woman does. I still can't believe he's single. I wonder if he has a curved dick or something."

If only it were that simple. But how can I even consider starting something with Damien when every night I'm claimed by someone else, a man I want more than my next breath? A man who kills without even the barest hint of remorse.

The moral conflict tears at me. My wolf hunts animal abusers, monsters who torture the innocent animals I heal. Part of me thinks they deserve what they get. The other part of me, the doctor who took an oath to do no harm, recoils from the violence. How can I crave his touch when I know what those hands have done?

Shadow and Ghost lope ahead across the open meadow, their pace easy and relaxed. A deer lifts its head from grazing about thirty yards out, ears swiveling toward us.

I stop, grabbing Maren's arm. "Look."

The deer watches us for a moment, then goes back to nibbling grass. Shadow and Ghost glance at it with zero interest and keep moving toward the slope that leads down to my backyard.

Maren starts walking again. "Your animals are so chill about everything."

"They see wildlife every day. It's background noise at this point." I match her stride as we cross toward the low foothill. "Damien's response kind of reminded me of Elk Fest. I think he might have some underlying anger issues. I don't need another man like that in my life. Caleb was more than enough."

"Yeah, you don't need that shit, for sure. But it was kinda hot when he flattened Pearson without breaking a sweat. A woman should be able to protect herself, but having a man who turns into the Incredible Hulk when his woman is threatened gets my panties wet any day of the week."

"Is there anything that doesn't get your panties wet?"

Maren shields her eyes against the morning sun. "The thought of your ex showing up here unannounced last night dries me right the fuck up. I'm glad Damien showed up when he did, possible anger issues or not."

"Me too. As long as he doesn't turn on me. But I don't think Damien's like that. He has this quiet intensity about him. Intense but mellow. If that makes any sense."

"Yeah, quiet intensity beats explosive rage any day. And there's nothing wrong with mellow. It can be okay with the right guy. Look at JT. He's a big teddy bear. A teddy bear with some hot-as-fuck kinks, but did you ever think I'd last almost two years with someone like him?"

I hip-check her as we start down the last slope into the backyard. "Never in a million years."

"Seriously, Lu, I'm just glad you're at least considering something with some-one. You've been alone too long. You deserve to be happy."

"I am happy." The words sound hollow even as they leave my mouth.

Maren ducks under a low branch that crosses the path, holding it up so it doesn't snap back at me.

"Content isn't the same as happy. When's the last time someone made your heart race? Made you laugh until your sides hurt? Or made you feel like you're the most important person in their world? Besides me."

My wolf makes my heart race in a way that leaves me breathless. There's no laughter in our encounters, only raw, consuming need and satisfaction. In those moments, I do feel like the most important person in his world. But is that love or obsession? Is there even a difference with him?

It was different with Damien. Conversation that challenged and intrigued me. The security of his protection when he'd defended me against Caleb. He could offer me a real relationship, a normal life. Everything my wolf can't give me, no matter how much I'm starting to wish he could.

"Maybe you're right."

As we crest the final dip before the house, that familiar sensation washes over me.

I'm being watched. Again.

Awareness prickles my skin, and I scan the treeline. It feels different today, more intense than usual. Like last night on the porch.

Not at all like my wolf.

"Of course I'm right. You heard her say that, Shadow. You're my witness." Maren rubs her hands over Shadow's back, and he wriggles with delight. Ghost stands nearby, watching. Maren turns to him, her energy shifting, her voice dropping, and her movements gentling as she holds out her hand.

I watch with bated breath as he inches closer, one slow step at a time. He ducks his head, and her hand finds the spot behind his ears, tracing her fingers along his neck. The tight coil of his posture unwinds. He leans into her touch the way he always does, the way every creature seems to when she works her Maren magic on them.

I try to shake off the feeling of being watched as we approach the back of the house, but my gaze keeps drifting to the shadows between the trees to the west.

The back door of the sanctuary building bursts open, and Tate comes running out, chasing after a blur of gray and black fur.

"Ricky, get back here!"

But the raccoon is already bounding toward us with surprising speed.

"Oh, for fuck's sake," Maren mutters as Ricky makes a beeline straight for her.

He launches himself at her, scrambling up her body like she's a tree. His hands make a grab for her boobs, and she blocks him while trying to maintain her balance.

She holds him at arm's length as he chitters. "Why are his paws covered in peanut butter?"

"Sorry!" Tate pants as he reaches us, his glasses askew. "I gave him a frozen pop while I cleaned their enclosure. The door must not have latched."

"Why can't you be a normal raccoon?" Maren sighs as Ricky wriggles in her grasp, his paws flailing.

"Here, let me take him." I laugh, and she hands him over.

The moment Ricky is in my arms, his sticky paws move toward my breasts. I grab them before he can make contact, holding them against his body with a stern look. He meets my eyes with a challenging gaze of his own before letting out a small sigh and resting his head on my chest.

"Nice try, buddy." He looks up at me with those dark, mischievous eyes that get me every time.

Maren heads toward the house. "I'm going to take a shower. I hope you have eggs because I'm in the mood for an omelet."

"Hey, Shadow. Hey, Ghost." Tate crouches to greet the wolves. Shadow goes to him for pets, while Ghost maintains his cautious distance but doesn't retreat. Shadow's aggressive with most men, except for a handful. He's never forgotten the men who killed his mother in front of him when he was a pup. And before coming here, Ghost had only known cruelty at the hands of humans.

I look down at Ricky in my arms, his body warm against mine. The conflicting feelings I've been wrestling with all morning come rushing back.

Back to the incredible feeling of my wolf's partial weight on me last night. And then to Damien's kiss. Both men spark wild, forbidden feelings within me. But how do I reconcile my burgeoning feelings for someone who represents safety and normalcy with my craving for someone who embodies danger and darkness?

I don't understand how I'm developing feelings for Damien when all I want is more from my wolf.

Then again, maybe that's why.

Chapter Two

Damien

I lean back in my chair, my gaze fixed on the bank of monitors mounted on the wall of my Denver office. I haven't been here for weeks, but I needed to handle a few things that couldn't be done remotely, so I flew down before dawn.

The central screen shows Luna's kitchen, where she and Maren sit at the table, still flushed from their morning hike. Steam rises from their coffee cups as they dig into a frittata and toast. I'd watched Luna shower after their return, water cascading over her perfect body, and then move through her kitchen with that grace that never fails to captivate me.

If she knew about the cameras in her bathroom, she'd castrate me. I'd installed them with her security system months ago. I wanted access to her everywhere, including her private spaces. I felt no remorse at the time. Still don't, if I'm honest. But now that my obsession has grown into love, there's a twinge of guilt for invading her privacy.

She's aware her wolf hacks into the sanctuary's cameras and scolds him for being a creep, but she doesn't know the number of cameras and that they're inside her bedroom and bathroom.

She also doesn't know I'm her wolf. The masked stalker and serial killer who comes to her in the darkness. The man who ties her up, chokes her, and fucks her until she's sobbing and coming on my cock so many times, she nearly passes out.

I've taken steps to hide my identity. The silver wolf mask covers most of my face except my mouth, hiding the silver threading through my hair at the temples, which I've heard Luna tell Maren she loves. I use a different soap. No aftershave.

And I go to extreme lengths to disguise my voice. What started out as a way to anonymously take her, claim her, and make her mine has now spiraled into a duplicitous double life that I'm losing control of.

The struggle to keep my identities separate is reaching a breaking point. The lines are blurred, and I won't be able to keep them separate much longer. Not if I want more with Luna than just what we have in the dark. Heat, passion, and a connection that defies logic.

When it began, she didn't know Damien Wolfe, so it was easier for the mask to conceal my identity. Now that we're spending more time together in daylight, she's noticing the cracks in my carefully crafted facade.

Once she discovers my deception—that her dark, masked, serial killer lover is also her billionaire neighbor who donated a quarter of a million dollar security system to her wildlife sanctuary and paid off both her mortgage and student loans—the betrayal might be too much.

Who the fuck am I kidding?

I'll lose her. And that can't happen. Living without Luna Foster—her light, her goodness, her warmth—isn't an option.

"We need to figure out an outdoor space for Titus."

The sound of Luna's beautiful voice through the speakers draws me out of my thoughts.

"He's come a long way, but he's getting depressed being kept inside."

"He didn't hiss at me when I touched him yesterday." Maren takes a bite of her toast. "I was starting to think you were the only one he'd ever let touch him."

"He still hisses at me most of the time, too."

Luna leans back in her chair and sweeps a damp strand of her long blonde hair behind her ear. My hand twitches. I want to reach through the screen, wind those strands around my fingers, and feel the silk of them again. Heat crawls up my neck and settles in my chest, then drops lower. My pulse kicks up, drumming in my throat, my wrists, everywhere.

"But then you do whatever Luna voodoo you do on animals, and he rolls over and lets you rub his belly."

Luna laughs, and the sound wraps around me. When we're tangled together in the dark, she gives me other sounds. Broken moans and desperate gasps that drive me to the edge of my sanity. Those sounds burn through me, set my blood on fire, but this laugh—this laugh—I want to chase, capture, and coax it from her lips again and again.

"I've been pricing out materials for an enclosure. Something separate from the wolf area and far enough from the barn that the horses won't spook. And away from Gertie's outdoor pen."

"Because that goat's already got enough attitude without a bobcat making her paranoid." Maren takes a bite of her eggs. "How much are we talking?"

"More than I have." Luna sighs, defeat written into the sag of her shoulders. "I still think I should talk to the bank about another mortgage."

"No, Lu, don't get yourself into that again." The words come out firm and protective. "Are there any more grants we can apply for? I'll fill out the paperwork."

"I don't think we can get more from the state, but we can try for a few more federal grants. They're not for wildlife, but considering we have a handful of domestic animals, we might be able to sneak in under their guidelines."

"What about a fundraiser?"

"Maybe. But we need to get it built before the heavy snow starts. Otherwise, we'll have to wait until spring. I can't bear the thought of him going through the entire winter in that indoor cage." Luna's chin lifts, determination hardening her features. "Maybe I can get a small mortgage so we can get it built, and then we can have a fundraiser in the spring so I can pay it off."

Maren lifts her coffee cup, and she takes a long sip, watching Luna over the rim. "I said this a while back, but why don't you hit Damien up? Go to his foundation?"

"No." Luna shakes her head, defiance flickering in her eyes. "He's already donated the security system. I'm not going to take advantage of his generosity like that."

"Then take advantage of your relationship with him. The man is a billionaire, and he kissed you last night."

"No, Maren. One kiss doesn't make a relationship. I don't know if it even meant anything. And he's done enough. I'll figure it out. I always do."

"Well, let me know what you need me to do." Maren sighs, then her lips curve into a smirk. "If I've gotta blow someone, I will."

Luna snorts as she takes another bite of her frittata.

"Does JT know you make those kinds of offers?"

"He knows I'll do anything for you and these animals."

"Well, I don't think that'll be necessary, but I appreciate the offer."

"I'll do it. Not Damien, though. I'll leave that to you." Maren's teasing grin turns serious. "Speaking of figuring things out, we never finished talking about Caleb showing up last night. That asshole has some balls violating the restraining order. I would've killed to see Damien throw him out."

The veins in my temple throb, sending sharp pulses through my skull as Hunter's name leaves Maren's lips.

Luna frowns. "I don't want to think about him right now."

"You should call Karen so it's on record in case anything..." Maren trails off, and my hands clench into fists.

Cade strides into my office without knocking, interrupting the overlapping fantasies of Caleb's pain as his warm blood coats my hands.

My COO's short salt and pepper hair is perfectly styled, his charcoal suit immaculate despite the early hour. He moves like a man twenty years younger than fifty-five, thanks to decades of discipline that started in the Rangers.

"We need to discuss tonight's target." He settles into the chair across from my desk as I lower the camera's volume. "Julian Pembroke. You sure you want to grab him from the parking garage?"

Dragging my attention from Luna's image on the screen requires conscious effort. My eyes want to drift back.

"There's minimal foot traffic after 8 PM. Put the cameras on a loop, and it'll be a clean entry and exit. Why are you even asking me about this? You don't usually worry about how I grab them?"

"You've been a little distracted."

"I've stopped leaving corpses to be found. I'm following disposal protocols again. Everything's contained." My impression of his pissed-off voice is so off the mark, it fails to elicit even a subtle change in his expression.

"Thank fuck. I'm glad you decided I was right. What changed your mind?"

"Not you."

"Dr. Foster tired of the sheriff's visits?"

Fucker!

Luna asked me to stop leaving bodies on her property. Demanded it. So I started leaving them on various trailheads in Rocky Mountain National Park. I wanted her to know when an abuser paid the price for his or her crimes, but she didn't appreciate my gifts or Sheriff Mills' repeated visits after the bodies were discovered. So I stopped, determined to heed her wishes. Now, Cade is back to handling the cleanup and disposal. I'll have to find some other way to show her my devotion when I've eliminated the filth that makes her cry.

Besides, the sheriff is a better detective than I gave her credit for. And ever since Pearson's body was found, after our altercation at Elk Fest, Mills has been sniffing around me.

"Let's take a break from anyone in Luna's files for a while, unless a gruesome or urgent case comes in. We should focus more on targets out of state."

He nods. "Any particular area in mind?"

"East Coast. Florida to Maine."

"Our East Coast list is long." Cade takes out his phone, and his thumbs move across the screen. "There are lots of abusers in New England. Good call. I'll get started on a priority list today."

Death rolls off his tongue like quarterly reports—clean, organized, and stripped of emotion.

"Are you going to be able to tear yourself away from the doctor for the trips?"

I give him a look cold enough to frost glass. "Let me worry about my time with Luna. Just be prepared to assist."

Cade and I are both licensed pilots. When we have a target outside Colorado, he flies my plane while I handle the hunting and capture. The kills themselves and the disposal—those always happen here. On familiar ground where we control every variable.

"We need to talk about Caleb Hunter."

"Dr. Foster's ex? What about him?"

"He showed up at her house last night, before our dinner. Grabbed her arm and threatened her." Rage kicks through my system like adrenaline. My hand curls into a fist on the desk. "I threw him out, but he's a problem that needs solving."

"How?"

"Permanently."

"Damien." Cade leans forward, his voice taking on that lecturing quality I hate. "We don't kill innocents. Animal abusers. Child predators, when we come across them. The genuine monsters of the world. That's our code. That's what separates us from common murderers."

"He's an asshole who threatened Luna."

"We can't kill him just because he's a shitty person."

Cade is right, but the visceral need to eliminate any threat to her drowns out the logical part of my brain.

"He threatened her. He is a threat to her. Therefore, he's forfeited his right to breathe."

"Then we watch him." Cade leans back in the chair.

"You weren't able to find him two months ago. You said he was a ghost with no digital footprint for over a year."

"But now he's shown his face. I'll backtrack. You should have called me last night. I could've gotten a jump on it. What kind of vehicle does he drive?"

"I didn't notice. Check the exterior cameras and get the plate. Track him. I want eyes on him twenty-four seven until I decide what I want to do with him."

My eyes drift back to the screen behind Cade's head. Luna and Maren have finished eating but are still at the table talking. Something Maren says makes Luna throw back her head and laugh, and my chest tightens again. Her friend can be a little much sometimes, but the joy she brings to Luna's life is priceless.

Luna's fingers drift to her mouth as she speaks, and my lips pulse with the echo of hers, a phantom sensation that won't quit. I can still taste the sweetness clinging to her tongue, along with the small catch in her breath when I pulled her closer and she melted against me.

That kiss didn't just change everything. It obliterated me, stripping away every lie I'd told myself, then rebuilt me from the wreckage.

My father's voice echoes in my head. Weakness, attachment, and vulnerability. All the things he beat out of me by the time I was ten. I've spent years building walls no one could scale, convinced that part of me had been burned away with everything else in the wasteland of my childhood, long before I understood what it was.

Love.

I roll the word around in my mind like broken glass, cutting myself on its edges. What pulses inside my chest defies every clinical definition I know. It's not possession, though I want to own every breath Luna takes. It's not obsession, though she consumes every waking thought. It's something that gnaws at my bones, a fever that burns without breaking.

The realization explodes inside my skull and leaves me bleeding and raw. She's pulled me under her spell, and I'm suffocating on the sweetness of it. I'm fucking drowning in her. There's no surface to break through, and no air to breathe that isn't her.

"You seem more distracted than usual today."

Cade's voice pulls me back. My head jerks, and my gaze snaps to his face. But he's not looking at me. His eyes are locked on the screen.

On Maren.

His expression holds that same granite composure he wears like armor. It only cracks when his daughter Mary Jane enters a conversation or during those rare childhood visits when she'd light up his office with her presence. She turned twenty-two recently, though I haven't seen her in years.

But then his face shifts as Maren crosses the kitchen, his eyes tracking her with the intensity of a hunter watching prey, absorbing every detail and every angle. The naked desire in his gaze is unsettling. I'm seeing something he didn't intend to share, something that wasn't meant for witnesses.

What the fuck?

This can't be the first time he's seen her. He monitors Luna's system, checking the camera feeds every couple of days to ensure nothing is amiss. Except for the ones inside Luna's house. Those belong to me alone. But Maren lives all over that sanctuary. He's had to see her dozens, if not hundreds, of times by now.

I file that observation away for later consideration. Whatever obsession is brewing behind Cade's eyes, it's the last thing Maren needs in her life. It spells trouble for a woman who isn't even aware she's being hunted.

"You're the one who seems distracted."

His head snaps toward me, eyes flashing with irritation I've seen maybe a handful of times in twenty-five years, the look he saves for when I've crossed a line he didn't know he'd drawn.

"How'd dinner go last night?" The question comes out smooth, designed to pull attention away from his fixation on Maren.

"Mind your own fucking business, Cade."

His eyebrows rise, but his expression remains otherwise unaffected.

Luna's mouth crashes through my memory—soft, yielding, perfect—then the crushing weight of guilt follows like a tidal wave. Every lie I've fed her sits heavy in my chest, two sides of myself at war until I can't breathe. My tie constricts around my throat. I tear it free.

Both versions of myself want her with equal desperation. The polished executive wants her laughter over wine and her smile when she heals an animal in her care. The wolf wants her gasps in the dark and her back arching under his touch.

But beneath both burns something more fundamental. The need for her to see through every mask and choose to stay.

"Just do your fucking job." I turn my attention back to the monitors.

Cade doesn't back down. Never has. Not since that night twenty-five years ago when he walked in on something he wasn't supposed to see. I was twenty-one and still perfecting my methods, still green and careless enough that my COO pieced together what his young boss did when the sun went down. He figured out what lived beneath my skin, what I became when no one was watching.

"I was thinking about Desert Storm yesterday."

I freeze. Cade rarely brings up his military service, and never the incident that ended his career. The classified mission that went sideways, the one that left him with blood on his hands and a discharge that looked honorable on paper but destroyed everything he'd worked for.

"Why?"

"Because it reminded me why I do this. Why I help you." His voice takes on that haunted quality it gets when he talks about the war. "Some people deserve to die, Damien. They trade away their right to breathe when they choose cruelty."

It's the same conversation we had that night in 2000, when he walked into my office after hours and found me cleaning blood from under my fingernails. Instead of calling the police, he'd looked me in the eye and said, "You're going to need help if you want to keep doing this without getting caught."

He was thirty then, already carved hollow by things he'd done in service to his country. I was a kid with too much blood money and vengeance that ate me alive from the inside. He became my right hand, my cleaner, and the voice of reason when mine drowned in fury. Twenty-five years later, he's the closest thing I have to family.

Which makes his protective behavior both touching and fucking infuriating.

"I know what I'm doing with Luna."

"Do you?" His gray eyes search my face. "Your survival is my business, Damien, and you're getting careless. All for a woman you barely know."

I look back at the screen, where Luna is filling the dishwasher, but the tension in her shoulders remains. That bastard of an ex is still affecting her even when he's not here, and that strengthens my resolve to hunt him down, wrap my hands around his throat and feel his pulse stutter and fade.

"I know every fucking inch of her, Cade. And she's everything."

The confession tastes like freedom, but speaking it out loud doesn't solve the problem burning through my veins. It just makes it more real. It confirms what I've been trying to deny and that I was lying through my teeth a second ago. I'm way in over my head.

"I don't know what the fuck to do."

"Start by not killing her ex-boyfriend." He doesn't miss a beat. "We've avoided killing innocent civilians for twenty-five years. Let's not start now."

"He's not innocent." My jaw clenches so tight that a dull ache spreads toward my temple. "I want every available resource focused on finding him. Wolfe Technologies has the most advanced AI tracking system in the world."

"And then what?"

Silence stretches between us. We both know the answer. I'll watch him and wait for him to give me a reason for what's already decided. If he so much as looks at Luna wrong again, he's a dead man.

"One more thing." I glance back at the screen, but Luna's kitchen sits empty now. "Make an anonymous donation to Luna's sanctuary. One hundred thousand. Enough to build her bobcat enclosure and then some."

Cade raises an eyebrow. "Anonymous how? She'll ask questions about a donation that large."

With a few quick strokes on my keyboard, the screen changes to inside the sanctuary's main room. Luna is going about her morning business of greeting and feeding the animals.

"Figure it out. Not the same trust we used to pay off her debts. And make sure she can't trace it back to me." She shouldn't have to struggle when I have more money than I can spend in ten lifetimes. "And do it today."

"This is only going to make her more suspicious if she digs."

"She won't. She needs the money too much to question its source." At least, I hope she won't. But even if she does, it's worth the risk to see the worry about that bobcat disappear from her beautiful face.

Cade clears his throat as his eyebrow arches. "If you're done mooning, can we hit today's highlights?"

I drag my attention back to business as we prepare for the morning meetings that pulled me to Denver, away from the mountains where my heart lives. But my eyes keep shifting to the screen over Cade's shoulder. Luna is feeding what looks like oatmeal to that pervy raccoon of hers, as he keeps trying to grab her breasts.

Part of my mind stays fixed on the impossible problem of loving someone who doesn't know I'm deceiving her. When she finds out that her wolf and Damien are the same man, she'll run from me. Never forgive me.

And I'd rather live with this aching deception than lose her. Even if it destroys me.

Chapter Three

Damien

The lingering scent of death permeates the air in the basement. It should make me gag, but all it does is give me purpose and excitement. Even after forty years, the scent of the girls who died screaming within these walls at Jeremiah Morrison's hands still clings to the stone foundation. Tonight, it mingles with Julian Pembroke's terror, sweat, and the metallic tang of fresh blood.

I've spilled more blood in this basement in four months than Morrison did in two years. But I don't kill innocents. Only monsters.

Julian sways from the ceiling beam, suspended by chains I installed last week. They creak as he twists, blood trickling from his shackled wrists down his forearms. The silver wolf mask covers my face, its familiar weight a comfort as I circle my prey.

Through the eyeholes, I study the man who's been running an illegal fighting ring for exotic cats in warehouses across Colorado.

"You know what you did."

My voice cuts through the basement's silence, and Julian's broken face snaps toward the sound. Cold satisfaction spreads through my chest at the terror that floods his eyes.

"Please." Blood and saliva bubble at the corner of his split lip. "I don't know what you're talking about."

The lie hits me like a match to gasoline. Heat floods through my chest and down into my hands, fingers curling into fists so tight my knuckles go white.

I've spent weeks documenting his crimes. The starved jaguars forced to fight to the death, the mountain lions with broken bones left to suffer, and the young lynx bred in captivity for one purpose. All so rich assholes could bet on which magnificent creature would die first.

I pick up the cattle prod from my table of tools. "Let me refresh your memory."

The electricity arcs across his ribs, and his screams echo off the stone walls, vibrating through my bones, awakening the same primal satisfaction I feel when Luna arches beneath me.

"The warehouse in Commerce City." I move the prod to his thigh. "Twenty-three big cats found dead. Some still in their cages, others torn apart in your fighting pit."

Another jolt. Julian convulses against the chains, his body a symphony of pain that I conduct like a maestro.

"You made them fight to the death, then didn't even bother to dispose of their ravaged bodies." The rage builds in my voice despite my efforts to stay controlled. "Beautiful, powerful creatures reduced to entertainment for degenerates with too much money."

I place the prod back on the table and select a pair of bolt cutters. Metal reflects the dim light, and Julian's face drains of what little color remains.

"No, no, please—"

The bolt cutters bite through the flesh and bone of his index finger. The wet, grinding sound carries through the basement. Julian's scream splits the air, high and desperate, the sound of a man discovering what real pain means. Blood sprays across my black shirt, warm droplets soaking into the fabric in patterns that look almost artistic. My pulse kicks up, heat spreading through my chest and down my arms.

"That was for Diablo." I collect the severed digit, tossing it onto the workbench. "The jaguar you starved for two weeks before his final fight."

His middle finger is next. Julian's eyes bulge until the whites show all around, veins standing out on his forehead like rope beneath his skin. When the metal shears through the bone, his head whips back and forth, the tendons in his neck going taut. The howl that rips from his throat hits something deep inside me, satisfying a craving that nothing else touches.

"That's for the pregnant lynx you forced into the pit."

Julian's consciousness wavers as I work through my list. Each animal he tortured earns him the loss of a finger, each crime extracted from his body piece by piece. The smelling salts become necessary when his mind tries to shut down, tries to flee into unconsciousness. I snap the capsule under his nose, dragging him back to the present. He doesn't get to escape. The creatures in his arena never got that mercy.

"Do you know what the beautiful thing about pain is?" I select a serrated blade from my collection. "How it clarifies priorities. All those things that seemed important before—money, power, reputation—they become meaningless when you're drowning in agony."

I drag the knife across his chest, the blade parting skin like scissors through silk. Blood wells up in the cut's wake, a deep red line that blooms wider. The wound goes deep enough to sear nerve endings but misses anything vital. He needs to feel this.

His body jerks against the chains, metal rattling against metal. Fresh waves of pain hit him, and broken sobs rip from his throat. The sounds are raw and animal-like, and my pulse hammers harder. My fingers clench around the knife handle as his tears cut tracks through the filth coating his face, mixing with the crimson mess until everything runs together. Each gasping breath, each whimpered plea pays down a debt owed to creatures who never got the chance to beg.

I bring my face close to his, the mask filling his field of vision. "You're going to die slowly, piece by piece, like those cats did. And when you're begging for death, I'm going to remind you about every innocent animal that suffered because of your greed."

The next hour is a masterpiece of controlled violence. My pulse hammers against my throat as I carve justice into Julian's flesh, keeping him balanced on the knife's edge between consciousness and oblivion.

Blood roars in my ears with each slice of the blade, my hands steady as electricity crawls up my spine, every nerve ending alive with purpose. I reach for my mini blowtorch. Sweat trickles down my temples as I drag the flame across his skin, the smell of burning flesh filling my nostrils. Each burn, each cut becomes an offering to the beautiful creatures he destroyed.

The tiger cubs born in captivity and killed for sport, the elderly cougar who lasted three minutes against a younger opponent, and the beautiful snow leopard who died of infected wounds because veterinary care cut into profits.

When Julian is more blood than man, his consciousness hanging by a thread, I lift the silver mask from my face. Cool air hits my sweat-slicked skin as his battered eyes fight to focus. Recognition dawns behind the blood and swelling, his pupils dilating with fresh terror.

"Damien... Wolfe?" Blood foams at the corners of his mouth with each syllable.

"My Luna could have healed all of them if given the chance, but she'll never know about them or you because it would make her cry. And for that, you'll burn in hell."

I grab his hair, forcing his head back as I reach for my knife again. I drive the blade through his left eye. It enters with a soft pop and a whisper of resistance before sliding home. His body jerks once, twice, then hangs limp from the chains.

My breathing sounds thunderous in the sudden quiet. I step back, wiping the blade on my sleeve. My breathing slows. The knife handle is warm and slick in my palm. For the first time tonight, my shoulders relax, and my jaw unclenches.

I pull out my phone and dial Cade. "Come and get him."

"On my way down."

Cade's footsteps echo on the stairs a minute later. His eyes sweep the room, pausing on the crimson spatter on my clothes and across the wall, the still-warm body suspended in the center. He reaches into his pocket for latex gloves, his fingers sliding into them before reaching up and releasing Pembroke's wrists from the chains.

"Messier than usual."

"He deserved it." I'm already stripping off my blood-soaked clothes, stuffing them into the incinerator bag. I check my watch and curse. "Fuck. Luna is probably asleep."

I hate having to wake her up, but I need her. She's the only peace I can hope for.

"Then you better get moving. Wouldn't want to keep the doctor waiting."

His tone carries an edge that makes my head whip toward him, especially after our conversation today, but his expression reveals nothing, other than a slight tightness around his eyes.

"Problem?"

"I'm curious how you compartmentalize this." He gestures at Julian's corpse. "How you go from torturing a man to death to whatever it is you do with her? She appears unharmed, but how do you shake off this violence when you put your hands on her?"

It's not difficult. The violence satisfies one part of me, while Luna feeds another. I can't survive without either of them now, but I don't expect Cade to understand that.

"I've been compartmentalizing for twenty-five years," I remind him.

"Not like this. Not with someone you..."

Not with someone I love.

The question is far too personal, but I decide to answer.

"Being in her presence, her very existence, chases away the violence."

He nods and gets to work as I head upstairs to shower. The hot water strips away the basement's stench while I scrub with the soap and shampoo I always use before I go to her. No cologne, no designer products, just clean flesh that won't betray my double identity. My reflection stares back from the steamed mirror. This double life has to end soon, but tonight I need to lose myself in Luna without the fear of her discovering the truth.

Athena greets me when I exit the bathroom, demanding attention I'm happy to give. My pulse shifts as I scratch behind her ears, my blood cooling from the fever pitch of violence.

The drive and short walk to Luna's sanctuary complete the transformation from killer to lover.

By the time I reach her back door, Julian Pembroke is a closed chapter. There's only Luna, waiting for me with her warm body and that beautiful smile that makes me believe I might be more than just a monster after all.

Chapter Four

Luna

I wake with a start, my eyes adjusting to the darkness of my bedroom. My heart leaps into my throat as I make out the familiar silhouette standing at the foot of my bed. Towering shoulders, lean hips, and the unmistakable silver wolf mask glinting in the moonlight.

My body responds before my mind fully wakes. My lips part on a soft exhale, and heat unfurls through me like opening petals, starting in my chest and spiraling lower until it pools warm and insistent between my thighs. The familiar ache of want burns beneath my skin as I drink in the sight of him standing like a dark sentinel at the end of the bed.

He's positioned himself in the shadows, the way he always does. I've never gotten a clear look at him, not in all the nights we've done this. Not really. He ensures that. Always staying where the light barely touches him, taking his pleasure from me in the dark, where I can't truly see him, where his identity remains concealed by shadow and silver.

Even in our most intimate moments, when he's buried deep inside me and his body hovers over me, my eyes can only catch fragments. The burning intensity of his stare behind that carved metal, and the way his jaw clenches as he's about to fill me with his come. The shadows offer me glimpses, maddening pieces that make me desperate for more, but never satisfaction. Never enough to truly know him.

He refuses to let me turn on any lights. Not the bedside lamp, not the bathroom light, nothing that might illuminate him properly. Only a handful of times has there been more than just pale moonlight to see him by.

Like the time in my office after he'd killed Odell Pearson. But my small desk lamp did nothing to offer more than what I'd already seen in the shadows of my kitchen or bedroom or living room. He knows how to wield darkness like a tool, how to give me his body while revealing none of the truths that matter.

The air in the room shifts, charged with an electric tension that makes the hairs on my arms stand up. I stretch beneath the sheets, arching enough to let him see how his presence affects me, the hard peaks of my nipples pressing against the thin cotton of my pajamas.

Doubt had tugged at me until I fell asleep, thinking he might not visit tonight. But he always shows. Except for a handful of times, he's come to me every night since we've started this... what? Affair? I'm not even sure what to call it.

But here he is, watching me from behind that wolf's face. Fire trails across my skin under his stare. My thighs clench at the memory of last night. His shirt whispered across my nipples, his body grazing mine, like a gift before he'd pulled away and left me aching for what he'd offered and stolen back, leaving me wanting and unsure if I'd ever have it again.

A sharp pang of longing twists behind my ribs. I force it down. This thing we have has rules, and wanting more isn't one of them. But that truth leaves a gaping wound where my heart keeps forgetting its place.

I push it away. It's better to focus on what's real—the hunger pouring off him in waves despite his stillness and the wild beat of my pulse against my throat. I sit up, and the sheets slide down, gather at my waist, and expose skin around my neck, marked with the shape of his fingers. I lock eyes with him, holding that masked stare without flinching.

"You're late."

"I had business to attend to tonight."

I arch a brow. "You mean you killed someone?"

"Do you really want to know?"

The smirk on his lips is visible even in the dim light. It makes me want to slap him or spread my legs for him. Maybe both.

Of course, he killed someone. The tension radiating off him is palpable on the nights he kills, the air around him thick with it. At first, those nights were brutal, his touch rough and punishing. But now, that tension seems to dissipate minutes after he gets here, after he's inside me, as if being in my presence, in my body, calms him.

I glance over at Shadow, who sits on the floor waiting for attention. His relaxed posture is the reason I trust the man standing in front of me. If he meant me harm, Shadow would protect me.

"He knows I'll never hurt you, Luna," he says, as if reading my thoughts. "At least not any more than you want me to."

My body's response is instant, my nipples tightening even further beneath the thin fabric of my pajamas until every breath scrapes them raw. When did I become a woman who craves a killer's touch? And when did my prayers change from "keep him away" to "bring him back"?

His gaze drags down my body like fingertips, claiming what it sees. My core throbs with need, slick and ready for a man who's carved himself into almost every corner of my life. I crave him, his hands on my skin, and his weight pinning me down. I want to feel crushed beneath him until breathing becomes a luxury.

The mask keeps his secrets locked away. He could tell me his name and let me see the face that haunts my dreams. Instead, he feeds me darkness, and I swallow it whole, starving for more.

Damien tries to surface in my thoughts, but I bury him where he belongs. Not now. Not when my wolf stands before me like some dark god, beautiful and fierce behind that mask, danger radiating from every muscle, and looking at me like I'm his next meal.

This moment belongs to the man who makes me forget every rule I've ever lived by. Sanity feels overrated when he's close enough to touch, all power and control and dark promise.

He scoops up the cats sprawled across my comforter, their sleepy protests cut short by a snap of his fingers toward the hallway.

"Out. What I'm about to do to her is not for your innocent wolfy eyes."

Shadow exits the room without hesitation, and my other wolf closes the door behind him. My heartbeat echoes in the sudden quiet.

"Take off your clothes." He moves to the foot of the bed again. "Then lie back."

The command flows through my bloodstream like liquid fire. My heart skips, then races, a flutter beneath my ribs as my fingers find the first button of my pajama top. The smooth plastic slips against my fingertips once, twice, before I manage to work it free.

"Slowly. We're in no rush, little doe."

The air between us thickens. I draw a steady breath and fight to still my trembling hands. The second button slides free, then the third, each release punctuated by the taut flex of his jaw beneath the mask.

The fabric whispers against my skin as I roll my shoulders, letting it slip down my arms and pool behind me. Cool air dances across my bare nipples, and I suck in a breath. A strangled sound escapes him. His shoulders rise and fall with each breath, and those dangerous hands curl against his thighs.

I hold his stare as I inch down the mattress, kicking away the tangled sheets. My thumbs hook into the waistband of my pajama bottoms, and I arch my back, sliding them past my hips and down the length of my legs until nothing remains between us but air and want.

I settle against the pillows and let my knees drift apart. His eyes burn through the mask's slits, and a dark heat pulses between my legs. The outline of his cock pressing against his jeans becomes more pronounced, and want coils in my belly.

"Touch yourself." His voice cracks with impatience.

My hand brushes over my stomach before dipping between my thighs, finding warmth and wetness waiting for me there. My fingers drown in the slick evidence of my arousal, gliding through the most sensitive part of me with ease.

I circle my clit, teasing myself, awakening every nerve. Each slow pass sends sparks up my spine.

"Like this?"

My breath stutters, and my head falls back against the pillows, baring my throat to him as I surrender to the sensation.

"Just like that."

The words sound painful through the deep growl rumbling in his chest as it rises and falls in rapid pants beneath his dark shirt, his powerful body frozen in place as he watches me.

My fingers drift lower, collecting the proof of how much I need this. Need him. The cool air of the bedroom brushes my exposed skin, raising goosebumps along my inner thighs. I gather my arousal before returning to circle my aching clit, drawing out each stroke. My free hand drifts up to my breast, palming the weight of it before capturing the nipple between eager fingers. The dual sensations, the gentle pinch at my breast and the glide of my fingers below, threaten to undo me.

I flick my fingers, creating delicious friction against my swollen flesh. His eyes devour me from behind the mask, a predatory gaze that electrifies every inch of my bare skin.

He shifts his weight, hands balled into fists. The air vibrates with his restraint. My eyes lock on his hands as they move to his zipper and tug his jeans open. His cock springs free—thick and hard, with a bead of moisture at the tip that makes my tongue dart across my lips.

He steps forward, leaning over the bed. He pushes my fingers away, replacing them with his own, swiping his fingertips through my arousal, and gathering my wetness on his hand before plunging two fingers inside me. I gasp, my spine curving as I rise to meet him, my body welcoming the invasion.

"Yes..."

The hiss escapes my lips, filling the quiet room. My legs tremble as I rock into his touch, chasing the pressure that promises everything.

When his fingers slip away, emptiness floods the space they left behind. A whimper slips out before I can stop it. My fingers return to my clit, taking over where his left off, circling that sensitive bud while he fists his length with fingers still wet from my body, our movements falling into perfect sync. His hand on his cock makes my breath catch.

"Are you going to come on me when I come for you?" My voice is ragged and desperate.

"Only inside you, Luna." Each word fights past gritted teeth as he works himself with long, measured strokes. "Your mouth, your cunt, and your ass. Nowhere else."

His crude words push me closer to the edge, the possessiveness in his tone setting fire to my veins. I moan, my back arching off the bed as my fingers move quicker, my other hand pinching my nipple harder, until pleasure and pain blur together.

"That's it, beautiful." He presses his shins against the mattress, his fist pumping faster. "Show me how good it feels."

The world narrows to just this man. I'm drowning in sensation now, my body moving on instinct as my hips chase my touch. Each breath scrapes from my throat. Sweat beads on my chest as heat blooms beneath my skin.

He freezes, his muscles locking as his climax threatens. A growl tears from his chest as his fingers circle the base of his cock in a punishing grip, fighting his own release. Every line of his face speaks of desperate need barely held in check.

His rigid control strips away mine, and the coil in my belly snaps without warning. White-hot pleasure crashes through every nerve as my back bows off the bed, and I surrender to its tide. My fingers dance against my swollen flesh, and my voice shatters, my walls pulsing around emptiness, desperate to be filled.

My hips buck against my hand, chasing each aftershock as I come with a cry that I wish could be his name. He stands frozen except for the harsh rise and fall of his chest.

As I fight to catch my breath, trying to gather my scattered senses, he walks around the bed. One finger trails along my inner thigh, gathering proof of what he's done to me before bringing it to my face. He paints my bottom lip with my own arousal.

A lazy smile curves my mouth despite my trembling limbs. His touch is gentle as he traces my cheek with the same wet finger.

"You're so fucking beautiful, Luna."

"So are you,"

My hand lifts toward his cock without thought, barely grazing hot skin before I catch myself. The rules are clear. I can only touch when permitted.

He captures my fingers in his grip. "Time to bind your hands, little doe."

My breath hitches, and I scramble to my knees, turning away from him as I bring my hands behind my back. The cold plastic surrounds my wrists, and the zip tie tightens. A little jolt of fear mingles with my excitement.

His hands guide me off the bed, steadying me as I find my balance without the use of my arms, before steering me toward the chair in the corner by the window.

"What are we doing?"

"I want you on your knees, but the ground will be too low."

The ottoman in front is the perfect height. He helps me climb onto it, positioning my body where he wants it. Then he's there, hard and heavy against my lips, demanding entry.

I part my mouth and take him in. The weight of him on my tongue, and the masculine taste and scent of him, make me dizzy with desire. My tongue swirls around his crown, and I relax my throat to welcome more of him as he slides deeper. He groans, one hand coming to rest on the back of my head, not steering, not pushing, but his fingers curved there like he needs the anchor as much as I do.

"That's it." His voice grates out, all gravel and want. "Take me deeper."

His hips start a steady rhythm. I hollow my cheeks around him. Air whistles through his teeth as his cock glides smooth and wet along my tongue with each stroke.

My position—helpless, bound, and filled with his taste—sends a thrill through me. I've never wanted to submit to anyone before. But with him, I want this. Want to surrender every piece of myself.

His free hand lifts, brushing a strand of hair from my face, tucking it behind my ear with careful fingers. The gentleness of that touch, while his cock fills my mouth, while I'm tied and kneeling, makes my heart stutter.

I redouble my efforts, swirling my tongue around the sensitive head before swallowing him deep. Every stroke becomes deliberate, calculated to unravel him the way he's unraveled me.

My own need pulses hot and insistent, an echo of what I'm doing to him, pressing at my core.

"Good girl." The words rasp out as he pulls me back.

The praise crashes through me. My heart slams against my ribs. Heat floods between my legs, instant and undeniable. I've never considered myself a woman with a praise kink, but coming from him, those words unlock something I didn't know existed inside me, desires I've never acknowledged. They reach into my chest and twist, remake me into someone desperate to hear them again, to earn them through submission and surrender, to become everything he needs me to be.

His composure cracks, and his hips drive forward with new force, each thrust hitting the back of my throat. His hand curves around the back of my skull, fingers tangling in my hair, directing my head where he wants it. No more pretense of letting me set the pace. He takes over, claims my mouth, and uses it for his pleasure. I yield completely, molding myself to his demands, letting him fuck my mouth while his breathing disintegrates into ragged, broken sounds above me.

"That's it, beautiful. I'm close." The words come out through clenched teeth.

I whimper, the sound vibrating around his cock. His hips jerk, snapping forward as control abandons him.

"Luna!" My name wrenches from his throat.

He pulses against my tongue, and heat floods my mouth as he empties himself with a shudder that racks his entire body. I breathe through my nose and swallow everything he gives me, taking every drop, as pride swells in my chest at the way I've shattered his composure.

When the last tremor passes, he steps back and tucks himself away. I tip my face up to meet his gaze, satisfaction curving my mouth as his chest rises and falls in an uneven rhythm. His hands shake as he works his zipper. Then his palm finds my cheek, thumb tracing my swollen lips, gentle now where moments ago there was only hunger.

"Now it's my turn."

***

He helps me onto wobbly legs and guides me back to the bed. My heart pounds, desire rebuilding within me, a slow-burning fire spreading through my body. I climb onto my knees on the mattress, my bound wrists making balance a challenge, but he steadies me.

The plastic around my wrists reminds me of how exposed I am. Fear and excitement tangle in my stomach, each feeding the other until I can't tell where one ends and the other begins.

This is our ritual. Our game. The pattern we've fallen into night after night. And though I'd never admit it aloud, never confess it even in my own thoughts most of the time, I crave this—the way he strips away my control, the moment when I stop having to make decisions and exist only to feel what he gives me.

"You're so beautiful like this, Luna." Warmth infuses his words as his palm traces the curve of my spine, sliding down to cup my ass. His hand presses between my shoulder blades as he grips the zip tie to guide my descent. "Face down, ass up."

I sink forward, pressing my cheek and chest to the cool sheets, my bound hands resting in the small of my back. The position bares everything—my arousal, my need, the way my body weeps for his attention.

The mattress shifts under his weight as he kneels behind me. His rough palms spread me open, and I feel his stare like a physical touch on my most intimate places.

Shame died somewhere between the first night and now. All that remains is the wild, desperate need that's been clawing at me since he appeared in my life.

His mouth finds me, his wicked tongue diving deep. I cry out as he devours me with broad strokes and long, languid licks, tasting every fold and crease before focusing on the bundle of nerves that makes stars explode behind my eyelids. Each pass of his tongue steals my breath and leaves me gasping.

"Oh God." My fingers curl into helpless fists behind me. "That feels... incredible."

He hums against my flesh, the vibration spreading through my core. His strong hands grip my thighs, holding me open as he works me with devastating skill. When his tongue dips inside, mimicking what's to come, I push back against his face, begging for more.

Every time I get close, he retreats, letting the tension coil tighter until I can't stand it, backing off just enough to keep me teetering on the edge. I whimper in frustration, trying to move my hips to direct his attention where I need it most, but his grip is firm and unyielding.

"Stop teasing me." Pride dissolves under the weight of need. "Please let me come."

His tongue circles my clit before his lips close around it, sucking with gentle pressure. The sensation rockets through me, my thighs shaking and my breath reduced to desperate gasps as release rushes toward me.

Before I fall, his mouth withdraws, and I scream my frustration into the sheets. Then, the blunt head of his cock presses against my entrance, hot and insistent. I push back, lost to my hunger.

His first deep thrust steals my breath as he buries himself to the hilt.

"Fuck," I choke out.

He fills every space inside me. The stretch and the fullness overwhelm me, bordering on too much and not enough.

"God, you feel like perfection." His hands roam the curve of my ass, up to my bound wrists, then back down to grip my hips. "So fucking tight and wet for me."

He sets a pace that unravels me stroke by stroke. Each withdrawal drags against my inner walls, making me gasp. Every return thrust drives deeper, claiming more of me. The room fills with the wet sound of our bodies sliding together, his harsh breathing, and my voice climbing toward desperation.

His thrusts turn savage as his restraint abandons him. His fingers bite into my flesh, and the headboard thuds against the wall. I arch lower, spine curving to take him deeper, my hips slamming back to meet each punishing stroke. This is possession stripped to its essence. No gentleness and no apology.

This is what I crave from him. This honesty of desire, his mask stripped away to reveal pure need.

His hand climbs my spine to fist in my hair. He yanks my head back, using it as leverage to drive deeper.

"Take every fucking inch of me."

The new angle finds nerves that make my vision white out. Each thrust pushes me closer to the edge, my inner walls clamping down, trying to keep him buried inside me.

Words die in my throat, replaced by animalistic cries. Sweat slicks our skin, the musky scent of sex hanging heavy in the air, as the coil in my belly winds tighter with each brutal stroke.

When I think I'll die from the pleasure, he slows to a tease. He curls over me, his heart beating a wild rhythm against my back, his hot breath against my neck. His lips brush the shell of my ear.

"Come for me." His free hand snakes around to find my clit. "Come on my cock, Luna."

The command triggers the release I've been fighting for, pushing me over the edge I've been teetering on. I shatter, my walls rippling around him, pleasure exploding through every cell. He groans against my neck, hips stuttering as his own release claims him, flooding my core, the warm pulse of him marking me in the most primitive way.

My body melts into the mattress as the last tremors fade. He withdraws, and his hands move to my bound wrists, snapping the zip-tie with his fingers, a casual display of strength that should terrify me. But when those same hands soothe the angry marks on my skin, the contradiction makes my breath catch.

"You're a goddess, little doe." He helps me roll onto my side, arranging my limbs on the bed.

I smile up at him, exhaustion tugging at my consciousness. The space between us feels charged with unspoken things, especially the kiss that never comes. The absence of that simple intimacy feels like a wound sometimes. But I don't ask. Don't push. Not anymore. I'm too hesitant to upset this delicate balance we've found.

He stands, adjusting his clothes. "Don't fall asleep on me, beautiful. We're only getting started."

Hours blur together in a haze of touch and surrender. When it's over and he's gone, I lie sprawled across tangled bedding, every muscle humming with the aftershocks. My mind floats in that space between satisfaction and dreams.

My eyelids grow heavy, and sleep pulls at me. I should get up and pee. As a doctor, I know better than to fall asleep with his semen warm and sticky inside me. Last month's UTI should be reminder enough.

But my body refuses to move. His warmth still coats my thighs, and something primal in me wants to keep it there, this proof of what we've done, and this piece of him that lingers when everything else about him disappears with the dawn.

As consciousness slips away, I wonder if I'm losing my mind, letting a masked stranger possess me so completely. But the thought dissolves, washed away by the echo of his voice, his touch, and his promise to return.

Chapter Five

Luna

I push through the double doors to the treatment area, my arms loaded with bags from the feed store and pharmacy, plus the mail I grabbed from the post office. Exhaustion weighs heavily on my shoulders from this morning's errands, and all I want is to get these supplies sorted and maybe steal five minutes to myself. The familiar antiseptic smell hits me, mingling with something else, something sweet and chemical that makes my nose wrinkle.

Nail polish?

"What do you think?" Maren holds up two bottles. "Hooker red or bashful blue?"

I stop dead in my tracks, blinking at the scene before me. What the hell?

She's sitting on a stool in front of the main treatment table, while Ricky sits in front of her with what looks like an iced peanut butter pop clutched in one paw, picking at the eye of the stuffed monkey I gave him last week with the other.

I squint at the treat. "Where did he get that? We were out of pops after Tate's attempted bribe the other day."

"I had some bananas on my counter that had gone too soft, so I picked up some natural peanut butter on my way home last night and made them."

A laugh bubbles up from my chest despite my fatigue. "I had the same idea! I picked up bananas and peanut butter today too. When I told him what they were for, the produce manager at the store in Estes gave me a bunch that were turning at a discount."

"Good. Half of what I made is already gone. Zorro's had two, I had to give Shadow and Ghost each two, Winston had one, and this is Ricky's second."

I set the bags on the opposite counter, watching in amazement as Ricky continues his methodical destruction of his toy while enjoying his treat, his usual chaos replaced by focused concentration. For once, he's not making grabby gestures at Maren's chest or lunging forward with his usual manic energy. The distraction monkey is actually working.

"What are you doing?"

"Trimming his nails. But I want to paint them, too."

"You can't paint a raccoon's claws."

"Why not?" She examines the polish bottles with serious consideration. "Raccoons should look pretty, too."

"The chemicals in that are dangerous, and he's just going to scratch and bite it off."

"Don't worry, it's the kid-friendly kind. Non-toxic."

My brain stutters for a moment. "Wait a minute. Hooker Red is kid-friendly?"

Maren snorts in a way that always means trouble. "Eh... that's what I call it because it looks like the color a prostitute would leave around a john's dick."

Jesus Christ. Sometimes I forget how crude she can be until she drops bombs like that in casual conversation.

I reach for the bottle. "Let me see it."

Maren offers it with a dramatic sigh. "Can you believe this, Rick? She doesn't trust me. I'm hurt." He chatters back as if he understands the entire conversation, his little tongue struggling with the sticky peanut butter as he licks his pop.

The corners of my mouth twitch upward, fighting a smile as I read the ingredients. They all look safe enough if he chews on his claws. I hand the bottle back to her.

"Okay, fine, but use the blue because Ricky is a boy."

"So sexist. I think the red would bring out his eyes." She sets the red polish aside and pulls his paw from his monkey. "Come on, Rick, Mom said we can do this."

Ricky looks up and then lifts his hand to wave his pop at me, and my smile widens.

I busy myself unpacking the bags. Raccoons, as a rule, don't appreciate getting their claws trimmed. Their fight-or-flight instinct kicks in on the spot. Zorro needs to be sedated before we can go anywhere near his claws, but Ricky came to us as a baby, barely a few weeks old, when a car killed his mom, so he's always had his trimmed. Even the sound of the little Dremel tool Maren is using doesn't faze him.

I lean my hip against the counter, sorting through the mail. Bills, supply catalogs, donation letters—the usual mix. My bank statement sits at the bottom, the envelope already torn along one edge. I slide my finger under the seal, expecting the usual thin balance after grant payments trickle in and expenses drain out.

One hundred thousand dollars.

I blink hard, certain my eyes are playing tricks on me. But the numbers don't change. My hands shake, and the paper trembles between my fingers. It's more than I've ever seen in my account at any one time.

"Maren." My voice comes out strangled.

"What?"

"Look at this." I thrust the statement toward her.

She glances over, and her eyes widen. "Holy shit. What the fuck is that?"

"I have no idea. I need to call the bank." My fingers fumble with my phone, nearly dropping it twice before I manage to pull up the number and hit dial.

Hold music drones through the speaker while Maren abandons Ricky mid-manicure and crowds beside me, peering at the statement over my shoulder. After what feels like hours, a voice cuts through the synthetic orchestra.

"Ms. Foster? Yes, I can see the deposit you're asking about. It came in by wire transfer from an anonymous donor."

Air rushes from my lungs in a ragged burst. "Is it from the same anonymous private trust that handled my previous transactions?"

Keys click through the phone speaker as she searches. "No. It's a different tax ID. Also, I see there's a message here that says it's for 'bobcat enclosure.'"

"Thank you." I end the call before she can say more, turning to face Maren's stunned expression.

"What the actual fuck, Lu? Who the hell knows about Titus' enclosure?"

"I don't know." My voice sounds like it's coming from underwater.

"Do you think it could be Damien?" Her face mirrors the confusion spinning through my head.

"I don't know."

Apparently, that's all I'm capable of saying at the moment.

My mind races, trying to make sense of this. I told him about Titus when I showed him around the sanctuary, but that was almost two months ago.

Should I call him? What if it wasn't him? That would be awkward as hell. Heat crawls up my neck at the thought of that conversation. Him thinking I'm fishing for money, or worse, expecting it.

"You know what?" Maren drops back onto the stool in front of Ricky. "Who the fuck cares who donated it? Titus is getting his enclosure, and with that kind of cash, we can build him a bobcat palace complete with heated rocks, a fucking waterfall, and maybe even a disco ball for when he wants to get his groove on."

I give her a look like she's lost her mind. "A disco ball?"

"Hey, don't knock it until you've seen a bobcat dance. I bet Titus has some moves."

I'm grateful for her humor, but my mind keeps spinning. Could Damien have done this? But why hide behind anonymity? The questions pile up like puzzle pieces that don't fit, though underneath the confusion, relief floods through me. We can build Titus his enclosure.

The last of Ricky's popsicle disappears with a satisfied pop of his lips. He wipes his sticky palm on his fur before seizing his monkey, his claws working to separate one of the arms from its fabric body.

"At least the monkey seems to be working." I nod toward Maren's chest. "I need to order more of those. Maybe a whole case."

"Yeah, he's hardly noticed my boobs at all today. It's almost insulting." She captures another of Ricky's paws for trimming.

Footsteps echo in the hallway outside. Then, Sarah, one of our young volunteers, pokes her head through the door. Her usually cheerful expression looks strained.

"Luna? The sheriff is here to see you."

Maren scowls. "I'm over her showing up here unannounced all the time."

"You and me both." I turn to see Karen standing in the doorway behind Sarah. Shit.

I need to remind the staff of the visitor protocols, but given recent events, Karen showing up unannounced has become the norm.

"Hey, Karen. What's up?"

Her gray eyes take in Maren's nail polish operation with amused bewilderment.

"Luna. Maren. Sorry to drop by and interrupt... whatever this is."

"Just Ricky's spa day." I rest the bank statement on the counter and lead her into the hallway. "How can I help you?"

"Have you ever had a case that dealt with Vance Krueger, an animal abuser down in Walsenburg?"

The name sends a chill down my spine. Vance Krueger—even his name sounds like something that would crawl out from under a rock.

"No, Walsenburg is outside my jurisdiction. There's a sanctuary in Trinidad that's closer, but I've heard of him. A friend in animal services down there told me about him. Why?"

"He's disappeared. Didn't show up for a parole hearing. Been missing for weeks now."

I process her words, bewilderment giving way to a creeping sense of dread that makes it hard to breathe.

"What does that have to do with me? Criminals failing to show up for hearings happens all the time."

"It got me thinking. About the bodies that were dropped here on your property and around the county. We have absolutely nothing to go on in our investigation. So I started looking into other cases of animal abuse in the state." Karen's voice shifts to the animated tone I often heard growing up, when she'd tell Grandpa about cases she was working on. "Over eighty suspects have gone missing in the last two years. So, I went wider and checked nationally. In the past four years, over three hundred animal abuse suspects nationwide have disappeared without a trace. And that's only the ones that were reported."

Blood drains from my face, taking with it all the warmth. Could my wolf have killed all of them? No... that's impossible. Isn't it?

"That's unbelievable," I force out, my voice sounding distant. "But I still don't understand what it has to do with me. You're not here to question me about Damien again, are you?"

"No. Something still doesn't sit right about his arrival coinciding with all these bodies, but there doesn't appear to be any connection I can find."

Relief hits me hard. Her previous suspicion of Damien had turned my blood cold, because he's not the killer. My wolf is.

"Okay, so, again, what does Krueger's disappearance have to do with me?"

"Can I get a list of every perpetrator you've dealt with on all your cases, whether or not they went through animal services or the courts? I know some come in without county or law enforcement involvement."

My pulse hammers against my throat like it's trying to escape.

"Why?"

"I want to see if there are any missing persons who have a connection to your sanctuary so I can get a sense of the bigger picture."

Karen's request sends panic shooting through me.

"I understand why you'd want that information, but I'm obligated to keep patient records private unless there's a valid legal reason not to."

Karen's brows furrow. "Luna, animal medical records are not subject to HIPAA laws."

"You're right, technically, but they are subject to state privacy laws. Veterinary-patient-client privilege exists in Colorado, unless it's in connection with an investigation of animal cruelty."

"It is an investigation of animal cruelty."

"Karen, with all due respect, no, it isn't. Your investigation concerns missing persons."

Her face hardens, displeasure written in every line as she realizes I know the statutes.

"Luna, this could help solve multiple murders. Why wouldn't you want to share something that might save lives?"

"It's not that." *I don't want you to catch him.* "You're asking for personally identifiable information about the animals' owners."

"I can have them subpoenaed, but I really don't want to go through that hassle."

My arms cross over my chest as her threat settles in the space between us. "There's no need for that, Karen. Let me talk to my attorney and find out what I can legally give you."

The hard edges on Karen's face soften. "Thank you. Now, have you felt anyone watching you again? Any sense that someone's been around the property?"

Only my wolf.

"No. Nothing."

"Good. Stay diligent and call me if anything changes." Karen's expression opens up. "Luna, please get in touch after you consult with your attorney. I really could use your help on this."

Karen leaves, and Maren and Ricky emerge from where they'd been eavesdropping, Ricky's nails now trimmed but bare of polish.

"Well, that was intense." Maren cradles Ricky against her chest, and true to form, one of his paws is clutching her breast while the other yanks on the tail of the stuffed monkey tucked under his arm.

"What happened to his blue nail polish?"

"Lost interest. Your conversation was far more fascinating. Though it's batshit crazy that she seems to suspect Damien of running some kind of nationwide animal abuser death squad. Or that it's tied to you and the sanctuary."

The truth lodges between my ribs and refuses to move. It is tied to me. Not through Damien, but through my wolf. Could he have killed them all? The scope of it makes my head spin.

And now Karen won't let this go. She'll keep digging, keep pushing, until she uncovers the truth. Until she finds him.

The thought of him being caught and caged sends a wave of panic through me. What does it say about me that I'm more worried about his safety than the hundreds of missing people who might have died at his hands?

Ricky chitters, reaching for my hand as if sensing my distress. I let him take my fingers, and his warm paw grounds me, pulling me back to the present.

Even as I focus on his touch, dread settles in my bones. Karen's getting too close and asking too many questions.

And somewhere out there, my wolf is still hunting.

Chapter Six

Damien

I watch them from across Elkhorn Avenue, my hands buried deep in my jacket pockets as snowflakes drift around me. The remnants of last night's snow cling to the edges of the sidewalk and gather in the corners of storefronts, turning to gray slush where foot traffic has worn it thin.

Luna and Maren weave between the scattered tourists browsing the shops. The crowds are thin now that peak season has passed, but enough bodies drift between us that I have to keep shifting positions every few minutes to keep them in view.

They laugh about something, Luna's head thrown back in that unguarded way that makes my chest tight. Even from this distance, the mountain air's bite shows in her flushed cheeks, and snowflakes dust her blonde hair like scattered diamonds in the early afternoon light. Her cream-colored coat wraps around jeans and faux-fur, knee-high boots that showcase every curve of her legs.

I've been following them for twenty minutes now, lurking behind parked cars and skulking in doorways like some lovesick creep. This isn't me. Damien Wolfe doesn't stalk women through mountain towns. But I can't seem to help myself.

My phone vibrates in my pocket. My EA, Tiffany, with some crisis about the foundation gala, no doubt. I let it buzz. The only things that exist right now are Luna's joy and her laughter floating over the muted sounds of the sparse street traffic.

They duck into a clothing store, and I cross the street, my dress shoes sliding on the wet pavement before finding grip. Why the fuck didn't I wear boots?

I position myself near Notchtop Bakery & Café, using the window's reflection to monitor the boutique entrance. The barista shoots me suspicious glances as I hover without ordering, but I don't give a shit.

Since I kissed Luna last week and then punished her later as her masked wolf, I've been unraveling, thread by agonizing thread. The memory of how she trembled under my hands that night plays on repeat in my head, replaying in vivid detail at the worst possible moments.

Fuck! Heat rushes through my body, and my cock hardens against my zipper until I have to shift my stance to ease the pressure building there.

The boutique door chimes as they emerge with small shopping bags, still deep in conversation. What is it that women talk about all the time?

Wind whips down the street, sending snow spiraling around their boots. Luna tugs her coat closer while saying something that makes Maren snort with laughter, the sound carrying despite the distance. They head toward the art galleries, and I follow, keeping to the far side of the street.

This duplicity is killing me. Each night I'm with her, the compulsion to tear off the mask and show her who I am grows stronger. Two sides of myself fight for control, and she's trapped in the middle without knowing it.

They pause outside Mountain Traditions Gallery, voices low as they debate going inside. A middle-aged couple walks toward them from the other direction, pushing Luna and Maren closer to the building's front windows.

This is a perfect opportunity. I can walk over and act as if the meeting is pure coincidence.

My pulse pounds against my collar with the same intensity I feel before a kill.

Fuck! Get it together, Wolfe.

I stride across the street, navigating patches of gray slush while my footsteps echo off wet concrete.

"Luna? Is that you?"

Both women turn toward me, and Luna's face lights up. The urge to press her against the gallery's window and kiss her breathless pounds through my veins like a second heartbeat. It's all I think about now that I've tasted her. Her hazel eyes soften, her lips curving into a smile, and warmth spreads beneath my ribs.

"Damien, hi!" Small puffs of breath escape her lips. "What are you doing here?"

Maren eyes me with a sly smile.

"Had lunch with a friend." It's not a lie. Cade and I had lunch, and he's the closest thing I have to a friend. "Though I have to say, running into you two is the highlight of my day."

Maren adjusts her hat over her dark hair with an eye roll. "Smooth, Wolfe."

A young couple pushing a stroller approaches behind them. The sidewalk's too narrow for everyone, giving me the perfect excuse to place my hand on Luna's hip and ease her toward the door. The touch shoots electricity through me, and I fight not to let my fingers linger. She smells like wildflowers and peaches, that scent that makes me want to bury my face in her neck right here on the street.

"What brings you ladies here in the middle of the workweek?" The question sounds casual, but I already know the answer. I've been tracking them since they left the sanctuary two hours ago.

"Taking a much-needed break." Luna shivers as the wind picks up, sending her hair across her face as more flakes swirl around us.

"Yeah, Ethan's covering for us so we can have a girl's day."

This is my moment. It's now or never.

"I'm glad I ran into you. I was going to call." My eyes drink in every detail of Luna's face in the afternoon light, memorizing the way the snowflakes stick to her lashes and how the cold brings out the pink in her cheeks. She's more beautiful in daylight than in moonlight, if that's possible.

"I have a gala on Saturday night for my foundation. It's our annual fundraising event before the winter holidays."

"Sounds fancy." Maren glances between us. The gleam in her eyes says she knows where this is going.

I keep my focus on Luna. "I was wondering if you'd like to attend with me. As my date."

The invitation floats between us in the frigid air, and I stop breathing. This is my test. Will she choose me despite her masked wolf's warnings? More than that, it's my desperate attempt to pull her into my real world, to have her beside me in the light instead of only in the shadows.

Please say yes. Or no. Just save us both from this madness.

"Where's it being held?" Maren asks.

"The Sentinel Tower's ballroom."

She whistles. "Isn't that Denver's tallest building?"

"Yes. The Wolfe Group's headquarters is in the Tower." My attention returns to Luna. "I should have called sooner. I've wanted to since our dinner. I understand if it's too short notice to get someone to cover the sanctuary."

"Luna always has backup to cover. And I happen to have Saturday night free. What are the odds?"

"Can you stop talking for me, please?" Luna's expression shifts between exasperation and amusement as she faces her friend. "And aren't you taking Estella into Denver on Saturday?"

"That's during the day. We'll be back in plenty of time for you to go rub elbows with Denver's elite and raise money for animals."

I have to admire Maren's strategy. Making it about the animals is the surest way to get Luna to agree. Even though she's hijacking our conversation, I'm reminded of why I like her.

Snow falls thicker now, dusting our shoulders and hair white. Luna brushes flakes from her face. Watching her do something so simple shouldn't steal the air from my lungs, but it does.

"I'd be honored if you'd be my date for the evening." The words scrape my throat, rough and loaded with the hope I can't quite hide.

She catches her lower lip between her teeth and peers up at me through snow-wet lashes.

"I'd love to." Her acceptance nearly drops me to my knees. "Anything that helps animals, count me in."

Satisfaction and anger collide in my bloodstream. Satisfaction because she chose me. Anger because she's defying her wolf's warnings about other men touching her. That rebellion will have consequences tonight.

And make no mistake, on Saturday night, I will touch her everywhere.

"Perfect." I have to clear my throat to get the word out. "It's black tie. I hope that's okay."

A couple approaches from behind me, wanting to enter the gallery, and we all shuffle on the narrow sidewalk to accommodate them.

"She may look like a complete disaster most days at the sanctuary," Maren says as we resettle. "But trust me, she cleans up real fucking good."

"Thanks for that ringing endorsement, Mar. Really feeling the love here."

"I think you always look beautiful." Color blooms across Luna's cheekbones. "So, I'll pick you up at six."

"It's a date."

Those three words slam into me with unexpected force. A predatory hunger roars to life in my chest, all teeth and claws and possessive need, erasing everything but the need to claim what she's offering.

I lean down and kiss her cheek, my lips lingering a moment too long. Her skin is soft and cool, and her breath hitches as she leans into my touch. When I pull back, her eyes have gone soft and unfocused.

"I'll see you Saturday." I step back before the need to claim her mouth tears through my self-control and exposes everything on this public street.

"See you Saturday."

I'm halfway down the block when I hear Maren's voice. "Girl, that man wants to eat you alive. And from the look on your face, you'd let him."

Luna's mortified "Maren!" makes me grin like an idiot. I pull my coat tighter against the wind.

I already do, Maren. And she already does.

Saturday can't come fast enough. And tonight... tonight she'll again pay for saying yes to another man, even though that man is me.

My hands shake as I picture it. Luna spread beneath me, her voice breaking as she begs, first for more, then for mercy. The sounds she'll make when I drive her to the edge again and again, until tears streak her cheeks and her voice gives out. I won't stop. Not until every piece of her fractures and crumbles.

This punishment will be for me. For that sick satisfaction I get from watching her break apart under my hands, even knowing I'll put her back together.

It's unfair the way I punish her for indiscretions that I trick her into committing. The injustice of that should bother me, but all I can think about is her in a gown and the feel of her on my arm as I introduce her to my world. She may be an easygoing wildlife veterinarian who saves every broken creature she finds, but she has an innate elegance that puts most socialites to shame.

She's a far better person than most of the people who will attend the gala.

For the first time in my life, Damien Wolfe feels like more than the mask I wear during business hours. With Luna at my side, he might actually become real.

———◆———

The soft murmur of Cade's voice draws my attention away from the bank of monitors displaying feeds from around Estes Park. He uses that voice only with one person.

He's seated at the breakfast bar, laptop open, speaking into his headset. Through the floor-to-ceiling windows of our rented Stanley Hotel residence, snow continues to fall in lazy spirals, adding to the already thick blanket covering the streets.

"I know you want to go to Cancun with your friends, MJ, but winter break would be a perfect time for you to visit Colorado." Cade's tone is gentler than I've heard it in months, the harsh edge softened as he leans back in his chair. "When's the last time we spent more than a weekend together?"

I glance at him from my position at the dining room table to see something I rarely witness—the stoic mask slipping from his face. Twenty-two years old, and his daughter still has the power to make him vulnerable. It's both fascinating and unsettling.

"Dad, I'm an adult now." Mary Jane's voice carries through his headset, tinny but animated. "Besides, you're always working. What would we even do for two weeks?"

Cade's jaw tightens, but his voice remains controlled. "I could take time off. We could go skiing, or—"

"Or I could get a tan in Mexico with my girlfriends." She pauses. "Please, Dad? Spring break is forever away, and this might be my last chance to travel with everyone before we graduate."

Cade's shoulders drop, revealing the disappointment he's trying to hide in the set of his mouth.

"Fine. But you text me when you get there. And every day you're gone. Cancun can be dangerous for tourists, especially a group of twenty-something girls by themselves. If a day goes by that I don't hear from you, I'll fly down there. And you don't want that, MJ, trust me."

"I will! Thank you, Dad. Love you!"

Cade sits motionless for a moment, staring at his laptop screen. The harsh lines return to his face like armor sliding back into place, but I caught that glimpse of the father beneath the soldier, the man who would move mountains for his daughter but settles for phone calls and brief visits.

He closes the laptop and turns toward me, his expression once again unreadable.

"I'm sending two men to Cancun to keep an eye on her."

I nod. Part of his compensation package allows him to use members of Wolfe Group's private security force when needed. Our teams provide security for some of the wealthiest, most influential people in the world.

"Why don't you take a couple of weeks off and go down yourself?"

"Because MJ doesn't want her uncool father cramping her style."

My mouth curves into a smirk. "I don't blame her. You are completely uncool."

"Fuck you."

"Don't feel bad, old man. Kids grow up. They move on. It's what they do."

He reaches for his tea, his movements tight with irritation. The man's a former Army Ranger who chooses oolong tea over coffee. I'll never understand it.

My attention shifts back to the monitors. Luna stands in front of a boutique mirror, holding up different scarves. First a dark one, then something lighter. The black and white feed makes it impossible to tell what colors she's considering.

Maren hovers behind her, pointing at something off-camera. Luna shakes her head and puts the scarf back on the rack.

She'd mumbled something about shopping today while I carried her sated, exhausted body to bed last night, boneless and still trembling from what I'd done to her on her kitchen counter.

So, I hacked into Estes Park's public webcam system. Perks of having Wolfe Technologies wire the whole damn town, and I always build backdoor entrances into every system my company touches.

"Why are you doing this from here? You could have hacked the public cameras from your house in Aspen Ridge."

I keep my eyes on the screens. "Range limitations."

"It's the internet. There are no range limitations."

"I wouldn't have been close enough to run into her on the street."

The hair on the back of my neck rises as he processes what I just admitted.

"So, you rent an entire house for what, a few hours?"

"What do you care? It's my money. Why did you follow me here anyway?"

"Because we need to go over the last details for the gala, and trying to nail you down since the good doctor came into your life is like herding cats. If I'm not in the same room as you, I'll never get the answers I need." He opens the laptop again, fingers already moving across the keys. "Let's do this. I have to get back to the office."

The video call with Tiffany takes forty-three minutes. She runs through the guest list, seating charts, and menu selections. Cade chimes in occasionally about security protocols.

I give the required responses while half my attention stays on Luna, who's moved to a different store.

"The mayor's office confirmed." Tiffany looks over a list on her desk. "Along with both senators."

"What about the Governor?"

Luna tries on a pair of fuzzy mittens, holding her hands up to examine them.

"He RSVP'd last week."

"Good. Are we done?"

The call wraps up. Cade closes his laptop and begins packing up, which means I can stop dividing my focus. Now I can watch Luna browse without pretending to care about hors d'oeuvres versus canapés.

"I asked Luna to go with me."

The words tumble out of my mouth before I even realize I'm speaking. Cade goes very still, the kind of stillness that precedes rare explosive action.

"What? Is that why you wanted to run into her?"

"Yes."

"Jesus Christ." Cade moves to stand in front of the dining table where I've spread out my equipment. His expression hardens. I'm tempted to tell him his face will freeze that way, but given his current mood, I doubt he'd appreciate my humor.

"You're introducing her to your world? To Denver's high society, while there's an active murder investigation, of your making, by the way, tied to her sanctuary? You don't want that kind of scandal anywhere near the foundation."

"I want her there." The words come out as possessively as I intend. The truth is carved into my bones now. "She belongs with me."

Cade runs a hand down his face, his frustration with me bleeding through. "You're dragging her deeper into your life even as she drowns in your secrets. If the truth ever comes out about your other life, she'll be caught in the blast radius. It'll get her arrested as an accessory. If she means as much to you as you say she does, then you need to make protecting her a priority."

Blood roars in my ears.

"Protecting her is all that matters."

What I do puts everyone in my life at risk. Cade and I are both damned already, and we agreed long ago that drawing others into our twisted world was a mistake. It's the reason neither of us has maintained a permanent relationship. Cade avoids them for the same reason he didn't fight harder for MJ when his ex took her. Keeping his daughter close would taint her life if our actions ever came to light. The scandal, the investigation, the media circus—she'd be buried under it all.

My avoidance is different. My parents didn't just damage me. They demolished my capacity to connect with people in any meaningful way. It's the reason I never intended Luna to be more than a physical release. I wouldn't even consider the possibility at the start. But she worked her way inside me like water finding cracks in stone. That light of hers reached something I thought had died long ago and coaxed it back into beating.

"This isn't obsession anymore. You're in love with her."

"Yes." The snarl rips from my throat. "I told you the other day that she's everything."

"You've been saying that for a while, almost since the beginning. I didn't realize that meant you were in love with her."

"Neither did I." The confession feels like swallowing acid. I've spent weeks trying to understand these new feelings, this overwhelming need that goes beyond possession into something vulnerable and terrifying.

"What are you going to do? You don't know how to have a normal relationship." His tone is matter-of-fact, not cruel, but it still cuts. "And you're deceiving her about who you are. You'll have to tell her the truth if there's any chance for the two of you to have a relationship."

"You think I don't fucking know that?"

"Are you sure you can trust her with the truth?"

"Yes. I trust her as much as I trust you."

For once, Cade is unable to hide the surprise on his face.

"She knows what I've done and hasn't betrayed me yet."

He crosses his arms over his broad chest, the movement pulling his black sweater tight across his shoulders. "She's been lying to the sheriff, covering for you, but for how long? What happens when the veterinarian who took an oath to 'do no harm' decides she can't be complicit in murder?"

I'm on my feet before the sentence ends, the chair tipping back and hitting the floor behind me. He stops talking.

"She won't say anything. Luna understands why I do it, even if she doesn't condone it. She has darkness in her too."

"Does she? Or are you projecting what you want to see?" Cade doesn't back down, doesn't even blink. All our years together have earned him that right, but it doesn't mean I have to like it.

I step closer, warning flashing in my eyes. "Watch your fucking mouth, Cade."

Something in my expression must convince him to dial it back because he sighs, the sound heavy with resignation.

"You need to get on board with this. I'll tell her the truth. I'm not sure when yet, but I will."

"Are you positive you can trust her?"

"Yes. I told you she won't betray me."

I know this with the same absolute certainty I know my own heartbeat—because that heartbeat belongs to her now. She's gotten into my blood, under my skin, and into places that have never been touched by another person.

Forty-six years of being convinced that I was broken at my core, that whatever's wrong with me made loving someone an impossibility, and then she walks into my life and proves me wrong with every breath she takes.

"Promises made under duress tend to have expiration dates." Cade's voice carries that quiet concern that reminds me why I trust him above all others. "I haven't seen you lose control like this since you were only starting out."

The comparison stings because it's accurate. I walk back to the monitors, needing the anchor of watching Luna. She's moved to the jewelry counter now, leaning over a display case with interest. I've never seen her wear jewelry except for the small diamond studs in her ears. A detail I've meant to ask about but always get distracted by other parts of her body.

"She's different. I'm getting tired of telling you that."

"Different enough to stand by you when she learns the truth of who you really are?"

His words press down on me, but I can't tear my gaze away from Luna on the monitor. She and Maren leave the boutique, crossing the street to the restaurant. With quick keystrokes, I access the internal cameras, amazed as always by how lax most companies' cybersecurity is.

Luna settles at a high table across from Maren, the snow-dusted windows creating a perfect backdrop behind her. Even through the grainy security feed, she's breathtaking.

"Damien." The urgency in Cade's voice compels me to look at him. "I've said this before, but it bears repeating. Inserting yourself into Dr. Foster's life as Damien Wolfe while visiting her as her masked stalker was reckless for a hundred different reasons. Now you're bringing her into your public life? When she learns the truth, the betrayal is going to be devastating. It's going to be a fucking disaster."

The word "betrayal" is the only part of his speech that registers. He's right, and the prospect of seeing it in her eyes is agonizing. I've let this go too far, but I don't know how to backtrack without destroying us both.

My phone sits on the table beside the monitoring equipment, and I reach for it, pulling up Luna's contact. I feel like I'm spiraling out of control, and she's the only thing that calms the chaos in me now. She has an inexplicable soothing effect on me, quieting the savage beast that lives under my skin even when I'm buried deep inside her body and my control snaps.

I move to the sofa, angling one of the monitors so I can watch her while I type. My thumbs move across the screen almost without conscious thought.

Me

Thinking about you.

On the monitor, she checks her phone, a smile curving her lips, before she types back.

Luna

> You saw me an hour ago.

Me

> Too long. I'm already looking forward to Saturday night.

Luna bites her lip as she reads my message, shifting in her seat. She types back with one hand while picking at her salad with the other. Maren says something that makes Luna nod.

Luna

> Fair warning: I have no idea how to act at fancy galas. I might embarrass you.

I can already picture how every man in that ballroom will want what belongs to me.

Me

> Impossible. You'll be the most beautiful woman there.

She smiles, glancing around as if checking that no one can see her reaction before typing again.

Luna

> Flattery will get you everywhere, Mr. Wolfe. Should I be worried about what kind of crowd you run with?

I smile.

Me

> The kind that will be jealous they're not going home with you.

Luna fans herself with her napkin, and I have to adjust myself through my jeans, my arousal spiking at her reaction.

Luna

> You're terrible. And I'm blushing in public.

Me

> Good. I like knowing I can affect you even when I'm not there.

Luna sets her phone down and takes a long sip of water. Her lips press together, but the corners twitch upward. She's fighting a smile.

"Are you texting her right now? While we're discussing how to keep us all out of prison?"

I set the phone aside. Every muscle in my body coils with tension, demanding I go to her, be near her, and touch her.

"This conversation is over, Cade. You've made your point. I have no emotional capacity to be with her. But that doesn't fucking matter because I'm in love with her. She's permanent. She'll know the whole truth soon, for better or for worse. And the gala is happening. She's coming with me."

He stares at me for a long moment. "I'll go to the grave for you if it ever comes to that, Damien. You know that. But for all our sakes, I hope she's as trustworthy as you think she is."

He stands, grabs his laptop, and heads toward the door. He pauses with his hand on the knob.

"She's already lied to the police for you. Already compromised herself. Now you're going to burden her with the knowledge of your true identity? How much more are you going to ask her to carry before you're satisfied?"

The door closes behind him with a soft click, leaving me alone with the monitors and the weight of his words. I sink back into the sofa cushions, staring at the feed of Luna finishing her lunch. She's laughing again at something Maren says, unaware that I'm watching every micro-expression cross her face. God, I love how much she laughs. The sound would be musical if I could hear it through the cameras.

Outside, the snow continues to fall, blanketing the streets in pristine white that tire tracks and footprints will soon mar. Just like the purity I'm destroying in Luna with every secret I keep and every lie of omission.

My love for her, this all-consuming need that's devoured obsession and morphed into a force that dictates my every breath, is dangerous in ways I haven't experienced since I was seventeen and still learning boundaries I shouldn't cross. Back then, it was about power and control, about making the first predators I knew bleed for what they'd done.

Now it's different. More complicated. I'm chasing the possibility of being truly seen by another human being, the chance to lay myself bare—every scar, every kill, every twisted impulse—and have her choose me anyway. Not despite the broken pieces, but with full knowledge of the wreckage underneath the polished version I show the world. The man whose hands know the texture of a dying heartbeat.

I thought my obsession with Luna was overwhelming, consuming every rational thought. But this love is worse, sucking me under like quicksand.

Saturday night is another step in my careful progression of leading Luna toward the truth. My seduction of her, not as the wolf whose existence confines itself to her bedroom, but as Damien, the man who can offer her the world if she'll accept the darkness that comes with it.

The question that haunts me, the one I can't answer despite Cade's concerns, is which version of me she'll choose when the masks fall away.

And what I'll do if she chooses neither.

Chapter Seven

Luna

The fox kit's eyes watch me warily as I clean the infected wound on his hind leg. His mother paces in her cage, emitting occasional sharp barks of concern. The whole family was brought in this morning after a homeowner found them huddled under his deck—the mother limping badly, two kits showing signs of mange, and this little guy with what looks like an old bite wound.

"Easy, little one." I apply antibiotic ointment with careful fingers. "This will make you feel better."

The kit's siblings watch from behind their mom, pressed together for comfort. Wild foxes rarely tolerate human contact this well, but desperation and pain sometimes have a way of overriding natural instincts. The mother's leg was caught in an old snare, probably abandoned by some careless trapper years ago. She's been dragging it around long enough for the wire to embed itself into the muscle. I'm pretty sure I'm going to have to amputate it this afternoon, but I hope we can save this little guy's leg.

"Talking dirty to the patients again?" Maren appears beside me, arms crossed and grinning. "Ricky's gonna get jealous." She sets down a fresh bottle of saline solution. "Hey, I'm not judging. We all have our types, but a jealous raccoon ain't no joke."

Her words are light, but there's something tense about her today. I noticed it the minute she arrived this morning. Her smile is brittle and forced, like she's trying too hard to be her usual crude, sarcastic self. I've known Maren long enough to recognize when she's putting on a show.

I finish bandaging the kit's leg and place him back with his family. The mother grooms him, her rough tongue working over his fur in quick, anxious strokes.

I move to the sink to wash my hands. "Is something wrong?"

Maren shrugs, but her eyes don't meet mine. "Wrong? What could be wrong? Just living the dream, baby."

"Maren."

She fidgets with the hem of her scrub top and lets out a heavy sigh. "JT and I are fighting. Or maybe not fighting exactly. More like existing in the same space without actually connecting."

I dry my hands and turn to face her. "What's going on?"

"He hasn't been calling me as much when he's on the road." Her voice is smaller now, vulnerable in a way I've only heard from her a handful of times. "Used to be, he'd call every night when he stopped. We'd have phone sex or video sex before he crashed for the night. Now, when he calls, it's like he's checking off a box, you know? 'Hey, babe, still alive, talk to you later.'"

I lean against the counter, giving her my full attention. JT's been driving long haul for as long as he and Maren have been together. The distance and uncertainty of that lifestyle are hard on relationships.

"Maybe he's just tired? Those runs can be brutal."

"That's what I keep telling myself." Maren's laugh comes out wrong, all edges and no humor. "But even when he's home, he's not really there. He comes through the door, grabs a beer, and plants himself on the couch with the remote. We don't talk anymore. Last weekend, he watched football for two straight days. I could've been giving the mailman a lap dance in the doorway, and he wouldn't have noticed."

A snort escapes me before I can stop it. "The mailman would've appreciated it, though."

"Right?" She tries for a smile, but it falls apart before it fully forms. What replaces it makes my stomach drop—a frown that looks wrong on Maren's face. "I don't know what to do, Lu. Something's not right with him, but every time I try to bring it up, he says he's fine and changes the subject."

I reach for her, pulling her into a hug. She sags against me. "When's he due back?"

"Next Friday." Her words come out muffled against my shoulder. "He's hauling a load to Florida, then picking up something in New York on the way back."

I pull back enough to look at her face, hands still on her arms.

"Talk to him then. Don't let him brush you off with football and beer. You deserve better than that."

Maren nods, but the doubt is plain in her eyes. The worry that maybe the conversation she's dreading will confirm what she already suspects—that whatever they had is slipping away, mile by mile, highway by highway.

"Enough about my disaster of a love life." She steps back, shoulders straightening. Her cocky grin slides back into place like armor. "Let's talk about your hot date on Saturday."

I don't push. I know better than to press when she retreats behind that smile.

"It's just a fundraising gala, Maren."

"Who knows where it will lead?" She mock pouts. "I want to be the maid of honor at a fancy billionaire wedding someday. That's not too much to ask, is it? My picture in People magazine, my best friend swept off her feet by a guy who worships—"

"Okay, pump the brakes. You're getting way ahead of yourself. It's only our second date."

"Don't ruin my billionaire fantasy wedding, Lu. I'm living vicariously through you here. Let me have this."

She shifts her attention to the foxes, and the playfulness drops from her expression.

"Now what are we doing about Mama?"

I study the injured fox inside the cage, where she's still grooming her babies. "Prep the OR. That wire has to come out of her leg."

"Think she'll lose it?"

"Probably. But I won't know for sure until I get her under and can assess the full extent of the damage."

Maren grabs the cage, lifting it with care, and heads for the door.

"Can Tate watch the surgery? He's been dying to observe."

I follow her toward the surgical suite, my mind already running through the procedure.

"Yeah, that's fine. Tell him to put the phones on voicemail and scrub up."

She sets the cage down on the prep table and heads toward the lobby, a wicked grin spreading across her face.

"Hey, Tate! Guess what? You owe me that dinner!"

His enthusiastic reply makes me smile and chuckle. She knew I'd let him watch, but she conned him into betting on it first.

My thoughts drift to Saturday night as I prepare the anesthesia. If only I could just focus on Damien and the normal, uncomplicated relationship he's offering.

As much as I'm looking forward to the gala, to wearing a beautiful dress and pretending to be someone sophisticated and put-together, there's a part of me that's already aching for what comes after. For the party to end. For the dress to come off. For my wolf to come to me.

I'm falling for a man who won't let me see his face. A man who only comes to me in shadows. And I hate myself for wanting him more than the one who stands in the light.

Damien can offer me everything—dinners, dates, conversations over wine, the possibility of a real future. He's handsome and successful and kind, and he wants to be seen with me in public. He wants to take me to fancy events and introduce me to his friends, but when I close my eyes, it's not Damien's hands I imagine on my body. It's not his voice that makes my skin tingle with anticipation. If only I could choose between the man who could offer me everything and the one who offers me nothing but stolen moments in the dark.

But my heart, stubborn and foolish as it is, seems to have already made its choice. And I have no idea what to do about it.

I lean back in my chair, massaging my temples, unable to stare at the numbers on the computer screen for another minute. Flower and Honey, two of our permanent resident rabbits, keep me company, hanging out in the wicker bed on the corner of my desk. They twitch their noses at me as if sensing my frustration with the pile of invoices, payroll sheets, and new grant applications that never seems to shrink. But my nonprofit sanctuary needs all the grant money I can get my hands on.

I look up at the knock on my door as it opens, and Jenny bursts through, bouncing on her toes with excitement. She's carrying a long blue florist box tied with an elegant black ribbon.

"Special delivery!" She sets the box down on the only clear space left on my desk, jostling Honey, who thumps her hind leg in protest. "Sorry, lady."

I eye the box. "I didn't order anything."

"It's not from you, silly. Someone sent them *to* you." Jenny can barely contain her grin as she sits in the chair opposite my desk. "I'm betting they're from a certain handsome billionaire who's taking you to that gala on Saturday."

"How do you know about that?"

"Maren."

Of course.

"He's kinda old, but the man is seriously hot, Luna." She fans herself, and it reminds me of my best friend, who can't keep her mouth shut.

"He's more than twice your age, Jenny."

"When a man looks like that, age becomes irrelevant real quick."

"You've been hanging around Maren too much." I point at her, and she shrugs.

"Come on, open it! I want to see what kind of flowers billionaires send."

I pull the ribbon loose, my heart pounding with a thrill I can't deny. Why would Damien do this? The lid comes off easily, revealing tissue paper. I fold it back and—

My stomach drops. The breath leaves my lungs in a gasp.

Twelve long-stemmed black dahlias lie arranged in the box, but they're not beautiful. They're horrific. Someone hacked each stem apart, severing the flowers at jagged angles. Deep red fluid coats the shredded flowers, thick droplets clinging to the torn leaves, creating a small, dark puddle beneath the carnage. It has a faint metallic scent.

Jenny scrambles out of her chair. "What the hell is that?"

My hands shake as I drop the lid back onto the box.

"I need to call the florist." I grab my phone, searching for the number on the box.

The woman who answers sounds cheerful until I explain what arrived. Then her tone shifts to horror.

"Oh my goodness, that's awful. I'm so sorry. We would never send flowers in that condition. Someone must have altered them after they left here."

"Who bought them?"

I pace behind my desk while Jenny watches me with wide eyes.

"Let me check... A man paid cash for a dozen black dahlias this morning. I didn't take that order, but let me talk to my associate."

She puts me on hold, and Jenny and I exchange glances as I bite my lip. After a minute, she comes back on the line.

"He was tall. Wore sunglasses and a baseball cap. I'm sorry, she doesn't remember much else about him. He paid cash and took them with him, so we don't have a record of his name. I'm so sorry this happened."

"No problem. Thank you." I hang up and turn to Jenny, who's still staring at the box like it might explode. "Who delivered these to you?"

"Some guy. Maybe nineteen or twenty? He drove a white van." She wraps her arms around herself. "Luna, this is really creepy."

I'm already pulling up the security camera feed on my computer, grateful now to have them, rewinding the footage to fifteen minutes ago. I watch a young man pull up in a white van with no logo or writing and approach the main building carrying the box. When the camera catches his face, I don't recognize him.

"Have you ever seen him before?"

She leans in to look at the screen. "No. He had really bad acne, but I didn't pay much attention to him. He said he had a delivery for Luna Foster and left. Didn't even make me sign for it."

I rewind the footage, trying to catch a glimpse of the van's license plate, but the space where it should be is empty.

"No plates," I say more to myself than to Jenny.

She moves closer to me. "Luna, who would do something like this?"

I grab my phone again and dial Karen's number.

"Hi Luna, what's up?"

"Hi Karen. I need to report something." I try to keep my voice steady.

"What's going on?"

"I received a package today. Flowers that have been destroyed and covered in what appears to be blood. Someone who isn't affiliated with the florist made the delivery, and there's no way to trace who sent them."

There's a pause, and I can hear her shifting in the background.

"Hold on a sec. Tim, I'm heading to Luna's sanctuary. She's gotten an odd delivery. No, not another dead body. Okay, Luna, were there any threats accompanying the package? A card or a note?"

"No, nothing like that. This doesn't feel like the person who left the bodies."

"I'm on my way. Don't touch anything else in that box, and if you have security footage, pull it up for me to review."

"Already done. Thank you, Karen."

Jenny and I stand in awkward silence, both of us avoiding looking at the box. Honey has moved in front of Flower, her small body rigid.

"I'm gonna go back to work." Jenny gestures toward the door.

I nod. "Don't worry about this, Jenny. I'm sure it's nothing."

She doesn't look convinced, poor thing, but I can hardly blame her. She walks out of my office, leaving the door open, and I sink back into my chair. I close my eyes and rub my temples again when I hear Maren's angry voice from down the hall.

"What the actual fuck?"

Maren appears in my doorway like a storm cloud, her eyes blazing as she takes in the box on my desk.

"This is some fucked-up bullshit, Lu." She takes a peek inside the box. "Shit, is that blood?"

"I'm pretty sure it is."

"I need to sit down."

She lifts Honey and Flower from their wicker bed and goes to the sofa, where she collapses, cradling the rabbits against her chest like furry shields.

Neither of us knows what to say, but she stays with me until Karen arrives half an hour later.

"Luna." She steps into my office, her eyes zeroing in on the box. She pulls latex gloves from her jacket pocket and lifts the lid again. "This is definitely an escalation."

She examines the contents, making notes on a small notepad while Maren mutters something sarcastic under her breath. I catch her eye and give her a sharp look.

"Any idea who might have sent this to you?"

"No."

"Do the dahlias mean anything to you?"

"Not black ones. Red dahlias are my favorite flower, but no one knows that except Maren and... Caleb." I glance at Maren, who's watching me while Flower explores the space between her knees and the arm of the sofa.

Karen's pen stops moving. "Caleb, your ex?"

"Yeah."

"Have you heard from him recently?"

Oops. I never told her about his visit, did I?

"He showed up a few weeks ago."

The silence in the room is deafening. Even the rabbits seem to pause their movements. Maren and I exchange a glance.

"Luna." Karen's voice carries that warning tone cops use when they know you're about to admit something significant. "What happened?"

I fidget with a pen on my desk, rolling it between my fingers. "It wasn't a big deal. He dropped by and wanted to talk about getting back together. I said no. He wanted me to drop the restraining order against him. Get it off the record. He was fired after I filed it, and, from what I understand, no other law firm will touch him. Apparently, even Daddy's money and reputation couldn't help with that."

"Was that all that happened?" Karen continues making notes on her pad.

"No. He got a little heated about it, but Damien showed up and made him leave before anything really happened."

"A little heated?" Maren scoffs. "That piece of shit threatened you."

Karen looks over at her and then back at me as she crosses her arms.

"Wait a minute. Let's back up a minute. He threatened you?"

"A little. But Damien handled it. He threw him out."

"And what was Damien Wolfe doing here?"

"I invited him to dinner. What does that have to do with anything?"

"I didn't realize you were that close."

"It was dinner. Neighbors can have dinner together."

Suspicion clouds Karen's features. "Why didn't you tell me about this?"

"Honestly? Because it slipped my mind?"

Damien kissed me, and that wiped away any memory of much else, except the visit from my wolf later.

Maren snorts from the couch, and I shoot her another warning glare. As usual, it has no effect on her.

"Don't you have something to do?"

"I am." She holds up Flower. "I'm socializing with our resident rabbits."

Now it's my turn to snort, but I hold back.

Karen leans forward in her chair, her expression stern. "Luna, this is exactly the kind of escalating behavior that can lead to serious violence. You should have called me immediately."

"I know, I know." I rub my forehead, tension coiling at the base of my skull. "I... Damien seemed to handle it, and I thought that was the end of it."

"Do you think these could be from him?" Karen taps her pen against the box.

I lean back in my chair, considering, before I shake my head. "He's clearly still angry about our breakup and the restraining order. But this..." I gesture at the destroyed flowers. "This seems more elaborate than his usual style. Caleb's more of a show-up-drunk-and-yell-at-you-then-threaten-you kind of guy, not a send-mutilated-flowers-through-a-third-party type."

"But you can't be sure."

"No. I can't be sure."

Karen closes the box and picks it up, slipping it into a large evidence bag before tossing her gloves in the trash.

"I'm taking this to have it processed for fingerprints. We'll see what we can find. Email me that security footage, and I'll have forensics take a look. Run the kid's face through facial rec." She looks at me, her expression stern. "Luna, if Caleb contacts you again—if anyone contacts you in a way that makes you uncomfortable—you call me. No more letting Damien Wolfe or anyone else handle it for you."

"I will." But I wonder how much my promises mean these days. I've assured Karen several times that I'd reach out if something unusual happens, but there's so much unusual in my life, I'd be calling her constantly if I followed through with my promise.

After she leaves, I feel drained. I walk over to the couch and sink beside Maren. She hands me Honey. The rabbit's warm, solid weight against my chest is just what I need.

"I'm so over all this crazy," she murmurs as I let my head drop onto her shoulder. "First, your may or may not be stalker, then the dead bodies, then Caleb, all these mysterious donations and payoffs, and now this."

"When you say it like that, it sounds like a lot."

Humor seems safer than acknowledging the weight of everything she catalogued. Less brutal than letting it all crash down on me at once.

"It's more shit than on the soap operas Estella watches."

She pushes to her feet, shifting Flower over her shoulder before taking Honey from me. I stretch out sideways on the sofa, letting my head rest on the arm. The warmth left over from Maren's body seeps into my every muscle.

"I'll take these ladies back to their cage. You stay put. Decompress for a bit." Maren pauses at the door and turns back. "I want a greasy cheeseburger and fries for dinner. I'll go to Nancy's. And I'm staying here tonight. What do you want from the diner?"

Her words hit me like a gift I didn't know I needed. I hadn't wanted to ask, but the thought of being alone tonight makes my stomach clench. My wolf will find his way around Maren's presence, but he never stays until morning.

"Get me a spinach salad with chicken and a side of fries, please."

The office is too quiet without Maren. I glance over at my desk, where the stack of paperwork mocks me with its importance. I should get back to work. But my limbs refuse to cooperate. My body is heavy, drained by the day's events and all the complications threading through what should be a simple life.

The thought of sitting at my desk feels like too much right now. I'll deal with it all tomorrow when I'm clearer, when the image of black dahlias splattered with red isn't burned into my retinas.

I close my eyes and try to push away the creeping anxiety that's been building all afternoon. Those flowers were meant to frighten me, to send some kind of message I don't understand. The deliberate destruction, the blood, the untraceable delivery—it feels personal.

I'm so tired of drama. I just want a normal day where the biggest crisis is Ricky and his boob obsession.

Is that too much to ask? One quiet, drama-free day where I can focus on the animals who depend on me without worrying about Karen and her investigation, or threatening ex-boyfriends, or whoever turned beautiful flowers into something horrific?

The sanctuary has always been my refuge, my way of making sense of a world that often seems senseless. But lately, it feels like chaos keeps finding me no matter what I do. And I'm not sure how much more I can take.

Chapter Eight

Luna

The deep rumble of Damien's voice floats up from downstairs as I fasten my second earring, a final touch to an outfit I've spent far too long selecting.

My heart does that ridiculous flutter it always does when he's near. I smooth down the fabric of my dress, checking my reflection one last time. The woman staring back looks elegant and polished, a far cry from my usual self, covered in animal fur and bodily fluids I can't always identify.

Maren's laughter drifts up the stairs, followed by Damien's lower, controlled responses. I can't make out their words, but the familiarity in Maren's tone makes me smile. She never treats anyone with undue reverence, not even billionaires, but she sure is under his spell. Not that I can blame her.

I hope she'll be alright alone here tonight. We're both still on edge about the flower delivery two days ago. I've heard nothing from Karen about the investigation. I didn't mention it to my wolf, but I wonder if I should have. He's so adept at stalking; perhaps he could have found whoever it was. But I worry about what he might do to the person if he found them, especially Caleb. I have no desire to see my ex ever again, but if he's the one who did this, I don't want him to die for it. And I worry about Maren being here alone until we know something more.

I step into my heels and make my way downstairs, gripping the railing as I descend. The conversation below stops as I come into view. Damien stands in my living room, magnificent in a tailored tuxedo, underneath a gray wool coat that accentuates his broad shoulders and lean waist. His dark eyes find me, and the weight of his stare sends a shiver racing down my spine.

"Thanks for taking care of the critters tonight," I say to Maren when I reach the bottom of the stairs, trying to sound casual despite the way my pulse races under Damien's scrutiny. His gaze follows me as I walk toward him, and the intensity of his stare is a heavy heat that makes it hard to breathe.

Maren whistles. "Damn, girl. I was right. You clean up good."

"Are you sure you're okay being alone?"

She waves me off. "Bitch, please, I'm fine. I'm just glad I don't have to drive home in this snow. Are you sure you'll make it down to Denver?"

"Yes, we're taking my helicopter."

The casual way he mentions it reminds me of the vast difference between our worlds. I run a wildlife sanctuary on a shoestring budget while he casually owns aircraft.

Maren lets out a laugh. "Of course, you have a helicopter. Let me guess, you've got a plane sitting around too."

His eyes never leave my face.

"Two."

His stare presses against my skin until I want to squirm, look away, fidget, or do something to break the connection, but I force myself to stay still. He looks at me like he's memorizing every detail, like he can see past my dress to what lies beneath.

"Where do you keep it?" I ask to cut through whatever this is between us.

"I have a heliport on my property. It's around the side of the house, so you didn't see it the day you were there."

"You came here to pick me up only to drive straight back to your house?" Disbelief colors my voice. "I could've driven over there."

"Not in this weather. The roads are too slick."

"I do have a truck with four-wheel drive. And I've driven in Colorado weather my whole life."

"Not anymore. Not as long as I'm around."

I want to bristle at his presumption, but his commanding response makes my body react. Heat floods my core, and my nipples tighten against the fabric of my dress. The tone of authority in his voice is similar to my wolf's, and my traitorous body responds in predictable fashion.

Shit.

"We'll be fine here too." Maren's voice cuts through the charged silence. "I'm going to give Ricky a little boob action, then we're going to watch a rom-com."

I chuckle as I look over at Ricky lying on the sofa, sliding over the cushions, back and forth from one end of the couch to the other.

"You should put him in his cage for the night."

"Nah, I like his company when he's not being too handsy. Besides, he's been pulling at the fur on his lower belly. I think something might be stressing him."

My veterinarian brain kicks into gear, concern overriding everything else.

"When did he start pulling on his fur? Why didn't you tell me?"

"I noticed it yesterday. I meant to mention it, but the day went crazy when that bighorn sheep came in."

I walk over and crouch in front of Ricky, where he's flat on his back, scratching at his belly. My mind is already cataloging possible causes—parasites, infection, or stress.

"What's the matter with your tummy, Rick?" I push his hand away and start feeling around his abdomen. He takes the opportunity to reach over and squeeze my breast. "Ow. Stop it." I look up at Maren. "We should do an ultrasound."

"I set some time aside in the schedule for one Monday morning. Don't worry, he'll be fine for tonight. I'll let him cop a feel or two, and he'll fall asleep watching the movie."

Out of the corner of my eye, Ricky's paw moves toward my chest again, but I stand before he can strike. As I rise, I catch Damien's amused expression.

He extends a hand. "Ready to go?"

I nod, my stomach flipping at the thought of what the evening holds. "Let me grab my coat."

Damien helps me into it, his fingers brushing the nape of my neck as I lift my hair.

"You look beautiful, Luna." The heat of his breath fans across my ear, and goosebumps race over my skin.

"Don't wait up." I smile at Maren as we head to the door.

"Oh, I won't. You kids have fun."

Damien's hand finds the small of my back as he guides me out. The cold air wraps around me, erasing the warmth of the house in a single breath. Snow falls in fat, lazy flakes. Damien parked his sleek black Range Rover in front of the porch steps, which is perfect, so I don't have to walk in the snow in my heels.

"Here." He opens the passenger door for me, holding out his hand. "Let me help you."

I'm capable of getting into a car on my own, but his old-fashioned courtesy is sweet.

He walks around to the driver's side, sliding into the seat, and the car suddenly feels much smaller. The vanilla and amber woody scent of him wraps around me, making my mouth water.

I'm constantly aroused by this man. Heat spreads through my body at his nearness, pooling low in my abdomen while my heart hammers against my ribs. My skin tingles with awareness from sharing this small space with him.

"I need to check on Athena real quick before we leave. I hope you don't mind."

"Of course not. But didn't you leave her at your house a few minutes ago?"

"No. I was in Denver for most of the day. I flew up to pick you up."

"Oh, Damien. You didn't have to do that. I could have driven down."

"I'll always pick you up."

I reach over and touch his hand, calloused and warm on the steering wheel. A slight tremor runs through his fingers, matching the unsteady rhythm of my own pulse.

Snow crunches beneath the tires as we wind along the five-minute stretch of road separating our properties. He turns in the long driveway, and the headlights sweep across snow-laden pines before revealing the Victorian's towering silhouette. In the dark, it looks haunted, though the lights glowing in several windows make it a little less scary.

"I've never seen lights on inside this place. Every time I trespassed, it was during the day. How are the renovations coming along?"

"Slow. The property isn't on the historical register, but the permitting has turned into a nightmare. The exterior is finished. Finally. The inside wiring is done, but we're still waiting on approvals for plumbing before the cosmetic work can even start. My designers compose resignation letters for entertainment."

He helps me out of the car and guides me up the front steps. The heavy oak door opens with a groan, revealing a grand foyer with scuffed hardwood floors and walls stripped of their wallpaper.

"The county wanted me to demolish it. Every delay feels like punishment for refusing."

"That sounds incredibly frustrating. But its nefarious reputation freaks people out around here."

The skittering of nails on hardwood echoes before the blue-gray pitbull appears, tail wagging and a purple bow around her neck this time.

"There's that beautiful girl!" I crouch as she bounds toward me, her whole body wiggling with joy. I scratch behind her ears and have to lean back to prevent her from licking my face and destroying my makeup. "How are you, sweet thing? Are you being good for your daddy?"

"She misses you." The tenderness in his voice pulls my attention away from the dog. I tip my head back to look at him and find he's watching us with an expression that's gone soft around the edges. "She enjoyed visiting your place and now whines when we pass your property on our walks."

"Aww, is that so?" I stand up. Athena stays pressed against my legs. "She's welcome at the sanctuary any time. She and Shadow get along so well. He and Ghost would love to have her for a sleepover sometime."

Damien reaches down to pat Athena's head. "I think she'd like that, but she's a needy girl. You might end up with her in your bed before you can stop her."

"My bed is full of animals now. I have three cats and one wolf in my bed every night." *Two wolves.* "The more the merrier."

I hope the heat rising in my cheeks isn't noticeable in the low light.

His mouth curves into that maddening half-smile. "Are you saying you're not discerning about who you let in your bed?"

"Nope. Not when they have fur and keep me warm."

"I'll remember that. Let me get her fed and watered. I'll be right back. Come on, girl."

Their footsteps fade into the depths of the house, leaving me alone in the foyer. I turn in a slow circle, taking in what remains of something once beautiful. The exposed plaster and paint-stripped woodwork remind me of the house's troubled history. A shiver runs up my spine.

I wrap my arms around myself, trying to shake the sensation of invisible eyes watching me. The phantom scent of death lingers in the air. As fascinated as I've always been with the property, how can Damien sleep here night after night with all the weight of this place pressing down? How many young girls had drawn their last breath within these walls?

"Ready?" Damien returns, Athena hot on his heels. Even the temptation of food can't pull her away from her favorite person.

"Yes." I exhale and push my unease down.

"You look beautiful, Luna." The heat in his eyes matches the warmth spreading through my chest, down to places that have no business responding to just the sound of his voice.

"You told me that already." I smile despite myself. "But thank you. I don't mind hearing it again."

He takes a step closer, his gaze dropping to my mouth. For a moment I think he's going to kiss me. Then his expression shifts, closing off, and he clears his throat while checking his watch.

"We should go. The pilot's waiting."

After one final scratch behind Athena's ears and a promise to visit soon, we head back out into the snow. Instead of returning to the car, Damien leads me around the side of the house on an asphalt path that is clear of snow. The snowflakes melt as soon as they land on it.

"Hot mix asphalt. Necessary safety precaution in the mountains," he says, like he can read my mind.

As we round the house, a sleek black helicopter comes into view, sitting on a landing pad, its blades already turning.

The engine's pitch rises, drowning out everything else. I have to lean in. "I've never been on a helicopter before."

His gaze locks onto mine. "I want to introduce you to many new things, Luna."

Heat floods my skin. My breath catches, not from the icy air biting at my cheeks, but from the way he's looking at me. Like he means more than helicopters and new experiences.

"Anything at all you want to try." He shifts closer.

"Anything?"

The challenge slips out before I can stop it. His eyes go dark, almost black.

"Anything."

Damien helps me into the helicopter, his hand firm on my waist, and I can't help but compare his touch to my wolf's. There's something in the way he grips me that is almost identical. Confident and possessive.

Why can't I stop comparing them? Why do I try to find similarities between them? They're so different. Damien is controlled and polished. My wolf is raw passion and animal hunger.

Yet as we lift into the snowy night sky, I find myself studying Damien's profile. The strong jaw, the perfect nose, the crinkles at the corners of his eyes. And those sexy silver streaks at his temples. I've never seen more than my wolf's mouth and the shadows of his eyes. His mask and the darkness he insists on always obscure the rest. Damien's square jaw seems similar, and for a split second, I think I see more, but then it's gone as he leans forward to speak to the pilot.

I inhale a shaky breath as my mind goes places it shouldn't, to ridiculous suspicions and an even crazier place, as I picture what it would be like to have both of them.

Jesus, what's happening to me? Now I'm contemplating threesomes. Maren would be so proud.

I need to get ahold of my libido before it gets me into more trouble than I'm already in.

I push the thought away and focus on the wonder of flying through the night in a private helicopter with a billionaire who, it seems, more and more bears a striking, unnerving resemblance to my wolf.

Chapter Nine

Damien

The ballroom pulses with wealth and ostentation. Crystal chandeliers cast their glow over Denver's elite, all dressed in their finest, champagne flutes in hand, checkbooks at the ready. I keep a possessive hand at the small of Luna's back as we move through the crowd, the silk of her dress warm beneath my palm.

Every eye in the room turns to her. I can't blame them. She's stunning tonight. The deep emerald dress hugs her curves like it was made for her body alone, her blonde hair cascading in loose waves over her shoulders. She doesn't realize how she outshines every woman here, her beauty unadorned by the calculated artifice that plagues these events.

"The turnout is incredible." Luna's wide eyes survey the room. "You must be pleased."

I force a smile, the muscles in my jaw tightening. "Numbers mean donations. Donations mean more animals we can help."

"But you hate this part, don't you?" Her voice is low, meant only for me. "The schmoozing?"

I look at her, surprised by her perception. Most women I've brought to these events are too dazzled by the glamor to notice my discomfort.

"Is it that obvious?"

She smiles, and I can't look away. "Only to someone who's paying attention."

The thought of her watching me and studying me sends a primitive satisfaction through my gut before panic follows in its wake. Does she see the truth lurking beneath this facade?

"Damien! There you are."

I turn to see Cade approaching, champagne in hand, his tuxedo as impeccable as mine.

"Cade." I shake his hand, though I don't know why. We saw each other four hours ago. "I'd like you to meet Dr. Luna Foster. Luna, this is Cade Crawford, my COO and the man who actually runs my companies while I pretend to work."

Cade's lips pull tight at the corners, the closest his face gets to a genuine smile. But his eyes are busy, scanning from me to Luna with the kind of scrutiny that misses nothing.

"Dr. Foster, it's a pleasure." He takes her hand, and his expression softens a fraction despite whatever reservations are churning behind his eyes. "Damien speaks of little else these days."

Subtle, Cade. Real fucking subtle.

"I hope he's been editing the embarrassing parts. Like my being a Peeping Tom." Luna's smile is warm and confident as she glances between us. "And please call me Luna. 'Doctor' makes me feel like I should be wearing scrubs instead of this dress."

"You look beautiful in anything." I've lost count of how many times I've told her tonight, but somehow the words feel inadequate each time. She's stunning in a way that scatters my senses and makes me want to abandon this entire event and take her somewhere private. Somewhere I can taste every inch of her warm, silken skin.

Luna blushes, and Cade raises an eyebrow at me. I'm never this open or unguarded. Especially not at events like this, where every word might be overheard, analyzed, and reported in tomorrow's society pages.

"I've heard about your wildlife sanctuary." Cade pivots, guiding us away from the awkward tension my compliment created. "Damien tells me you've revolutionized rehabilitation techniques for injured animals."

"That's an exaggeration," Luna says, though she stands a little straighter. "But we've had some success with methods that minimize human imprinting during treatment. The goal is always to return them to the wild as true wild animals, not creatures dependent on humans. I don't always succeed at that, though."

Her face lights up as she speaks, and I'm transfixed. This is the same passion I see in her eyes when I'm with her in the dark, when she arches against me, when she begs for release. But this... this is different, too. Pure. Untainted by the deception I've woven between us.

"Cade, would you mind getting Luna a drink? I need to speak to the mayor about something." I spot the politician across the room, then turn back to Luna. "I'll introduce you to him later, but I need to speak about some business now, and I don't want to bore you."

"Of course." Cade nods, understanding the subtext. This is my way of giving him a chance to spend time with Luna without me hovering like a possessive bastard. He holds out his arm to her. "Shall we?"

"Lead the way."

I catch his eye and hold it for a beat longer than necessary.

You better fucking watch your step, Cade.

His mouth quirks upward, that rare, but familiar smirk that tells me he's received the warning loud and clear.

My chest tightens with conflicting emotions as he leads her toward the bar. Part of me hates to see her walk away with another man, even Cade.

Though I trust Luna, and nothing he says will change my mind about her, I still need his opinion. No one reads people better than he does, and his investigative instincts are unparalleled.

Chapter Ten

Luna

Cade leads me toward the bar as Damien disappears into the crowd, swallowed by the mass of tuxedos and evening gowns. My stomach tightens, watching him walk away. Part of me wants to stay glued to his side in this sea of unfamiliar faces and designer dresses, but I push the impulse aside and focus on Cade.

The man beside me is not what I expected when Damien told me about his COO on the helicopter ride. He could have walked straight out of a military recruitment poster. Tall, broad-shouldered, and as intense as, if not more so than, Damien, with steel-gray eyes that seem to catalog every detail about me in the span of a heartbeat. His handshake was firm but not crushing, his smile genuine but measured.

Damien told me he was ten years older, but if it weren't for his head full of cropped salt and pepper hair and the crows' feet at the corners of his eyes, I'd never have thought he was in his mid-to-late fifties. Like Damien, he's handsome and has aged well. The kind of man who gets better with time instead of just older.

He guides me through the throng of guests with confident, controlled movements. People part for him, though I notice several women giving him appreciative glances. He seems oblivious to the attention, his focus on navigating us through the crowd.

"So, what's your poison?" He asks as we reach the bar, gesturing to the impressive array of top-shelf liquor. "I'd suggest something strong to deal with this crowd."

I consider the options, then decide to go with my instincts. "Whiskey. Neat."

His eyebrows rise, and for the first time, his smile reaches his eyes. "Make that two," he tells the bartender.

The amber liquid burns as it slides down my throat, warming me from the inside out. Cade watches me drain half the glass without flinching, and I catch the subtle dip of his chin, like I've passed some kind of test I didn't know I was taking.

"You're not what I expected." He swirls his own drink.

"What did you expect?"

"Someone more..." He pauses, searching for the right word. "Delicate. Damien described you as fierce, but most people hear 'veterinarian' and picture someone gentle."

"I am gentle. With animals." I take another sip. "Humans are a different story."

His laugh is low, rumbling from deep in his chest. "I can see why Damien likes you."

The way he says it makes me pause. I study his face. At the same time, his gaze travels across my features—forehead, cheekbones, and jaw. Not hostile, but not warm either.

I take a sip of my drink. "How long have you worked for him?"

He leans against the bar, casual but alert. "Twenty-five years, give or take. We met when I was fresh out of the Army."

"What kind of work do you do for him? I mean, I know about the security systems, but Damien mentioned you run all his businesses."

"I handle whatever needs handling. Damien's brilliant, but he gets... focused. He needs someone to manage the details while he's busy changing the world." There's affection in his voice, but something else too. Worry, maybe?

"That sounds like a big responsibility."

"Not really. He's a good man, Luna." Cade's expression grows serious. "Better than he gives himself credit for."

The intensity in his voice surprises me. There's real emotion there, controlled but unmistakable. "You really care about him."

"He's family. The only family I have besides my daughter." His jaw tightens. "That's why I'm protective of him. And why I need to know that anyone in his life has his best interests at heart."

My breath catches. This casual conversation suddenly feels less casual.

"Ahh. So that's what this is? You vetting me, Cade?"

"Not exactly." He takes a sip of his whiskey, those eyes never leaving mine. "There isn't one thing I or anyone on this planet could say that would change Damien's mind about you. He's quite smitten."

"So, what do you want to know? Are you asking if my intentions are honorable?"

"Something like that."

I finish my whiskey and set the glass down. "I care about Damien. More than I should, considering we haven't known each other long. But I'm not after his money, if that's what you're worried about."

"Money's the least of my concerns." His gaze doesn't waver. "Damien doesn't let people close. On the rare occasions he does, it's significant."

A defensive prickle runs through me. "I get the feeling you don't approve of my being here."

Cade signals the bartender for another round. "It's not about approval. It's about what happens when you step into his world. It can be complicated."

"Complicated how?"

He hands me a fresh glass, his fingers brushing mine. They're calloused and scarred, hands that have seen violence and hard use. "Let's just say Damien often has dealings with certain types of people. Not the kind you meet at charity galas. You get close to him, you're exposed to that world whether you want to be or not."

The temperature in the room hasn't changed, but goosebumps pebble along my arms anyway.

"Are you trying to scare me?"

"I'm trying to prepare you." His voice is gentle but firm. "If you're going to be in his life, you need to understand what that means."

"I'm stronger than I look."

"I'm beginning to see that." He studies me over his glass. "Tell me about your sanctuary. Damien says you're doing important work there."

The change of subject is deliberate, giving us both a chance to step back from the intensity. My shoulders relax as we move to safer ground.

"We rehabilitate injured and abused wildlife and provide sanctuary for animals that can't be released. Nothing glamorous, but it matters." I smile, thinking about Maren at home with Ricky.

"Can't be easy work."

"It's not always easy, no. But these animals deserve advocates, people willing to fight for them when they can't fight for themselves."

"That's exactly what Damien said you'd say."

"He talks about me?"

"I told you, he speaks of little else." His expression shifts, and the wariness fades from his eyes. "He's different since he met you. I don't think I've ever seen him this... invested in someone."

Warmth spreads through my chest, though his word choice is a little odd. "I enjoy spending time with him too."

"Good. He deserves that."

We stand in silence for a moment, watching the elegant crowd swirl around us. A string quartet plays in one corner while couples dance on the polished floor. The tension from earlier has dissolved, replaced by something that feels like an understanding between us.

"Can I ask you something?"

"Shoot."

"Earlier, you said Damien doesn't let people close. What about you? You seem just as guarded."

His laugh is rueful. "Occupational hazard. When your job is keeping someone safe, you learn to see threats everywhere."

"That must be exhausting."

"It can be." He drains his whiskey. "But some people are worth protecting."

I think about my wolf again, the secrets I keep to protect him, the lies I've told Karen, and the darkness I've discovered in myself.

"I understand that feeling."

Cade's eyes sharpen, and I cringe. The alcohol is making my tongue too loose. A commotion near the entrance draws our attention. A small crowd gathers around a distinguished man with silver hair.

"Looks like the governor's arrived. Damien will want to speak with him."

I scan the room until I spot Damien still deep in conversation with Denver's mayor and several other men in suits. Even across the crowded ballroom, he's magnetic—commanding attention without effort.

"He looks like he's in his element, but he hates every second of this, doesn't he?"

"He would rather eat glass. But he does it for the animals. He's become even more passionate about them since meeting you."

I blush, grateful for the dim lighting. "You're quite the confusing wingman, Cade."

"I don't peddle in bullshit, Luna. I tell it like it is. Damien's interest in you is genuine."

A waiter approaches with a tray of canapés, and I realize I haven't eaten since this morning. I grab two toast points with something pink smeared on top. The tiny portions of fancy food disappear before I can taste them, making me wish for a real meal.

Cade's gaze follows another waiter crossing the room before returning to me. "Not much substance to the food at events like this."

"I keep waiting for the actual dinner part of this party." I eye another passing tray, and Cade's expression shifts. Not quite a smile, but close.

"There'll be a five-course meal later, but each course will be smaller than what you'd feed a child. I always eat before these things."

"Good to know for next time." The words slip out before I can stop them, and I flush. There's no guarantee Damien will invite me to one of these events again.

"There will be. A next time." It's like he spotted my doubt the moment it surfaced. "Damien's not letting you go anywhere."

The steel-edged certainty in those words should raise every warning flag I have. Instead, my heart beats faster, my pulse jumping with what feels like anticipation.

"I've never seen him look at anyone the way he looks at you." Cade pauses, his fingers tracing the rim of his glass in slow circles. The statement feels odd considering he's only seen us together for less than five minutes. "Damien doesn't do anything halfway. When he commits to something—or someone—it's absolute." He sets the glass down with a soft clink. "The question is whether you're prepared for that level of devotion."

I think about my wolf's hands on my body, the possessive way he touches me, claims me. The way Damien's eyes follow my every movement when we're together.

"I'm learning to be."

"Good." He nods, and I get the sense I've passed whatever test he's been giving me. "Because he's going to need someone strong enough to stand beside him, not behind him."

"Do I strike you as the kind of woman who stands behind anyone?"

"Not at all. The fact that you rehabilitate dangerous animals for a living and you're going toe-to-toe with me right now makes it clear you can hold your own." The last traces of his earlier wariness melt away. "Most people find me intimidating."

"You are. But so am I when the situation calls for it."

Across the room, Damien's head turns. Our eyes meet through the crowd, and heat spreads across my chest, crawling up my neck. He leans toward the mayor, his mouth moving, but his attention stays locked on me. Then he's cutting through the clusters of guests, closing the distance between us.

"He's coming back." My hands find the fabric of my dress, smoothing wrinkles that aren't there.

"Probably worried I'm scaring you off."

"I don't scare easily."

Cade studies me, his gaze assessing. "No, it appears you don't. If I may be so bold to say, I think you might be exactly what he needs."

A brunette intercepts Damien. She's stunning, all curves and confidence in a red dress that leaves nothing to the imagination.

"Oh, that's not good." Cade signals the bartender. "That's his ex. We better go save him before he tosses her out on her ass."

His tone is casual, almost amused rather than urgent. He slides a champagne flute toward me.

"Come on. Let's go rescue your man."

Chapter Eleven

Damien

I never let Luna out of my sight as I make my way through the crowd, shaking hands and accepting congratulations on another successful benefit. Last year's event raised over five million for the foundation. We're on track to exceed that tonight.

"Damien Wolfe, as I live and breathe."

The voice hits me like a cascade of ice water as Francesca Vega steps in front of me, blocking my path back to Luna. She stands closer than appropriate, her red dress cut in a dramatic V that draws attention to the cleavage she's spent considerable money perfecting. Her smile promises things I have zero interest in.

"Francesca. I didn't know you were in Denver. Or that you were on the guest list."

Nothing in my tone gives away the irritation at seeing my ex. If you can even call her an ex. Ours wasn't a relationship. It was a fuckfest that turned into a shitshow of epic proportions. We fucked for three weeks, longer than I've fucked any other woman, other than Luna. But when it had run its course for me and I stopped answering her calls, she didn't take it well, to say the least. It took months for me to get her off my back, and it was only after I introduced her to an acquaintance who was into her kinks that she stopped harassing me.

"I flew in yesterday. When I heard about the benefit, I simply had to attend. Tiffany was so gracious to extend the last-minute invitation."

I need to have a talk with my EA.

She places her hand on my arm, her red nails standing out against the black of my tux. "You know how I adore your passion for animals."

I remove her hand. Every part of me recoils from the contact, from any touch but Luna's.

"Your donation is always appreciated. If you'll excuse me—"

"Don't be so cold, darling." She steps closer, the scent of her heavy perfume making me want to step back, but Damien Wolfe doesn't retreat. "We had such fun together. Don't you miss me... even a little?"

I spot Luna with Cade over her shoulder. The way she carries herself, confident and at ease despite the opulent surroundings, makes Francesca's practiced seduction seem cheap and tawdry in comparison.

"No, I don't. It was six years ago, Francesca. We've both moved on."

Her smile falters, then hardens. "Have we?" She turns, following my gaze to Luna. "Ah. Not your usual type, is she?"

Luna and Cade reach us before I can respond. My hand moves to Luna's back without thought, settling low, fingers splayed wide. The touch anchors me as her scent wraps around me. My breathing evens out. The tension in my shoulders loosens. And yes, everyone watching will know exactly what this means.

Mine.

"Luna, this is Francesca Vega. We knew each other some years ago." The past tense is deliberate. "Francesca, Dr. Luna Foster."

Francesca's gaze slides over Luna from head to toe. Her lips curve into something that might be called a smile if it held any warmth.

"A doctor? How impressive." Francesca's tone makes it clear she finds it anything but. "What kind of medicine do you practice?"

"I'm a wildlife veterinarian." Luna's smile is unwavering. "I run a sanctuary for injured and rehabilitating wild animals."

"A veterinarian?" Francesca's eyebrows rise. "How... untamed. I suppose someone has to look after the wild things."

My jaw tightens, anger rising at Francesca's condescending snub of what Luna does, but Luna laughs. The sound is genuine, not forced or awkward, and it catches Francesca off guard.

"Definitely untamed. Last month, I had to remove shotgun pellets from the rear end of a 400-pound black bear." Luna takes a sip of her champagne, her eyes dancing with amusement. "But I do get to wear much more comfortable shoes to work than these heels. That's a definite perk."

Cade chuckles under his breath, and even I can't help the smile that tugs at the corner of my mouth, despite the unwelcome reminder of Luna's injury. Francesca's face hardens for a split second before her social mask snaps back into place.

"How fascinating. Damien has always had such diverse tastes." She turns to me, disregarding Luna. "We must catch up properly before I leave town. Call me."

"I'm afraid my schedule is quite full. Perhaps next time you're in Denver."

Which will hopefully be never.

Francesca's smile doesn't reach her eyes. "You always did play hard to get, darling. It's what made the chase so delicious." She glances at Luna again. "Enjoy the benefit, Dr. Foster. I hope some of these wealthy patrons can spare a thought for your bears."

With that parting shot, she slinks away into the crowd, the exaggerated sway of her hips doing nothing for me.

Luna watches her go. "Well, she's delightful. Former girlfriend?"

"Briefly," I admit. "It was over quickly once I realized she saw animals as accessories rather than living beings."

Luna's posture doesn't change. No jealousy tightens her features, and no insecurity creeps into her expression.

"I'm going to guess a tiny purse dog she dyed red to match her outfit?"

The accuracy of her guess startles a laugh out of me. "A Pomeranian. And it was pink."

"Even worse." She sighs, her sympathy for the dog obvious. "Well, she's certainly beautiful."

"She's nothing compared to you."

It's happening more and more. This loss of control, this honesty that slips past my walls.

Color blooms across her cheeks. Her gaze drops, then rises to meet mine.

"Smooth talker."

I move into her space, close enough to catch the hitch in her breathing.

"Not smooth. Honest."

Her lips part. The blush spreads down to her collarbone, visible above the neckline of her dress. She toys with the stem of her glass, suddenly fascinated by it.

"You're staring," she whispers.

"I know."

———— ◆ ————

For the next hour, Luna accompanies me as I make my way around the room, introducing her as I play the role of the charming host, thanking donors, discussing the foundation's achievements, and shaking hands with politicians and celebrities whose support lends credibility to our cause.

Luna is magnificent, moving through the crowd with effortless grace. When the governor pulls me aside, she assures me she'll be fine. It takes longer than I anticipated, and when I return to the ballroom, I see her engaged in an animated conversation with a photographer whose work we've featured in our campaigns.

I can't take my eyes off her as she uses her hands to demonstrate something that looks like the wingspan of a bird of prey, given her gestures. The photographer grins like she's just made his entire night. Everyone she talks to comes away smiling. She has that effect on people. On animals. On me.

But watching her captivate another man makes my hands curl into fists at my sides. The photographer is harmless. Cade mentioned something about a husband, but that knowledge does nothing to stop the heat climbing up my neck. Logic doesn't touch this. Sharing her feels like bleeding out in slow motion.

I want her attention. All of it. Only on me.

I start moving without conscious thought, determined to reclaim what's mine when Cade appears at my elbow.

"A word?"

We move to a quieter corner of the ballroom. It's only because I'm eager to hear what he thinks after the time he spent with Luna that I let him delay me, but my gaze stays on her.

Cade glances toward her, then back to me. "She's remarkable."

"Yes, she is." I don't bother hiding the pride, the hunger, and the possessiveness in my voice.

"That's the problem, Damien. You're in too deep. I can see it in how you look at her. This definitely isn't only about sex anymore."

"I already told you that."

"But I don't know if I'd call it love either. It's different seeing you with her in person, rather than watching you watch her through monitors like some lovesick stalker." He meets my gaze. "You're losing it. The look you were giving that photographer—it's the same look you get right before you kill someone."

"Don't be ridiculous."

"I'm serious. You looked ready to walk over there and rip his head off with your bare hands."

Because I was.

"Your point?"

"My point is, you can't hide yourself from her much longer. Not when you're two seconds from murdering harmless photographers. So, what's your plan? She's not stupid, Damien. I've seen her studying you tonight, like she's trying to make sense of what she's seeing."

I rake my hand through my hair. How many times are we going to have this conversation?

"I'm working on it, Cade. So back the fuck off. I'll tell her when I'm ready."

"When? Because this thing between you two—" He gestures between Luna and me. "—is a lit fuse, and it's going to explode in your face. All our faces."

"I said I'll handle it." The words come out steady, but my gut tells a different story.

Cade sighs. "Now that I've met her, I see why she's captivated you. She's everything you said she was. Brilliant, passionate, genuine, but you need to pull it together."

Luna approaches, a glass of champagne in her hand, her eyes bright.

"There you are. I was thinking you'd abandoned me to the wolves."

I'm the only wolf in your life, little doe.

"Never. Just fulfilling my duties as host."

"Well, you're very good at it, even if you hate every minute." She touches my arm, and even through the layers of my tuxedo, the heat of her fingers seeps into my skin. Her touch is the worst kind of agony, but I want to drown in the pain. "I met Senator Howard. He told me the foundation is funding a new wildlife corridor through three counties. That's incredible, Damien. Why didn't you tell me?"

Admiration flickers in her expression, and it reaches straight through my ribs and squeezes. When she looks at me like that, like I'm someone worthy of her respect and her affection, I almost believe it myself. I forget the darkness, the blood on my hands, and the lies I've built between us. For a few moments, at least.

"It still has to clear state and federal hurdles. I don't like tempting fate." I hold out my hand. "Dance with me."

The words stop her mid-sip. She blinks, not expecting the invitation. After a moment's pause, she places the glass on a server's tray and slides her fingers into mine. Her touch is warm, with the barest tremor running through it.

"I should warn you, I'm terrible at dancing like this." She steps closer. "Put on some Taylor Swift or Rihanna, and I'll show you moves that'll make your head spin, but this fancy footwork?" She glances down between us. "You might be sorry you didn't wear steel-toed shoes."

I guide her onto the polished floor. "I'll take my chances."

She barely reaches my shoulders, her hand small and delicate in mine. Despite her protests, her movements are graceful, her body responding to my lead like we've done this a thousand times before.

The orchestra swells with something slow and haunting. She settles into my arms, her free hand coming to rest over my racing heart.

"See?" I guide her through a simple turn. "Not terrible at all."

Her lips quirk up at the corners. "That's your expertise talking. I'm just trying not to maim you."

A sound escapes me, something between amusement and disbelief. When was the last time someone made me smile at one of these events?

"You could step on both my feet, and I wouldn't care."

"Don't say I didn't warn you."

We drift together across the floor, her body molding to mine like she belongs there. Heat radiates from every point where we touch—my palm against her back, our fingers intertwined, the whisper of space between her chest and mine. The urge to close that distance claws at me. I want to crush her against me until I can feel her heart hammering against my own and press my face into the curve of her neck where her perfume mingles with something uniquely her. I want to wrap myself in her until she's all that remains, until everything else fades into nothing.

But I can't. Not here. Not now.

Even as I tell myself that, I pull her closer. My hand spreads wider across her back, feeling every breath she takes.

"Thank you for bringing me tonight." Her voice flows between us, soft and private. "I can tell these events aren't your thing, but what you're doing for animals... it matters, Damien. It really does."

"You know what matters?"

"What?"

"This. How good you feel in my arms." The confession tumbles out unfiltered. "How right this feels."

She stumbles. A small misstep, but I catch her, steadying her against me. Her face flames red. "You can't say things like that."

"Why not?" I dip my head until my lips brush her temple. "It's true."

Her fingers curl into my jacket, gripping the fabric. "Because you make it very hard to remember this is..."

"What?" I prompt when she trails off.

She looks up at me, conflict written across her features. "I don't know anymore."

"Good." I hold her gaze with mine. "Because I stopped knowing the moment I met you."

I'm moving before I can think better of it. The space between us vanishes, inch by inch, until her breath ghosts across my lips. Warm. Sweet. My pulse pounds in my ears.

I need to taste her again. The need claws through me, sharper than hunger, more vital than air.

"Luna." Her name escapes, hoarse and desperate.

She lifts her face to mine, and the light catches in her eyes, hazel depths flecked with gold and green. Open, trusting, and so beautiful the rest of the ballroom fades into meaningless noise. At this moment, she's the only real thing in my world. Everything I want and everything I fear I'm destined to lose. The ground shifts beneath my feet, and I'm falling, not gracefully, not with control, but like a man stepping off the edge of the world.

I press my lips to hers, the softest touch, designed to look innocent to any casual observer, but the moment our mouths connect, lightning shoots through my bloodstream and scrambles every coherent thought. The careful control I've built crumbles to ash.

Her quick intake of breath vibrates against my mouth, and that tiny sound shoots straight to my cock. I bite down hard on the inside of my cheek to keep from making a sound that would scandalize half the room.

She draws back a fraction, her brows pulling together in the way they do when she's thinking too hard.

"Should you be doing that here? In public?"

"Why not?"

My arm tightens around her waist, drawing her against me until there's no question of distance, no pretense of casual affection. The logical part of my brain that governs these situations has gone silent. All that remains is the need to mark her as mine in front of every damn person in this room.

"Because you don't want people to get the wrong idea about us."

"And what idea is that? That you're my date and you're beautiful and I—"

The words slam into an invisible wall.

I love you.

The declaration hovers there, desperate to escape, but speaking it now would detonate everything between us. "I'm crazy about you?"

"Damien." She breathes my name, and her entire face transforms, her eyes going soft and liquid, and pupils expanding until they swallow the hazel.

"I don't care what people think, Luna. I've been dying to kiss you all night. Since you walked down those stairs in that dress and made me forget how to breathe."

A war plays out across her face. Her lips part on a shaky exhale, her tongue darting out to wet her bottom lip. Want radiates from every inch of her. Every line of her body says yes, but something invisible holds her back, some chain of guilt wrapped around her conscience. She thinks she's betraying him. Her wolf.

You're not betraying anyone, little doe. You're kissing the same man.

Her fingers clutch my shoulder. The air between us hums with electricity, stretched so tight one wrong breath could shatter it. Then she lifts her chin, eyes falling closed, lips parting in unmistakable invitation.

I don't make her wait.

My mouth finds hers. The kiss begins soft, a question more than a statement, but she answers by pressing closer, and the careful restraint I've been clinging to dissolves. Her lips are warm silk, sweet with champagne and the unique taste that belongs only to her.

A sound escapes her lips, and my body responds like she's thrown a switch. Arousal slams through my system like a sledgehammer. Blood rushes south so fast it leaves me dizzy. That tiny, breathless moan rewires every circuit in my brain.

Her soft curves fit against my hard lines, silk and heat melding to me until there's no space left between us. Her heartbeat hammers against my chest, rapid and wild, matching the chaos in my own veins.

This. This is what I've kept from us with my masks and lies. The knowledge sits like acid in my stomach. I'm the architect of my own hell.

I keep the kiss as gentle and controlled as I'm capable of, but a wild current of need pulses beneath the surface, a riptide that could pull us both under if I give it an inch. I can taste her want. It's there, sweet and desperate on her tongue. I feel it in the bite of her nails into my shoulder and the way she tilts her head and opens for me, inviting me deeper into the wet heat of her mouth.

I deepen the kiss by degrees. A gentle pull of her bottom lip between mine, the slide of my tongue against hers, and the change in angle that lets me explore the corners of her mouth. Every small gasp she makes, every shift of her body closer to mine, stokes the fire building in my chest until it threatens to consume me.

When we finally surface, the world feels different. Her breathing stutters out in quick, shallow pants that echo mine. Her lips look claimed. Swollen, darker, and thoroughly kissed. The sight of them is so beautiful it's hard to look away. The war I witnessed play out in her eyes has ended, leaving only desire, hot enough to reduce me to ash.

"Wow."

The single syllable floats between us as she lifts trembling fingers to her mouth, like she needs proof of what just happened.

Wow, indeed.

Chapter Twelve

Luna

I step out of the ladies' room after freshening up, my mind still spinning from the evening—the opulence, the people, the way Damien kept me tucked against his side all night. The way other women looked at him. The way he looked only at me.

The gala is winding down, but as host, Damien needs to stay until the end. After our first dance, dinner was served, giving me space to pull myself together and quiet the heat still burning under my skin. But then he asked me to dance again after dinner and kissed me a second time, deeper and hungrier than the first. When the music stopped, I fled to the bathroom, my composure hanging by a thread.

Damien kisses me like he wants to consume me. No one's ever kissed me like that. A deep, soul-consuming kiss that leaves a person breathless and weak, trembling with aftershocks.

I can still feel it, still taste it. The man kisses how I imagine he fucks. Slow and tender. So very different from my wolf.

"There you are."

I gasp as Damien's lips and warm breath brush against my ear as he steps up behind me.

"I was beginning to worry. You'd been in there so long."

I turn to find his blue-gray eyes studying me with an intensity that quickens my pulse. "I needed a moment to myself."

With his hand on my lower back, he leads me out of the hallway and back into the ballroom. "Did you enjoy the gala?"

"I did, but I'm not used to this world."

"You fit in perfectly." His lips curve into that half-smile that sends heat spiraling through me every time.

There are still some stragglers in the ballroom, but almost everyone is gone. Cade walks up to us as Damien leads me toward the coat check room.

"You two heading out?"

"Yes. You and Tiffany can wrap it up."

Cade nods before turning to me, taking my hand. "It was lovely to meet you, Luna. Your presence made this night bearable." He leans toward me. "And just between us, you're way too good for him."

His words sound teasing, but there's something deeper, a dangerous undercurrent that seems to lurk beneath them. Damien tenses beside me.

"Yes, she is. Now, let go of her hand before I break yours off."

Cade drops my fingers and steps back. The look that passes between the two men is loaded with a history I'm not part of, a silent conversation happening in the space of a few seconds. Then Damien's shoulders drop, tension bleeding away.

"It was nice to meet you, Cade." I inject warmth into my voice, trying to smooth over whatever happened.

Cade's expression returns to a mask of professional composure.

"You two have a good night."

⁂

Damien guides me away. I consider asking him what that was all about, but it's none of my business.

He retrieves our coats but tosses them over his arm rather than offering me mine. He leads me down a hallway and around a corner toward a bank of private elevators, the ones that we used when we landed on the roof earlier.

"How about a nightcap before I take you home?" His voice is casual, but his eyes burn with intention. "My penthouse is on the top floor. I have an excellent view of the city."

I hesitate. I should decline. Tomorrow is Sunday, so it will only be Maren and me, and I need to check Ricky's tummy. But more than that, my wolf will come to my bed in a few hours, and the kisses with Damien already feel like a betrayal. Is it smart to spend any more time with him?

Self-preservation screams at me to refuse and ask him to take me home.

"One drink," I say instead, and Damien's smile widens. Warmth floods my chest, pooling behind my ribs until I can barely breathe.

As we near the elevator, a metal wall-mounted pad beside it scans Damien's eye, and the doors open.

"These only go to my private floors." We step inside, and the doors close.

Silence wraps around us, broken only by the elevator's mechanical hum. My pulse kicks up, a betrayal of nerves I can't quite swallow down. His presence fills the small space, the mirrored walls reflecting him from every angle. His profile, his hands, and the way he watches me as the numbers beside the door climb, each floor bringing us deeper into dangerous territory.

Maren's words from the other day echo inside my head.

"His penthouse is in the same building. Win-win. Just head on upstairs, and I'll let you fill in the blanks..."

Yeah, this is a mistake.

"Having second thoughts?"

Is the man a mind reader?

My hands tremble as I grip the handrail, desperate for something to steady myself against this tide of want threatening to sweep away my better judgment. Every second of silence stretches the tension tighter, like a violin string about to snap. I need an escape route, something light and safe.

I tilt my face up to meet his gaze, painting on a smile. "I'm wondering if you have a spare pair of slippers. These heels weren't designed for actual walking, and I'm pretty sure I left a trail of sequins from the ballroom to the elevator."

His laugh breaks through the charged air between us. "Good. The place could use a little sparkle. Too much marble and steel, not enough personality."

The elevator slows to a stop, and the doors slide open. My breath catches as his world unfolds before me in sweeping grandeur, soaring ceilings, and an expanse of clean lines claiming the entire top floor. He hit the mark about the marble and steel. For all its undeniable elegance, the space carries a chill. It's too pristine, too perfect, like a museum where visitors aren't meant to linger.

Floor-to-ceiling windows frame the city like a living painting, Denver's lights twinkling against the night sky. The snowstorm adds a dreamy quality to the view, turning the night ethereal. Dense waves of white cascade past the glass, each flake luminous against the darkness, backlit by the city's thousand windows that feel like glowing eyes.

"Oh," I move toward the windows as if pulled by the sight. "This is—"

"The view makes it worth the ridiculous price tag."

I laugh, appreciating his attempt at humility even though we both know what "ridiculous" means in Damien Wolfe terms.

"You weren't exaggerating about the view."

He comes up behind me, standing close. Not touching, but near enough that his warmth radiates against my back. "What's your poison? Whiskey? Wine?"

"Whiskey. Neat."

I follow his reflection in the window as he moves to a bar in the corner and selects a bottle, pouring two generous measures into crystal tumblers. His movements are fluid and controlled, like everything about him.

Everything except for the moments when I catch him looking at me. In those unguarded seconds, hunger blazes raw and undisguised in his eyes, and my skin goes hot, nerve endings firing like live wires beneath the surface.

"Here."

He hands me my drink. Our fingers brush during the exchange, and electricity skitters up my arm at the brief contact.

"Thank you." I take a cautious sip and can't suppress a small sound of appreciation. The whiskey is rich and complex, sliding down my throat with only a pleasant burn. "This is exceptional."

"It should be. It's a thirty-year single malt from a small distillery in the Scottish Highlands. Only a few hundred bottles are made each year." He stands beside me now, both of us facing the view. "I discovered it on a trip years ago and bought their entire stock for that season."

I laugh, shaking my head. "Of course you did."

"What does that mean?" There's an edge to his voice now.

"Just that it's a very Damien Wolfe thing to do. Find something rare and beautiful and then acquire it."

He turns to face me, his expression unreadable. "Is that how you see me? As someone who collects beautiful things?"

I meet his gaze. "I think you're someone who knows what he wants and isn't afraid to go after it."

"And what if what I want isn't for sale?" His voice drops lower, and my skin flushes with sudden heat.

"Then I imagine you find other ways to get it." I take another sip of whiskey. "It's peaceful up this high. Though I prefer my view of the mountains and forest."

He turns to me and takes the still half-full glass from my hand, setting it aside with his empty one.

"Stay tonight."

My heart skips several beats. "Damien—"

"The snow's getting worse." He nods toward the window. "I'll take you back if it's what you really want, but I'd love for you to stay."

Hope lights his features, but underneath runs a current of desire and want so heavy my throat tightens.

"I have plenty of guest rooms if that's what you're worried about."

But his eyes tell a different story. He doesn't want me in a guest room. He wants me in his bed.

"I should get back. The animals—"

"Maren is there." He reaches for my hand, and his thumb brushes the pulse point on my wrist, making me tremble. "Stay, Luna."

I want to. God, how I want to. But my wolf will come for me tonight, and if I'm not there, there's no telling what he might do.

"I can't." I hate the regret in my voice.

Damien's gaze burns with intensity. My pulse hammers as he leans in, giving me time to pull away, and when I don't, his mouth meets mine.

The first brush of his lips is light, a whisper of contact that makes my breath hitch. Tentative, careful, like our first kiss on the dance floor. They're sinfully soft, a stark contrast to the hard body pressing close. His chest is solid muscle beneath the thin fabric of his shirt. My pulse roars in my ears. I tilt forward until the warmth pouring off him surrounds me and beckons me nearer. My hands flatten against the smooth cotton of his shirt. Underneath my palm, his heart pounds a wild rhythm, the force of it pulsing against my fingers.

His tongue sweeps along my lower lip, seeking rather than taking. I part for him, and a low growl escapes his throat, vibrating between us. His hands slide down my spine to settle at the small of my back, pulling me against him until our hips meet. My breath catches, and my legs turn liquid beneath me.

Stop. Pull away.

The words echo in my head, but my hands betray me, my treacherous fingers reaching up for the silver threading his temples, the hair I've been dying to touch since setting my damn eyes on him.

His impeccable styling, so pristine an hour ago, crumbles beneath my touch, and satisfaction blazes through me, as intoxicating as the whiskey on his breath.

Desire unfurls, restraint melting like honey between us as the kiss deepens. We breathe together, sharing the same heated air, mouths fusing in an unhurried rhythm. His teeth catch my upper lip, applying enough pressure to make me gasp.

His arms lock around me, and the hard outline of his arousal presses against my abdomen. My back curves toward him, my body arching of its own accord. He growls low in his throat and pushes me backward, step by step, until glass meets my spine. The sudden chill against my bare skin makes me gasp, the contrast of the cold window and my scorching flesh enough to steal my breath.

He tilts my chin up, drawing me back to his mouth, and a slow fire ignites. The gentle pressure becomes something richer as the kiss turns languid. This is what I love about kissing, tongue stroking tongue in a dance that echoes deeper hungers.

His hands slide into my hair before trailing down my neck and spine, leaving goosebumps in their wake, to grip my hips. His fingers dig in, sending sparks across my skin. The touch burns familiar, like my body already knows the shape of his hands. My nails find the nape of his neck as he claims my mouth with his.

He breaks away to trace my jaw with his lips.

"Damien..." His name escapes on a breath.

"Do you want to stop?" His question vibrates against my skin, sending shivers cascading down my spine.

My mind screams to flee, to remember the wolf waiting at home, but fire races through my veins, drowning out reason, even as guilt claws at my throat.

"We should slow down."

He draws back and meets my eyes. He's no longer the composed executive but a man raw and unleashed.

"Slow down." His lips twist with dark promise. "Not stop."

My thoughts scatter as he sinks down. The powerful, untouchable Damien Wolfe on his knees before me. Air vanishes from my lungs.

His fingertips ghost beneath my dress, trailing heat up my calves, then my thighs. My core clenches as my dress climbs higher, and my chest stutters. He's going to expose me here, pressed against glass, while the city lights witness everything.

His fingers dance higher on my thighs, burning away every coherent thought about why this is madness. Silk bunches at my waist, the fabric caught on the flare of my hips.

"Tell me to stop, Luna." His thumbs graze the lace of my panties. "Tell me, and I will."

My stomach tightens. I should insist he take me home, where in only a few hours I'll be coming so hard I'll forget all about Damien Wolfe. But my voice has fled, and the words won't come.

"Your silence tells me everything." His fingers curl into the waistband. "But I need to hear you say it, Luna. I need to know you want this as much as I do."

The formality and his insistence on my explicit consent move me in ways I don't expect. My chin drops.

"I want this. But I'm terrified."

"Of me?" Lines crease between his brows.

"Of how much I want you. Of what this means."

Warmth softens his features even as his eyes flame hotter. "We don't have to define this right now. Tonight is for pleasure. Yours and mine."

The lace whispers down my legs, a slow glide that makes my pulse stutter. His eyes stay fixed on mine, refusing to look away even as the fabric drops. Cool air kisses my exposed flesh, raising goosebumps across my skin. But the real tremors begin when Damien's lips press against my thigh.

"Step out."

My feet obey before my brain processes the command. I lift one foot, then the other, careful not to let my heels slip off. He pockets the lace with a grin that burns heat into my cheeks.

Arousal gathers between my thighs, impossible to hide. The exact moment he catches the scent, his nose twitches and eyes go black as they track the flush spreading across my skin.

"Beautiful."

His palm climbs my calf, leaving fire in its wake. My mouth opens, but his breath against my center steals every word.

"Let me make you feel good, Luna." Dark eyes hold mine from below. "I want you to come apart for me. Will you let me?"

His request, this seeking of permission I'm not used to, even after I stand here bare before him, proves more intoxicating than his touch.

"Yes." My fingers dive into his hair again. "Please."

He parts me with gentle fingers, opening me to his gaze. A whimper tears from my lips as his tongue tastes me for the first time. My head meets the glass behind me with a soft thud.

Damien's touch carries tenderness wrapped in demand, nothing like my wolf's devouring need. Even in gentler moments, he's never this careful. He's always hungry.

No! Stop thinking about him here.

My fingers clutch Damien's hair, anchoring me, as heat gathers low in my belly. The dark and silver strands tangle around my knuckles, and my knees shake with the effort to hold me upright.

He lifts my right leg over his shoulder, my thigh pressing against his cheek. He stills, his nose grazing the most sensitive part of me, then he teases with a soft flick of his tongue against it before moving lower.

"So sweet." The words vibrate against my flesh. "Always so fucking sweet."

Familiarity echoes in those words, but then his tongue finds my clit, and all thought dissolves. My hips surge forward, seeking more pressure, more friction.

"Patience." One hand traces my calf, and the other caresses the thigh beside his face. "We're going to take this slow, remember?"

A moan tears free, pleasure and torment battling in my chest.

"Damien. Please..."

"Please, what? Tell me what you need."

All thought scatters as his breath warms my center.

"More. I need more."

"Like this?" His tongue traces one slow path from my entrance to my clit. A cry rips from my chest, fingers clawing at his hair.

"Yes! Like that, please don't stop."

But he maintains that maddening pace, gentle strokes that wind tension tighter at the base of my spine.

As release hovers within reach, when I balance on the knife's edge, he withdraws. His nose nudges my clit, his breath a whisper against my wet flesh, pulling me back from the brink.

"Damien." Desperation bleeds through my voice. "Why are you teasing me?"

"Because I want to savor this." His lips ghost over my thigh. "I want to remember every sound you make, every tremble of your thighs, every tug of your fingers in my hair. And my name on your lips when you come for me."

The raw intimacy of his words brings tears to my eyes. "Please. I need to—"

"Not yet." His voice is firm but gentle. "Not until you're so desperate that you'll scream my name when you fall apart."

He dives back in with renewed purpose, his tongue setting a lazy rhythm that steals my breath. A strong hand lifts my remaining leg, spreading me wide across his shoulders.

"Oh."

The sound catches in my throat as my fingers clench his hair. His palms cup my ass, holding me steady against the glass.

"I've got you, Luna. I won't let you fall." His tongue delves inside me. "I'll never let you fall."

Those words send tremors through my frame. My body quivers between cold glass and molten heat.

His finger traces my slick folds before sliding deep. A second joins the first, and I arch at the delicious pressure.

He gathers my wetness on the digits before pulling out and sliding lower. His finger circles the tight ring of muscle at the back, pushing inside. The new stretch makes me gasp.

"Oh, God."

My wolf takes my ass with force and hunger, but never with this careful exploration.

I need to stop this. I'm betraying him. But Damien's tongue against my clit and finger working deeper erases everything except raw feeling.

My thighs shake against his shoulders, yet he never wavers. Each deliberate flick of his tongue, each gentle thrust of his finger, winds the coil inside me tighter. He works a second finger inside, opening me further. The stretch burns, stoking the inferno in my core.

His tongue traces gentle circles around my clit, and it's maddening because I crave speed, pressure, and force. But part of me never wants this soft worship to end. He finds every sensitive spot as if he's mapped my body before, as if he knows exactly how to unravel me.

Pressure mounts like a gathering storm.

"Damien. I'm close. So close."

My wolf's brutality has trained my body to expect domination, and this tenderness leaves me hanging.

"Please." My voice splinters. "I need more."

His teeth capture my clit, and reality explodes. Heat and sensation consume everything as my orgasm tears through me in savage waves. My body convulses against his mouth while a scream rips from my throat, his name echoing off the walls of his penthouse. I sag against the window, my chest heaving, his lips and tongue still pulling, wringing the last of it out of me until I have to press both palms to his head and push him away because I can't take anymore.

"Beautiful." He turns his face, murmuring against my still quivering thigh. "So fucking beautiful when you come."

His fingers slide free, and he presses a soft kiss to my still-throbbing clit. The contact draws another whimper, another ripple of pleasure-pain. Then he helps me down, steadying me on trembling legs before rising to his feet.

When he's at his full height again, I'm struck by the contrast between us. He stands in his tuxedo, composed, though his hair is sexily wild from where I'd tugged on it, his mouth and chin glistening with my arousal.

For a moment, I gape at him, at how together he still looks while I'm wrecked. He leans in and kisses me, letting me taste myself on his lips. His tongue traces mine, sharing the evidence of my pleasure, and I moan into his mouth.

When he breaks the kiss, his eyes have darkened to near black, pupils swallowing the blue-gray until only hunger remains. "Stay. Let me take you to bed. Let me spend the night showing you how good I can make you feel."

My pulse jolts, and the temptation is overwhelming. My body hums with residual pleasure, aching for more. But guilt coils in my stomach like a serpent, joined by the familiar prickle of being watched.

My head snaps toward the glass windows, scanning the night sky for a masked figure that couldn't possibly be there because we're sixty stories up.

In the window's reflection, I see myself. I'm a tangle of messy hair and a rumpled dress hiked up around my waist, knees still unsteady, my nakedness exposed to all of Denver spread below. I yank the fabric down, my hands trembling. If letting Damien bring me to climax with his mouth isn't betrayal enough, displaying what belongs to my wolf for the world to see will earn me punishment I can't imagine.

"Are you alright?" Confusion creases Damien's brow.

I turn back to him, my throat tight. "I can't stay, Damien. Not tonight."

His expression flickers. Startled, hurt, then a flash of disappointment before he tucks it away. But not before I catch a dangerous glint in his eyes.

"I want to." I reach up to touch his face, his cheek damp and slightly stubbled against my palm, a masculine contrast to his otherwise smooth appearance. "I do. But we should take this slow. This thing between us... It's still so new."

He catches my hand, turning it to press a kiss to my palm. The gesture is tender, at odds with the hunger still burning in his eyes.

"Is there someone else?" His voice is carefully neutral.

The question catches me off guard. How does he know? How could he possibly suspect?

"No." The lie is necessary, but it still leaves an acrid taste in my mouth. How can I explain my wolf to him? He'll think I'm crazy. Or worse, he'll think I'm a whore who lets a man press her against his windows and devour her while she lets masked strangers into her bed.

Disappointment returns to his eyes, and for a moment, I think he sees straight through my deception. But he nods, steps back, and allows me to straighten my dress.

"I'll take you home. Let me call the pilot."

He pulls his phone out of his pocket and walks toward the kitchen as I smooth my dress. My legs still tremble, my body humming with the echoes of the intense climax he gave me. I bear his mark now, invisible to anyone else but undeniable to me, and the realization sends another sharp pang of regret through me.

I'm already claimed.

What will my wolf do when he comes to me tonight? How will he punish me? Because he will.

Part of me wants him to. Part of me anticipates the rough, jealous sex that might follow if he discovers my betrayal. But another part of me is afraid. His possessiveness has always excited me before, but there's an edge to it sometimes that still terrifies me.

Damien returns to where I stand by the window. "The pilot will be ready in ten minutes." His composure is back in place, his desire contained, though I can still see the bulge in his tailored pants. "Can I get you anything while we wait?"

"No, thank you. I'm fine."

He nods, keeping his distance. The air between us is charged with everything neither of us will voice. With the pleasure he gave me and the pleasure I'm denying him. The tension becomes unbearable.

"I should use your bathroom before we go."

"Of course. Down the hall. First door on the right."

⋅◦⋅

I splash cold water on my cheeks, trying to clear my head. My reflection in the mirror tells the story of the night. My lips swollen from Damien's kisses, my hair a mess, my eyes still dark with residual desire. I look thoroughly debauched, and we didn't even make it to his bedroom.

What the hell am I doing?

The hunger in Damien's eyes demolishes every defense I've built, and the terrifying truth is that I want to let him take me to bed. But my wolf haunts every breath I take.

The guilt sits on my chest like a boulder, crushing the air from my lungs, and hot and accusing tears gather behind my eyes. I let Damien's hands and mouth give me the pleasure I reserve only for my wolf. I gave him pieces of myself that belong to another man. A man whose face remains a mystery but whose touch I crave like oxygen.

I swipe my fingertips beneath my eyes, catching the moisture before it can fall. When did I become this person? This woman who kneels for a shadow, who gives her body to someone who won't even show her his eyes? But the bitter voice in my head whispers back. What right does he have to my fidelity when he hides behind metal and refuses to let me know him?

The thought of him discovering tonight's betrayal sends ripples of anticipation skittering down my spine, part terror, part thrill.

When I return to the main room, Damien is still standing by the window, staring out at the snow. He turns as I approach, holding out my coat, helping me into it. The heat of his body presses against my back, and the warmth of his breath stirs the hair at my nape. Hunger still pulses from him in waves, making the air between us electric with anticipation.

"Ready?"

I nod. As we step into the elevator, I catch his reflection in the polished doors. He's watching me with that same intensity as before, his eyes dark and ravenous. But that anger still lingers there too.

It sends a shiver through me, and not entirely of fear. In that moment, he looks so much like my wolf that I almost gasp. The way his jaw clenches, the way his eyes narrow, the barely contained violence in his posture.

But that's insane. It's my guilty conscience playing tricks on me. It has to be.

The elevator doors slide open onto the helipad, where the snow is falling harder now.

"Watch your step." He helps me navigate the slippery surface, guiding me to the waiting helicopter.

"Is it safe to fly back?"

"I'd never put you in danger, Luna."

I'm aware of his strength as he steadies me, his arm wrapping around my waist when I slip. For a brief moment, I'm pressed against the solid wall of his chest, and the memory of what happened in his penthouse sends a fresh wave of remorse through me.

"Thank you." The wind whipping across the rooftop swallows my voice.

He climbs into the helicopter behind me, and we settle in for the ride. I lean back in my seat as Denver falls away beneath us, the city lights blurring through the falling snow. My body still hums from Damien's touch, and my mind races with questions I'm afraid to ask.

As the helicopter turns toward the mountains, toward my sanctuary, I wrap my arms around myself, suddenly cold despite the cabin's heating. Tonight has set something in motion that I can't stop, a collision course between my two worlds.

My mind drifts to what's coming when I get home. Despite my best intentions, I'm caught between two powerful men.

One who's made it clear he wants to possess me.

And one who already does.

Chapter Thirteen

Luna

The helicopter ride back to my sanctuary is quiet. Damien sits across from me now, no longer pressed against my side as he was on the journey into the city. The distance between us feels deliberate, calculated, but his gaze rarely leaves me.

We land on his property, and he drives me the short distance to my house, dropping me at my door with the gentleman's manners he wears like his expensive tux. But there was nothing gentlemanly about the way he had me against his window less than an hour ago, dress hiked up around my waist, his mouth between my thighs, coaxing sounds from me that I only make for my wolf.

The soft glow from behind the living room curtains suggests Maren is still awake.

I turn to look at him. "Thank you for tonight."

His mouth curves into a dangerous smile. "My pleasure."

"Damien—"

"Next time..." He steps closer, the faint scent of my arousal still clinging to him. "I'll have you in my bed, Luna. And you won't leave it until morning."

It's not a question. There's no room for negotiation. It's pure, unwavering certainty delivered by a man who's used to getting what he wants. The worst part is how my body once again betrays me, responding to his dominance with a fresh surge of want.

"Goodnight, Damien." I force the words past the knot in my throat.

He leans closer, and my breath catches. For one moment, I think he's going to kiss me, going to make me taste myself on his tongue again. Instead, he stops just shy of contact, his breath ghosting across my lips like a promise.

"Goodnight, Luna," he whispers, then steps back and strides to his SUV.

I stay frozen on my porch until his taillights disappear into the swirling snow. Only then do my lungs remember how to work, releasing the breath I've been holding in a shaky exhale as I fumble for my keys.

The living room is lit only by the light of the TV. Maren is asleep on the couch with Ricky curled up on her chest, his fingers wrapped around her left breast. The sight makes me chuckle despite the turmoil inside me. I grab the throw blanket from the back of the armchair and drape it over both of them. Ricky stirs, his eyes opening to slits, then he snuggles closer to Maren and drifts back to sleep.

I make my way into the dining room, pulling a bottle of Jameson out of the hutch before pouring myself a glass, needing some liquid courage for what I know is coming. I swallow it down in one gulp, coughing as it burns my throat.

I don't know how long I stand there before I head upstairs, each step feeling heavier than the last. The guilt comes in waves as I strip off my dress and step into the shower. The warm water beats down on my shoulders as I scrub every inch of my skin, as if I could wash away what happened. As if I could wash away Damien's scent, his touch, the evidence of my betrayal.

Because that's what it feels like more and more. Betrayal. Kissing Damien wasn't a betrayal of my wolf. Not really. But letting Damien make me come with his tongue is.

Why didn't I stop it?

But even as the regret washes over me, there's something else. Excitement. Exhilaration. The image of Damien on his knees before me, his eyes burning with hunger as he looked up at me, makes my heart race all over again.

And beneath it all, confusion.

Because I'm falling for him. How is that even possible when I have such strong feelings for my wolf? How can I have such intense feelings for two different men?

I step out of the shower and wrap a towel around myself, wiping the steam from the mirror. My reflection stares back at me, flushed and bright-eyed despite the late hour. I look different. Changed.

With a sigh, I pull on a silk robe and run a brush through my hair before walking into my bedroom. The room is dark, but I don't bother with the lights, my eyes already adjusting to the dim glow filtering through the curtains.

My skin erupts in goosebumps from my scalp to my toes, and the tiny hairs on my neck rise as fear ripples through me.

He's here.

A stillness in the corner of the room, motionless, waiting, radiating a presence that makes every instinct scream danger.

"Did you have a good time at your gala, little doe?"

His voice comes out of the darkness, low and hard. I freeze, my heart hammering against my ribs.

"Yes." I swallow. "It was nice."

He steps forward into the faint strip of moonlight slicing through my curtains. His mask gleams, covering the upper half of his face. But his mouth, that beautiful mouth that has never once kissed me, is visible, twisting into a smirk that makes my stomach drop.

"Nice," he echoes, the word sounding dangerous on his lips. "And after? Was that nice too?"

My blood runs cold. How does he always know?

"I don't know what you mean." I retreat a step as he advances.

"Don't lie to me, Luna." He erases the remaining space until his presence overwhelms me, that intoxicating, clean, masculine scent that makes my treacherous body respond. My core pulses, my body softening and readying for him.

I swallow hard. "We had a drink at his place after the benefit."

His hand comes up, fingers brushing my jaw with unexpected softness. Then his grip tightens, forcing my chin up.

"You have to be quiet tonight, little doe." His voice gets quieter but somehow more menacing. "We don't want to wake Maren, do we?"

My body spins before I can answer, and cold plastic snaps around my wrists as the zip ties lock tight.

"Wait—"

"Shhh." His warm breath brushes against my ear. "Quiet, remember? Unless you want her to come up here and find you like this."

The mental image makes me flush with arousal rather than embarrassment. He knows the right buttons to push, the correct combination to make me respond to him.

"Now." He turns me towards him, his hands moving to the belt of my robe. "Let me see that beautiful body."

He works the knot loose and pushes the silk from my shoulders. The fabric catches on my bound wrists, leaving me exposed while the robe hangs useless behind me. He steps back to take in the view.

"Turn around."

I hesitate, and his hand lifts to circle my throat. No pressure, just weight, a reminder of the power he has over me.

"Turn. Around."

I do as I'm told, shivering as the cool air touches my damp skin. Fabric rustles behind me, and then cool steel presses against my skin as he cuts my robe, so it falls from my wrists.

Shit! He brought his knife.

He's only used it a handful of times since that first night. But it still scares the fuck out of me every time.

The blade slides away with a whisper, replaced by his palms on my hips, his thumbs finding the dimples above my tailbone. Then one hand moves lower, fingers sliding between my thighs from behind until his middle finger glides through my slick folds.

I gasp at the contact, my body already responding to his touch.

"Wet." He withdraws his hand. "You're always so ready for me, Luna? But is this for me? Or because you let another man touch you?"

I stay silent because a lie would taste wrong on my tongue, but the truth might shatter whatever fragile thing exists between us. Will honesty finally kill this twisted dance we do in the dark?

"You let him do something. Tell me what."

The slap lands hard across my ass when I don't respond fast enough, echoing through the room. I bite down on my lip to stop the sound threatening to break free.

"Tell me."

"He... he went down on me." The confession tumbles out breathless, tangled with heat I can't forget.

"Where?"

"In his living room. Against his window."

My body tenses as I brace for rage and brutality. Instead, a sound that almost resembles approval rumbles from his chest.

"Did you come?" My hesitation earns me another slap, this one stinging worse than the first. "Did you come for him, Luna?"

"Yes." My voice cracks on the word.

"How many times?"

"Once."

He holds perfectly still behind me, hands anchored on my hips while seconds tick by. Then he's guiding me forward, pushing me toward the bed.

"On your knees. Face down, ass up."

I struggle onto the bed with my wrists bound. This spread-out position always brings a familiar mix of fear and anticipation.

The metallic clink of his belt opening fills the quiet room, followed by the sound of his zipper. The bed shifts as he climbs on, kneeling behind me. His hands find my hips again, gripping hard enough that I know I'll wear his fingerprints tomorrow.

"You're mine, Luna. Say it." He drives into me without warning. I bury my face in the duvet, crying out as my body stretches around his thickness.

"I'm yours," I manage between broken breaths as he moves.

His rhythm is punishment, each thrust shoving me forward on the mattress. I press my face into the pillow to muffle the sounds trying to escape while he takes me with relentless force. The zip ties bite into my wrists as I strain against them, the sharp ache mixing with pleasure when he hits that spot inside me over and over.

"Did you want him to fuck you like this?" His hand twists into my hair, yanking my head back. "Did you?"

"I don't know," I gasp, the truth spilling out.

"But you let him put his mouth on my pussy. You wanted it."

"Yes."

His pace turns savage, each thrust driving my body forward. Pleasure and pain crash together, tearing gasps from me with every stroke.

"You're mine, Luna. Say it!"

"Yours." The word tears out of me because denying it would be a lie.

"Again."

"Yours."

He slams into me, burying himself to the hilt. Then he drapes himself over my body, his chest pressed to my back, his mouth at my ear. "What's mine?"

"My pussy." The words come out sharp and clear, too loud in the quiet room, and he clamps his hand over my mouth.

"Don't wake Maren." He sinks his teeth into my earlobe. "What else is mine, little doe?"

"Every part of me," I sob when he removes his hand.

He makes a pleased sound deep in his throat, his punishing rhythm unchanged. His fingers slide down to circle my throat, and his grip tightens, cutting off my air.

"That's right, Luna. Every part of you is mine. Remember that the next time another man tries to touch you."

The words brand themselves into my brain whether I want them there or not. There's something about how he claims me and controls me that goes beyond anything I've felt before. My body responds to his roughness even as my mind questions why I need this, why I hunger for what only this masked man gives me.

Then he shifts his angle, and thought dissolves under the wave of sensation. Heat coils tight in my belly, winding tighter with each brutal thrust until I'm balanced on the edge of breaking.

"Are you going to come?" His voice splinters, betraying how close he is. "Are you going to come on my cock after coming on his tongue?"

He loosens his fingers, and the sound that escapes me is small and broken.

"Yes."

The room tilts, and my body knows nothing but the ache, the building wave and the desperate climb, the pressure coiling tighter and tighter, pulling me toward some sharp precipice I can't escape.

His grip tightens around my throat again as he drives into me without mercy. My lungs burn for air while my vision starts to dim at the edges.

"Do it. Come for me, Luna. Show me you're mine and only mine."

His command and the sudden rush of oxygen when he releases me send me tumbling over the cliff. My body contracts around him in waves, pleasure tearing through me like wildfire. I sink my teeth into the duvet to trap my scream, every muscle seizing with the force of my climax.

Before the tremors fade, he pulls out and flips me onto my back in one swift motion. My tied hands wedge beneath me, trapped under the curve of my back, but something about it feels almost gentle despite the brutality seconds before. I squirm, trying to shift my arms to something less painful, but my own weight locks them in place.

He positions himself at my entrance, but instead of the violent thrust I expect, he slides into me with agonizing slowness, inch by inch, his masked gaze never leaving my face as he watches my reaction.

"What are you doing?" The words come out breathless, confusion clouding my thoughts at this departure from our usual dynamic.

He doesn't answer. Instead, he withdraws until only his tip remains, then sinks back in, slow and deliberate. The next thrust goes deeper, stretching me further.

Then another, each one reaching places the previous stroke didn't. His hand moves to cup my face, palm warm against my cheek. His thumb finds my lower lip, tracing the curve with a gentleness that doesn't belong here, doesn't fit with anything I know about us.

"Is this how you wanted him to fuck you tonight, little doe? Gentle? Slow?"

His cock glides slowly, almost leisurely, along my inner walls, the sensation making my eyes flutter.

"Yes."

"Don't you like how I fuck you?" He slams into me once with his usual force before slowing again.

"I love it," I gasp.

"Then why would you want him to fuck you like this?"

"I want you to fuck me like this." My admission is raw and honest.

He continues his slow rhythm, withdrawing until only the tip remains before sinking back in to the hilt.

"I'm not a gentle man, Luna. I told you that right from the beginning."

But his careful movements tell a different story. I arch beneath him, seeking more contact.

"I know. And I want every brutal thing you do to me. But I want to touch you. I want to kiss you. I want to feel your skin against mine as you move inside me, just like this. But you won't give it to me."

A sob breaks free before I can stop it. It sounds like the cries he pulls from me when pleasure overwhelms, but this one carries something heavier. Grief mixed with want.

"You don't know what you're asking for." A growl tears through his teeth. "Knowing who I am will change everything.

"There's nothing wrong with change. Change can be good."

"Not when it means losing you."

"You won't lose me. I've given you every part of me. Why isn't it enough?"

This talking while he moves inside me is so incredibly erotic. The intimacy of it strips me bare in ways his hands never could. He continues his slow, purposeful rhythm, his body suspended above mine while his arms create a cage of heat and muscle around me.

All I want is for him to collapse onto me, skin to skin.

Why won't he kiss me? Why is my mouth good enough for his cock but not his lips?

"Please." My voice cracks with need for something I can't name.

His thumb brushes my lip again. "Not yet. Not like this."

The words confuse me, but I can't focus on them because he shifts his angle, finding the spot that makes my spine arch. Pressure builds again, slower this time but somehow deeper.

"Come with me. Give me one more, little doe."

The command pulls me toward the edge, and when his hand slips between us to circle my clit, I shatter. This orgasm rolls through me in long, gentle pulses while he finally lets go, his body trembling above me as he spills inside me.

We stay joined for several heartbeats. His forehead drops to my shoulder while his frame hovers just out of contact as our breathing settles. Then he pulls out, leaving cold air where his warmth had been.

He climbs off the bed and turns me to my side, snapping the zip tie with his fingers. My wrists fall free, and he rubs the red marks left behind, working away the ache.

"Why weren't you more brutal with me tonight? After what I did?"

He ignores my question, doesn't even acknowledge I spoke. Instead, he adjusts his clothing, getting ready to vanish like he always does. But tonight something's different. His hands move with less certainty than usual.

"Will you ever tell me who you are?"

He stills, his back to me. "Do you really want to know?"

"Yes." My voice doesn't waver. "I want to know who you..." My throat constricts around the words. "I want more than this. More than these stolen moments in the dark."

He turns halfway toward me, the mask catching what little light filters through the room.

"I won't share you with another man. You're fucking mine."

"Then trust me with who you are."

"I'm a killer, Luna. That won't change. If you really want to know who I am, you'll have to live with the consequences. Live with knowing that the man you let inside you every night often kills with those hands before they touch you."

I plant my palms on the mattress and push myself up. My hair falls across my face, and I push it back with trembling fingers.

"You think I don't know that? You think I don't struggle with that? I'm waiting for the night you show up here covered in blood." My voice cracks on the last word, but I force myself to keep going. "And do you want to know the worst part? I hate that I don't care enough to stop this. I'll always want your hands on me. I don't ever want to go back to living without them."

The mask turns his face into an impenetrable wall, and it makes me want to scream because I can sense the storm of emotions he's hiding beneath it.

"Listen to me." His voice drops to something deadly quiet. "This is the last time I'm going to say this, Luna. If another man ever puts his hands on you, his mouth on you, or his cock inside you, I'll come here dripping in his blood and fuck you until it covers every inch of your skin."

And then he's gone, slipping into the night like the phantom he is, leaving only silence and the lingering echo of his threat.

I curl onto my side and pull the blanket over my bare skin. My body aches in all the right places, marked by his touch. His words won't stop resonating through the hollow space he left behind.

Nothing about tonight makes sense. I should be covered in bruises, barely able to move. When Damien kissed me, jealousy turned my wolf into something savage. Tonight, after I let Damien taste me, my wolf drove into me like he wanted to leave permanent marks. And he did. I feel every brutal second of it radiating through my body. But halfway through, something shifted in him. The savagery bled away, replaced by movements that felt like worship. Like he was cherishing me.

I squeeze my eyes shut. The room falls into stillness, waiting for footsteps that won't come back until tomorrow night. The scent of him lingers in the air. I pull the blanket tighter around me, suddenly aware of how alone I am. How alone I always am after he leaves.

Why can't he trust me with the truth hiding behind that mask?

My breath stutters because now I know with crystal clarity what this knot in my chest really is. This isn't just a physical need anymore. This stopped being about sex a long time ago. Somewhere between the fear and the pleasure, between his violence and his surprising gentleness, I fell in love with him.

It took Damien's mouth on me to understand that I'd already given my heart to someone else.

I'm in love with a killer whose face I've never seen.

How fucked up is that?

But there's Damien too. He fills different spaces in my chest. Brilliant and controlled, he treats me like I'm something worth protecting rather than conquering. He respects my work, seems to care about animals as much as I do, and he makes me laugh and think and want.

I'm torn between them. Two different men, yet both make my pulse race and my thoughts tangle into knots. One thrives in shadow; the other in light. One takes, the other gives. Both have pieces of me I'm not sure I can reclaim.

My chest tightens. I press my palm between my breasts, trying to ease the pressure building there. This can't continue. Something has to break, either them or me.

Sleep pulls at me—the gala, Damien's mouth, my wolf's claiming all blending into exhaustion. But consciousness refuses to fade completely. A whisper surfaces in the darkness of my mind, the question I've buried beneath rationalization and denial.

What if there is no choice to make?

The thought is absurd. That's why I keep dismissing it. Yet there are these ever-present, recurring moments when something feels familiar. The way Damien's eyes darkened when I refused to stay at his penthouse. My wolf's hands tonight, gentle where I expected brutality, tender after my betrayal. The way both men look at me like I'm air and they're drowning.

It's a dangerous thought, one that could shatter the delicate balance of my complicated life. But as sleep claims me, I can't quite push it away. No matter how insane it is.

Chapter Fourteen

Luna

I run the ultrasound wand over Ricky's belly, my eyes glued to the screen. Under anesthesia, he is the least active he's ever been. My boobs are safe as I try to see what is going on inside him.

I let my mind drift to Saturday night. Daylight has a way of making the impossible seem foolish, like childhood fears that dissolve with the sunrise. In this bright examination room, I can push down the wild theories and convince myself I'm seeing connections that don't exist. There is no way Damien and my wolf are the same man. I'm seeing things I want to see. Things I wish were true.

I frown as the issue inside Ricky's belly comes into focus as Maren walks up behind me.

"What's the verdict, doc?"

I point to the screen. "It looks like he's got a kidney stone."

"Fuck! Where the heck would he get that? Can raccoons get kidney stones?"

"It's not common, but yes, they can. It's not very large, but I can see why it's bothering him, especially when he pees."

"Poor perv."

"Shit." I sit back in my chair. "I don't have a lithotripter."

"That's the machine that uses shock waves to break it apart?"

"Yeah."

I rack my brain, thinking about what I can do. The surprise anonymous donation we received for Titus is gone. I used most of it for the new enclosure, but I also had some unexpected expenses, including having to replace the barn roof after part of it caved in during a nasty storm two weeks ago. It was a miraculous gift that came at the perfect moment.

"CSU has one, right? Call them and see if they'll let you use it."

"It won't be free, Maren. I can't afford this."

"Can't afford what?" A deep voice cuts through our conversation. My gaze jerks to the doorway. Damien stands there, bouquet gripped in one hand. His eyes lock onto mine, questioning.

My lips curve into a smile. "Hey, what are you doing here?"

"I have some unexpected business that's come up out of town. I have to leave this evening, but I wanted to see you. What can't you afford?"

I turn my chair to face him. "Ricky has a kidney stone. And I don't have the equipment here to treat it."

"And CSU has it?"

I nod. "They'll give me a discount because I'm an alum, but it's still an incredibly expensive treatment."

"I know several people on the Board of Regents. I can make a call."

Maren shoos me from my chair, taking over the task of wiping the gel from Ricky's belly. I walk over to Damien.

"I can't ask you to do that."

"You're not asking."

"Are you sure?"

Ricky needs this treatment, and pride won't get it for him. I'll take help from anyone, even the man who had his face buried between my thighs two nights ago.

"Of course. I couldn't live with myself if your favorite resident raccoon suffered when I can do something to help."

"I don't have favorites. I love both Ricky and Zorro."

A slow smile spreads across Damien's face, and he shakes his head. His eyes crinkle, and warmth melts into his expression, like he finds my defensive response endearing rather than convincing.

"I'll call today before I leave."

"Thank you, Damien. I don't know how I can ever repay you for this."

He closes the distance between us and leans down, his breath ghosting across my lips. I breathe him in—that clean, masculine vanilla and amber scent that triggers the same visceral response I get from my wolf's nearness. My belly clenches, and want coils tight inside me.

"I'll take another kiss."

I shoot a quick look at Maren, who's ignoring us, and a smile curves my lips. Damien's face carries such naked hope. How can I refuse? The combination of his usual commanding presence with this moment of vulnerability makes him impossible to resist.

I stretch up and press my lips to his in the briefest contact, barely more than a breath.

"Thank you, Mr. Wolfe."

When I step away, Damien's head jerks, his eyelids fluttering like he's been jolted awake. His irises have disappeared into black pools that pin me in place with their intensity.

"Okay, you two, pervy raccoon coming through." Maren approaches with a groggy Ricky in her arms. "I'll put him back in his cage to rest."

I guide Damien out of the way with my hand on his arm so Maren can get by. His muscles jump under my touch.

"Thanks, Maren. I'll come check on him in a little bit."

The moment she disappears around the corner, Damien's composure shatters. The flowers slip from his hand and hit the floor, petals scattering in every direction as he spins me around and presses me against the door. His hands lock onto my hips and lift, hauling me upward until my feet leave the ground. The wood behind me is solid and cool against my spine, while his body radiates heat in front, pinning me in place.

He takes my mouth like he's been starving for it. His tongue slides past my lips with maddening slowness, each movement calculated to drive me insane. My heartbeat turns chaotic, thundering in my ears. The scent of him overwhelms my senses—expensive cologne mixed with something darker, more primal.

I whimper in his mouth as my hands fist in his hair. The kiss shifts from desperate to reverent, so gentle it makes my throat tight with emotion. He's worshipping me with his mouth, and the tenderness threatens to break me apart.

His moan vibrates against my lips, and he deepens the kiss until the world narrows to this moment, this man, this perfect collision of want and need. He tilts his head and claims me deeper, until my lungs scream for air I can't spare. I wrench my mouth away, gasping.

"My god, Damien." The words scrape out of me between harsh breaths. My chest rises and falls as I try to anchor myself back in reality.

"I've been dying to do that again since Saturday night." His voice comes out rough, and he clears his throat as my fingers drift to my swollen lips.

He kisses me like he's drowning, like I'm oxygen and salvation wrapped into one. This is the kind of kiss I crave. The kind that devours and claims and leaves nothing untouched.

My wolf owns my body with his touch, his possession, and his relentless hunger. But there are parts of me he's never claimed. My heart, my soul, and the pieces that exist beyond flesh and bone. I ache for him to consume those too, to kiss me like his very existence depends on the connection between our mouths.

But Damien kissed me with that exact desperation, and the knowledge crushes my chest, pressing against my lungs until breathing hurts.

He eases me down the door, his hands steady on my waist as my feet find solid ground. My legs feel like water—without his touch grounding me, I'd end up in a puddle on the floor.

"I want you, Luna. In case that wasn't clear before, I hope I've left no doubt in your mind."

"Jesus, Damien. Message received."

His mouth curves in satisfaction, and he leans down to capture my lips again. This kiss carries the same devastating tenderness as the last, and I melt into it with the same desperate hunger, giving him everything I have to offer.

He releases my lips but doesn't pull away, his breath still warm against my mouth.

"Can I call you?"

My head moves up and down because words have abandoned me. My throat feels too tight, my brain too scrambled to form coherent speech.

"And can I take you out again when I get back?"

Another nod is all I can manage. His expression shifts from hopeful to radiant, and the smile that takes over his face should be illegal. All I can think about is hauling him next door, shoving him onto my bed, and spending hours exploring every inch of his body.

Oh shit! I'm totally fucked!

⊷◆⊶

The morning light streams through the window over the kitchen sink as I crack eggs into a bowl. Like every morning, my body is sore in all the right places. My wolf was relentless last night. I don't know how the man does it. He must pop Viagra like candy.

Even now, hours later, I can still feel the touch of his hands, the way he whispered my name in that gravelly voice that makes my core clench.

But it's Damien's kisses that keep creeping into my thoughts, no matter how hard I try to push them away. The memory of his mouth on mine, tender and consuming all at once, makes my heart race in a completely different way than my wolf's brutal possession does.

I roll my neck, trying to shake the headache blooming. It's been there since yesterday morning, a dull throb behind my eyes that won't quit. I'm probably just tired. Since my wolf came into my life, exhaustion is my body's new normal.

The girls wander into the kitchen, meowing and demanding breakfast.

"Morning, babies."

I pour their kibble into three separate bowls, and they dive in as Shadow waits at his spot beside the island. He's always so patient, letting me feed them first.

I grab his bowl and fill it with the raw meat mixture I prepare for him, setting it down near the door. He needs to be fed apart from them, or they'll try to steal some bites.

"There you go, handsome." I scratch behind his ears as he begins to eat.

I go back to my eggs, but my mind won't shut up this morning. After those soul-stealing kisses with Damien three days ago, I again expected punishment from my wolf. I know he hacks into the sanctuary's cameras, so I braced myself for the brutal fucking he delivers when his jealousy flares.

Instead, he surprised me. The last few days, yes, he was rough and relentless as always, but now, even when he's brutal, he touches me like I'm something beloved and breakable all at once.

This is the problem. In the darkness, with my wolf's hands on my body, I can think of nothing else. He drives away every rational thought, every doubt, every longing for something more. But in the light of day, Damien creeps back into my mind with his intense eyes and devastating kisses, and I'm torn between two different kinds of need.

I want the raw passion my wolf gives me, but I also want what Damien offers. A real relationship. Someone who wants more than my body, someone who looks at me like I'm the center of his universe.

The front door opens and closes, followed by Maren's voice echoing through the house.

"Luna! Where the hell are you? I need coffee and food before I deal with any horny animals today!"

"In the kitchen."

I'm glad she's here and grateful for the distraction. I grab two more eggs out of the fridge and add them to the bowl, pouring them into the heated pan, the sizzle filling the room.

Maren appears in the kitchen archway, shaking snow off her head.

"You couldn't have done that on the front porch?"

She gives me a sheepish smile. "Sorry, it's freaking cold out there today. I'm staying for a few days because I don't want to deal with that road. I think they might close it." She eyes the pan of scrambled eggs with obvious interest. "Please tell me you're making enough for two."

"Of course. Toast?"

"You're a goddess."

She grabs two slices of bread and drops them in the toaster, then leans against the counter. A wicked grin spreads across her face.

"So... want to tell me about that hot and heavy lip-lock you and Mr. Tall, Dark, and Loaded shared Monday afternoon?"

Maren's been gone for the last few days. She left before Damien did on Monday. Her grandmother had cataract surgery, and she's been staying with Estella during her recovery.

"Can't you just call him Damien?" I stir the eggs, keeping my eyes on the pan.

"No, I like coming up with fun nicknames for him. Especially because it bothers you so much."

"How old are you?"

"Not as old as you."

The toaster pops up, and Maren transfers the toast to a plate before adding two more slices of bread.

"You're only four months younger than I am."

"And it feels like a lifetime sometimes. Now quit stalling. And don't give me that innocent act. The entire volunteer staff saw you two going at it like teenagers. Jenny actually fanned herself with a clipboard, and Tate, God bless him, made some very inappropriate noises that I'm pretty sure violated several workplace harassment policies."

"We were not 'going at it.'"

"Honey, the man had you pressed against that door like he was trying to fuck you through your clothes. We all got hot and bothered watching." She grins wider. "So spill. All you'd give me Sunday morning was that you had a 'nice' time, but based on that kiss, I think Luna had a 'really good' time."

I turn off the burner and divide the eggs between two plates, buying myself time. There's no point in lying to her.

"Okay, fine." I hand her a plate. "Things got a little heated Saturday night."

The second set of toast pops up, and I grab it, slathering butter on both pieces while I figure out how much to tell her.

Maren's eyes light up with interest as she takes a bite of eggs.

"I knew you were lying when you wouldn't spill. Now define 'heated.'"

Warmth creeps over my skin at the memory. "I let him go down on me in his penthouse."

The fork clatters against Maren's plate.

"Luna fucking Marie... So, how was it?"

I exhale a long breath. "Glorious. Mind-blowing. Heart-stopping."

"Shit. I can't believe you kept this to yourself for almost five days."

"I know. But I needed some time to wrap my head around it. And we were both a little busy. How's Estella?"

"She's fine. Takes more than that to slow her down." She waves her hand as if she's swatting away the question. "And we are never too busy for that conversation. You grab me, shove me in a closet, and say, 'Mar, Damien Wolfe ate my pussy so good last night, I saw God.'"

She picks up her fork and resumes eating.

"I'll remember that next time."

"But the real question is why you stopped there. Why didn't you ride him into next week?"

I push eggs around my plate, my appetite gone. The nausea crawls up my throat again, the same feeling that's been plaguing me, along with the headaches.

"I don't know."

We both look toward the window at the sound of a massive white delivery truck rumbling up the driveway with "MedCore Systems" emblazoned on the side.

"What the hell?" I set down my fork.

Cold seeps through my jacket the instant we step outside. Snow packs beneath our boots as Maren and I head toward the truck. Two men in coats and coveralls lean together over a clipboard, their breath misting in the frigid air.

"Excuse me. Can I help you?"

The older of the two men approaches us, his cheeks red from the cold.

"You Luna Foster?"

"Yes, that's me."

"We've got a delivery for you. Lithotripter, model XL-5000. Where do you want us to set it up?"

My mouth falls open. "I'm sorry, there must be some mistake. I didn't order a lithotripter."

The man checks his clipboard again. "Says here it was ordered yesterday for Sage & Summit Wildlife Sanctuary. Paid in full by the Wolfe Foundation, including installation and setup."

The ground shifts under my feet.

"Holy shit, Lu." Maren lets out a low whistle. "Your pussy must taste like pure gold."

"Maren!" My face burns despite the cold air.

But she's grinning like the Cheshire Cat.

"I mean, damn, girl. Most guys buy flowers or jewelry. Your man buys you a half-million-dollar piece of medical equipment. That's some next-level courting right there."

The deliveryman clears his throat. "So, where do you want us to put it?"

I'm still reeling, my mind struggling to process what's happening. Damien was only supposed to make a call to see if CSU would let me use their machine for free. Instead, he bought me one. An actual lithotripter that I can use whenever I need it, for any animal that needs treatment.

"The main building." I point toward the sanctuary.

The men begin unloading their equipment.

"Where are we going to put that behemoth?" Maren asks as we watch them.

"I don't know."

I pull out my phone with shaking hands. I need to call Damien. I need to understand why he would do something so generous and overwhelming.

"You know what this means, right?" Maren bumps my shoulder with hers.

"That I'm going to be paying Damien back for the rest of my life?"

"That man is crazy about you. And after that kiss on Monday and your Saturday night escapades... holy shit, Lu, you're as far gone as he is."

My heart clenches because she's right. I am falling for Damien fast and hard, and in ways that terrify me.

But how can I give my heart to him when it belongs to someone else?

Chapter Fifteen

Damien

My phone buzzes, and Luna's name appears on the screen. I lean back in my chair and press the button to close the shades because she thinks I'm in Tokyo, and it's just past ten in the evening there. Thank fuck, I decorated my Denver office in a minimalist Asian style.

The lithotripter must have arrived. I brace myself for either reaction she may have, fury or appreciation.

I accept the call, and even through my phone's small screen, she's breathtaking. She's standing on her front porch. Her blonde hair is blowing gently around her face, cheeks flushed pink from the cold, and those incredible doe eyes are wide with something between gratitude and disbelief.

"Hello, beautiful."

"Damien." Her voice is breathless. "I... the lithotripter arrived."

She runs a hand through her hair, a nervous gesture I've memorized from countless nights of watching her. The guilt gnaws at my chest as I take in every detail of her face on my screen. She has no idea I'm not in Tokyo. No clue that in twelve hours, I'll be losing myself inside her again with a wolf mask on my face.

"Did they set it up?" I force my voice to remain casual.

"Damien, you can't. This is too much. It's a half-million-dollar machine. I can't accept this."

"Luna—"

"No. This is too generous. Too expensive. I don't know how I can ever repay you for something like this."

I walk over to sit on the sofa. "You don't owe me anything. There are no strings attached to this gift, Luna. None."

"But why? I only needed to use CSU's machine. Why would you do something like this?"

Because I love you.

"What you do is important," I say instead. "You shouldn't have to compromise your animals' care because you don't have the right equipment."

There's silence on the other end, and she bites her lower lip the way she does when she's thinking.

"I wanted to do this for you. Let me."

"Damien." Her voice is soft and vulnerable. "I don't know what to say."

"Say you'll still let me take you out when I get back." The lie burns my throat as I watch her face on the screen.

"Yes, Damien." Her lips curve into a smile. "I told you, call me when you get home."

Relief floods through me. "Good. I'm looking forward to it."

"You didn't say how long you'll be gone?"

"I don't know yet." The lies pour off my tongue with such ease these days, I don't know what's true anymore. Except this woman. "But I'll call you when I get back into town."

"Be safe." The genuine concern in her voice makes me feel like absolute shit for lying to her.

"I will. And Luna?"

"Yeah?"

"Thank you."

"For what?" Her face is a mask of beautiful confusion.

"For letting me be part of your world."

Her eyes drop from the camera to focus on something off-screen. Several heartbeats pass. When she finally looks back, her expression has shifted. It's softer, unguarded, and vulnerable in a way that squeezes my heart.

"Thank you for wanting to be."

———————◄O►————————

Luna is standing in front of the window of the enclosed porch when I approach the back of the house. Though the lights are off, the moon's glow makes her look like something I don't deserve to touch. Her hair is loose, tumbling over her shoulders, and she sways on her feet, an empty wine glass dangling from her fingers. Two half-emptied bottles sit on the coffee table, casualties of her and Maren's celebration. Those two drink a lot.

Cold November air rushes past me as the back door creaks open, and I step inside. She startles, whirling toward me, her hand flying to her chest.

"Jesus, you're like a steal... stealth ninja sometimes."

The words tumble together with wine-softened edges, her tongue catching on consonants that usually come so crisp and clear. She's adorable when she's had too much to drink.

I ease the door shut behind me and take in the flush that the wine has painted across her cheeks and the liquid shine coating her eyes, free of the careful tension that usually guards her expression.

There's something so free about her like this, uninhibited in a way that makes her breathtaking.

"It looks like you and Maren had quite the party."

"Yup."

She brings the glass to her mouth with the careful movements of someone trying not to appear drunk, tips it back with hope, then lets out a soft sound of disappointment. Her lips curve into a frown when nothing emerges, her bottom lip pushing out in a pout that makes me chuckle.

"What were you celebrating?" I ask, though I already know. Even if I hadn't been watching earlier, I'd know they were celebrating my donation for that little troublemaker raccoon of hers.

But seeing her so happy like this, so free from worry over one of her animals, I'd donate ten of them.

She drifts toward the sofa that stands between us, her hips swaying with each unsteady step while she grips the back cushions for balance.

"I want to tell you, but you probably know 'cause you're a creepy stalker. And..." She wags a finger at me. "You'll only act like a jealous prick because Damien donated it."

She's higher than she was on the Oxy after her bear attack.

The couches angle toward each other in an L, but leave enough space between them for me to wrap my fingers around her wrist and pull her through the gap.

"A prick, huh?" My lips curve into a smirk. I take the wineglass from her unsteady fingers and set it on the coffee table.

"Yes. You always act like a jealous prick, but you don't—" Her foot catches nothing but air, and my hands find her waist before she can fall. "You don't own me."

"That's where you're wrong, Luna." My voice drops to a growl, rough and dangerous. "And I think I have a right to be a jealous prick because you let Damien Wolfe put his mouth on *my* pussy." My hand slides beneath her sleep shirt, my fingertips grazing over the lace of her panties before I cup her through the delicate fabric.

Air rushes from her lungs. "I told you I was sorry."

"No, actually, you didn't." My thumb finds her clit, pressing until she arches into the contact like a flower bending toward sunlight.

"I didn't?" Her shoulders lift in a careless gesture, though her thighs tremble around my hand. "I wasn't sorry while he was doing it. Only after."

"I don't want to talk about Damien Wolfe's mouth on you, Luna."

She tilts her head, studying me with those eyes that see too much, even with the wine clouding her vision.

"What do you want?"

My finger slips past lace and into slick warmth. Her hips jerk, a moan rising from deep in her chest as I stroke through her arousal.

"I want this pussy wrapped around my cock for the rest of the night."

A shuddering, breathless "Yes" escapes her lips. She arches into my hand, seeking more friction as her eyes slip closed.

"Where's Maren?"

Her friend's presence won't change my plans. I've learned to improvise when she stays over.

"Sleeping." Luna whimpers, her hips rolling in rhythm with my finger as I move it inside her. "I... I couldn't sleep, so... so I came down to wait for you."

"Can you keep quiet? Or do I need to fuck you down here?"

"Down here." She gasps between shallow breaths. "But the wicker... It'll dig into me if you bend me over it."

"We're going to try something different tonight. Would you like that?"

Her eyes whip open, and her hips come to an abrupt stop. "What?"

I withdraw my finger and gather the hem of her nightshirt, lifting it over her head. She pushes her panties down her legs without hesitation, the fabric pooling at her feet, leaving her standing bare in front of me.

"Do I need to bind you?" My fingers drift along the ridge of her hipbone.

She swallows, fighting the alcohol haze. "I don't know. What are we doing?"

I back toward the couch, pulling her with me. Her confused gaze tracks my movements. When I settle onto the cushions, she remains standing, her balance wavering as moonlight spills across her breasts and the soft curve of her stomach.

Her eyes widen when I unbuckle my belt, the metallic click loud in the quiet room. Her breath quickens.

"What are you—"

I free myself from my pants, shoving them down my thighs. Her pupils expand as her gaze drops and locks onto my cock, standing hard and proud. Her tongue darts across her lips as she leans forward, gravity and desire pulling her toward her knees.

"No." My hands catch her hips before she can drop to the floor. "Not like that."

Her eyebrows draw together as she looks down at me from this unfamiliar angle.

"But you never..." Her words fade into the space between us, desire and bewilderment warring across her features. "You always bend me over something or push me against—"

"Tonight's different." I tighten my grip on her hips, drawing her closer. "Tonight I want to watch your face while you take what you need from me."

Her breath stops short. She sways, and I steady her. "I don't understand."

"You will."

Her eyes shimmer with want and desperation as realization dawns.

"I think I might be too drunk to have my hands tied. I don't think I can balance without them."

"Trust me."

I anchor my hands on her hips, fingertips exploring the silk of her naked skin. She nods without hesitation.

"Be a good girl and brace your hands on my shoulders."

A surprised gasp escapes her lips. "You're letting me touch you?" Delight floods her expression as if I've offered her something priceless.

"We're about to have a lesson in trust."

"I'll never betray your trust." The conviction in her voice reaches into my chest and grips hard.

I maneuver her over my lap, supporting her weight as she settles one knee on each side of my thighs, her body creating a perfect frame around mine.

She grips my shoulders like a lifeline, her fingers bunching the fabric of my shirt while I position her hips above mine, her hands trembling against me through the cotton barrier.

She hovers there, uncertain.

"I've got you." My hands curve around her hips, thumbs settling into the soft hollow beneath her ribs. "Take your time."

Her teeth sink into her bottom lip, concentration replacing confusion as she angles her hips. The first brush of contact makes us both gasp. I ease her down, watching wonder bloom across her face as I stretch and fill her. Her lips part around a fractured sound that's half moan, half sob.

"Oh God." Moisture gathers on her lashes. "Why are you letting me—"

The question fragments, her mind struggling to reconcile this power when all she's known with me is surrender.

"You're going to take what you need from me tonight." The words tear out of me, ragged at the edges, as her heat engulfs me. Her thighs quiver as she takes me deeper. Once I'm buried to the hilt, she lifts her hands from my shoulders and meets my gaze with eyes that hold nothing but absolute trust. Without her hands to brace herself, she floats in my grip alone.

I adjust my hold, one hand gripping her waist while the other spreads across the small of her back. "Trust me to keep you steady."

"I trust you." Those three words wrap around my heart like a caress.

"Move, Luna." My hands guide her into motion's first tentative steps. "Take what you want."

She rests her palms on her thighs and begins to move, rolling her hips against me with careful exploration before finding her rhythm and growing bold. Her head falls back in surrender.

"I can't believe you're—" A sob tears from her chest, mixing with her moans. "You've never given me this."

This pace is nothing like our usual frantic fucking. Each movement is sensual, deliberate, and almost worshipful.

"You're the most beautiful thing I've ever seen." The words come out rough as she moves over me.

"Flatterer." Her laugh comes in breathless gasps, but when she lifts her head to meet my eyes, warmth spreads across her features at my words. "I love being able to see your eyes through that mask like this."

"What do you see in them?"

"Hunger. Always hunger. But something else tonight..." She circles her hips in a motion that pulls a sharp breath from me. "Something softer."

I let her lead, and she moves with increasing confidence. Every roll of her hips tears growls from deep in my throat. She rides me with nothing but faith between us, no hands for balance, trusting my grip to keep her from falling.

Her head tips back again. Moonlight spills through the windows, illuminating the swell of her breasts as they move with her rhythm. I lean forward to capture one nipple between my lips.

"Yes!"

The sound tears from her throat. Her spine arches, pushing her breast deeper into the heat of my mouth. My tongue sweeps around the sensitive bud, and her body answers—a violent shudder rolling through her core, her hips jerking out of tempo. A visible tremor runs from her chest down to where we're joined. Her thighs squeeze tight against my hips, and I release her nipple with a soft pop.

"No, please don't stop." The plea breaks from between her lips.

"That's it, beautiful. Fuck my cock."

I capture her other nipple, unable to deny her or myself, teasing the sensitive bud with my tongue and teeth. Her hips stutter again, losing their rhythm for a heartbeat before she finds it again. The muscles of her stomach ripple, tightening and releasing with each pass of my tongue.

"My cock," she breathes, claiming what's already hers.

"Your cock." The words rumble against her flesh before I release her. "My cock is yours, Luna. Every part of me is yours."

She lifts her head and meets my eyes. "Except the one I truly want."

"What part is that?"

"Your heart." She breathes the admission into the space between us.

You fucking have it, Luna. You fucking have it.

The truth claws up my throat, demanding escape, but I swallow it back down. Instead, my eyes devour her, the way she moves over me, the moonlight painting her skin silver, before my gaze drops to where we're joined.

She looks down. "What are you looking at?"

"You."

I can't look away from where she's stretched around my length, how her body opens to take me, and how her arousal coats my cock in slick heat. My thumb finds her clit and traces lazy circles around the swollen bud.

"We fit together perfectly," she breathes. "Like our bodies were made for each other."

She's so fucking beautiful like this, powerful and vulnerable at once.

"They are, little doe."

Her eyes lock with mine, and grief shadows her expression. "I wish you'd let me see your face. I know you're beautiful under there." Air shudders through her lips. "God, you feel so good. Different tonight. Deeper somehow."

She bears down harder, chasing her orgasm. Her inner walls flutter and pulse around me, the telltale signs of her approaching climax.

"Why won't you let me touch you?" The words break as they leave her mouth, her hands clenching into tight fists that tremble against her thighs.

The question burns through my mind as she rocks over me, her heat gripping my cock like warm silk.

Why won't I let her touch me?

Because her hands on my naked flesh would destroy every defense I've built. I'll be lost to her. Once she strips away cloth and barriers, I'll have nothing left to hide behind. The mask isn't just hiding my face. It's protecting the last shred of distance I can maintain.

Until I can tell her the truth.

"I can't, Luna." My hips drive upward, and her strangled cry bounces off the windows. "I'll—"

"You'll what?" Her gaze pierces through the mask's eyeholes, searching for answers I can't give.

"You have no idea what you're asking for."

"Then show me." Her rhythm turns wild, desperate hunger driving each movement. "Show me what I'm asking for."

Her plea unleashes something feral in me. I thrust up hard, with brutal force, ripping a broken sound from her throat.

"Oh God." The moan tears from her throat. "Right there."

Pleasure carves beautiful, devastating lines across her face.

"I need you." The admission crumbles between her desperate gasps for air. "All of you. Not just this."

"You have more of me than anyone ever has."

"But not enough." Her pace turns frantic as she chases her release. "I want to touch you everywhere. Kiss you. I want to wake up next to you. See you in the daylight. I want—oh god, I'm gonna come."

"Come for me, Luna."

Her movements jerk as pleasure crashes over her. Her spine curves into a perfect arc, and she comes with a strangled cry, her entire body convulsing while her walls clamp around me, drawing out my own release as she rides each rolling wave of ecstasy. With a low growl, I thrust up into her one final time and explode, flooding her with my release.

We stay locked together for long moments, both gasping as we drift back from the edge of oblivion. Her eyes flutter open as awareness seeps through layers of wine and bliss.

"Why?" she whispers. "Why did you give me that?"

Because watching you take your pleasure from me was everything. And sometimes even monsters want to give instead of take.

"That was..." Her voice dissolves into a satisfied hum.

Perfect.

But that's not true. Perfect would include her lips against mine and her palms tracing paths across the bare skin I keep hidden.

Before I give in to the temptation, I stand, keeping her steady in my arms as I slip from her warmth. A small sound of loss escapes her throat.

"Quiet. Or I'll gag you."

She snickers again, the alcohol in her system making her bold. "Promises... promises."

Luna Foster is adorable when she's drunk.

She stands on unsteady legs, collecting her clothes from the floor as I fasten my pants and guide her into the house and upstairs.

Her bedroom door clicks shut behind us. She tumbles onto the bed and sprawls back, her blonde hair spreading across the pillow, letting her thighs fall open. She draws lazy circles around one nipple while her other hand slides down her stomach to where my come still glistens between her thighs.

"You're not leaving yet, are you?"

I reposition her so the moonlight from her window bathes her bare skin.

"Nope. Arms up."

She grips the headboard slats. Alcohol softens her gaze, but trust radiates from every curve of her body.

I pull the zip ties from my pocket, the plastic clicking as I secure her wrists to the wood.

"Perfect." My fingers glide down her inner arms, her skin pebbling beneath my touch. "Now I'm going to taste every inch of you."

My mouth finds her throat first, lips tracing over her racing pulse. She arches beneath me as I trail my lips lower, over her collarbone, the valley between her breasts, and the smooth expanse of her stomach.

"Please." She lifts her hips.

My hands spread her thighs wider, and I lower my head. Footsteps echo in the hallway, and my body goes rigid.

Fuck!

Luna's head shoots up, lips parting in surprise. My fingers snap the zip ties, and my hand clamps over her mouth.

"Quiet. You don't want us to get caught, do you?"

Blood roars in my ears.

"Lu?" Maren's voice drifts through the door.

I drag the covers over Luna's exposed body, up to her chin, and spring from the mattress. The doorknob turns, and I dive across the room, pressing my spine to the wall behind the door as it opens.

"Luna?" Maren's voice is thick with sleep. "You okay? Thought I heard voices."

Luna blinks hard. "What?" The word comes out strangled. She coughs to clear her throat. "Yeah. Just a weird dream. I think I was talking in my sleep. Sorry if I woke you."

Maren yawns. "You sure? It sounded like—"

"I'm fine. Promise. Too much wine."

"Tell me about it. My head's already pounding. Why are the cats and Shadow in the hall?"

The cats streak into the room and launch themselves onto the bed, purring as they settle around Luna. Shadow pads through the doorway, nostrils flaring. My muscles coil as he pauses, but then he ambles to his bed and lies down.

"I got up for water earlier. Guess I didn't notice they were still out there."

Maren yawns again. "Okay. Night."

The door clicks shut. Footsteps fade down the hall, followed by another door closing.

I count to thirty before moving. Luna lies frozen beneath the covers, her eyes reflecting what little light filters through the window.

"That was close." Her words slip out on an exhale.

"A little too close." I shoo the cats away and pull the covers back down, exposing her to the cool air. "Where were we?"

"Are you sure we should do this?" Her knees fall apart even as doubt colors her voice.

"We'll have to keep you quiet."

I snatch her panties from the floor, not sure how Maren missed them, and stuff the fabric between Luna's lips.

Her eyes flare wide, then darken as her lids grow heavy with want.

I zip-tie her hands to the headboard again and settle between her thighs, my hands gripping to anchor her. The first sweep of my tongue causes her to shudder, and she moans behind the gag.

"Quiet." My breath ghosts over her skin.

Over the next hour, three more climaxes tear through her. Two from my mouth and one from my cock buried deep inside her. I crawl up her trembling body, and her eyes flutter open, glazed and sated. I remove her gag, and she sighs, her pink tongue moistening her lips.

"Stay." Her hand reaches for me before she remembers. It drops to the mattress. "Please stay tonight."

The soft plea in her voice threatens to shatter my resolve. Everything inside me screams to tear away the mask, the clothes, the lies, and give her everything she's asking for.

"I just want to touch your hair once when your head's between my thighs. I bet it's so soft."

The longing in her voice cuts deep. She wants such simple intimacies, things I deny her because of my own shortcomings.

Alcohol and exhaustion start to pull her under. Her breathing deepens, evening out as sleep claims her.

I slip out of the house and back through the woods, guilt gnawing at me for every secret I'm keeping. Truth's walls are closing in, and when they crash down, I'll lose more than my mask.

Chapter Sixteen

Luna

The cold air bites at my cheeks as I climb out of my truck outside Hansen's General Store, my boots crunching on the thin layer of snow that accumulated overnight. Not much—maybe an inch—but enough to make the roads treacherous and coat the sidewalks in a slick, dangerous sheen. Thanksgiving is less than a week away, and winter is still a month away, but it already feels like it, with snow coming at least a couple of days a week now.

I slip as I step away from the truck, catching myself on the door handle. She feels like she's on her last legs, and I suspect I'm going to have to get a new one in the spring. But I can't bring myself to let her go. She was Grandpa's truck and is the last real tangible thing I have of him, aside from the sanctuary.

As I close the door, that familiar prickle of awareness, the one I'm so used to now that it's stopped bothering me most of the time, crawls up my spine.

I'm being watched.

Damn it, wolf! Can't you just stop being a creep?

I pause, scanning the street. My eyes sweep across the snow-dusted buildings, the parked cars, and the bare winter trees lining Main Street. Nothing moves except the occasional snowflake drifting from the gray sky above.

I shake my head and trudge toward the store entrance as I swallow back a yawn. The exhaustion that's now a constant companion refuses to lift. Besides my wolf's nightly visits, my bladder has decided sleep is overrated, dragging me out of bed multiple times a night to pee. I'd been sure another UTI was brewing, but the test came back clean. No infection.

My muscles ache from last night and this morning's work. A coyote with a mangled paw needed surgery, and I spent hours hunched over the surgical table. Though exhausted, I'm happy knowing he won't lose it as long as I can keep any infection at bay.

I push through the heavy glass door to the store, the familiar chime announcing my arrival. The warmth envelops me, along with the comforting scent of coffee and the faint mustiness of old wooden shelves that have stood here since before I was born. I stomp my boots on the worn mat, shaking off the snow.

"Luna!" Betty Hansen looks up from behind the counter, her silver hair catching the overhead lights. "Those medical supplies you ordered came in yesterday. Let me grab them for you."

"Thanks, Betty." I unwrap my scarf and unzip my coat, grateful for the heat coming from the old radiators along the walls.

She disappears into the back room, and I make my way to the counter, passing shelves stocked with everything from canned goods to fishing tackle. This place tries to be everything to everyone in our small town, and somehow it manages. Most of the time.

I stare out the front window at Main Street. All of downtown Aspen Ridge stretches before me—the post office next door, Nancy's Diner with its faded red awning, the library across the street, and the gas station on the corner. That's it. The entirety of our bustling metropolis.

There's something about the simplicity of it that I love. There aren't many places like this anymore that haven't died off due to the growth of the surrounding cities.

"Luna, honey!"

I turn to see Eleanor and Frank pushing through the front door, Eleanor's rhinestone glasses glinting under the fluorescent lights as she navigates the slippery threshold.

"Hi, Eleanor. Hi, Frank." I wave as they bring another gust of cold air that makes the door chimes dance.

Frank catches Eleanor's elbow as she almost loses her footing on a patch of slush tracked in by previous customers. Probably me.

"Careful there." He steadies her.

"We were finishing lunch at Nancy's when we saw your truck pull up." Eleanor bustles over with that purposeful energy she's famous for, brushing snow from her wool coat. "How are you? Haven't seen you in town much." She gives me a once-over, her sharp eyes cataloging every detail, though I see the concern in them. "You look all healed up from your run-in with your bear, thank goodness."

I give her a reassuring smile. "It was over a month ago now. And I'm good. All healed up."

Eleanor's expression shifts, becoming more serious as she glances around the store, then leans closer. "I'm glad we ran into you, honey, because I owe you an apology."

"What for?"

Frank moves to browse the hardware section, giving us women our space to talk, but I catch him listening from the corner of my eye.

"That ex of yours—Caleb—came into the post office a few weeks ago, slithering around like the snake he is." Eleanor's mouth purses with distaste. "I told him to get lost and leave you alone because you had a new beau. I mentioned Damien Wolfe." She wrings her hands, her usual confidence wavering. "But then Maren told me he went to your place and threatened you. I'm so sorry if I caused any trouble."

I'd rather forget Caleb and his visit, especially since I still haven't heard from Karen about those flowers, and it's been almost two weeks. My lips curve into a forced smile. "Eleanor, it's okay. It's not your fault."

"But if I hadn't opened my big mouth—"

"Caleb would've come by, regardless. It had nothing to do with your mentioning Damien. Besides, Damien showed up and threw him out on his ass."

Frank snorts from the hardware aisle. "Wish I could've seen that."

"You and Maren both." I chuckle as he peeks around the endcap and gives me a thumbs-up.

Ever since Maren's comment, I can't help but see the old man from UP every time I look at him.

"How's that security system working out? The one Damien installed for you?" Eleanor asks.

"It's been a lifesaver. I caught a poacher trying to get into the wolf enclosure last week."

"No!" Eleanor's hand flies to her chest. "What happened?"

"Found himself staring down the barrel of my shotgun until Karen arrived." I'm unable to keep the hint of satisfaction from my voice. "He wasn't so tough then."

Frank chuckles, abandoning his perusal of screws and bolts to rejoin us. "That'll teach 'em to mess with Luna Foster. Bet he pissed himself."

"Frank!" Eleanor swats at him. "Language."

I can't help but smile at their familiar banter. They've been married for fifty-four years and still act like newlyweds half the time.

"Maren mentioned something about a fancy Denver gala you attended with Damien, too." I can already see where this is heading. Maren needs to learn to keep her trap shut. She's becoming more of a gossip than Eleanor.

"Yes. It was lovely. He raised over ten million dollars for his foundation."

"So are you two seeing each other?" Eleanor prods with the tenacity of a bloodhound.

The door chimes again, and Karen steps inside, stomping snow off her boots. Saved by the bell.

"Luna!" She zeroes in on me before the door closes behind her. "I saw your truck outside. I was planning to stop by the sanctuary later." She smiles at Eleanor and Frank. "Afternoon, Eleanor. Frank."

This is about the flowers. It has to be. I keep my expression neutral, but my fingers curl into my palms. Betty emerges from the back room at that moment, the box of medical supplies in her arms.

"Here we are, dear." Her gaze lands on Karen. "Sheriff Mills! How are you?"

"Doing well, Betty." Karen's smile appears on cue, then her eyes drift back to me. "Mind if I borrow you for a minute, Luna?"

Betty sets the box on the counter. "I'll ring these up when you're ready."

Eleanor clears her throat. "We should get back to the post office, Frank. The afternoon mail won't sort itself."

"Of course," he replies with an obedient nod.

The door chimes as they leave, bringing in another gust of cold air that makes me shiver despite my coat.

I turn my attention back to Karen. "Did you find out who bought the flowers?"

She sighs, and the lines around her mouth deepen. "No. But we did find the delivery kid. Even though he removed his plates, we got a hit on facial rec from your camera footage."

"What did he say? Who is he?"

"Some local kid from Denver. Said a man offered him five hundred dollars to drive his father's van, remove its license plates, and deliver the box to you."

"What did the man look like?"

Karen leans against the counter beside me, drumming her fingers against it. "Same description as the girl at the flower shop. Sunglasses, baseball cap, no remarkable or memorable physical characteristics."

"So you have nothing?"

"Unfortunately, no." She glances over at Betty, who's making a show of organizing receipts behind the register, trying to give us the appearance of privacy while still being close enough to eavesdrop. Karen lowers her voice and leans closer. "I did seek out Caleb, though, and I couldn't find him."

A knot forms in my belly. "What do you mean you couldn't find him?"

"He's got an address in Boulder, an apartment, but it doesn't appear he's staying there. I spoke to his parents, and they said he's out of town on business and has been for months, including the date of your flower delivery."

"Business? I thought he was unemployed."

"Apparently, he works for his father in some capacity." Karen pauses, and I can see her debating how much to tell me. "The state suspended Caleb's law license."

"I didn't know that. Because of the restraining order?"

No wonder he's so angry.

"Not necessarily. I contacted the Colorado State Bar, but they said the records are sealed and inaccessible without a court order."

"That doesn't sound good."

"No. But I have no justification for getting one. Or to subpoena his phone records, and with his parents' statements, it's a dead end." I hear the frustration in her voice.

"Was that blood on the flowers?"

"Yes. Animal blood."

Heartbreak and grief hit me at once, knocking the air from my lungs. My throat closes as images flood my mind of some innocent animal terrified, in pain, and bleeding for this monster's twisted message. I swallow hard against the sob that threatens to break free. The cruelty of it, the senseless waste, makes me want to curl up and weep until there's nothing left inside me.

"I know I keep asking every time I see you, but do you still feel anyone watching you?"

Just my wolf, but his presence comforts rather than frightens me now.

"Not since the night Caleb came by."

"What about Damien Wolfe?"

"What about him?"

"I heard you attended some fancy gala in Denver with him."

Jesus. Small-town gossip is a real pain in the ass sometimes.

"Yes. We've been dating casually."

Karen nods, and I see some of the tension leave her shoulders.

"Stay aware, Luna. And report anything unusual. I promised your grandfather I'd look after you when he was gone."

The mention of Grandpa opens a dull wound in my chest. Two days ago was the sixth anniversary of his death. I spent it the same way I always do. Shadow and I hiked up to Triangle Mountain, one of his favorite places in the world. That's where I scattered his ashes, and every year since, we make the trek back. It's a three-hour round-trip hike under normal conditions, but this year the falling snow added another forty minutes to our time.

Maren worries when I go up there in winter conditions, convinced I'll slip on ice or get caught in a storm, but being on that mountain makes me feel connected to him again.

My throat closes, and I have to force it open before words will come. "I know. I appreciate everything you do, Karen."

She heads for the door, then pauses with her hand on the handle. "I'll let you know if we come up with anything at all in the investigation. Be careful driving home—those roads are getting slick."

After she leaves, I turn back to Betty. She's fascinated by her computer screen, clicking through what looks like the same email over and over, but we both know she was listening. Just as we both know that Eleanor will be privy to the details of my conversation with Karen by the end of the day. I could ask Betty to keep this conversation private, but the request would be futile. In Aspen Ridge, secrets have a half-life measured in hours, not days.

Betty chats about her granddaughter's upcoming wedding while she rings everything up. I make appropriate responses, but my mind is elsewhere.

She hands me the box. "You take care, Luna."

"I will. You too. Say hi to Harry for me."

I pull my coat closed, steeling myself for the cold, before pushing through the doors. The snow has picked up, large flakes now drifting down from the darkening sky.

And the feeling hits me again, stronger than before. I pause beside my truck, box in hand, and scan the street. The sensation ripples along my skin like electricity, raising the fine hairs on my arms. But unlike earlier, this feels different. Darker. More menacing.

Maybe it isn't my wolf watching me.

No, it has to be. This is what he does, but uncertainty gnaws at me. The watching presence feels wrong in a way that makes my stomach clench with genuine fear instead of that twisted excitement I've grown accustomed to.

I fumble with my keys, dropping them once in my haste to get into the truck, and I curse under my breath. When I get the door open, I toss the box across the seat and climb inside as quickly as possible.

The engine turns over on the second try, and I waste no time pulling away from the curb. In my rearview mirror, Main Street looks the same as always. Quiet, peaceful, and covered in a light dusting of snow. But the feeling of being watched doesn't fade until I'm well outside the town limits.

Chapter Seventeen

Luna

I stretch as I roll over. Sunlight filters through the curtains, casting my bedroom in a soft golden glow that belies the ferocity of last night. The sheets are tangled around my legs, and I can still feel the grip of his hands on my hips, my wrists, and my throat.

My wolf is gone, as always. I don't remember his leaving. I think I might have passed out after that last orgasm. Stretching, I wince at the delicious soreness in my body. It's the price I pay for our nights together, and one I'll always accept.

Something feels different this morning, though. I swing my legs over the side of the bed, and as soon as I stand, a sharp cramp seizes my lower abdomen. My hands grip the edge of the nightstand, knuckles white, until the pain releases its hold.

The first step sends warmth trickling down my inner thigh. I freeze, one foot on the hardwood floor, the other still on the rug beside the bed.

"What the hell?" I drop my gaze to see a trail of dark blood on my pale skin.

The bathroom light is too bright as I examine myself and try to make sense of what my body is telling me. The bleeding is vaginal, but my period isn't due for another two weeks. Last night replays in my mind. It was the same roughness we both crave, but nothing new, nothing violent enough to explain what I'm seeing.

I look at the clock, and it's a little after 8 AM. Shit. What happened to my alarm? Did I forget to set it?

I grab my phone and dial my doctor's office.

"Dr. Ritchie's office, how can I help you?" The receptionist's cheerful voice makes me cringe.

"Hi, this is Luna Foster. I need to see Dr. Ritchie. It's urgent."

"Oh, Luna!" Her tone immediately warms with recognition. "Let me check the schedule. How urgent are we talking? Today urgent or this week urgent?"

"Today would be best." I grab a pair of jeans from my dresser drawer. "I'm having some unexpected bleeding."

"Say no more. Let me see... We had a cancellation at ten thirty. Would that work?"

"Perfect. Thank you." I hang up, relieved but anxious.

After a shower, feeding the babies, and some toast because that's all I can stomach, I head next door.

Maren's in the treatment room, bathing one of our small ferrets. They're not old enough to adopt out yet, but she's already found and vetted families for most of them. Her brown eyes lift to meet mine as I enter.

"Hey, I was about to come over and make sure you were alive." She doesn't miss a beat as she lathers soap down the ferret's back. "Mr. Whiskers here had a little accident in his cage. Didn't you, buddy?" She scratches behind his ears, earning a contented chitter. "I think trying that solid food yesterday was too soon."

"I was worried it might be. And sorry for being late. Long night."

One perfectly sculpted eyebrow arches, and a knowing smirk plays across her lips. "You have a lot of those these days."

I ignore her and lean against the doorframe. "I need to run some errands this morning. How are the roads?"

"Fine. Snow's all melted. Are you going down to Estes?"

"Yeah, do you need something?"

She grabs a towel from the warming rack by the oversized sink.

"No, but if you wanted to stop by Rocky Mountain Chocolate Factory and grab me some of their chocolate-dipped Bavarian pretzels, I wouldn't argue with you."

She wraps Mr. Whiskers in the heated towel like a burrito, leaving only his pointed face visible.

"I can probably do that." I chuckle, then wince as another cramp rolls through me.

Maren misses nothing. Her hands pause mid-wrap, and her brown eyes sharpen as they sweep my face. "Are you sure you're okay? You look a little pale."

"Yeah. Just tired."

I'm not ready to tell her about the blood or my doctor's appointment until I know what's going on with my body.

She rubs Mr. Whiskers' fur, and he wiggles, chittering his approval. But Maren's attention stays split between him and me, concern etched across her features.

"Grab some of those fancy dog treats they have while you're there. Shadow loves those."

"Shadow's a wolf, not a dog."

"He still likes them. And so does Ghost, and he's half dog." She cradles the bundled ferret against her chest. "Don't be a mean, stingy mommy and not get your babies the fancy treats."

I push off the doorframe without answering her because we both know I'd forgo eating myself to give my animals treats, especially Shadow.

"Grab some money out of my wallet if you need—"

"I got it. Thanks for holding down the fort."

"No worries. Ethan will be here by ten, and Tate's coming in after class. We'll be fine."

"Thanks, Maren. Really."

"Yeah, yeah. You're the best, Maren. What would I do without you, Maren?" she says in a playful imitation of my voice. "Save the praise for my Christmas bonus, which I will want in chocolate-covered Bavarian pretzels."

"Duly noted." I back toward the door before she notices the rigid way I'm holding myself together. "You really are an angel, Mar."

"Tell that to Estella. She showed up last night when JT and I were in the middle of one of our role-plays. If she thought I was going to hell for my behavior before, I reinforced it when she caught me wearing a strap-on."

Somehow, Maren's words don't shock me. I guess she and JT patched things up. I'll have to remember to ask her about it later, when my body isn't staging some kind of revolt.

"That's what you get for giving your grandmother a key to your apartment."

Her scoff echoes all the way down the hall. "Did you hear that, Mr. Whiskers? Like she's one to talk."

The words stop me cold, but I force myself to keep moving. There's no way Maren knows. She's many things. Observant, intuitive, and possessing an almost uncanny ability to know when I'm lying, but actual mind reading isn't part of her skill set. Though it's strange that her normally infallible bullshit detector hasn't seen through me and the secrets I'm keeping.

The next cramp almost brings me to my knees against the corridor wall. It feels like someone's twisting my uterus. My breath comes in shallow gasps. Dizziness sweeps over me, and the overhead lights flicker, or maybe that's my vision wavering.

I push away from the wall, though my body protests every movement, making it three more steps before the nausea surges.

Something is seriously wrong. I don't know what yet, but I can make it, one foot in front of the other. Get outside, get to my truck, and get to Estes so I can figure out what the hell is happening to my body.

That's all I have to manage.

———— ◄O► ————

The examination room is cold, or maybe it's just me. I sit on the paper-covered table in the thin gown, staring at the anatomical poster on the wall while waiting for the doctor to return with my test results. The stirrups are already put away, the examination is over, but I still feel exposed.

When the door opens, Dr. Ritchie enters with my chart. She's in her late fifties, with copper hair and kind eyes behind tortoiseshell glasses. The concern in those eyes makes my stomach ache more than it already does.

"Luna." She sits on the rolling stool across from me. "How are you feeling now? Any more cramping since the exam?"

"A little. It comes and goes. So what's going on? Is it some kind of tear or..."

She folds her hands over my chart. "You have some minor vaginal bruising, but no tearing. Nothing that would cause the bleeding you're experiencing." She pauses, her dark eyes searching my face. "But is there anything you want to talk about?"

"No."

She doesn't move, doesn't fidget, and doesn't break eye contact. I caught the way her gaze hesitated over the fading bruises on my hips and scattered along my inner thighs during my exam.

The silence stretches. Outside the room, phones ring and footsteps echo down the hallway—the sounds of the clinic going about its business, but inside these four walls we exist in a bubble separate from all of that. She waits, patient and calm, giving me space to fill the quiet with whatever I'm willing to share.

I don't.

"All right." The words come out measured and careful. She's been treating me since I was a teenager, long enough to know I don't play games with my health. When something's wrong, I speak up. When I need answers, I ask. "That said, the bruising isn't my concern today."

My hands grip the examination table, the paper crinkling beneath my palms.

"What do you mean?"

She studies me for a moment, then continues. "Your blood work shows elevated hCG levels. Combined with the bleeding and cramping..." She pauses, her voice gentling. "You're experiencing an early miscarriage."

"Miscarriage?" I echo, the word sounding wrong, impossible. "But I'm on birth control. I can't be—I wasn't—"

"No birth control is 100% effective." She speaks with the patience of someone who's watched this shock play out too many times to count. "Based on your hormone levels, you were about six weeks along. Many women don't even know they're pregnant at this stage. I'm assuming that's the case with you."

I stare at her, my mind racing back through the past weeks, counting days, searching for signs I might have missed. "Are you sure?" Maybe it's... something else."

"I ran the test twice to confirm the results. Your hCG levels are elevated well above the normal range. There's no ambiguity here."

"But I didn't miss any pills," I protest, as if arguing will somehow change the reality. "I've been careful."

"Pills can fail for many reasons. Other medications, illness, timing variations." She leans forward, her tone remaining steady. "And if you've been on antibiotics recently."

Shit! How could I be so stupid?

"I had a UTI almost two months ago. I self-prescribed."

She gives me that look over her glasses, the one that reminds me that even as a doctor, I'm technically not supposed to self-prescribe meds.

I hold up a hand before she can speak. "I already know what you're going to say, but I've been so busy. I ran the urinalysis myself and had amoxicillin on hand."

"Luna, I know how busy you get up there, but you still should have called me even if you couldn't make it down here." She rolls the stool closer, removing her glasses to clean them, a gesture she does to gather her patience. "Next time, call and send me the results so I can add them to your chart. I can prescribe something from that if needed."

I nod, feeling like a scolded child.

She replaces her glasses, focusing on me with renewed intensity. "But that also raises another concern as to why you're getting UTIs."

I bite my lip. "I started a relationship a couple of months ago, after not being sexually active for over a year. I'm usually good about peeing after sex, but not always. And the relationship is new, so..."

"You're caught up in it, I get it. But if it keeps happening, there might be something more going on, and we should run some tests. Any worries about STIs?"

"No. We're exclusive."

At least I think we are. If I don't count my indiscretion with Damien.

The clinical discussion feels surreal against the backdrop of what I've just learned. I rub my temples, trying to soothe the chaos in my head and the headache pounding behind my eyes.

"How could I not have known I was pregnant? I'm a doctor, for Christ's sake."

"A veterinarian," she reminds me, her voice gentle but firm. "And six weeks is very early. Some nausea, maybe fatigue, subtle changes you might attribute to stress or your normal cycle. It's very common not to realize."

I nod, but the gesture feels mechanical. My mind is still reeling, trying to process this new reality.

"So what happens now? What do I need to do? Do I need a D&C?"

"No, that won't be necessary. The pregnancy has terminated on its own. Your body will finish the process naturally over the next several days to a week. You'll experience cramping and bleeding that will feel similar to a very heavy period."

The straightforward medical explanation makes it sound so ordinary, so manageable. But nothing about this feels ordinary.

"How much pain should I expect?"

I'm a grown woman, a doctor; I shouldn't need reassurance about pain tolerance. But my brain won't cooperate, my thoughts scattering before I can piece them together into anything coherent.

"The cramping can be significant. Rest when you need to. Use heating pads. Over-the-counter pain relievers should help." The prescription pad tears with a soft ripping sound as she hands me the slip. "This is for something stronger if you need it. Call me if the bleeding becomes severe or if you develop a fever. And no intercourse for at least two weeks, possibly longer. Your body needs time to heal."

Two weeks.

How am I going to tell my wolf? He comes every night and never takes no for an answer. It's part of our unspoken arrangement. I'm always available to him. Always his.

"Luna?" Dr. Ritchie's voice cuts through my thoughts. "Are you alright?"

My eyes snap back into focus, finding her concerned expression across the small room. "Sorry. Thinking about logistics."

"Logistics?" Her brow furrows.

"With my partner." The word feels wrong for what he is to me. "He's very persistent."

Dr. Ritchie's expression sharpens. The shift happens so fast I almost miss it. "Persistent as in he won't respect your medical need to abstain?"

"No, no. It's not like that. He would never..." Though would he? "Our relationship is very physical. It's a big part of how we connect."

"I see." Her tone suggests she understands more than I've said. "Well, this isn't optional, Luna. Your body needs time to heal. If your partner can't understand and respect that, then—"

"He will. Of course he will."

Even as I say it, my mind questions if it's true. Will he understand? Will he stay away? Or will he simply take what he wants, as he always does?

"Good." Dr. Ritchie studies me carefully. "Luna, it's normal to have complex feelings about this, even if the pregnancy wasn't planned. Some women experience grief, relief, and confusion, often all at once."

"I don't know what I feel."

"That's okay too." She places a gentle hand on my arm. "Be patient with yourself. You've received shocking news."

"I never thought about having children." I surprise myself with the confession. "Not seriously. My work has always been enough."

"And now?"

"Now I don't know." I blink back unexpected tears. "It wasn't real to me until this moment, and now... now it's already gone."

"Would you like to talk to someone? I can refer you to a counselor who specializes in pregnancy loss."

I shake my head before she can finish. "I'll be fine." The lie comes easily, a reflex.

"It's not always about 'fine' or 'not fine.' Sometimes it's about having someone objective to process with. Someone who understands what you're going through."

"I just need some time." I shift on the examination table, the paper crinkling beneath me. "And my friend, Maren, had one when we were in college, so I can talk to her if I need someone."

"Take Dr. Mosier's info anyway." She plucks a business card from the holder on the counter. "And Luna? If there's anything else going on, anything you want to talk about, I'm here."

I slide off the table, eager to end this conversation.

"No. That's okay. Thank you for fitting me in today."

"Of course." She moves to the supply cabinet and retrieves a tri-fold brochure, setting it on the chair next to my folded clothes. "This has information about what's typical after a miscarriage at six weeks. The bleeding you're experiencing now should gradually decrease, though some women have intermittent spotting. Your body is doing what it needs to do. But certain symptoms shouldn't be ignored. Soaking through multiple pads in a short time, fever, dizziness that doesn't improve, or pain that gets worse instead of better. Any of those symptoms requires immediate medical attention. And Luna?"

I pause in reaching for my clothes. "Yes?"

"I say this purely out of concern as your doctor and, I hope, as something of a friend. Be careful with this relationship. Everyone deserves to be treated with care and respect, especially in their most vulnerable moments." She's not speaking as a doctor anymore. The words are too unguarded for that. "Call me anytime. If your symptoms worsen, or if you just need to talk."

"Thank you." I don't meet her eyes. "But really, everything's fine."

Except that nothing feels fine anymore.

Twenty minutes later, I sit in my truck in the parking lot, keys in the ignition, but the engine is silent. My hands grip the steering wheel until my fingers ache.

A baby.

I was carrying a baby. His baby. The result of all those nights when he claimed me. Filled me. When he whispered dark, possessive things against my skin as he came inside me, over and over again. I never thought. I never worried.

How could I be so stupid?

"What would you have been?" I whisper to the void inside me.

Boy or girl? Would you have had those dark, piercing eyes of his? That cocky smile?

Would I have even been a good mother?

I try to imagine telling him. Will he laugh it off? Will he be furious? Or will he just say, "Lay back and spread your legs, little doe."

Will this change anything? Will he even care, or am I only a body to him, a vessel for his pleasure? In all our time together, his face hidden behind that wolf mask, I've never known what he thinks or what he feels beyond desire and possession.

A sob escapes me, surprising in its intensity. I press my hand against my mouth to stifle it, but more follow. I'm crying for a baby I never knew existed until it was already gone. I'm crying for the mess my life has become, caught between two men—one I can see but don't truly know, and one I know intimately but have never truly seen.

Most of all, I'm crying because beneath the shock and confusion, there's a hollow ache of loss that I never expected to feel. Something was growing inside me, something created in darkness and passion, and now it's gone.

I rest my forehead against the steering wheel and let the tears come, mourning a future I never even had the chance to consider.

Chapter Eighteen

Luna

I haven't moved from my bed for the past four hours. The sheets are twisted around my legs like restraints, and I can't bring myself to care. My body feels hollowed out, not only from the miscarriage, but from the months of secrets I've been carrying.

The front door opens downstairs, followed by Maren's familiar voice echoing through the house. I texted her to let her know I wasn't feeling well as soon as I got home. Her reply emojis asked if I was okay, and when I said I needed some rest, she said she and Ethan had it covered. I'm so glad he was here today.

"Lu? You up there?"

Her footsteps thunder up the stairs, and she appears in my doorway, her dark hair starting to fall out of her ponytail. She only looks like that after she's had to fend off Ricky's wandering paws too many times. Concern is etched across her features, and when she takes one look at me curled up like a broken bird, her expression shifts from casual worry to alarm.

"Hey, what's going on, Lu?" She sits on the bed, and the mattress dips under her weight. Her gaze searches my face, cataloging every detail. The puffiness around my eyes, the pale cast to my skin, and the way I'm clutching my pillow like a lifeline.

The words stick in my throat like thorns. I've rehearsed them a dozen times in my head since this morning, knowing I have to tell her and my wolf, but now that it's here, I can barely breathe around the truth.

I push on my hands to sit up.

"I had a miscarriage."

Her mouth drops open, and under different circumstances, her expression would be comical, like something out of a cartoon. But there's nothing funny about this moment. And she's been through it herself, so she knows how devastating it is to lose a baby you didn't plan. In an instant, she's throwing her arms around me, pulling my head against her chest.

"Oh, fuck, Lu." Her voice drops to a whisper against my hair. "What happened? When did— Is this where you went today?"

I lean into her. She's solid and warm and everything I need right now. "Yeah. I woke up bleeding this morning."

"Why didn't you tell me?"

Her arms lock tighter, her heartbeat steady beneath my cheek, and my breathing finds the rhythm of hers.

"I wanted to find out what it was first, before I worried you."

"Did you know you were pregnant?" Her voice goes soft, each word placed with care.

"No."

She pulls back to look at me. "Can I ask the obvious?"

My stomach clenches. This is my moment of truth. Well, part of it. The part I can safely share without revealing serial killers and dead bodies.

"I thought you said you aren't having sex with the Wolfe?"

I nearly choke on my tongue. "What? Who?"

"The Wolfe. That's what I've started calling Damien in my head, since you seem to dislike all my other saucy nicknames for him. It's my running joke with myself." She looks sheepish, like someone caught her talking to herself in public. "You know, because he's all brooding and intense and has that whole lone wolf vibe. And, duh, the name."

"Maren, do not call Damien the wolf." The irony of her nickname squeezes my throat until I can barely breathe.

"Is it his? I thought you only let him—"

"The baby wasn't Damien's."

Her mouth opens, then closes, confusion crossing her features. "Oh."

"It's a long story."

She kicks off her shoes, then climbs under the covers beside me, settling against the headboard and pulling me into her arms. She tucks my head under her chin, and some of the tension leaves my body as I sag against her.

This is why I love Maren Rodriguez with my entire heart. Why she's the best friend I've ever had, and why I would drive off a cliff with her like Thelma and Louise. Because she'd do the same for me. And she always knows what I need more than I do most of the time.

She rests her head on the top of mine. "Hit me with it."

I take a shaky breath. Where do I even start? And how much can I tell her?

"So, as it turns out, I wasn't paranoid when I felt someone was watching me?"

Her body tenses beneath me. "Fuck! But you—" She cuts herself off and takes a deep breath, releasing it slowly. "Okay, I'm going to refrain from tearing you a new asshole until I know all the facts. Continue."

I know how hard that is for her, so I hug her tighter to let her know I appreciate her restraint. She squeezes me back.

"Okay, I really did think I was being paranoid at first. But then I started seeing a flickering in the woods, like the moonlight shining on metal. I convinced myself it was my imagination." I tilt my face up to look at her. "Until one night. I woke up and found a man standing in the backyard, looking up at me. So, I grabbed my shotgun and went outside to confront him."

"You what? Jesus fucking Christ, Luna, you could have been murdered."

"I know, I know." I sigh, the sound heavy with everything I don't know how to explain. "Anyway, when I stepped outside, he was standing in front of the porch. He was wearing this silver wolf mask."

Maren's eyes widen. "A wolf mask? Are you shitting me right now?"

"No." I shake my head before she can get another word out. "I know what you're going to say. Don't. Anyway, he was standing there. I had the gun pointed right at him, and he didn't even flinch."

"Who does that?"

"I know, right?"

"So what happened?"

"I asked him what he wanted."

"And? What did he say?"

I close my eyes as I answer. "Me."

"That's creepy as fuck."

"I was fucking terrified, Mar. Like shaking-can't-breathe terrified. But the weird thing is, at the same time I wasn't. I know that makes no sense." Pulling away, I sit up, twisting my hands together in my lap. "I thought I might piss myself, but there was also this... pull. Like something inside me was being dragged toward him. A magnet I couldn't fight."

"Okay... And then what happened?"

"He strode up the porch steps, so I shot him."

Maren sputters and releases me, sitting forward and looking at me like I've sprouted a second head.

"Are you freaking kidding me?" Behind her horrified expression, I detect a hint of amused pride. "So, why didn't I have to come help you bury a dead body?"

The way she asks is so sincere, I actually laugh because I know she'd do it in a heartbeat.

"I missed."

"You always hit your targets."

"He moved so fast. One second he was standing there. Next he had the shotgun. Ripped it right out of my hands. The shot went wide, barely clearing his shoulder. He burned his hand on the barrel."

She sits back. "Shit, Lu." I give her a weak shrug. Emotions cycle through her face—shock, concern, disbelief. "So, what happened after he took the gun away from you?"

Heat floods my cheeks, and her eyes narrow to slits. "Hey. We don't do embarrassed. Not with each other."

She's right, so I let it all spill out, starting with all the times I felt watched. Seeing him at the edge of the yard, stripping in front of the window when I was drunk, and finally, what I let him do to me after confronting him on the porch.

Maren sits up straighter. "Hold up. You let a masked stranger—"

"I know how it sounds."

"—finger-bang you on your front porch after he stalked you? And you didn't tell me?"

"When you put it like that, it sounds even worse." I bury my face in my hands. "But the way he touched me, God, Maren, I've never felt anything like it."

"Okay, we're going to come back to the stranger finger-fucking in a minute. Because, as horrified as I am in reality, it's also kinda hot and dirty fantasy material for me. But what happened after that? Please tell me you called Sheriff Mills."

I shake my head, telling her the rest. How he came back the next night and the next. How he bypasses Damien's security system, hacks into the cameras, and seems to always know what I've done.

I tell her how he comes to me every single night and takes me apart before putting me back together, leaving me wrecked and wanting more. About the things I let him do and the things I beg him to do. I hold nothing back—well, almost nothing—and the relief of speaking the words out loud, of not carrying this alone anymore, crashes over me so hard my eyes blur.

Maren yanks the elastic from her ponytail, her curly hair tumbling free around her shoulders. She tosses the hair tie onto the nightstand, where it bounces once and disappears over the edge. Both hands rake through the long chocolate strands, nails scraping against her scalp, and she exhales a long, slow breath that sounds like a deflating balloon.

"Everyone calls me the queen of bad decisions. You kicked me out and took the crown. He really comes every night?"

"Yes."

"Christ. I don't know whether to be horrified or jealous of that. No wonder you're fucking exhausted all the time." She shakes her head. "You know I'm all for wild, dirty sex with strangers, but this is kinda off the charts for you. And a little fucking scary. No, make that a lot."

"I'm not afraid of him, Mar. I was at first. The first couple of nights, I was terrified he was going to kill me. But the way he touched me, I knew he wasn't here to hurt me. Just to claim me."

She catches her bottom lip between her teeth, studying my face. "I never would've pegged you as a woman into erotic asphyxiation. Zip ties? Breath play? That's more my style."

"I know, right?" I say again.

She scrunches her nose like an angry kitten. "Hey, we don't judge each other's kinks. Especially now. I think you've bypassed me."

She has no idea.

"So who is he?"

Oh, shit. Here it comes.

"I don't know."

Her eyes narrow, and her voice lowers. "How do you not know? You've been fucking him for months, right?"

"Yes."

"So why don't you know who he is?"

"He always keeps the mask on and refuses to tell me his name. And he only takes me in the dark, except he positions me so the moonlight comes through the curtains and hits my skin. He tells me I look beautiful bathed in it."

"That's kind of sweet, I guess, in a masked stalker, serial killer kind of way." She stops, her face going serious. "He's not a serial killer, is he? Fuck, I know I joke about this shit a lot, Lu, but he isn't one, right?"

I freeze and hope she doesn't notice. Thankfully, she's rubbing her hands over her face, trying to digest everything I've told her. There's no way I'm telling Maren that part of the story. That I'll take to the grave.

"Maren, seriously?"

She leans back against the pillow again. "So, what do you call him?"

I knew this question was coming. I run my fingers through my hair and sit back against the pillow.

"At first, my watcher. Now I call him my wolf." The last word comes out soft, loaded with emotion I'm not ready to admit. "Because of the mask."

"Your wolf." She repeats it without inflection. "No wonder you flinched when I called Damien that."

I stare at the ceiling, letting my mind wander down that familiar path of suspicion and doubt.

"So this all started around the same time you met Damien, too, right? You don't think it's him, do you? I mean, that would be totally fucking twisted of him."

I'm relieved she asks because I have to say it to someone.

"Sometimes I think... but then I convince myself I'm crazy and imagining things, almost like I want them to be the same person. Yeah, they're both huge. Similar height, similar build. Similar overwhelming presence. But they don't walk the same, they don't sound the same, and they don't smell the same. He won't let me turn on the lights. I can only see hints of him, so I don't know if I'm just imagining that they seem similar. Damien always wears really strong cologne, and my wolf smells more natural, like soap and pine and sex. I just want to breathe him in all the time. I want to crawl inside that scent and live there."

"But the wolf mask?" Maren's eyebrows shoot up. "Doesn't that seem like too much of a coincidence?"

"Maren, I'm known across three states as the wolf whisperer."

"Okay, fair point. Whoever he is could have picked the mask because of your reputation. But what about taste? Do they taste the same? And I'm talking about kissing here, not—"

She makes a crude gesture that needs no explanation.

My shoulders drop. "I don't know. I've kissed Damien, but my wolf doesn't kiss me. Not on the mouth. I don't know what his lips taste like. Or how they feel on mine."

"Oh, Lu."

The familiar ache of disappointment returns. I sigh and let my head fall forward, knowing I've kept so much from Maren, and it just adds one more layer of confusion and guilt to what I'm already feeling. Her hand glides through my hair and comes around to rest on the back of my neck.

"Hey, no judgment, but I don't understand what's going on with you and how you got here."

I sit back and let all the rest pour out of me. She stops asking questions and listens in the way only Maren can when she lets the sarcastic armor she always wears fall.

It takes almost an hour to empty myself of everything I've been holding in. But when the last word leaves my mouth, the relief crashes over me like a wave. The weight that's been crushing my chest for months—it lifts. I can breathe again. She stares at me with the same dazed expression I've been wearing since the doctor's office.

"So, let me get this right. You've been having nonstop sex for months with a guy who wears a wolf mask, ties you up, fucks you like an animal, chokes you, won't kiss you, but tells you he's never letting you go? Did I get that right?"

"That about sums it up. I know how crazy this all is, Mar. All the reasons it's insane. Trust me, there is nothing you can say that I haven't said to myself already a hundred times."

"Obviously, it failed, but you do use protection, right? Please tell me you use protection with someone whose identity you don't know."

I cringe. She's going to kick my ass.

"I've been on the pill for years, but other than that, he refuses to wear a condom. Says he wants to feel all of me. And I let him, Maren. I let him come inside me every single night."

"Are you out of your goddamn mind?"

She looks like she wants to shake me until my teeth rattle.

"I know." That's all I have. Two words on repeat. I'm as pissed at my recklessness as she is.

"Does this guy hurt you?"

"Not in the way you mean. He's rough, but he's never actually hurt me. It's more like..." I struggle to find the right words. "Like he worships me through the brutality. If that makes any sense."

She doesn't answer, only raises an expectant eyebrow that tells me to continue.

"Lately, he's been different. He still won't kiss me, but he lets me feel the barest hint of his weight, and his touches have become more reverent. Like I'm something he's afraid of losing."

"Do you guys actually talk, or is it just sex?"

"At first, it was just sex. Pure, primal fucking for hours with barely any words exchanged. Grunts and groans and orgasms until I was literally overflowing with his come." My skin flushes at the memory. "He'd tell me I was his, that I'd never have another man inside me but him. How good I felt wrapped around him, how sweet I tasted, and how he couldn't get enough of me."

"Fuck! Why can't I have a man say shit like that to me? JT and I need to talk." She's trying to pull us out of the heaviness, so I laugh, but it sounds as forced as it feels. "And now?"

Even though I'm laying myself bare for her, I still can't tell her everything. I can't expose him like that. And I can't put that burden on Maren.

"We joke around a little now. Tease each other." I pause, struggling with how much I can reveal. "But honestly, it's still mostly sex. We can't keep our hands off each other. Well, he can't keep his hands off me."

"And you're in love with him."

My head slumps forward again. "Yes. Which is so fucked up I can't even process it." Tears well up in my eyes. "How do you love someone whose face you've never seen? A man who won't even kiss you?"

"What about Damien?"

"That's the worst part. I think I have genuine feelings for Damien, too." I wipe my fingertips under my eyes. "I started seeing him because he reminded me of my wolf in some ways. The intensity, the way he looks at me like he wants to devour me."

"So you really don't think they're the same person?"

"I don't know anymore, Mar. I don't trust my own judgment at all. How can I?"

"Have you thought about confronting him?"

"And say what? Are you Damien?"

"Yeah."

"He's incredibly jealous of Damien. Loses it when I go out with him. There's no way..." Her eyes blaze with anger. "Don't look at me like that. I told you he doesn't hurt me. He gets rougher, but we both like it rough."

She doesn't look convinced, but she nods. "How the fuck did I miss this? I knew something was up with you. But I wanted to give you space. Let you come to me when you were ready. That's what we do. But I'm the one who catches everything." She runs a hand through her hair, tugging at the ends. "I'm fucking losing my touch."

I grab her hand, interlacing our fingers together and squeezing. "I twisted myself in knots to keep you from finding out."

"Wait." Her eyes go wide. "That night I came into your bedroom—when I thought I heard voices. Was he here?"

I nod. "Behind the door."

"Son of a bitch. What kind of freaking best friend am I? And why didn't Shadow blow his cover?"

"Shadow trusted him from the start. It's why I trusted him."

"I thought I saw your panties on the floor that night. And I swore I heard you moaning after I went back to bed."

"Why didn't you say anything?"

"Because what you do with your vagina is none of my damn business, Lu. Every woman's got a right to take care of herself without her best friend demanding a play-by-play. Though you know I'm always down for that."

I snort and rest my head on her shoulder. "I'm sorry I lied and kept it from you. I wanted to tell you so many times."

She leans her head against the top of mine. "So where does that leave you now?"

"On the train to crazy town." I try to laugh, but the sound comes out hollow and wrong.

"I think you've been on it for a while."

"I don't know what to do, Mar. I'm torn between two men who couldn't be more different, except for the way they make me feel. And now..." My hand drifts to my stomach. "There's this."

"Does he know? About the miscarriage?"

"Not yet. I have no way of getting in touch with him. I have to wait for him to show up. He'll come tonight expecting to fuck me, and I won't be able to."

"Will he take no for an answer?"

"He never has before. That's part of what I love about him. The way he just takes what he wants. Makes me take it."

"What about Damien? Are you going to tell him?"

I feel the weight of all these secrets crushing down on me. "I don't know."

"If you're not that serious and you aren't fucking him at the same time, you don't owe it to Damien to tell him."

"If I want something real with him, I need to be honest. I can't build a relationship on lies. But how do I tell him I've been having sex with a masked stranger every night while dating him?" I curl up smaller, pulling my knees to my chest. "I need to end things with my wolf if I want to be with Damien. But I don't know if I can. I don't know if my heart will let me."

I don't know if my wolf will let me either. I'm terrified he'll hurt Damien, but I keep that to myself.

Her expression softens, and she tucks my hair behind my ear. I lean my face into her palm.

"I'm so sorry about the baby, Lu. Just because you didn't know doesn't mean it isn't gutting."

I go quiet, trying to sort through the mess of feelings tangled inside me. More tears blur my vision. "I don't know how I feel. I had no idea, but now that it's gone... part of me is wrecked. Not only because it was mine, but because it was his."

She nods, and something passes between us. An understanding that doesn't need words. Senior year, the guy she was dating, the one she thought was *the one*, left her the second she told him she was pregnant. She fell apart. Then she lost the baby a month later. God, I'm dragging her back through all of that. I'm a terrible friend.

"If things between us end, and they probably will because we can't keep going like this without destroying each other, at least if I'd had his baby, I'd always have something of him." The tears come harder now. "How sick is that?"

She wraps her arms around me again. "It's not sick, Lu. It's human."

"I'm so fucked, Mar. I've gone so far down this road I can't even see the way back anymore."

"Well, for what it's worth, I think you need to tell your wolf the truth. First, because you can't have sex while you're still miscarrying. And if he fucking doesn't take no for an answer, I will kill him, and they'll never find his body."

I laugh and cringe at the same time. Her words are almost unbearably ironic.

"But what if he ends it? I'm not ready for that. It'll break me, even if breaking is probably the healthiest thing that could happen."

I sag against her, and her arms tighten as fresh tears stream down my cheeks. A wave of grief, held back all day by numbness, releases, washing over me in waves.

Maren holds me through it all, her presence an anchor in the storm of my emotions. She doesn't try to fix anything or offer empty reassurances.

She just holds me, and for now, that's enough.

Chapter Nineteen

Damien

Luna is still awake when I arrive, even though it's after midnight. She's usually asleep by now. I'm late tonight because I had a target who needed my attention. Cade is disposing of what's left of him now as I come to my little doe, desperate and aching for her.

I push open the door. She's sitting on the bed in the dark, bathed in nothing but a thin sliver of moonlight cutting through the gap in her curtains. The look on her face stops me cold. This isn't the breathless anticipation I've come to expect. This is emptiness. A void where emotion should be.

Her gaze lifts to mine, and I'm struck by how wrung out she looks. Exhaustion is carved into every line of her face, weighing down her shoulders.

I spent the entire day trapped in my Denver office, hammering out the final details of a new acquisition, which meant I only caught an early exchange with Maren about errands before my day spiraled into back-to-back meetings. Then I had to attend to my target. But I should have checked the cameras and looked in on her. Because the way she's sitting here, the emptiness in her eyes—it sets off every alarm bell in my head. Something is very wrong.

I know how to make it right, though. And it involves my cock inside her cunt.

I shoo Shadow and the cats out of the room and close the door. In three long strides, I'm in front of her, my hand already at my belt, impatient as always.

"Stand up. Take that off."

She rises, but when my hands move to the sash of her robe, she steps back. "Wait."

I go still, my head tilting. Did I hear her right?

"Wait?"

"I can't tonight. I... something's happened."

I step closer, lifting my hand to cup her pale cheek. "What's happened?"

"I saw my doctor today. I woke up bleeding this morning."

"Your period has never stopped me before, you know that."

"It isn't my period."

My body goes rigid as last night replays in fragments. Her gasps, the way she arched beneath me, and how I held her down when she tried to move away from the intensity.

I drop my hand from her face. "Did I hurt you last night?"

"No. It has nothing to do with that." She takes a deep breath. "I was pregnant. Six weeks. I didn't know, I swear I didn't know, but I'm not anymore. I'm having a miscarriage."

Pregnant.

The word ricochets through my skull like a bullet.

Luna was pregnant with my child.

Blood roars in my ears. My hands flex open and closed at my sides, fingers grasping at empty air, desperate for something tangible to hold onto, to control. My pants are half-undone, and my cock is already hard, ready to take her as I always do. Now I feel exposed, caught in a moment I don't know how to respond to.

For the first time in her presence, my cock deflates.

"Say something." The words break in her throat. Her eyes go wide, pleading with me, searching my face for any reaction she can read.

What the fuck am I supposed to say?

That I'm sorry? That I'm angry? That somewhere deep inside the monster I've become is howling with what... grief?

My hands move to her waist without conscious thought. My body operates on instinct while my mind refuses to function. I need her. Need her to calm the beast that's clawing to get out.

"I'll go easy." My cock hasn't completely softened. It pushes against her belly through the fabric between us, making my desire obvious. "But I need you, Luna."

Fury flashes across her face, and she shoves both palms hard against my chest, catching me completely off guard. I rock back on my heels.

"No. Didn't you hear what I said? I'm having a miscarriage. I can't have sex with you tonight. I can't have sex for at least two weeks."

Two weeks.

The words land like a prison sentence. Two weeks without losing myself inside her body, without feeling her fall apart underneath me, around me. Two weeks without the only thing that makes me feel human.

"My body needs to heal."

I turn away, fumbling with my pants, trying to cage the beast that still demands I take her. My hands shake, and my fingers won't cooperate. Her stare burns into my spine.

"So that's it? You have nothing to say?" Her voice climbs, sharp with anger. "I tell you I was carrying your child, that I'm losing it right now, and you can't even say you're sorry?"

I spin to face her, rage burning through my veins. "Sorry for what? Something we didn't know about? Something that was never supposed to happen?"

The words come out harsh, but I can't pull them back. Can't make them gentle. This isn't what we do. What we have exists in the realm of flesh and possession, of dominance and surrender. Not this. Not loss and grief and things neither of us can control.

"Sorry that I'm hurting." Her voice rises to match mine. "Sorry that I'm losing something that was part of both of us, even if neither of us knew it was there."

I cross the space between us in two strides, using every inch of my height advantage to loom over her the way I do when I want to intimidate. She doesn't cower.

"Is that what you want? Pretty words about a clump of cells that never had a chance? Would that make you feel better, Luna?"

Her eyes fill with tears, and my stomach turns over. I've made her cry before. In passion. In surrender. But never like this. Never with words meant to wound. The woman I love is hurting, bleeding in front of me, looking for comfort I don't know how to give.

"You want to know what would help? Knowing I matter to you. That I'm more than a body you use and then leave behind."

Her words find their mark, cutting through the man beneath the monster. We've talked about this. I told her she means everything. How does she not understand?

I love you!

The words lodge in my throat, thick and choking.

Why else would I come to you night after night, reveal the darkest parts of myself, and trust you with the beast that lives inside me?

"You think that's all this is?" My voice drops, turning dangerous. "After everything I've said to you? Everything I've shown you?"

She doesn't flinch from my anger, doesn't back down. "You've shown me your cock. You hide your face behind that mask and your body beneath those clothes. You won't show me anything real. Do you have any idea how that makes me feel? You strip me bare, body and soul. You tell me I'm yours, that you'll never let me go. But the second something real happens, you stand there with your pants undone, pissed off because you can't get what you came for."

Her words penetrate the red haze of my anger, leaving clarity in their wake. She's right. Whatever twisted path I've been walking with her—this moment demands more. Something I'm not sure I'm capable of giving her. But I take her hand, driven by the sudden need to undo the damage. "Come." I guide her toward the bed. "Lie down."

She hesitates, suspicion clear in her eyes.

"No sex. I won't touch you that way. Just lie down. Please."

The "please" feels foreign on my tongue. When have I ever asked instead of commanded? When have I ever given her a choice?

Her face registers her surprise, but she lets me lead her to the bed. I arrange the pillows behind her, my hands fumbling with the task. I pull the covers up to her waist, then adjust the curtains to keep the moonlight only on her before I sit beside her, placing one hand flat against her stomach. I've touched her everywhere, claimed every part of her with greedy hands, but never like this. Never with a touch this careful, this tentative.

She stares at me like I'm someone she doesn't recognize, and it cuts deeper than any blade.

"Does it hurt now?"

"A little. It comes and goes, like bad cramps."

I move my hand in slow circles over her abdomen, applying the lightest pressure. I know how to make her come undone, how to break her down until she's pleading with me, but this—this simple act of comfort—feels like speaking a language I never learned.

"I don't know what to say, Luna. I never considered pregnancy a viable possibility."

"Neither did I. I'm on birth control."

"Which obviously failed."

"Obviously." She echoes my sarcasm. "It was probably the antibiotics I took for my UTI or after my bear attack. I didn't even think about it, but it can interfere with birth control. Not that it would've mattered. You'll never wear a condom."

"No, I won't. But if I'd known there was a chance, I would've brought you a dozen cases of the morning-after pill."

She sighs. "It's my fault. I'm a doctor, and I know better. I should have thought about it and insisted you wear a condom while I was on the antibiotics."

"I wouldn't have worn one, Luna."

"Well, it doesn't matter anymore now, does it? There's no more baby."

Silence settles between us, and inside me a war rages. Anger at her for getting pregnant. Anger at myself for being careless. Fear that this ruptures what we have, that the raw connection we've built will twist into something unrecognizable. And underneath all of it, grief I have no business feeling.

"Are you sad?"

I have to ask because the need to understand what's happening inside her overrides everything else.

"I think so." She exhales. "Not in the way I would be if I'd known about it, if I'd had time to imagine a future with it. But there's this emptiness that wasn't there before. Like a door closed on something that could have been."

I nod. A door closed. A future that never had a chance to exist. A version of me that might have been a father, a notion so absurd it would be laughable if it didn't ache so badly.

What kind of father would I have been? Would I have removed the mask? Stopped killing? Would I have buried that part of myself, become someone new for the sake of an innocent life?

"Will you be alright? Physically, I mean."

"I'll be fine. It's very early, so my body's handling it like a heavy period." She pauses. "But no sex for at least two weeks. Maybe longer."

The reminder sends a fresh surge of frustration through me. Two weeks without the only form of connection I truly understand. Two weeks of this awkward tenderness I'm not equipped for.

Yet, the thought of hurting her is unbearable.

"I'll wait."

"You will?"

Her disbelief stings, and my eyes narrow behind the mask. "You think I'd hurt you? Force you?"

Her gaze sweeps over the mask as she hesitates. "I wasn't sure you'd stay away. That you'd be able to."

I want to argue, but my initial reaction condemns me. My cock still throbs with want, even now. If she offered herself, would I have the strength to refuse?

"I fucking want you desperately, Luna." My voice drops, taking on the rough edge I know reaches her. "Every fucking hour of every day. But not at the expense of your health. Never that."

Her face softens with relief, then clouds with doubt. "I wasn't sure. Since I can't see your reaction behind that mask. I thought maybe you'd see me as broken now. Damaged."

My hand leaves her stomach and finds her face, cupping her cheek, her skin warm against my palm.

"You're still perfect. Still mine. Nothing about this changes that."

"Nothing?" She pushes back.

I weigh the question, fighting the instinct to offer platitudes. "Maybe it changes how I see us. The potential consequences of what we do. What we are."

"And what are we to each other?"

The question catches me unprepared. What are we? Lovers? Predator and prey? Two broken people seeking oblivion in each other's bodies? I've never had to define it before. I've never loved someone the way I love her, but how do I tell her that without revealing who I am?

"More than I intended. And less than you deserve."

I stand, needing distance. The intimacy of the moment presses in on me, threatening to suffocate me. "You should rest. I'll go."

"Don't." She reaches her hand out. "Stay with me tonight. For a little while."

I stop, caught between conflicting impulses. This is the moment. I could tell her who I am and end all the lies right here. But her body is rejecting what we created together. Dumping my confession on top of that seems like the worst kind of selfishness.

"Please." Her voice comes out small and fractured. "I don't want to be alone right now."

The naked need in her voice splinters my chest wide open. Every intention I had to leave evaporates. How can I walk away when she's asking for this one thing? This basic comfort?

I nod once. "The mask stays." I cut off the question forming in her eyes before she can voice it.

She's not fast enough to hide the way her shoulders drop, the disappointment that flashes across her face.

"I know."

I stretch out along the bed, propping myself against the headboard. The comforter creates a barrier between us, her beneath and me above. She shifts down into the blankets and rolls to face me.

"I'm sorry." I force the words past years of emotional armor. "Not for something we didn't plan, but for your pain. For your loss."

"It's our loss."

Tears well in her eyes, and I brush my fingers against her cheek, then slide them through the soft strands of her hair. She sighs and closes her eyes. My body still aches for her, but it's manageable now, subdued by something stronger, by the overwhelming love I feel for her.

As her breathing evens out and she drifts toward sleep, I battle new demons. My mind cycles through images of what might have been. Luna swollen with my child, a blonde-haired infant with her eyes and my damned bloodline.

Mine

The child would have been mine. Like Luna is.

The cruel truth mocks me. Maybe it's better this way. But what kind of man finds relief in the loss of his unborn child?

I'm a killer. A man who stalks prey in the night and hides his face even from the woman he loves. What right do I have to mourn the loss of a child I never intended to make? What right do I have to imagine myself as anyone's father?

But this pregnancy changes everything. It makes this real in a way I never expected. All this time, I've kept myself split in two. Damien Wolfe, the billionaire trying to court Luna with normalcy. And her masked lover, her wolf, who gives her nothing more than brutal passion in the dark of night.

Two separate men. Two separate relationships.

But my body betrayed that careful division. My seed grew inside her, a biological truth that mocks the lie I've been living. And now there's a loss that binds us together in yet another way, a shared grief for something that never had the chance to be.

She deserves better than me. Better than these fucking mind games.

Luna shifts closer, murmuring something in her sleep.

"I'm here, little doe. I'm not going anywhere."

For tonight at least, I can give her this.

————◆————

Luna stirs, her eyes blinking open. I've watched her for hours, the rise and fall of her chest, memorizing the way her eyelashes cast shadows on her cheeks in the dim morning light.

"You stayed." Surprise colors her voice.

"I said I would."

She sits up, then winces, her hand going to her lower abdomen. The gesture—so small, so full of pain—cleaves something open inside me. Rage mingles with helplessness, both fighting for dominance and neither winning.

I push off the bed, unable to remain still. My legs carry me to the window, then back to the door, then to the foot of the bed. The room feels too small, the walls pressing in. My hands ball into fists and release, over and over, every muscle in my body screaming for a target I don't have.

"You're angry."

There's no point in denying it. "Yes."

"At me?"

I stop pacing to look at her. "Why would I be angry at you?"

She shrugs, the motion small and uncertain. "For getting pregnant. For losing it. For not being able to give you what you need right now."

Her words trigger another wave of rage, but it's aimed at myself, at making her believe she's the problem.

Yes, I was angry at first. At both of us for letting this happen. Until I understood it was inevitable. With how often I come inside her and how much I need to mark her that way, my seed was bound to take root.

I cross to the bed in three strides. I grasp the hair at the back of her head, tilting it back so her eyes meet mine. She gasps at the sting, but no sound follows.

"Listen to me. I'm not angry with you. I'm angry at the situation." I struggle to put words to the chaos inside me. "At feeling helpless."

"I know the feeling." Her smile cracks at the edges. "I feel like my body betrayed us both."

"No." The word comes out sharp, like a shard of glass. "Don't say that."

"But it's true. First, I got pregnant when I shouldn't have been able to, and then my body rejected it. And now we can't even—"

"Stop." I tighten my fingers in her hair, then wrap my other hand around her throat. I don't cut off her air, but I need her attention. "This isn't your fault, Luna. Don't you dare fucking blame yourself. If anything, I did this to you by being too fucking brutal."

"Rough sex doesn't cause miscarriages. It happens sometimes. My body just couldn't sustain it."

My grip on her hair tightens. "I said stop. Don't you ever fucking blame yourself for this again, Luna. Not ever."

She blinks up at me, eyes wide.

"I mean it." The words pour out, unstoppable now. "If you do, I swear, when I can finally fuck you again, you won't be able to walk for a week. You understand me?"

Pain flashes across her face, and regret crashes through me. This is what I know. Dominance, possession, and control. But it's not what she needs right now.

"That was..." I release her, stepping back. "I shouldn't have said that."

To my surprise, a small smile curves her lips, even as she rubs at her scalp.

"That's the first normal thing you've said since I told you."

I tilt my head, confused.

"That sounded like you. Like the man who comes to me and takes what he wants. Not this careful stranger who's been tiptoeing around me."

Her words strike a chord. She's right. I've been performing a role I don't know how to play. The understanding lover. The supportive partner. Roles beyond the mask I wear.

"I don't know how to do this. I don't know how to comfort you. How to be with you without being inside you."

"I know. What we have is only physical."

Her words rip through my chest. A piece of me tears open—hot, bleeding, and raw. The need to correct her burns through me like acid.

"It's more than that. It's always been more than that."

"Has it? Because right now, when we can't have that, I don't know what's left."

Her words knock the air from my lungs. Is she right? Is our connection nothing more than lust, dominance, and submission? Does that mean she could never love me back? The thought hollows me out.

"There's more." I force the words out, though I can't define what that "more" might be.

"Then show me. Because I need something to hold on to right now."

I stand frozen, caught between who I am and who she needs me to be.

"All I know is taking you, Luna. I don't know how to be gentle."

"You don't have to be gentle. You just have to be here."

I watch her for a long moment before moving back to the bed, settling beside her again. I take her hand in mine, the gesture awkward and careful. Nothing like the demanding and rough way I usually touch her. Her hand feels small in mine. Breakable.

The need to hold her burns through me. I want to bury my face in her hair and inhale her scent while I pull her tight against my chest.

"I'm here." The words scrape from my throat. "And I'll keep coming back. Every night. Even if I can't have you."

"Promise?"

Everything she's feeling lives in her eyes. Pain, fear, and need, exposed and unguarded.

"I promise."

The words feel like a vow, binding me more than any contract I've ever signed.

We sit in silence, watching the sun climb over the horizon through the sliver in her curtains. In a few minutes, I'll have to leave before the world wakes. Before the light is too bright to hide my identity.

But for now, I sit beside her, holding her hand, learning a new way to possess her that has nothing to do with flesh and everything to do with presence.

And somewhere deep inside, behind walls I've spent years fortifying, I mourn the loss of something I never knew I wanted until it was already gone.

Chapter Twenty

Damien

I knock on Luna's door, then step back, forcing my expression into the controlled mask of daytime Damien. Friendly but not intimate, as long as you don't count the night on her porch, the night in my penthouse, or against the door in the sanctuary.

I spot Maren through the front window. She's wrestling with a Christmas tree, a strand of lights tangled around her arm, and what looks like a ferret on her shoulder.

I glance around at the snow-covered landscape. Aspen Ridge received its first significant snow of the season last night, over eleven inches, and it blankets the entire sanctuary in a pristine layer of white. The road is closed from Estes Park, so I took the helicopter up here on a whim to bring Luna and Maren lunch.

I'd been watching on the cameras as they hauled out Christmas decorations, but Luna seemed indifferent, while Maren's cheerfulness felt forced. Not that I could blame them.

The knowledge of Luna's miscarriage still sits in my chest like a stone. It's a unique kind of hell, knowing her pain through one persona while being kept in the dark in another. But I can't rush her. She'll tell Damien when she's ready. If she's ready.

Maren answers the door. Her eyes travel over me, calculating, as if trying to piece together who stands in front of her.

When I went back and watched the footage from the day Luna miscarried, their discussion in her bedroom was enlightening. They both suspect I'm her wolf. I'm not surprised, but it doesn't make revealing myself to Luna any easier.

Maren's eyes narrow, but then she catches sight of the insulated bags I'm carrying, and her face lights up. "Oh my God, is that Giacomo's? I think you might be my actual hero."

"Thought you two could use some comfort food. Is that a ferret with its head down your shirt?"

She looks down and pulls his small head from where it's burrowing into her cleavage, sighing, almost as if she hadn't noticed.

"Story of my life. Come on in."

She walks away, and I stamp snow from my boots before stepping inside. "Christmas decorations, huh? How's it going?"

"It'd be going better if these monsters would stop helping." She sets the ferret down on the floor and then gestures toward Ricky, who's rooting around under the partially decorated tree. "I swear to God, perv, if you don't stop sabotaging that tree, there will be no boob action for you today!"

Shadow and Ghost sleep in beds on either side of the fireplace. Neither bothers to get up and greet me. My eyes find Luna. She's curled on the sofa, wrapped in a thick blanket, with her calico cat on her lap and the black and white one behind her head. The fat one is nowhere to be seen. For some reason, I can never seem to remember their names.

Luna chuckles as she sips tea, but her face is paler than usual, her vibrant energy dimmed.

"Hey." I smile as I approach her. "I seem to remember you mentioning that Giacomo's butternut squash ravioli with sage butter is one of your favorites."

She looks up, attempting a smile that doesn't quite reach her eyes. "You didn't have to do that."

"I wanted to." I set the bags on the coffee table, fighting the urge to brush the hair from her face, my fingers aching to touch her, to pull her into my arms and comfort her. It's a foreign feeling for me, this need to nurture. "Are you okay? You seem a little off."

She shrugs, placing her teacup down, and then draws the blanket closer. "I'm fine. Just tired."

It's a lie, of course. I know how she feels. Devastated, empty, and confused. The urge to break character, to tell her I know everything, overwhelms me.

"You don't seem fine." I sit beside her, leaving space between us. "Is there anything I can do?"

A crash tears my eyes from her face. The ferret darts out from under the tree, ornaments rolling in its wake.

"That's it!" Maren throws her hands up. "These troublemakers are coming with me while I grab some plates and utensils. Come on, Ricky. You too, Frank." She scoops up both animals, and the ferret dives straight down the front of her shirt again, while Ricky's hand grabs for her breast. "Damn it, Lu. Can't you find animals that don't want to feel me up?" She walks toward the kitchen while trying to extract the ferret.

"Admit it, it's the most action you get when JT's away."

Maren's snort echoes down the short hallway between the kitchen and the living room.

Once she's gone, Luna's guard drops for a second, and pain flashes across her face before she blinks it away.

"So, the raccoon seems to be doing better?"

Her lips curve. I've learned that asking about her animals is the easiest way to make her smile.

"No more kidney stones. He passed all the fragments. Thanks to you. But we'll have to keep monitoring him." She shifts in her seat, settling into the topic. "Once an animal develops kidney stones, recurrence is pretty common. We'll need to adjust his diet too. Raccoons go crazy for nuts, but those increase the risk of stones."

"The care you give these animals, Luna—it's remarkable." My voice drops lower, softer. I have to be careful here. I don't want her to recognize it. "You have this incredible capacity for love. You deserve to have someone give all of that back to you. And more."

She stares out at the falling snow, fingers stroking the calico cat's fur.

"Luna." I keep my voice soft. "Something's wrong. I can tell. Are you sure you don't want to talk about it?"

"It's nothing you need to worry about."

"I do worry about you." I allow more of my true feelings to show than I normally would as daytime Damien.

She turns to study my face. Now that I know her suspicions, every time she looks at me, it makes me wonder what she sees.

"I'm dealing with some health issues."

My heart races. This is it. She's going to tell me. "What kind of health issues? Is it serious?"

She opens her mouth, then closes it, seeming to reconsider. "I haven't been feeling well. It'll pass."

The disappointment is sharp. I nod, respecting her choice even as it tears at me. But I also appreciate that she keeps our loss to herself. "Well, I'm here. Whatever you need."

We sit in silence, watching the snow. Through the window, I notice a pair of raccoons waddling through the powder, one chasing the other in what appears to be some sort of mating ritual.

Luna notices them too, and something shifts in her expression. "Do you know raccoons can have sex for hours?"

I choke out a laugh. I swear this woman can shock me like no one else. "Excuse me?"

Her cheeks flush pink, but she plows ahead. "Yeah. Maren and I sat on my back porch one time and watched two of them having sex in the backyard. It was like a train wreck. We couldn't look away." She seems relieved to talk about anything other than herself. "Not all of it was intercourse. There was quite a bit of foreplay too, but it went on for at least two hours. I think Maren was jealous."

"I totally was," Maren calls from the kitchen.

I study Luna's face. This is the first glimpse of the real Luna I've seen to-day—quirky, unfiltered, and unexpected. The ache of missing her settles deep in my bones. Not her body, but just her. And I can't help myself; I let a bit of my nighttime persona slip through.

"You sound surprised a man is capable of that." My voice drops lower. "Have you never had sex for hours, Luna? Never had someone make you come so many times you lose count? Who gets inside you and won't stop until you're begging? If that's the case, you haven't had sex with the right men."

Her eyes widen, and for a second, I worry I've gone too far. Let too much of my other self show.

"Jesus, Damien." Color floods her cheeks.

"You're the one who brought up raccoon sex." I hold her gaze, allowing a slow smile to spread across my lips. "And the one who seems fascinated by their stamina."

The tension between us shifts, electric now rather than awkward. I can see the wheels turning in her mind, making connections she's not quite ready to acknowledge. Maren returns with plates and utensils.

"Let's plate this feast up." She's oblivious to or purposely ignoring the charged atmosphere. "I left the little monsters locked in the bathroom for now. They can have their freedom back after we eat."

I help her plate up the food, grateful for the interruption. We eat in compan-ionable silence, with bursts of short conversation about the upcoming Christmas holidays, Maren's grandmother's arthritis acting up now that the snow's arrived en masse, and the animals. It always seems to segue back to the animals.

My gaze keeps drifting to Luna the entire time, to the subtle changes in her face. The way her eyes light up when discussing her animals, the pain receding for those moments. This is the Luna I've fallen for. The professional vet, the compassionate caretaker, and the woman who comes alive under my touch in the dark.

Maren stands when we're done, taking our plates and releasing the "trouble-makers."

"Alright, you horny little bastards, back to terrorizing the Christmas tree. But keep your paws off my goods!"

Ricky makes a beeline for Luna, carrying a stuffed monkey, climbing onto her lap, and reaching for her breast before she redirects his hand to the toy.

I raise an eyebrow. "Distraction technique?"

"It seems to work pretty well. But we've got a ways to go."

I take a deep breath. I can't push too hard, but I can't bear to see her suffering alone like this either.

"Luna, I know we haven't known each other that long, but I've made no secret about how I feel about you."

"I know, Damien."

"I want you to know if you want to talk, I'm here."

She looks at me, and for a moment I think she sees me, all of me. An almost sad smile tugs at her lips.

"Thank you, Damien. You really are a sweet man."

A derisive laugh wants to escape, but I swallow it down. I'm not a sweet man. I'm a man who's deceiving her. I lie to her every day and night in both my personas, and she deserves better.

"I'm sorry I'm shit company lately."

"I don't think you're shit company. Ricky obviously doesn't either." I nod toward the raccoon using her breasts as a pillow, his hands wrapped around his stuffed monkey, two fingers pulling at its nose. I'm pleased when she snorts.

She reaches for my hand, her fingers wrapping around mine.

"Why are you so good to me?"

Because I love you. Because the child you lost was mine. And I'm hurting too.

The words I long to say burn behind my teeth, desperate to escape. But I can't. Not now, when she's as fragile as spun glass. Not when she's grieving something we both lost, but only she has to carry.

Instead, I bring her hand to my lips, pressing a kiss to her knuckles.

"Because you deserve it."

Chapter Twenty-One

Luna

I drag the brush through Cotton's mane in long, steady strokes, finding comfort in the repetitive motion. This mindless routine is what I need right now. The familiar scent of hay and horse fills my nostrils, grounding me when everything else feels like it's floating away.

"Almost done with you, boy." I run my palm along his flank. He responds with a low whinny.

The barn door creaks open, letting in a gust of cold air and the sound of boots on straw. I don't need to turn around to know it's Damien. He changes the air when he enters a space. Thickens it, electrifies it, and makes it press against my skin. My pulse stumbles even though my thoughts are scattered elsewhere.

He's been coming to visit almost every day for the last week and a half. Just stopping by to say hi, bringing lunch, or bringing Athena to play with Shadow and Ghost. He doesn't stay long, and though it's a little strange, it's been nice.

"Maren told me where you were. I hope that's okay." His deep voice echoes in the wooden structure. "Thought you might need something warm."

I turn to see him carrying a steaming mug, snowflakes melting on the shoulders of his expensive coat. It's almost comical, this polished billionaire standing in my humble barn, looking like he stepped off a magazine cover. But that's Damien.

"Thanks." I accept the hot chocolate. Our fingers brush, and that familiar spark, the one I've been trying to ignore, rushes beneath my skin. The warmth spreads through my palms as I wrap both hands around the mug.

"Don't you ever work?"

"That's what I pay Cade for. I hardly ever go to my Denver office anymore. I prefer to work out of my office up here."

"You're spoiling me with all this attention. Bringing me lunch from Giacomo's, stopping by to bring me hot chocolate. I might get used to this. What's next? Mucking stalls?"

He chuckles, and the sound sends a pleasant shiver down my spine. "I draw the line at manure. Though for you..." He shrugs, leaving the sentence hanging with that hint of a smile that makes my stomach flutter.

He moves closer. "So, you seem better than you were last week."

"Yeah, I'm getting back to myself."

The words come easier now, less like a lie I'm telling myself. Healing happens in increments too small to measure day by day but visible when you step back and look at the whole picture. The crushing weight that settled on my chest after the miscarriage has lifted enough that I can breathe without conscious effort.

Maren has been my anchor through all of it, choosing to stay up here instead of going home to her apartment, claiming the mountain roads are too treacherous for her daily commute. We both know the weather is her excuse. She's here because she refuses to let me navigate this alone.

Still, Maren's protective presence doesn't stop my wolf from coming to me. He waits until she's in bed, until the last light disappears from under her door. I rarely see him anymore. Sleep takes me before he arrives, exhaustion winning over the part of me that wants to stay awake and wait for him. But when I wake in the morning, there's always a red dahlia bloom on the pillow next to my head. I never told him it's my favorite flower, but somehow he knows.

I take a sip of hot chocolate, the liquid rich and sweet. Of course, Damien would remember how I like it, another small detail that makes my chest tighten.

He grins. "Well, I'm glad to hear that."

That smile. It's dangerous.

"So, Christmas is right around the corner. Two weeks of holiday cheer bearing down on us."

"I actually love this time of year. Not because of the holidays, but because of how everything feels cleaner somehow when it's covered in snow. The mountains look different. More peaceful."

His smile is indulgent. "You're one of the few people I know who gets excited about winter in the mountains. Most people complain about the cold and flee to warmer climates."

"They're missing out. There's something magical about snow falling on the peaks." I glance toward the barn door, where I can see snowflakes drifting past. "It makes everything quiet. Muffled."

"Like the world's paused. Waiting for something."

I look at him, surprise flickering through me.

"That's exactly it."

His expression softens, the sharp edges of his usual composure melting away, and my heart skips a beat.

"You're different, Luna. You see beauty where others see inconvenience. I love that about you."

Love?

I'm unsure how to respond to his words, spoken with the casual, friendly tone people often use. But the intense look in his eyes makes me swallow, a nervous flutter vibrating in my stomach, so I take a sip of my hot chocolate.

His presence today offers a kind of comfort I'm not prepared for.

He moves before I realize what's coming. His hand lifts, and his fingers brush against my temple as he tucks a loose strand of hair behind my ear. His fingers linger against my cheek, and he leans down, his intention clear in his eyes.

"Damien."

I press my hand against his chest and step back, his warmth seeping through his sweater into my palm.

He stops, straightening to his full height. The confusion that flashes across his features morphs into hurt, restrained but impossible to miss.

"What's wrong?"

"I can't." My words disappear under the sound of horses shifting in their stalls.

"Can't what? Kiss me?" His voice stays level, but there's an edge underneath. "We've kissed before, Luna."

"I know, it's..." I set the mug down on a ledge. My hands shake. "It's complicated."

He crosses his arms, and his jaw tightens. "What's so complicated about two adults who are attracted to each other?"

"I'm not being fair to you." My throat closes around the words. "I haven't been honest."

Damien goes still, like predators do right before they strike.

"What do you mean?"

I'm about to shatter whatever we've been building between us, but I have to be honest.

"I've been seeing someone else."

The silence fills every corner of the barn. Damien's face goes blank—neutral in a way that's worse than if he'd gotten angry.

"Seeing someone else." He repeats slowly.

"Yes."

"While we've been..." He gestures between us, and the muscle in his jaw ticks. "While we've been whatever this is?"

"Yes."

I force myself to meet his eyes, but he looks away, staring at something beyond my shoulder. When he looks back, there's a storm brewing in those blue-gray depths.

"How long?"

"A few months. It's... It's complicated." I hate how inadequate the word sounds. "It started before you and I began this."

"But it continued." It's not a question.

"Yes."

He's quiet, and I watch him process this information. There's a look in his eyes I can't quite identify, but it resembles resignation, as if some part of him expected this.

"Is it serious?"

The question catches me off guard. "What do you mean?"

"I mean, are you in love with him?"

I open my mouth to deny it. The words stick in my throat. My hesitation answers for me.

"I see." There's no anger in his voice, just a deep sadness that wraps around my throat and squeezes.

I pick up my mug again. "I don't understand it myself."

"What don't you understand?"

The question is gentle and curious rather than accusatory.

"What we have is different from anything I've ever experienced. He's different."

"Different how?"

I struggle to find words for something I can't comprehend myself. "He makes me feel claimed. Like I belong to him completely." I blush at the admission. "I know how that sounds."

"It sounds honest. Tell me more about him."

The request surprises me. "Why?"

"Because I'm trying to understand. Help me understand what I'm competing with."

The vulnerability threading through his request pulls at a tender place buried inside me, and it compels me to be honest. "It's not a conventional relationship. He comes to me only at night."

His face shifts, an emotion crossing his features too fast for me to catch. I look down at my hands wrapped around the warm mug.

"I know how it sounds. Like some kind of fantasy. But it's real. He's real."

"I believe you. What does he give you that I can't?"

My gaze lifts. His face holds no judgment, only questions he wants answered. He's asking me to bare something private, something I've never put into words.

"Freedom. He takes all the control away from me, and somehow that feels like freedom. With him, I don't have to think or make decisions or worry about anything except feeling. He makes those choices for me."

Damien nods. "And that's what you want? To be controlled?"

"Yes. No. I don't know." I rake a hand through my hair with a sigh. "Not in every part of my life. Just in the bedroom. And I never thought I'd like something like that, but with him it's different. It's not about being weak or submissive. It's about trust. About letting someone else carry the weight for a while."

"And you trust him? This man who comes to you at night?"

"Completely."

There's no hesitation in my voice, and Damien's expression shifts. The lines around his eyes and mouth soften.

"But you can't have a life with him."

"No. He's not available for that."

"Why not?"

"He can't be part of my daylight world. What we have exists in shadows."

Damien studies my face. "That must be lonely."

The observation cracks me open. A fissure splits through my chest because he's right. "Yes. Sometimes it is."

"And yet you continue seeing him."

"Yes."

"Why?"

"Because when I'm with him, I feel more alive, more myself, than I ever have before. Even if it's only in the dark. Even if it can't last."

"And what about us, Luna? What do I make you feel?"

The question, though quiet, is loaded with meaning. I look at him, taking in the almost cruel beauty of his features, the intensity in his blue-gray eyes, and the way he holds himself with that carefully controlled power.

"Like I could build something real with you."

"But?"

"But I can't give you all of me when part of me belongs to someone else."

"Even if that someone else can never give you everything you need?"

"Even then."

He nods. "Who is he, Luna? Really?"

"I don't know."

The admission costs me. It sounds pathetic coming from a woman like me.

"Sometimes I think I do, but it's foolish." I tilt my head and study him. When I look at him like this in the daylight, in all his polish, I only see Damien. "Sometimes I think I'm falling in love with someone who doesn't fully exist outside of my bedroom."

"But you don't think that's what this is?"

"No. What I feel for him is real. What he makes me feel is real. Even if I can't have all of him."

Damien's hand rises to cup my cheek. His thumb traces the path of moisture I hadn't noticed escaping. The tenderness in that single gesture moves through me like a hairline crack spreading through glass.

"And how do you feel about me?"

The question comes out steady, but there's a fragility lurking beneath the surface, like he's bracing for a blow that might shatter him.

"I care about you. More than I should. More than is fair to either of you."

"But you can't choose."

"I don't know how to choose. What I feel for each of you... it's so different. It's like choosing between breathing and having a heartbeat. I need both to survive."

A dozen emotions flicker across his face. Pain, understanding, frustration. Then his expression settles into hard, unwavering determination.

"I have feelings for you too, Luna. Deep feelings. They've been growing stronger every day."

"I know. I'm sorry. I really am."

"I won't ask you to choose right now." More tears well in the corner of my eyes. "But I can't do this indefinitely. And I won't be anyone's second choice."

"I understand."

"Do you?" He cups my face in both hands now, his touch like a balm. And so familiar it makes my breath hitch. "Because I need you to know that what I'm offering you is real. A real relationship. A real future. Not just stolen moments in the dark."

"I know that too."

"Then figure out what you want. What you really want, Luna. Not what feels good in the moment, but what you truly need to be happy."

"And if I can't choose? If I can't choose between you?"

"Then maybe you don't have to. I should go. Give you time to think."

"Damien—"

He steps back, dropping his hands to his sides, before I can ask what he means.

"It's okay, Luna. I'm not angry. I'm hurt, yes, but I understand. You can't help who you love." He pauses at the barn door, snowflakes catching in his dark hair. "But don't take too long to decide. Some opportunities don't come twice."

I step forward. "Damien, what does that mean?"

Pain fills his eyes. The look of someone who's offered everything and watched it get rejected and torn apart. And there's knowledge in his gaze, knowledge that shouldn't be there, and my stomach plummets.

"Sometimes the choices you're afraid to make aren't choices at all."

Damien vanishes into the white curtain of swirling snow, leaving me alone with Cotton and his final words repeating in my head. The conversation went nothing like I expected. I was prepared for anger, for ultimatums, for the explosion that comes when hearts collide. Instead, he gave me understanding I don't deserve.

But his final words sit heavy in my chest. A promise or threat wrapped in riddles that I'm terrified to solve.

Chapter Twenty-Two

Damien

I adjust the plastic sheeting on the floor of my basement. Everything is in perfect order, as always. Everything is clean. Controlled. This is my domain, far beneath the polished facade of Damien Wolfe. Down here, I am the wolf.

My target tonight struggles against his restraints, eyes wide with terror above the duct tape covering his mouth. Travis Miller. Dog breeder. Or rather, the piece of shit who starved his animals when they didn't win shows and who beat them when they failed to meet his standards.

"Do you know why you're here, Travis?" I select a scalpel from my arranged tools.

Muffled screams tear from his throat, high-pitched and desperate. The table rocks as he struggles against his restraints. Tears stream down his cheeks, soaking the edges of the silver tape that seals his mouth.

"Don't bother trying to answer." I walk in a slow circle around him. His eyes lock on my face, on my wolf mask, and I reach up and adjust it. It weighs down on my face tonight. "The way you present yourself to the world as a respected breeder while creating suffering behind closed doors."

The irony of that statement stops me cold. Isn't that what I do?

This ritual should focus me. It should cleanse me, smooth over my jagged edges through the precision of pain. But tonight, every instrument on my table hums with accusation. My mind refuses to stay present. It keeps pulling me back to the barn. To the devastation on Luna's face as she confessed her infidelity—not realizing she was confessing to the very man she thought she was betraying.

I've been seeing someone else.

He makes me feel claimed. Like I belong to him completely.

He can't be part of my daylight world. What we have exists in shadows.

Because when I'm with him, I feel more alive, more myself, than I ever have before.

I can't give you all of me when part of me belongs to someone else.

I roll my shoulders and drag my focus back to the present. I can't afford distractions. Not here. Not now.

"I apologize." Travis stares at me in confusion. "I'm not myself tonight. But don't worry. I'll still give you the attention you deserve."

I light a cigarette even though I despise the taste and smell. But I do what I must to make them pay. Always torturing them the way they hurt their animals.

Smoke coils upward as I press the glowing tip against his right nipple, dragging it across skin already pale with fear. His back arches, and the scent of burning flesh fills the basement. He screams, muffled but harrowing, the table under him vibrating with each convulsion of his body.

One burn at a time, I work the cigarettes across his skin. His torso first, then the curve of his ribs, and then across his abdomen. The final burn goes to the head of his cock, deliberate and vicious. Each burn smokes black, the smell a twisted perfume in the dank basement air. His body trembles, slick with sweat and blood.

When the last cigarette burns down to ash, I set it aside and pick up my serrated knife. The blade is long, its teeth jagged like the broken promises of my past. I make the first cut, a precise slash over his bicep, drawing a ribbon of blood. His gagged screams rise once more, raw and keening, and it's music to my ears.

I lean in. "The puppy that was brought to Sage & Summit is going to live. Dr. Foster is extraordinarily good at what she does. Healing what monsters like you break."

At Luna's name, my chest tightens. The memory of her tears in the barn replays in my mind. The confusion in her eyes when I didn't rage at her confession. How could I? How could I condemn her for falling in love with both sides of me when that's all I've wanted?

Travis thrashes against his restraints, the movement jerking me back.

Focus, Wolfe. Stay present.

My pulse hammers against my skull. Air drags through my lungs too fast, too shallow. The blade wavers in my grip. The work that's always centered me, given me clarity—it's hollow now, powerless, as Luna fills every corner of my mind.

I miss touching her, kissing her, and the sounds she makes when she's breaking apart for me. I want to be there for her but can't, not in the way I should or the way she needs.

I press the blade to Travis' chest, deeper than I intended. His scream explodes past the duct tape. Blood flows faster than it should.

"Fuck." I reach for his shirt on the floor and jam it against the wound. "Not yet. Not like this."

I'm sloppy tonight. Distracted. This isn't how I work. This isn't me.

But who am I, really?

The controlled businessman who courts Luna in the day?

The masked lover who takes her in dark?

The killer who removes predators like Travis from the world?

The lines keep shifting and blurring since Luna entered my life.

My mind won't stay on the work. My hands move without purpose, graceless and disconnected, and the whole thing ends quicker than it should. There's no artistry, no finesse. The knife pierces his flesh in crude, functional strikes, lacking any elegance. When it's done, I stumble back, chest heaving, black fabric drenched and spattered. Travis Miller won't hurt another animal.

But there's no triumph. No satisfaction. Just vast, cold emptiness echoing through my chest.

I begin the meticulous process of cleaning my tools. That's the one thing I do myself. The rest I leave for Cade. I contemplate what I should bring Luna this time. She's asked me to stop with the "gifts" after kills. But I still want her to know when justice has been delivered for one of her animals. I could tell her outright, but that feels flat and empty.

And tonight is different. Tonight, we're both wounded.

I peel off my blood-soaked clothes and reach for my phone. Cade answers on the first ring.

"He's ready for disposal."

"That was quick. I'm on my way."

I head upstairs, into my office, where I pour a glass of whiskey. My mind drifts back two weeks, when Luna first told me about the miscarriage. The devastation threading through her voice. The way she sought comfort from a man who's never offered her tenderness in that persona, only possession.

I down half the glass in one swallow. The burn does nothing to quiet my thoughts.

My parents were monsters of a different sort. Cold, vicious, and emotionally barren. I learned early that love was conditional, that affection had to be earned, and that failure meant pain and abandonment. My father's fists. My mother's silence. The locked doors and empty rooms. I grew up without love, taught that attachment was weakness and vulnerability was a fatal flaw.

And then Luna walked into my life and shattered every lesson they'd carved into my bones. She accepts her masked lover, a serial killer, and welcomes him into her body and heart without hesitation. No questions. No judgment. Just open arms and unwavering trust.

Sure, Cade has always accepted me. But that's different. He knows the man behind the mask and understands the trauma that shaped me. He's my brother in every way that matters. His acceptance is duty mixed with genuine care, forged through years of shared violence.

Luna doesn't have that luxury. She only knows fragments, the mask, the violence, and the darkness I bring to her bed each night. And still, she opens herself to me. She looks at me like I'm worth something.

I drain the rest of the whiskey and pour another.

The truth sits heavy in my gut. For the first time in my life, I'm terrified. Terrified that when she sees the man beneath the mask, she'll realize what my parents always knew.

That I'm fundamentally unlovable.

By the time I reach Luna's property, it's after midnight. The mountain air is crisp and cold, the snow crunching beneath my feet as I make my way to the house.

I slip through the back door and toe off my boots, leaving them by the mat. I remove them now after Luna scolded me for traipsing dirt and snow on her clean floors. I move through the darkened house, navigating the space with ease now. The third stair creaks, so I skip it before stepping around the loose floorboard in the hallway. Her bedroom door needs oil on the hinges, making a soft squeaking sound every time it opens or closes. She keeps meaning to fix it. I should do it myself.

Maren stopped staying over when the road to Estes opened yesterday. Enough snow melted to make the drive safe again.

Luna left the door open tonight, and I find her curled under the covers, her blonde hair spilling across the purple pillowcase. She looks so small, so vulnerable. Her eyes flutter open as I approach.

"You came." A sleepy smile touches her lips, her words thick and slow.

I cup her cheek in my palm. She leans into it, her eyes drifting shut once more.

"Go back to sleep, little doe."

Her eyes open again, traveling across my mask. "Stay with me tonight?"

The usual routine would have me moving to the reading chair in the corner that has become my post. I watch over her through the night, a dark guardian ensuring nothing harms her. Sometimes she knows I'm here. Most nights, she sleeps unaware.

"Please."

I nod and move toward the chair.

"No." The word stops me mid-step. "Here." She touches the space next to her on the bed. "With me."

Every instinct tells me to keep the emotional distance the mask represents. But tonight, seeing the naked need in her expression, refusal isn't an option.

I lower myself onto the bed beside her, my back against the headboard. She shifts without hesitation, pressing her cheek against my thigh, her hand searching for mine. I entwine our fingers. Her skin is soft against my rough palm. She sighs, the sound carrying contentment, her eyes drifting closed as sleep pulls her back under.

I stare at our joined hands. The sight punches through my chest, tears open the walls I hide behind, and exposes the raw, vulnerable core I've spent a lifetime protecting.

I need to tell her the truth—that the men she's torn between exist in one body. Mine.

But not tonight. The excuse forms before I can stop it. She's not ready. She's still vulnerable from the miscarriage. Needs more time to process and heal.

But it's all a lie. It's been over two weeks. Her body has healed. Her emotional state improves daily. She's the strongest woman I know and can handle the truth, even though it would devastate her. But I can't make myself do it. I can't force the confession out, because telling her means losing her.

And I can't lose her.

Without Luna, I'm just what I've always been. A killer playing at humanity. A damaged thing my parents broke and never bothered to fix. She's the first person who makes me believe I could be something more than the sum of my trauma and violence.

I squeeze her hand, the pressure gentle. Her lips curve into a smile in her sleep. "I love you."

The confession falls into the quiet room. Three words that have never crossed my lips. Never been offered to another soul. Never seemed possible until now.

She doesn't hear me. But somehow, I hope she knows.

Chapter Twenty-Three

Luna

The water streams over my shoulders, hot enough to turn my skin pink. I tilt my head back and let it cascade over my face, washing away the sweat from my nightmare. The same one I've had every night since the miscarriage. Blood and wolf masks and empty cribs that morph into open graves.

I reach for my razor, propping my foot on the shower seat. The blade glides over my shin, and my stomach flips with anticipation. My appointment is this afternoon, and I already know what Dr. Ritchie will say. All clear to resume normal activities.

Normal activities.

As if anything about sex with my wolf can be called normal.

The bathroom door opens.

"Maren, I'm in the shower. Do you mind?"

"When has that ever stopped me?"

The toilet seat clatters down, and she settles onto it. I peek through the shower door. She dressed in her usual scrubs, her chocolate brown hair falling over her shoulders in curly waves.

Shit! When she wears her hair down and wild, she's readying for battle. She clutches a mug of coffee in her hand like a lifeline, and her expression is serious. Too serious for seven in the morning.

"What's wrong?"

"That's my question." She lifts the mug to her lips, her gaze tracking me through the clear glass. "You're shaving your legs."

"Yes. I do that periodically."

"You haven't shaved your legs in almost three weeks."

"How do you know that?"

"Because I know you. You get as furry as Shadow when you're depressed."

I drag the razor over my thigh in long, careful strokes.

"That's an exaggeration. And I'm not depressed. Talking to the counselor Dr. Ritchie referred me to has really helped."

Her face softens through the glass. "And you went for a bikini wax yesterday when you were in Estes."

"How the hell do you know all this?"

She takes another sip of her coffee, still staring at me. If it wasn't Maren, it would be weird.

"Trina called when you were running late."

"Should I be worried that you're stalking me? I've had one in my life, Mar. I'm done with it."

The bite in my voice echoes off the tile, and I hate the defensive sound of it.

"Luna." Just my name. Nothing else. The razor scrapes over my knee. "You're going to fuck him again."

It's not a question but an accusation wrapped in resignation. I swap the razor to my other hand and lift my arm, baring my armpit. The silence stretches between us, thick with all the words neither of us wants to say.

The toilet creaks as she shifts her weight.

"He could hurt you again."

My hand stills. "He didn't hurt me. My body—"

"I'm not talking about the miscarriage." Her voice softens, losing its sharp edge. "I'm talking about your heart, Lu. This creeper won't even tell you who he is. How can you trust him with your body when he won't trust you with his face?"

The water beats against my back, and I close my eyes. She's right, and I have no defense except the truth.

"I love him."

"Fuck." The word comes out on a long breath, and her mug bangs against the counter. "I know. That's what scares me."

I turn off the water and grab my towel, drying myself with the soft cotton. Maren's elbows rest on her knees, her face buried in her hands. When she looks up, genuine worry etches lines around her eyes.

"I know what I'm doing, Mar."

"Do you?" She stands, crossing her arms. "You're about to climb back into bed with a guy who got you pregnant and still won't tell you his name."

I step out of the shower, clutching the towel tighter.

"That's not fair."

"What he's doing to you isn't fair."

I push past her into the bedroom. She follows, her footsteps soft on the hardwood, dropping into the chair in the corner and propping her feet on the ottoman. Juniper abandons her perch on the windowsill, leaping down with a graceful arc despite her chubby body. She lands on Maren's lap and circles once before settling, purring loud enough to hear across the room.

I sink onto the edge of the bed. Shadow lifts his massive head from his bed, and his eyes lock on mine. He rises and lopes over, and I wrap my arms around his neck. He always knows when I need him. His fur is warm and solid, and I press my face against him, breathing in his familiar scent. Earth and woods and loyalty that never wavers.

"I have no choice." The words come out muffled against his fur. "I love him, Mar. I can't just turn that off."

"You do have a choice. You always have a choice."

I pull back, looking at her over Shadow's head. She's scratching behind Juniper's ears, and the cat's eyes are half-closed in contentment.

"I'll be careful. More careful than before."

"How? By asking him pretty please to tell you his name before you spread your legs?"

"Jesus, Maren."

"No, fuck that." She stops petting Juniper, and the cat chirps in protest. "You want me to sugar-coat this? Fine. Luna, my darling best friend, please consider the emotional ramifications of resuming sexual relations with your anonymous stalker."

I almost laugh, though the situation is far from amusing.

"You're such an ass."

"And you're deflecting." But her lips twitch, fighting a smile, before she reins it in and frowns. "I'm serious, Lu. I'm worried about you. Not only about you getting knocked up again, though that's high on my list of concerns, based on how often you let the man defile you without a fucking condom. I'm worried about what happens when this all blows up. Because it will. It has to."

Deep down, in the part of myself I keep locked away, I know she's right and this can't last. Eventually, the truth will crack open like an egg, and everything inside will spill out, raw and messy and impossible to put back together.

But not tonight. Please, not tonight.

"If everything is all clear, Dr. Ritchie is going to insert an IUD today. It's more effective than the pill. And I'll make him use protection."

Maren snorts. "You're a terrible liar. You never could keep a straight face. I still have no idea how you kept this a secret for so long."

Shadow shifts, resting his chin on my thigh. His eyes drift closed, but his body remains alert, attuned to every shift in my breathing, every hitch in my voice.

"What do you want me to say? That I'll end it? Cut him off?" My fingers dig into Shadow's fur, but he doesn't flinch. "I can't, Mar. I've tried. God, I've tried. But every night when he comes to me, when he touches me, I'm whole again. Like all the broken pieces inside me finally fit together."

"That's not love, Lu. That's addiction."

I want to argue, to defend myself, but what if she's right? What if what I feel for him isn't love?

No.

If I know one thing with absolute certainty in this whole shitshow, it's that I love my wolf. My heart is his as completely as my body.

Maren's face softens. She dislodges Juniper, who protests with an indignant meow, and stands. She crosses to the bed and sits beside me, her shoulder pressing against mine.

"I get it. I do. That feeling of being someone's entire world, even for a few hours. It's what we all want. God knows I do." Her hand finds mine, our fingers lacing together. "But you deserve more than scraps in the dark, babe. You deserve someone who'll stand beside you in the light."

Damien. She means Damien, even if she doesn't say it.

She squeezes my hand and stands.

"I'm going to make breakfast. You better have bread this time because I want French toast."

"Middle shelf in the pantry."

She heads for the door, then pauses, her hand on the frame. When she looks back, her eyes are bright with concern.

"Be careful tonight, Lu. Please. And for fuck's sake, make him wrap it up before you let him inside you again. I can't watch you go through another loss."

My throat tightens, and I nod because words feel impossible.

She lingers another moment, and her struggle plays out on her face. The urge to say more, to push harder, to physically stop me from making this choice. But she's Maren, and she knows when to hold on and when to let go.

"I love you, Mar."

"Love you, too, you reckless bitch." She disappears down the hallway, her footsteps echoing on the stairs. "Come on, pussies."

Juniper follows after her as Sage and Willow scamper off the duvet. Even Shadow abandons me for breakfast.

I sit on the bed, still wrapped in my towel. Through the window, I can see the snow-covered pines. Somewhere out there, he's watching. Waiting.

Tonight, he'll come to me, and I'll find out if we can get back what we had or if this loss broke us.

I love Maren for her worry, but I'm a grown woman. I can make my own choices, my own mistakes. I can walk into the fire with my eyes open and deal with the burns later.

Even if part of me wonders if I'll survive them.

I stand, dropping the towel, and move to my dresser. My reflection stares back at me from the mirror, a body that looks the same but feels forever changed.

———◆———

It's been eighteen days since I told him about the miscarriage. Eighteen nights of him visiting just to watch me sleep. The first night, he sat beside me on the bed. Then he moved across the room to the chair. The last few nights, he's been back beside me, our fingers threaded together.

I've spent the day in a state of nervous anticipation, checking the clock every few minutes as I went through the motions at the sanctuary, my heart tripping over its own beats.

Now I'm pacing between the sink and the stove, fresh from another shower, wearing nothing but a silk nightie that skims my thighs. The overhead lights are off, and the kitchen glows soft from the moon spilling silver through the window over the sink.

Tonight feels different, like a beginning. Or maybe a test.

The familiar beep of the alarm disarming freezes me in place. The enclosed porch door whispers open as I grip the kitchen counter. His footsteps echo on the tile before the soft thud of boots hitting the floor. He never tries to hide his approach when I'm awake. He wants me to know he's coming. Wants my anticipation to build with each step.

The window catches his silhouette in its glass, the wolf mask molded to his face like it belongs there. It's as familiar to me now as my own face, its sleek lines revealing nothing but the glint of his eyes behind it. And his mouth below it. He's dressed all in black, as always, his broad shoulders filling the doorway.

"Luna."

His growl ripples across my skin.

"You're late." I don't turn around, aiming for casual, but the tremor in my voice is unmistakable. "I was starting to think you weren't coming."

He steps closer, so close the heat of his chest burns through the fabric of my nightgown.

"I always come, little doe. Look at me."

I turn to face him. My body comes alive under his intense stare, nipples straining against the thin silk. My heart hammers in my throat.

"Dr. Ritchie cleared me." The words tumble out too quickly. "I'm healed. Everything's back to normal."

He remains silent and motionless, his predatory gaze fixed on me.

"Did you hear me?" I ask, frustration creeping into my voice as I step toward him. "I said we can... you can..." Why am I shy? This man has seen me, touched me, and taken me in ways that negate any shyness. "You can fuck me again."

"I heard you."

His voice is low and controlled. Too controlled.

Why is he standing there like carved stone?

"Don't you want me anymore?"

A growl rises from his chest, and my stomach flutters with relief. There's my wolf. There's the man I've been missing.

"Of course, I fucking want you. I've thought of nothing else."

"Then do it. Take what's yours."

He moves one step, closing the final distance between us. His thumbs slide under the slip at my waist, tugging it up, inch by inch, until the bare curve of my ass is exposed. His touch is light, too gentle. This isn't how he usually grabs me, with bruising force and desperate need.

"I won't break." I grip his hands, pressing them harder against my skin. He doesn't shake them off. Thank God. "I'm not fragile."

He tilts his head. "I know."

But there's still a hesitation in his grip.

"No." Frustration bubbles up inside me. This isn't what I want. This isn't what I need. "What happened to the man who can't wait to claim me?" I step back from his touch. "The one who rips my clothes off the second he gets here. The one who fucks me like he'll die if he doesn't?"

"He's still here." His voice is tight. "But things have changed, Luna."

My head whips from side to side. "No, they haven't. I'm still me. You're still you. And I still want you exactly as you are."

"Brutal? Selfish? Taking without thought?"

"Yes." I step closer to him again. "That's who you are with me. That's who I want you to be."

His hands clench at his sides. "And if I hurt you?"

"You won't." I reach for his jacket, hooking my fingers into the zipper and tugging it down, something I know better than to do. "Not in any way I don't want."

He grabs my wrists, stopping me. For a moment, I think he's going to push me away. Instead, he spins me around, pinning my arms behind my back.

"Is this what you want?" His breath is hot against my ear, and his grip anchors me in place, holding me captive in this exposed position, a vulnerability so delicious it leaves me dizzy. "To be handled roughly? To be used?"

"Yes." Desire floods through me. "God, yes."

Fabric rustles behind me, then cold plastic brushes my skin.

The zip ties that I now love.

He tightens them around my wrists, binding my hands together at the small of my back. The position forces my chest forward, my breasts straining against the silk.

"Like this?" His voice is darker now, more like the man I know.

My heart pounds. "Yes. Just like this."

His hand slides up my back, fisting in my hair, and pulling my head back. "And if I decide to bend you over that table and fuck you right now—ready or not—what then?"

"Do it."

I push back against him, his hard cock pressing into the small of my back.

There's a moment of stillness, then he pushes me forward until my hips meet the edge of the table. He spins me around and lifts me onto it, pushing me onto my back.

I gasp, my bound arms trapped beneath me, forcing my chest to arch upward as I try to adjust my position. The hard, unyielding table offers little comfort, and that's part of the thrill.

"Spread your legs." His voice drops to that dark, commanding pitch that raises goosebumps on my skin. He slides out of his jacket, the leather hitting the tile with a soft thud. "I need to taste you first."

My thighs fall open for him. No hesitation. The cool draft of night air grazes my center.

He kneels beside the table, pulling me toward him until my ass is at the edge. He pushes the silk up, exposing my bare sex to his gaze.

"Eighteen days." His hands grip my inner thighs, spreading them wider. "Eighteen fucking days without this."

Then his mask presses against my mound—cold metal shocking against warm flesh—and he buries his tongue inside me. The first flick sends a lightning bolt up my spine. I gasp, arching my back until everything but my shoulders lift off the wood.

"God. I've missed your mouth."

His hands clamp onto my hips, holding me still as his mouth and tongue move in perfect rhythm, long glides over my entrance, and sharp flicks around my clit until my legs tremble and my vision blurs. His mouth works me with the expertise of a man who knows exactly what drives me wild.

"So sweet." The vibration of his words sends fresh waves of pleasure through me. "I'll never live another day without you."

"Please." I don't know what I'm begging for. Except that I need more.

He lifts his head to look at me, his eyes gleaming behind the mask.

"Come for me, Luna."

His mouth returns to me with renewed intensity, his tongue relentless as one finger slides inside me, curving to find that devastating spot. Everything contracts to the sensation of his mouth, his finger, and the building pressure at my core that threatens to shatter me.

The orgasm rips through me, tearing a cry from my throat as my back arches off the table again. Pleasure detonates in waves, each one crashing harder than the last. My thighs clamp around his head. He growls, the vibration sending ripples of sensation through my core, as his tongue keeps working—licking, sucking, devouring—until my voice breaks on a plea.

"Please. Please, I can't—"

He pulls back then, his breathing harsh in the darkness. The back of his hand drags across his mouth in one rough swipe before his fingers adjust the mask's edge. His lips shine wet, and the sight of my release coating his mouth makes heat coil tight in my belly again, impossible and insistent.

My ribs expand and contract, lungs dragging in air that doesn't seem like enough. He reaches for the silk covering me and tears it open, the fabric giving way with a loud rip. Before I can process the sound, his hands clamp onto my hips. He spins me onto my stomach, pressing on my back until my upper body is flat against the wood, the surface cold against my overheated skin, making me gasp.

"Yes." The words fall from my lips like a prayer.

The metallic rasp of his zipper cuts through the silence. Then his palms slide down the backs of my thighs, rough and hot, and his fingers hook around my knees. He wrenches my legs apart, the motion pulling a gasp from my throat.

"Tell me you want this."

"I want this. I want you. Please."

A single finger drags through my folds, parting slick flesh. My hips lift, chasing the contact.

"Always so wet for me." Satisfaction purrs in his voice.

"Always," I push back, trying to increase the pressure, the friction, anything to ease the ache inside me. "Please, don't make me wait anymore."

The blunt head of his cock replaces his finger, pressing against my entrance—right there, so close—but he holds himself still. The pressure builds but doesn't breach, and my fingers curl into fists at the base of my spine.

"If it hurts, if it's too much, you tell me."

"Yes."

The lie falls from my lips without hesitation, and we both know that's what it is. I won't stop him. Not when he's splitting me open. Not when the burn threatens to tear me apart. That razor's edge between agony and ecstasy—that's where he makes me feel alive.

He drives in with one long stroke that empties my lungs. The cry rips from my throat as he fills every inch of me, the fullness almost too much, but God, the way my body yields to him feels like waking up from a nightmare I didn't know I was trapped in. My body has been waiting for exactly this.

A groan tears out of him, reverberating through his chest into my back.

"Fuck! So tight. So perfect."

He doesn't move, staying buried deep, giving me a moment to adjust. My inner walls flutter around him, trying to accommodate his size. Heat pools where we're joined, radiating outward.

"Move." The plea scrapes out of me. "Please move."

His answering thrust punches the air from my lungs all over again. Then his hips pull back, dragging almost all the way out before sliding forward again. Each thrust is deliberate, slow, and measured, like he's relearning my body.

Tears prick at the corners of my eyes—not from pain, but from the intensity of being completely filled, completely possessed. My inner muscles clench around him.

He hisses through his teeth. "Don't do that unless you want this to end before it starts."

I can't help it. My body has a mind of its own, tightening around him again.

His hand comes down on my ass.

"Behave."

The sharp, stinging slap sends a fresh wave of arousal through me. I whimper into the wood beneath my face.

His pace shifts, and the leash on his control snaps. Gentleness gives way to brutal force. His hips slam into me, the force jolting me forward on the table, wood scraping against my nipples, the friction painful and exquisite. My body rocks with each impact, need and relief colliding in every thrust. Each ragged breath I manage to pull in burns through my lungs, and with it comes the same undeniable truth.

I love this man and everything he does to me.

"Harder." I need him to stop treating me like I might shatter. I need him savage. "Please, harder."

A growl rips from his throat, and then he's gone. And I'm empty. I open my mouth to protest, but he's already spinning me again, flipping me onto my back. My bound arms twist beneath me, my wrists grinding into the hard surface, but the discomfort barely registers. I need him back. Need him to fill the hollow ache he left behind.

His hands hook under my knees, and he hauls me to the table's edge. In one motion, he shoves my thighs up and wide, folding me open. Cool air caresses my overheated flesh, and his gaze drops between my legs, hungry and possessive.

"Look at you." The words come out thick, reverence bleeding into possession. "So beautiful. So mine."

"Yes, yours." The word barely makes it out before he slams back inside, stealing my breath. "Only yours."

The angle changes everything. He hits deeper, striking places that make stars explode across my vision. His fingers dig crescents into my inner thighs, keeping me spread wide and vulnerable as he pistons into me. Each thrust comes harder, faster, and more savage than the one before. The wet slap of flesh meeting flesh ricochets off the kitchen walls, obscene and perfect.

His jaw locks, muscles jumping as his hips drive faster.

"It's not enough." My spine curves, lifting me toward him. "I'm not going to break. You don't have to treat me like glass."

Anger collides with challenge in his eyes, both swallowed by naked desire. He drops forward, his mouth finding my breast. His teeth scrape across my nipple, a teasing promise, then clamp down. The bite sends lightning through my nerves, pain that transforms mid-scream into something that makes my toes curl.

His hips never falter. He keeps pounding into me while his teeth and tongue work my nipple, and the combination fractures my thoughts. Pleasure and pain from both points of contact converge somewhere in my core, building into something that feels too big for my body to contain.

He releases my nipple and pushes himself upright. His hands abandon my thighs and lock onto my hips instead, fingers digging in as he tilts my pelvis up. The angle shifts, and he's stroking a place inside me that makes my eyes cross. Each thrust drags across that spot, over and over, and pressure coils tight in my lower belly. My muscles clench, pulling tighter and tighter as the orgasm gathers force.

"Are you close?" The strain in his voice makes the words come out rough and broken.

"Yes." I yank against the zip ties, wrists burning, desperate to touch him even as the restraint sends heat spiraling through me. "So close. Please don't stop."

"Look at me." I force my eyes up to meet his gaze through the wolf mask, the dark eyes behind it burning into mine. "I want to see your face when you come for me."

"Come inside me." The plea tears from my throat.

Some distant part of my brain, the part that sounds like Maren, screams, "What the fuck!"

This is reckless. We need protection. I finished my antibiotics, and my body's still healing. But rationality burned to ash the moment he touched me. I need to feel him come, need him to fill me and mark me and make me his all over again. The Plan B in my cabinet can handle tomorrow's worries.

His thumb finds my clit, circling, teasing, with the exact pressure to make my vision blur. His eyes never leave my face, and the intensity of that stare drags me closer to the precipice, my skin flushing hot then cold.

"Come for me now, Luna."

My body doesn't hesitate. The orgasm rips through me in brutal, violent waves as the scream tears from my chest. He keeps thrusting, prolonging each pulse of pleasure until my muscles turn liquid and my lungs can't pull in enough air.

He's still buried deep inside me, hard, and holding himself back from the edge. I squeeze my inner muscles around him, tight and intentional, and the growl that rumbles out of him rattles through my bones.

He pulls out, and his hands are on me, spinning me back onto my stomach like I weigh nothing, slapping my ass again. The table's surface hits my cheek, cold and unforgiving. His palm plants itself between my shoulder blades, pinning me flat while his other hand grips my hip, angling me how he wants me.

"Again." He slams back in, the pace turning wild and desperate. "I need to feel you come around me again."

"I can't." The words barely make it out, my voice shaking.

"You can." His hand leaves my hip and slides underneath, finding my oversensitive clit. "And you will."

His fingers start circling, each touch almost too much on nerves still firing. His other hand tangles in my hair, fisting the strands and pulling until my head lifts back, stretching my throat taut. Then his grip releases, and his fingers wrap around my throat. Pressure builds against my windpipe, stealing my oxygen bit by bit.

This is what I've been starving for. The knife-edge between safety and danger. The act of giving myself, my complete surrender, over to him until there's nothing left to hold back.

My pulse pounds against his fingertips as the familiar lightheadedness blooms. The oxygen deprivation heightens everything. His cock driving into me, his fingers circling my clit, the weight of his body dominant above mine.

"Remember this?" His breath scorches the side of my neck, and goosebumps erupt down my spine. "Remember how it feels when I control even your breath?"

Words won't form. My throat works uselessly under his grip. I manage the barest hint of a nod, jerky and desperate, as he pushes me further into that space where pleasure and panic become indistinguishable.

And in this moment, with my oxygen thinning, my body thrumming, and his hand around my throat, I know with absolute certainty that we've clawed our way back. This is who we are. This dangerous dance on the edge of too much. This perfect trust that he'll never hurt me.

Every muscle goes soft beneath him, even as tension coils tighter in my core, building toward another climax. His thrusts lose their rhythm, becoming wild and disjointed. His fingers move faster against my clit. Dark spots start appearing at the corners of my vision, multiplying and spreading. His hand opens, and he releases my throat. Air floods my lungs in a ragged, desperate gasp that sounds like drowning in reverse.

The sudden influx of oxygen, combined with the building pleasure, hurls me over the edge. My body convulses, my muscles seizing and releasing in waves I can't control. He buries himself to the hilt, the force driving him so deep a sharp ache blooms in my lower abdomen—pain and pleasure twisted together until they're inseparable. Heat floods my core as he empties himself inside me, and my name tears from his lips in a sound that's broken and worshipful.

He stays there, suspended above me. His body radiates heat like a furnace, wrapping me in his presence. The moment stretches and holds, both of us dragging in ragged breaths, our hearts pounding out of sync, suspended in the devastation left behind.

"You're mine." His voice comes out destroyed, the words pressed against my ear. "Your body is mine. Your pleasure is mine. Your very life is mine."

"Yes." Tears burn behind my eyes and spill over, tracking hot paths down my cheeks at the fierce possession in his voice. "Yours. All of me. Always."

"I will never live without you, Luna."

He straightens, rising to his full height. His fingers release my wrists from the restraints. Circulation slams back into my hands, a thousand tiny needles stabbing through numb flesh. I curl and uncurl my fingers, working feeling back into them, while he slides his hands under my shoulders and helps me roll onto my back.

His grip shifts to my waist, steadying me as I push myself upright. Then his palm lifts to my face, cupping my cheek with a gentleness that stands in stark contrast to what just happened. The tenderness splits me open, and fresh tears well up and spill over.

"Are you alright?"

Even through the mask, even with his face hidden, concern bleeds through every word.

"I'm perfect." I lean into his touch, the warmth of his palm centering me in my body again. My pulse begins to slow. "That was... We're going to be okay, aren't we?"

He doesn't respond right away. His thumb traces the curve of my cheekbone.

"Yes. We're going to be okay."

Relief crashes through me with enough force to make the room tilt.

My wolf has returned.

There's a new layer of tenderness beneath the savagery now, a protective care even in his roughest touches. But he's still mine.

Peace washes over me, a peace I haven't known since the miscarriage. We're different now, both of us changed by what we've lost, but the core of what connects us remains.

His hands drift across my body, reverent and slow, like he's memorizing terrain he was afraid he'd never touch again. I stare at his masked face, willing him to tear it away and show me the truth. Let me see the man underneath. But this, having him back, finding our way through the wreckage to each other. It's enough for now.

"Mine." The growl carries equal parts possession and oath.

"Yours." My eyes lock onto his and don't waver.

It's the truth. When I told Damien about my wolf, it hurt to know I had to let him go. But the decision was right. It had to be made.

For months, I've indulged in impossible fantasies that I could somehow have both men. That my paranoid suspicions about them being the same person would prove true. That reality would bend and let me keep everything I wanted.

Part of me still craves that fictional merger. The man who claims me in the dark, combined with the one who could offer me something resembling a future. Two incomplete halves forming one whole person.

But if I have to choose, there's only one choice to make. The man who makes me feel more alive is the only choice there is.

Chapter Twenty-Four

Luna

He presses his forehead to my back as I raise mine from the table, both of us gasping. Our reflection stares back from the window. I drink in the image. I love watching us this way. My skin flushed and damp, my hair plastered against my neck in sweaty tangles, shoulders trembling with residual tremors. I look absolutely wrecked, as wrecked as I feel. And the sight thrills me.

He pulls out, and his large hands trace the curve of my spine, his fingers gentle before he helps me stand, lifting me onto the table and sliding me back.

It's been a week since the doctor cleared me, and my wolf has spent every night inside me. We're back to how we were before. It seems I measure everything in my life these days in terms of before I lost our baby and after. I still feel the loss acutely, but his touch drowns everything out.

"It's so unsanitary what we do on this table." His lip curls up on one side as I twist my aching shoulders. "Can you untie my wrists? I'm getting stiff."

He reaches behind me and snaps the zip ties. I rub at the pink lines carved into my skin, but he's already tugging me closer to the table's edge. My arms shoot back, and I brace myself on my hands so I don't tumble backward.

"What the—" The words dissolve on my tongue as his thick finger glides along my slit, scooping up our combined orgasms and pushing them back inside, and a whimper escapes my lips. "What are you doing?"

"You don't seem to want to leak on the table. I'm helping you out."

"It would help me out better if you wiped it down with Lysol before you left." My eyes drift to his cock. It's softened but is still partially rigid. "How can you still be hard?"

He smirks, and his fingers flutter over my clit now. "Your pussy must be magical."

I shudder, fighting the distraction. "I'm serious. How is it physically possible for you to stay hard as long as you do? Do you take Viagra?"

His nostrils flare under the mask like a bull's. "I do not take fucking Viagra."

I laugh at the offended growl that rumbles through him. "Well, it has to be something artificial because no man can stay hard for that long without it becoming medically dangerous."

He leans in, his voice teasing as his fingers restart their gentle assault on my clit. "Aww, are you worried about my cock, little doe?"

"I'm worried about my cock." I curl my fingers around his shaft. He grunts and bucks his hips, pushing his erection deeper into my grip. "See how good it is when you let me keep my hands untied." I grin with a satisfied smile.

"Don't push it, Luna. And it's only a brief reprieve. I'm tying you to the headboard when we get upstairs."

He grunts out the last few words because one of my hands has found his balls, cupping and rolling them in my palm.

"Mmhmm." I brush the thumb of my other hand over his leaking tip. Then his words register, and my hand stills. "Wait. What did you say?"

"Huh?" He blinks as if I'm speaking a foreign language.

"Did you say we're going upstairs to have more sex?"

"Yes."

His dark eyes gleam as he tucks my hair behind my ear, a gentle touch that makes me shiver.

"No. I'm done for tonight. I have no more orgasms in me."

"Is that a challenge?"

He sweeps my hands away with ease and pushes his cock inside me in one smooth stroke. He's not fully erect again, but he's thick enough to stretch me, to fill me in a way that forces a gasp from my throat. With his length and girth, even half-hard, this man could wreck me.

My body clenches around him involuntarily. Traitor.

"See?" His hips roll, grinding deeper. "Your body disagrees."

I wrap my legs around him. "This doesn't prove anything."

"Doesn't it?" He withdraws halfway, then drives back in. His cock hardens with each thrust, growing inside me.

I bite my lip, trying to stifle the moan building in my chest. It escapes anyway. My eyes trace over his face, wishing I could see under the mask. Wishing he would show me all of himself.

His shirt is still buttoned. It always is. He's never removed it. Not once. The cotton might as well be armor for how it protects his secrets as fiercely as his mask.

I'm always fully naked, but he recently started removing his pants. The tattoos that peek out at his collar and beneath the hem of his shirt are hints of stories I can't read. When I take him in my mouth, he lifts the fabric just enough to watch, but never enough for me to see what's underneath.

His finger traces my clit, each circle timed to match his deep strokes. Slow waves of pleasure roll through me, building and cresting like the tide against the shore.

"Lay back, beautiful."

I sink against the table without hesitation, my arms settling at my sides. He fucks me like this a lot now, my hands free but forbidden to wander. The table's surface is hard against my spine as he moves inside me, each thrust sending tremors through my frame. His fingers trace patterns on my skin while his eyes devour my reactions. I drink in the sight of him above me, his jaw tight with control, lips parted, and eyes burning behind the mask.

"Wolf."

His hands freeze against my skin, and his entire body goes rigid.

Shit. Did I say that out loud?

I keep that name locked in my head, a secret between me and my heart. My wolf. Mine in ways that transcend names and faces. And as much as I want to see beneath the mask, I've grown to love it.

"What did you call me?"

His voice sounds different. Rougher, yes, but there's a tremor underneath. Layers of emotion I've never heard before. Surprise? Vulnerability? I can't tell with that damned mask hiding his face.

My heart slams against my ribs. The word sits there now, between us, impossible to take back.

"I called you wolf. That's what you told me to call you that first night."

"I thought you don't like the animal I am." His voice carries a new edge, raw and almost wounded.

"I never said that."

"You don't like it when I rut you like one."

The crude words send heat spiraling low in my abdomen. Because God help me, I more than like it. I love it. I love the way he takes me—wild and desperate and completely consuming. But that's not all I want.

"I never said that either. I—" My voice falters beneath his intensity. "I don't want you to always rut me from behind. I want to see you. Touch you. Feel you on top of me again."

He remains still. Frozen. Not even the rise and fall of breathing. Then he moves, lowering himself until the mask hovers inches from my face, and solid warmth presses against me from chest to hips.

For the first time.

Every point where our bodies meet ignites. His chest crushes my breasts, his stomach is flush against mine, warm and solid, and his weight settles over me like he's claiming all the space he's always kept between us.

My nerve endings fire in rapid succession, electricity arcing across every inch of contact. The dam I've built around my heart cracks. This is what I've been begging for through countless nights. What I've pleaded for in whispered desperation when he maintained that barrier, that distance.

Emotion slams into me with the force of a riptide, dragging me under. My throat seizes around a sob that won't stay down. Vision swimming, eyes burning,

I struggle to comprehend the enormity of what he's giving me. This intimacy he's guarded as fiercely as his identity. This closeness he's denied us both.

My thighs grip his hips, ankles locking at the small of his back, pulling him deeper. Tears break free and slide down my temples, disappearing into my hair. Not from hurt. From the devastating perfection of finally having what my soul has been screaming for.

"Don't try to remove my mask." His breath is hot against my lips—so close, so fucking close—each word edged with warning. "Don't betray my trust, Luna."

My lungs stutter, catching on the inhale. "Never."

Whatever demons hide behind that mask, whatever scars or secrets he's protecting, I won't violate that boundary. Not when he's offering me everything else.

My hand moves without conscious thought, sliding between our pressed bodies until my palm finds his chest. Heat bleeds through his cotton shirt, and underneath my fingertips, his heart hammers out a violent rhythm. The hunger to see his whole face consumes me, burning under my skin like a fever I can't break. An ache that's settled into my bones. But this—his weight, his heat, his trust—this is more than I dared hope for.

Through the mask's eye slits, his stare finds mine and holds. The hardness there softens, cracks, and a fragile uncertainty flickers in the dark depths, maybe fear of what I'll do with the vulnerability he's handing me like a loaded weapon. Then his voice roughens, dropping into a low rumble that vibrates through both our bodies.

"Fucking touch me."

The permission unleashes something wild in me. The sound that rips from my throat tangles triumph with relief and hunger so sharp it cuts. My fingers claw into his shirt, grabbing fistfuls of fabric. He hauls me upright as he stands, his arms banding around me like steel.

This embrace rewrites everything I thought I knew about touch. My body molds against his from chest to hip, and all of a sudden, I understand why I've felt hollow all this time. The emotions threaten to tear me apart from the inside—too much joy, too much rightness, too much everything at once.

The tears won't stop, tracking hot paths down my face. My breath stutters as every hard ridge and plane of his body presses against the soft curves of mine.

He's still thick and hard inside me, but he's gone motionless, holding me, watching and waiting for whatever comes next. I drag my tongue across my bottom lip and pull back, my pulse hammering as my shaking hands reach for his buttons. The first one resists my fumbling fingers before surrendering with a soft pop.

His touch whispers across my temples, fingers catching the moisture that reveals too much of my heart.

"Don't cry, little doe."

But I can't stop.

I attack the next button, and then the next. One by one, I work my way down, and the fabric parts under my touch, revealing more of his skin to my hungry gaze. The tattoos flow across his chest and stomach, intricate designs that beg my eyes to trace their patterns. A smattering of dark hair dusts his skin, and my lips curve of their own accord.

"Why are you smiling?"

"I just expected my wolf to have more fur."

I twirl my fingers through the sparse hair. He grunts, though I catch his lips twitching beneath the mask. Then he drives into me, one punishing thrust, deep enough to steal my breath, hard enough to make my toes curl.

When his shirt finally falls open, revealing his naked chest, I can't contain the sound that spills from my lips. He's more breathtaking than I imagined, all hard muscle and warm flesh. Darkness swallows most of him, but the moonlight coming through the window paints silver across his skin. Just enough.

"Jesus."

The word whispers out as I slide the fabric from his shoulders. His hands abandon me long enough to allow the shirt to fall and join the growing pile of clothes at our feet. Now he stands bare before me. Every inch of him exposed. Every line, every shadow, and every detail.

Finally.

The sight steals more than my breath—it leaves me speechless. My chest constricts so tight I forget how to breathe. My vision blurs again, emotions crashing over me in waves as the magnitude hits me. He hasn't just let me remove his clothes. He's lowering walls and barriers he's had in place since we began.

Beautiful doesn't begin to describe him. But it's the tattoos that stop my heart. They cover his chest, his shoulders, and his arms—a masterpiece of ink that tells a story I'm not sure I'm ready to understand. At the center of it all is a wolf, magnificent and terrible, standing defiant against a backdrop of flames and hellish landscape.

The wolf's fur is shades of gray, with burning embers seeming to dance along its coat where the hellfire touches. But it's the eyes that capture me. Ice-blue, unnaturally bright, piercing straight through to my soul. They're pupilless and otherworldly, creating a shocking contrast against the reds and oranges of the inferno surrounding it.

"My God."

I trace the outline of the wolf with trembling fingers. The ground beneath the wolf's paws is cracked obsidian rock, with molten lava visible through the fissures. The cracks extend outward across his chest like a shattered landscape, and I follow them with my eyes, taking in every devastating detail.

Behind and around the wolf, jagged rock formations twist upward in unnatural spirals, wrapping around his shoulders and down his arms. I look closer. The formations resemble human figures—warped, twisted, and frozen in moments of agony. It's disturbing and dark, emphasizing suffering and torment. But there's something beautiful about it too, in a painfully heartbreaking way. The wolf stands unbroken amidst the chaos, fierce and defiant. Whatever hell this represents, the wolf refuses to be conquered by it.

What could have happened to him?

The question burns in my throat, but I don't ask. Some stories are too painful to tell, too private to share. The fact that he's letting me see this much is gift enough.

My hands shake as they begin their exploration, trembling not from desire but from gratitude so profound it threatens to shatter me. I trace the landscape of his body with my fingers, learning every ridge and valley, every scar and imperfection that makes him real. My touch drifts along his collarbone, then slips down to the dip at the center of his chest.

Every touch feels sacred. The hard line of his sternum, the subtle rise and fall of his muscles, and the way his flesh responds to my exploration with minute tremors that mirror my own. My fingers continue trailing over the intricate details of the hellscape. He watches me through the mask, his gaze heavy and intense. When I lift my eyes to meet his, the tenderness waiting there shocks me. He looks stripped down, laid open in a way that goes deeper than skin. My chest tightens, and I forget how to breathe.

Instead of questions, I give him what I can. Acceptance, reverence, and desire. I press closer, wrapping my arms around his waist, pulling our bodies flush until no space remains between us. The wolf tattoo presses against my cheek as I bury my face in the warmth of his chest, breathing in his scent like it might sustain me.

The sound of his groan travels from his body to mine. His fingers dig into the flesh of my hips as he begins to move again. Each stroke builds on the last until I'm drowning in sensation that obliterates thought and leaves only pure need. I cling to him through each rolling wave of pleasure, our bodies finding their ancient rhythm until everything else fades to nothing.

I press my mouth to his throat, tasting the salt on his collarbone. My tongue darts out to capture the flavor before my lips continue their journey. They glide across the expanse of his chest, lingering over his thundering heart, and it seems to leap toward my touch. Each caress speaks all those silent, unspoken vows, promises I'm not brave enough to voice but desperate enough to write across his skin with my lips.

But then his hand fists in my hair, jerking my head back with enough force to make my eyes water. My pulse spikes at the sudden shift from tenderness to dominance.

"Please." I meet his eyes through the mask. Fire burns in his gaze, but beneath the anger is fear masquerading as rage, and my chest constricts. "You don't have to kiss me. I know you don't want to kiss me. But please... let me kiss you."

Each word is a fragile, exposed nerve, naked with need. I'm laying myself bare, admitting how much I want this connection, this intimacy that goes beyond the physical.

"Fuck, Luna."

His voice fractures around my name, raw and broken, and then his mouth crashes onto mine with bruising force. The impact steals the shocked sound that tries to escape my throat.

The bottom edge of his mask bites into my upper lip, sharp enough to draw blood, but the pain dissolves beneath the fierce hunger of his mouth. I part my lips, welcoming the sweep of his tongue and the brutal possession of his kiss. Our teeth scrape and clash, and our tongues battle for dominance, creating beautiful chaos between our mouths. It's messy and desperate and perfect.

I surrender to it, to him, letting him take what he needs while giving everything I have to offer. His taste floods my senses, achingly familiar. The pressure of his lips eases, and the kiss softens. My heart slams once against my ribs, forgetting its rhythm entirely.

And then it hits me like lightning, illuminating every shadow I've been hiding from. The nagging whispers I've silenced, the impossible theories I've called madness, and every instinct I've passed off as paranoia. It all crystallizes into devastating clarity.

I've kissed this mouth before.

My blood turns to ice even as my flesh burns, two impossible sensations warring in the same body. My hands slam against his chest, shoving him backward. He stumbles, catching himself as I drink in every detail of his masked face. His lips, swollen from our kiss, and his eyes holding truths that make my stomach drop.

"Damien?"

His name bleeds out of me, carrying the weight of every suspicion I've buried. It settles between us, changing everything with its simple existence. His eyes flash with panic before they turn black with rage, drowning any softness that existed moments before, replaced by something cold and dangerous.

"Did you just fucking call me his name?"

Betrayal laces every word, but I know the truth. The kiss still burning on my lips matches another in perfect, heart-stopping detail. The same combination of possession and worship that's haunted my dreams. The taste, the rhythm, the way his mouth claimed mine with reverence wrapped in hunger lit up every nerve with certainty.

It can't be. It can't be him.

But as I stare into those furious eyes, searching for evidence that I've lost my mind, the impossible becomes inevitable. Every strange moment and every whisper of recognition I dismissed clicks into place like puzzle pieces finding their home.

Lightning crackles in his heated gaze as he withdraws from my body, leaving an emptiness that echoes through my core. Without a word, he spins away and strides out my back door.

Buck naked.

"Wait!"

But the night has already swallowed him whole. Cold seeps into my bones as I sit bare on the unforgiving wood of my kitchen table, my mind fracturing under the reality of my revelation.

I'm not crazy.

Damien.

He's my watcher.

My stalker.

My wolf.

Chapter Twenty-Five

Luna

I'm curled up on the sofa in the enclosed porch, Shadow's head resting across my lap. His warmth seeps through my pajama pants, anchoring me while my thoughts threaten to drown me. Juniper, Willow, and Sage have arranged themselves around me in a protective circle. Juni is pressed against my hip, Willow is draped across the sofa behind my head, and Sage is kneading biscuits on the blanket covering my legs. They can sense the fragility of my emotional state, the way animals always can.

The frigid morning air outside seeps through the outdated, single-pane glass panels, which need replacing, but the cold inside me overshadows it. Everything hurts. Every tender spot on my skin and heart whispers something I don't want to hear. My body remembers what happened, my heart knows what it means, but I'm not prepared for either truth.

The tea in my mug turned cold hours ago. I haven't moved much since dawn broke, since the moment I sent that rambling text to Maren at five-thirty in the morning.

Me

> Need you. Come when you can. Everything's fucked.

My fingers stroke through Shadow's thick fur as my mind replays the moment over and over like a broken record stuck on the most devastating song ever written.

That kiss. That fucking kiss that unraveled everything I thought I knew about my life, about myself, about the man who's been claiming my body and soul for months.

Damien.

How could I have ignored my instincts and been so blind? I'm so goddamn stupid. A mask and a disguised voice were all it took to fool me.

Or did they?

From the start, I've had these nagging suspicions. But it was so ludicrous that my billionaire neighbor was the same man who stalked, watched, and fucked me. I should have listened to that niggling voice in the back of my head, the one that said it was too coincidental. The timing, their physicality, and that goddamn wolf mask.

Why did I insist on thinking I was just imagining it? Why didn't I recognize his fingers and tongue when Damien...

Shit! I have to be the stupidest woman on the planet.

But that kiss tore through every lie I'd been telling myself. He kissed me the way Damien did, his lips moving with that same reverence and unbearable tenderness. And I knew. Everything I'd been ignoring or burying or refusing to believe slammed into place at once. Each piece of evidence I'd overlooked or ignored burned through me, impossible to deny, and I nearly fell off my kitchen table.

Shadow lifts his head, ears perked forward, but settles back down when he recognizes the familiar rhythm of Maren's footsteps as she opens the front door without knocking. Her boots squeak on the hardwood floor as she strides through the house. I can feel her energy radiating through the air, that fierce protectiveness that makes her such an incredible friend and such a formidable enemy to anyone who crosses the people she loves.

I look up when the kitchen door opens, and she steps out before dropping into the chair across from me. She looks fresh and alert in her scrubs, her dark hair pulled back in a messy bun that somehow still manages to look effortlessly beautiful.

Her eyes widen when she sees me. "Jesus Christ, Lu, you look like absolute shit."

She kicks off her boots and props her feet on the coffee table. I shift and try to look less like the emotional wreck I am.

"Hello to you too, sunshine."

"Don't you 'hello sunshine' me." Her voice takes on that dangerous edge when she hasn't gotten enough sleep or when she and JT are fighting. "What's going on?" She gestures at my general state of dishevelment with a sweeping motion. Her expression hardens, that protective fury I know so well flashing in her eyes. "What the fuck did he do? Do I need to kill him?" I swallow hard, and whatever she sees on my face softens her. "And don't you dare try to downplay it or make excuses for him."

I nod, feeling the sting of tears behind my eyes. "I know who he is."

Maren sits up straighter, feet dropping to the floor, and her face goes through about seventeen different emotions in the span of three seconds. "Seriously? Did he finally take off that fucking mask?"

"No." I run a hand through my tangled hair, trying to order my thoughts. "But I know. He kissed me last night. And I knew."

"Knew what?" Maren shifts forward, elbows dropping to her knees. "Luna, who is he?"

I meet her eyes, seeing my devastation reflected at me. "It's Damien, Mar. You were right. I was right. It's been Damien this whole time."

The silence stretches between us, suffocating, filling every corner of the room. Sage meows and kneads my thigh under the blanket, sensing my distress.

"Holy fucking shit. That motherfucking manipulative, lying son of a bitch."

She launches to her feet, pacing the length of the porch, muttering curses that are so inventive, they could only come from Maren Rodriguez.

"I fucking knew it. I knew there was something there!"

She spins to face me, eyes blazing. Shadow's head jerks upright, Juni hisses, and Sage burrows under the blanket on my lap in response to her furious energy. Willow stretches behind my head, unfazed.

"You have such great instincts, Lu. We both should have listened to them. And the fucking timing. How he showed up in town right when your stalker started watching you—"

"My instincts suck." Bitterness coats every word, matching the white-hot pain in my chest. "I didn't listen to them. I mean, how could I ignore those moments when something felt... familiar? How could a mask and his disguising his voice fool me so completely?"

Maren drops back onto the seat with a sigh, her Aries rage burning out as fast as it ignited. "Because you wanted to be fooled. Because there was something freeing about not knowing, wasn't there?"

The truth of her words shatters my illusions. "With my wolf, I could be uninhibited. Surrender control. Let myself be vulnerable in ways I never allow with anyone else. And with Damien..." I trail off, memories flooding back. "With Damien, I was letting my guard down in a different way. He was patient and attentive. He never pushed for more than I was ready to give."

"Two sides of the same fucking coin. He gave you exactly what you needed in both personas. That fucking manipulative bastard."

"You said that already."

"And I'll say it again." She grabs one of the throw pillows and launches it across the room. It hits the window with a soft thud. "That motherfucking manipulative rat bastard."

"He lied to me." Pain and fury tangle in my throat, making each word jagged. "For months, Mar. He's been living this double life, manipulating me, and playing this sick game. Owning my body as my wolf while courting my heart as Damien. He watched me tear myself apart with guilt over 'betraying' him, and he enjoyed every second of my suffering. He loved punishing me for it."

"What do you mean, punishing you?" Her eyes narrow to slits, and her breathing slows. "Luna, I thought you said he didn't hurt you. Because if you've been lying to me about that, if he's been hurting you and you didn't tell me, I'm going to kick both your asses."

Even with the threat directed at me, the fierce protectiveness in her tone makes my chest ache with how much I love her.

"He doesn't hurt me, Mar. Not physically. But after I spent time with Damien, he was always different. Rougher. He never hid that he knew about Damien because he was always watching me, but I refused to put it together. I thought it was jealousy from my stalker, not him being jealous... of himself."

"That's pretty fucked up, even by my standards."

A bitter laugh bursts out of me. "He played me for a fool. Making me want both sides of him and then punishing me for developing feelings for his daylight persona."

Juni headbutts my elbow, her purr rumbling like a small motor. My fingers sink into her soft fur, and I focus on the rhythmic motion of petting her instead of the chaos in my head.

"Have you considered that maybe this wasn't some elaborate, cruel game?" Maren's voice loses its razor edge. Her jaw unclenches as she pushes past her rage to consider something else. "Maybe he didn't know how to tell you the truth once things went beyond crazy monkey sex?"

My jaw drops. "Are you seriously defending him right now? After everything I just told you?"

"Fuck no, I'm not defending him." She throws her hands up in protest. "What he did is completely fucked up, and he deserves to have his balls cut off and fed to him for it. I'll be the first in line to do it. But I'm trying to see the whole picture here, Lu. I've never seen your masked stalker, but I've seen how Damien looks at you. That man is completely gone for you."

"He let me grieve alone. He knew I lost our baby, and he just watched me suffer."

"Did he, though?" Maren leans forward. Her gaze pins me in place. "Because what I've seen is him bringing you lunch every damn day for the last couple weeks, checking on you, making sure you're eating and taking care of yourself, even though you didn't 'technically' tell Damien about the miscarriage. I can't even imagine how many miles he's put on that helicopter bringing takeout from Denver. Wait, do helicopters use miles or... never mind. Point is, he's been showing up for you this whole time. But not as the version you expected."

I go still. The righteous solid ground under my feet just turned to quicksand. Thanks for that, Maren.

"I don't know what to do." My voice cracks. "I'm so angry with him, Mar. What he did... the lies, the deception. He betrayed me, but I'm—"

"Still in love with him."

"Both versions of him." Tears well up and spill over. "I'm in love with the intense, patient man who remembers every animal's name here. And I'm in love with the primal, dominant force who knows my body better than I know it myself now." I look up at her, and desperation claws its way up my throat. "What does that say about me? That I can love someone who deceived me so completely?"

"It says you're human." Maren reaches across the space between us and grabs my hand, her grip tight. "It means your heart knows something your head hasn't caught up to yet." Her fingers squeeze harder. "But let me be crystal fucking clear about something, Luna Marie."

Oh, shit. My middle name again.

"If you want me to end him, I will. I don't give a shit that he's the hottest thing to walk this planet since they invented fire. You're my best friend. You're my sister. Say the word, and I'll castrate him with the dullest knife I can find and make him choke on his balls."

A laugh bursts out before I can stop it. Small and broken, but real. "Violence isn't the answer, Mar."

Her grin turns feral. "Maybe not, but it'd feel damn good." The smile fades, and her expression softens again. "So what now? Have you talked to him since you figured it out? What actually happened when you realized"

My stomach twists at the memory.

"When I recognized his kiss, I pulled away from him and said his name. He had the fucking audacity to growl at me, accusing me of calling out another man's name while he was inside me. When he saw the truth all over my face, he pulled out of me and walked out the back door. Completely naked."

"Wait a goddamn minute." Maren half-laughs, half-chokes. "You were fucking, and he got up and walked out of the bedroom?"

"No. We were in the kitchen. I was on the table."

Maren's gaze shoots to the doorway and to the kitchen table visible beyond it. Her face cycles through at least five different expressions. "How often do you two have sex on that table?"

"Uh... A lot."

"Are you fucking kidding me?" Her eyes snap back to mine. "I am never eating at that table again. Ever." Then her expression shifts, eyebrows shooting up. "Hold on, it was snowing last night. He really walked out? Naked? Into the snow?"

"As the day he was born. He left all his clothes behind."

Maren doubles over, arms wrapping around her stomach as laughter pours out of her. It comes in waves, each one louder than the last, shaking her whole body. I cross my arms and scowl at her. It's not that funny.

"You know what?" She forces herself upright, still gasping with laughter. "I'm really torn right now because I hate him. I hate him with every fiber of my being for what he's done to you. But I also kinda fucking love him too, because walking out naked into a snowstorm because you got caught in your own web of lies? That's some melodramatic bullshit right there."

"What do I do, Mar?"

She wipes beneath her eyes and studies me. Then her expression shifts, the humor draining from her features.

"Holy shit. That's how he got past your security. He installed the whole system himself. That takes serious balls."

"You're spending an awful lot of time bringing his balls into this conversation."

"That's because he's got some huge cojones, Lu. You're the woman who'd know. And it's brilliant, if you think about it. Completely fucked up, but brilliant."

"Whose side are you on?"

"Yours. Always fucking yours. And the next time I see him, he'll be lucky if I don't kick him in those apparently impressive balls of his. But you've got to give credit where it's due, Lu. The man went to great lengths to be with you."

I shove both hands through my hair and pull at the roots. "He waited for darkness. Every single time. Gave me the day to myself, like he was keeping his two lives in separate boxes. Until recently, when he started showing up as Damien."

"Getting greedy. Or maybe he just wanted to be with you outside the bedroom." Her gaze darts to the doorway, and her nose wrinkles. "Or kitchen."

"I don't know if he'll come back after last night." The thought has haunted me all morning. "I don't even know if I want him to. Or what I'll say if he does. I don't know if I want to scream at him or let him fuck my brains out."

"You can do both." Maren's wicked grin returns. "In fact, I highly recommend it. Angry sex is hot as fuck."

"Maren!" But I'm almost smiling now, which I suspect was her intent.

"What?" She shrugs. "I'm just saying, you've got options here. And as much as it pains me to say this, because I really do want to castrate him with garden shears, I think you need answers more than anything else right now."

"What if his explanations are worse? What if there's no coming back from this?"

"Then you'll survive it. You're the strongest person I know, Lu. You save animals that everyone else has given up on. You survived a bridge collapse that should have killed you. You survived losing a baby you didn't even know you wanted until it was gone. You can survive this, whatever happens."

Willow jumps from the back of the sofa to sit on Maren's lap. She must sense my mood leveling out and wants to say hello to her second favorite human.

"And if all else fails..." A dark smirk curves her lips as she strokes Willow. "We kill him and hide the body. I know some seriously remote spots in these mountains."

Oh, Jesus. The last thing these mountains need is more bodies.

"Do you want me to stay tonight? I can be your backup. Hide in the closet with a baseball bat or something. Maybe a tranquilizer gun. Yes." Her eyes light up. "We can tranq him, lock him in the recovery den, and torture him."

"Maren, dial back the kidnapping fantasies."

"Hey, kidnapping fantasies can be very hot with the right person, but I digress. We're talking about torturing your wolf."

"You're freaking me out a little. And I appreciate the offer, but this is something I need to handle myself." I pull in a deep breath, searching for courage somewhere in my chest. "Thank you, though. For listening. For not making me feel like a complete idiot."

"You're not an idiot for falling in love. And you're definitely not an idiot for having kinks that make you happy. If you want to get zip-tied, bent over, railed, and choked out until you forget your own name, I'm definitely not one to judge. As long as you have a safe word and he respects it. And you make him wrap it the fuck up."

"Jesus Christ, Mar. Tell me how you really feel about my sex life."

"Bitch, please, I've known you're a kinky slut since I walked in on Brad Worthington railing your ass after the CSU Thanksgiving bowl."

"I saw more of your ass than I ever wanted to during college too, you know."

"So you know how fabulous it is." She grins, then the smile fades. "You wanna know what I think?"

"Always."

"I think there's more to this story than you know yet. You need to hear him out before you decide anything." She leans forward again, holding my gaze. "And deep down, you already know what you want."

"Do I?"

"Luna, you soaked my shirt with snot and tears when you lost that baby. You never thought you wanted kids until you were pregnant with his. You weren't just destroyed by the miscarriage, but because the baby was his. Even if you couldn't say it then, you wanted a future with him." Maren's voice stays soft but steady.

"Now you know who he is. The only things standing between you and that future are anger, hurt feelings, and maybe a healthy dose of torture for good measure."

"You're oversimplifying it."

"Am I? Seems to me you've stumbled into something rare. Someone who sees all of you. The parts you show everyone and the parts you only let out in the dark." She pushes to her feet and stretches, her spine cracking. "Just think about it, okay? Before you torch everything because you're scared, hurt, and pissed off. That's my go-to move, and we both know how well that's worked out for me."

I nod, unable to push words past the knot in my throat. Sometimes I hate how well she knows me.

"Come on." She moves toward the kitchen door. "Let's get some food in you. But not at that table. You should burn it."

A smile pulls at my mouth even through the ache twisting in my chest. If she only knew how many times she's eaten breakfast at that exact table the morning after he'd had me sprawled across it the night before. I scrub it down every time, but the knowledge would freak her out, so I keep my mouth shut.

"Actually—" She stops in the doorway. "Maybe you should stay here today. Let me handle the sanctuary. I'll come get you if anything urgent comes up, but I think you need time to figure out what you're going to say to him tonight."

I push to my feet, moving Shadow's giant head and dispersing the cats. "No. I'll lose my mind sitting here obsessing. Besides, Ricky needs a final ultrasound to make sure there aren't any leftover kidney stone fragments."

She nods. "Okay. Maybe a little boob action from your favorite raccoon might just be what the doctor ordered."

I step forward and wrap my arms around her, crushing her in a hug until she squeaks. She squeezes back with everything she has, and the air leaves my lungs in a rush.

"Thanks, Mar. I love you so much."

"Yeah, you do. I'm fucking awesome." She tries for flip, but her voice comes out thick with emotion.

We head into the kitchen together. She insists on cooking while I perch at the counter, deliberately not looking at the table. Bacon sizzles in the pan while she fills the silence with complaints about JT being an ass and how they might be done. I knew he was the reason for her mood when she showed up. I can see the hurt she's trying to hide behind the irritation.

Men are the worst.

When the food's ready, she demands we take it back to the porch, and I go along with her need to avoid the scene of the crime. I watch her slip pieces of bacon to Shadow and the cats when she thinks I'm not paying attention.

My thoughts drift away from the food. Beyond all the lying, the manipulation, and the total implosion of my reality. I keep circling back to his kiss, to finally feeling his bare skin under my hands, tasting his mouth, and having him look at me like I was his entire world.

Before I said his name and shattered the illusion.

Chapter Twenty-Six

Damien

I stare at the bottom of my empty whiskey glass, watching the amber residue catch the morning light slanting through the tall windows behind my chair. My hand trembles enough that I notice.

My fingers, toes, and balls still throb from the frostbite I earned running naked through Luna's snow-covered property at one in the morning. At least I had the presence of mind to cup my cock with both hands during the sprint.

Thank fuck I parked halfway up Luna's driveway last night, the snow blocking my usual path through the woods. Less than a minute and a half from her back door to the Range Rover. I dove inside, calling Cade and telling him to drag my personal physician out of bed and get him on the helicopter. I've never been more grateful that I left the doors unlocked, considering I abandoned everything at Luna's, every piece of clothing I wore there except my goddamned socks.

They arrived a little after 3 AM, and the doctor left a few minutes ago, after giving me a three-hour lecture on the dangers of exposing my naked genitals to thirty-two-degree temperatures.

No fucking shit, Sherlock!

The frostbite might be mild, but every sting reminds me how catastrophically I ruined things with Luna. Running naked into a snowstorm was the least of my fuckups. My reasons for it, buried under the layers of lies and deception I've spun, outweigh it a hundred times over.

Cade sits rigid in the chair across my desk, arms locked over his chest, eyes sharp as vultures. The silence between us is thick and suffocating. Athena curls at my feet, her warm weight the only thing keeping me tethered. But she's restless, whining and thumping her tail, as if she can sense every jagged piece of my guilt.

"You gonna tell me what happened?" Cade's rough voice cuts through the noise in my head. "Or should I just watch you drink yourself stupid? You realize it's only 7 AM, right?"

I slam the glass down. The sharp crack echoes off the wood.

"She knows."

Cade doesn't even blink. "Course she does. Told you this would blow up in your face."

I surge to my feet. Athena lifts her head with a grunt as I stride to the window overlooking the helipad, each step a stabbing reminder of my stupidity.

"She said my name, Cade. Looked me dead in the eye and said, 'Damien.' She's had suspicions for a while, but the second I kissed her, everything clicked."

"Maybe you shouldn't have kissed her."

I spin toward him, heat exploding in my chest. "I fucking had to. I couldn't take it anymore."

Cade leans back, his expression unchanged. "What now?"

"Fuck if I know. Maybe I can convince her she's wrong." Even as the words leave my mouth, I hear how pathetic they sound.

"Why would you do that? I thought you were trying to come clean?"

"I am. But she's been through enough. She doesn't need my deception to add to it. Besides, she was overwhelmed, caught up in the moment. People say all kinds of shit during sex."

"Bullshit!" Cade stands, his presence suddenly dominating the room. "That woman's smarter than half the people we both know, and you've been playing a dangerous game for months. You really think she hasn't noticed how similar you are? The way you move, touch her, even fucking breathe? Christ, Damien. I'm shocked it took this long."

My hands ball into fists. I welcome the pain as my fingers ache. "I did what I had to do."

"You did what you wanted." His tone stays flat and factual. "You got obsessed, but you couldn't just watch from the shadows. You had to have her."

We've had this fucking conversation what feels like a dozen times, but I thought he finally understood that wanting Luna and loving her aren't choices I made. They're facts of my existence now.

"It wasn't supposed to be like this." I drag both hands through my hair and yank hard enough to hurt. "I was supposed to come clean first."

I drop onto the bench below the window. Athena pads over and nudges my foot. Pain shoots through the frostbitten flesh, and I jerk back. Fuck, I hope I can wear shoes.

"I blame my fucking parents for this. If I could kill them again, I would."

"Your parents were evil and got what they deserved." That's a first. He's always kept his opinion of what I did to himself. "But you're a forty-six-year-old man, and it's time you stopped blaming them for all your shitty choices. There's a point when you have to take responsibility for your own actions."

"You think I don't know this is all a hell of my own making?"

He crosses his arms over his chest. "Then man the fuck up."

I exhale, and months of buried secrets leave with the breath. "Luna's the only woman I've ever shown my real self to. Right from the start, I knew she could handle my darkness, even with all her light. Maybe because of it."

"So, you created two different versions of yourself?"

"I gave her what she needed. Her dark side wanted the wolf. But the rest of her wants someone normal."

"And what did you want? I'm serious, Damien. What did you want from her? Really?"

"At first? Just sex. To own her. Ruin her for anyone else but me. But the second she surrendered, I wanted every fucking part of her."

"That's not love, kid. That's control."

I surge to my feet. "Don't fucking lecture me about love. I've killed fifteen hundred fifty-seven people, Cade. Fifteen hundred fifty-seven pieces of human garbage who tortured innocent animals for fun. Their blood's on my hands, their screams are in my head, and I loved every fucking second of it. Someone who loves that kind of violence and carnage doesn't deserve to be on the receiving end of it. Especially from someone like her."

"For what it's worth, I believe she does... love you."

"Why?"

My voice cracks like I'm sixteen again instead of pushing fifty.

"Because you're not in fucking prison. She saw something worth protecting in you, or she would've turned you in." Cade sits again, his expression thoughtful. "So, what are you going to do?"

I lean forward, forearms braced on my knees, studying the grain of the floorboards. "I could go back tonight. Wear the mask, pretend she never said my name. Keep things the way they were."

"Did you miss the part where we established she's not an idiot?"

"I know that."

I've been carrying this secret like a weight, part of me hoping she'd see through the deception while another part dreaded this exact moment. But I wanted control over the reveal. Instead, she connected the dots because I couldn't keep my goddamn mouth off her.

"I guess you could try." His tone makes clear what he thinks of my odds. "How'd that work out for you last night when you nearly lost your nuts in the snow?"

The memory makes me flinch. "That wasn't my finest moment."

Her voice echoes in my head. The shock when she said my name, her eyes searching mine for confirmation. She spoke with such certainty, but instead of answering, I grabbed her hair and snarled at her like the wolf she called me. Then I ran into the night like a coward.

"I had to get out of there." I drag a hand down my face. "One more second and I was going to fucking lose it and vomit out the truth."

"I think your truth might be more than anyone should have to handle. But if anyone can, it's probably her."

"That's not fucking helping me, Cade. I don't know if I'm capable of being what she needs. What if all I know how to do is take and claim and destroy?"

"Then you figure out how to learn something else." He stands and crosses to the door, pausing at the threshold. "You've spent forty-six years convinced you're damaged beyond repair, but that woman proved you wrong. She chose you, Damien. Both versions of you, without even knowing it."

Athena whines and pushes her wet nose into my palm. Her love is simple and uncomplicated. She doesn't judge the killer in me. Doesn't care that I'm warped and broken. She only remembers I pulled her out of hell, and that's enough for her.

"Once she knows everything, once she sees that there's no separation between the man and the monster, she'll run."

"She might." His voice holds no false comfort. "Or she might not. But that's her choice to make."

Chapter Twenty-Seven

Luna

I hear him before I see him. Four quick tones as he disarms the security system, followed by the soft click of the lock disengaging and the whisper of the back door opening. Each sound feels amplified in the silence of my house, echoing the thunderous beating of my heart. I've been sitting here for hours, waiting, my body coiled tight as a spring. Shadow stirs at my feet, sitting up at the approaching footsteps.

This is it. The moment everything changes.

My hands shake as I grip the throw pillow in my lap. I've rehearsed this conversation a hundred times in my head, but now that he's here, now that I can hear his boots against my hardwood floor, every practiced word evaporates.

He appears in the archway between the hall and the living room, silent, imposing, and with that damn wolf mask covering his face. But tonight, everything is different. I've turned on all the lights in the living room. I won't let him hide behind shadows. Tonight, the mask doesn't represent mystery or forbidden desire. Tonight, it's a lie. A barrier. A fucking insult to everything I thought we had.

"Take. It. Off."

The words leave my mouth before he can speak, and some distant part of me registers surprise at how steady my voice sounds when everything inside me is screaming.

He stops mid-stride. Every muscle in his body locks into place, tension radiating from him in waves I can feel across the space between us. His shock pulses through the air, tangible even behind the silver barrier hiding his face.

"That's not how this works, Luna."

"It is tonight."

I push myself up from the couch, my movements deliberate despite the earthquake in my bones. My legs shake with the effort of supporting my weight, but I lock my knees and refuse to show weakness. The pillow tumbles to the floor.

"Take it off or leave. Those are your only options."

Shadow rises with me, a low growl rumbling in his chest, sensing the electrical charge of tension crackling between us. I cross my arms over my chest, trying to hold myself together.

"No more games, Damien. No more lies."

His name hangs in the air like a dropped bomb. For a moment that stretches into eternity, he doesn't move. He just stands there, this powerful, intimidating figure reduced to stillness by his own name.

One hand lifts halfway toward the mask, then drops back to his side.

"Luna—"

"No." The word slices between us. "You don't get to 'Luna' me right now. You don't get to use that voice, whichever voice you've decided to use tonight, and expect me to melt and forget. Take it off, Damien. Or get out."

His fingers twitch. The mask catches light from the fire, colors bleeding across the intricate surface, turning it into something beautiful and unbearable all at once.

"If I do this, there's no going back."

"There was no going back the moment I recognized your kiss." My throat tightens, but I force the words out. "So stop hiding behind that fucking mask and let me see you."

With deliberate slowness that makes my pulse spike, he reaches up with both hands and pulls the mask away.

My breath catches despite knowing exactly what I'll see. Even with the truth burning in my chest, seeing his face, Damien's face, in this context, in my living room where my masked lover has stood so many times before, feels surreal. The sharp planes of his cheekbones, the intensity of those dark eyes, and the mouth that I've kissed. It's him. It's been him all along.

A sob crawls up my throat. I've been such a fool.

"How could I have been so stupid?" The words I've been asking myself all day tear out of me, raw and bitter. I turn away from him, unable to look at that familiar face any longer. "I bet you got a good laugh out of that, didn't you? Fool your gullible little doe. As long as I don't show her my face or body or kiss her on the mouth, she'll never figure it out."

He moves behind me, his boots scraping on the hardwood.

"That's not true." His voice is rough. Real now, without the gravelly disguise he's been using for months. "Don't you ever fucking call yourself stupid, Luna. You're the smartest woman I know."

"Ha!" The laugh that escapes me is harsh and ugly. It doesn't sound like me at all. I spin to face him, my hair whipping across my shoulders. "Smart? Really? Because I feel like the world's biggest idiot right now."

His expression shifts, a flash of rage, or maybe anguish. I can't read it, and I'm past caring. I pace because standing still isn't an option. The energy crackling through my body has to go somewhere.

"When did you realize the truth? I know it wasn't last night. Not really."

"I've thought I was losing my mind for weeks... months." I wrap my arms around myself, trying to hold the pieces of my shattered world together. "There were so many similarities, so many coincidences. These moments of déjà vu that were too absurd to even contemplate."

I resume my pacing, moving from the couch to the window and back again, my sock-clad feet silent on the floor. Shadow paces with me, keeping himself between me and Damien.

"But I kept telling myself I was crazy, that it was impossible." My throat tightens. "I was so foolish. I feel like Lois Lane, too blind and too wrapped up in my own denial to see that Clark Kent was Superman. So stupid."

"I said, don't fucking call yourself that." His voice cracks like a whip, and Shadow's ears go flat, another growl rumbling deep in his chest.

The demanding edge in Damien's tone would have melted me before. Now it makes my blood boil.

"Why not? It's true." I turn away from him again, facing the darkened window where my reflection stares back at me—wild-haired, red-eyed, and broken. "I wanted you to be the same person. I ached for it. I berated myself for wanting it. Felt guilty for even thinking it."

"Luna—"

"That kiss." I cut him off as I spin back to face him. Tears threaten, but I refuse to let them fall. Not yet. "That's all it took. The kiss you've been denying me for months. One touch of your lips, and everything fell into place."

"Luna—"

"No! Shut up."

His jaw tightens, and he takes a step toward me, but I hold up my hand like a shield.

"Why did you do this to me?" Months of confusion and pain explode out of me. "Why the charade? Why couldn't you..." My breath hitches. "Why couldn't you be yourself with me from the beginning?"

He moves to my side table and sets the mask down, shrugging out of his leather jacket. He rakes his hands through those silver streaks at his temples, the ones I ache to grip.

"It's complicated."

I said the same thing to him a week ago. It carries the same hollow weight now as it did then.

"Bullshit."

I move closer, stepping into his space until I have to tilt my head back to hold his gaze. Heat radiates off his body, but I refuse to let it distract me.

"You made me fall in love with two different men, you bastard. Do you have any idea what that's done to me?" My voice cracks, but I push through. "The guilt I felt? I thought I was some kind of bitch, some kind of slut for having feelings for Damien, for letting him pursue me, kiss me, while my wolf was—"

The words catch in my throat as the full weight of his deception crashes over me. The intimate moments, the whispered confessions in the dark, the way I'd felt torn between two desires that were actually the same man playing games with my heart.

My stomach revolts.

"Oh, God." My hand clamps over my mouth. I stumble backward, my ass hitting the couch. The room tilts and spins. Bile burns the back of my throat. "I'm going to throw up."

"You're not a slut." His voice comes out soft but edged with steel. He steps toward me. "I'm growing weary of telling you not to say that kind of shit about yourself. I'm the monster here, and we both know it. You're perfect. Everything I never knew I needed."

"Don't." I jerk backward, keeping a space between us. "Don't you dare try to charm your way out of this. I've had enough of your silver tongue, Damien. Both versions of it."

He stops, but his whole body vibrates with tension. His gaze drops to my mouth, then my throat, then lower, and I feel it like a physical touch. He wants to touch me, and traitorous heat spreads through my belly, the same heat that's betrayed me before.

I sink onto the couch before my knees buckle. My elbows hit my thighs, and I bury my face in my hands. Shadow plops on the floor in front of me, nudging my hands with his nose.

"Why wouldn't you kiss me?" The question slips out, small and raw, but the pain behind it is enormous. "Why wouldn't you let me—"

My breath catches. I press my palm against my eye.

"I begged you. I fucking begged to feel your skin."

The memories crash over me. All those nights when I'd pleaded with him, desperate to connect on a deeper level. My hands reaching up in the darkness, his fingers catching my wrists. Pinning them. The word 'no' delivered in that cold, final tone.

Night after night after night.

My face burns, the remembered humiliation spreading like poison through my veins. I lift my head. Force myself to look at him, to hold his gaze even though everything in me wants to look away.

"Why wasn't I good enough for your bare skin? Why was my mouth good enough to fuck but not to kiss? Like some whore you used in the dark."

"Don't." His voice turns deadly quiet, his eyes burning with fury that steals the air from my lungs. He takes a predatory step toward the couch. "Don't you ever fucking call yourself a whore again, or I swear to God, Luna, I'll bend you over this couch and fuck your ass raw."

The crude threat should repel me, but instead it sends a shock of heat through my system. Even now, even in the middle of this devastating confrontation, my body betrays me again. I scramble to my feet. Shadow follows and puts himself between us.

"Then answer me!" I shout, refusing to be intimidated. "Tell me why you denied me!"

He turns and paces away, boots thudding against my floor, all coiled energy and barely restrained violence. A caged predator looking for an exit. When he wheels back around, grief carves itself into every line of his face. His mouth opens and closes as if the truth is choking him.

"Because I knew the second I kissed you, the second I let that part of my mask slip, I'd be lost. There'd be no coming back from it."

The width of my living room separates us, but it might as well be a canyon. Every muscle in his body screams with the effort it takes to stand there and bleed the truth out in front of me.

"It would've destroyed me." His voice drops to a whisper. He's stopped pacing, standing motionless, looking almost lost. "Opening myself up like that. Letting you see everything and then having you reject it." His hands dive into his hair, fingers tangling in the strands. "I wanted all those things. Fuck, Luna, I wanted to kiss you until you forgot your own name. Wanted your skin on mine with nothing between us. Wanted to make love to you with the lights on instead of just taking you in the dark." He drags a hand down his face. "But I'm a brutal asshole who takes what he wants and kills who he wants. I'll never deserve you."

The confession fills the space between us, more intimate than anything we've shared in the darkness of my bedroom.

"I didn't plan to kiss you that night after dinner." His jaw works, teeth grinding. "But I couldn't stop myself. You were so beautiful, so perfect, and I'd been starving for you. And it was exactly what I feared." He takes a step toward me. "One touch of your lips. One taste. That's all it took to ruin me."

My feet move before I decide to let them, closing the distance between us even as my brain screams warnings. Each step feels inevitable, like falling. Like gravity.

"But why pursue me that way at all?"

"Because those few hours at night were no longer enough. I wanted more than your body, Luna."

"You could've had it." My voice breaks, shattering the composure I'm trying to hold. "I offered you more of me so many times, and you always rejected me. But then you'd show up during the day as Damien. Bringing me coffee and making me laugh like some kind of..."

"Some kind of what?"

"Some kind of normal man who wanted something real with me." Tears burn my eyes, but I still refuse to let them fall. "Was any of it real? Or was I just some elaborate game to you?"

"All of it was real." His eyes search mine, black and bottomless. Desperation bleeds through his composure. Fear, too. Raw and unmistakable, as his chest rises and falls too fast. "Everything between us was real, and that's what's fucking destroyed me."

I want to believe him. The wanting aches in my bones. But I can't afford to trust anymore. I step back, widening the gap between us.

"What was your endgame? Did you think I'd never figure it out? That I'd sleep with Damien and not recognize you? Not know exactly how you feel inside me? How you move? How you fuck?"

His hands flex at his sides, and his throat works around the words he's trying to force out. When they finally come, they sound like they've been dragged over broken glass.

"I thought I could keep them separate. Have you both ways. Have you the way we are in the dark and still have what I crave in the light."

"And what is that, Damien? What is it you crave?"

"You." The word explodes out like he's been holding it back too long. He eliminates the last of the space between us in two strides, and then he's there, so close the heat and scent of him wrap around me. "Your smile. Your laugh. How alive you get when you talk about your animals. I want to be the man who makes you happy, not just the one who fucks you until you're sobbing. I want to be the man who fulfills every dark fantasy you have and every dream you'll ever have. I fucking want to be both."

The honesty in his words guts me. I stagger back, pressing my hand to my chest. Beneath it, my heart pounds, wild and chaotic.

"So, you fed me lies on both sides."

"What the fuck was I supposed to do?" His voice rises, anger sharpening the words. "You think I planned this? You think I wanted to fall in love with you?"

"Fall in love with me? Is that what this is? Love? Because it feels a lot more like manipulation."

His expression darkens. For a second, I see the dangerous man underneath. The killer who wears the mask.

"Don't do that, Luna. Don't twist this into something it's not."

"Then explain it to me!" My composure shatters. I surge forward and jab my finger into his chest. "Tell me why you did this to me!"

"Because I'm fucked up!" His hand shoots out and catches my wrist mid-jab, his grip firm and unyielding. "Because I'm dark and broken inside, and I don't know how to give you what you deserve! I knew this would blow up eventually, but I couldn't stop. By the time I realized I was in love with you, it was too late. I was in too deep. Letting you go wasn't an option. It never was."

He loves me. Or believes he does. But it fixes nothing. If anything, it makes everything worse.

I pull my hand free from his grip. "You fell in love with me. And your brilliant solution was to keep lying to me?"

I draw in a breath, steadying myself.

"Look, I get why you didn't tell me at first. You were stalking me, fucking me while wearing a mask. You admitted you're a serial killer. So yeah, in some sick way, I understand the initial deception. But later? After it became more than sex? Why keep lying? Why make me fall for two versions of you?"

"I'd never..." He tears at his hair again as he turns to face the window, and I worry he might actually tear it out. "You don't know what I come from, Luna. Love wasn't something I understood before I met you. I didn't know how to handle it. All I knew was that I needed you in every way possible. The dark parts of me needed to own you, possess every piece of you. But there was this other part. This part that wanted to make you smile. Be worthy of you. I thought I could give you both."

"By lying to me."

"By protecting you!" He wheels around to face me, his eyes wild. "Do you think I wanted you to know how depraved I really am? Wanted you to think about the blood on my hands every time I touched you?"

"I already knew the hands you touched me with were covered in blood, sometimes before you even came to me at night. But it didn't matter. I wanted your hands on me, anyway. I always accepted you, even when it cost me pieces of my soul to do it."

"Do you really think knowing the truth would've made you feel better? Do you feel better now, knowing it?"

"No. I feel betrayed and used."

"It's one thing, Luna, to know that the masked man you're fucking in secret is a killer. It's quite another to know he's also your neighbor. The seemingly civilized man who takes you to fancy galas and also devours you against the windows in his penthouse."

The weight of it all slams into me at once—the lies, the manipulation, the months of living in two different worlds with the same man. My shoulders cave inward, and my spine curves forward like I'm trying to fold myself in half.

"Knowing doesn't change anything."

He scoffs, and his mouth twists into a smile that makes him look like a different person, all hard edges and self-loathing. His eyes flash with bitter amusement, the kind that comes from watching your life burn down around you and finding it grimly funny.

"Now, who's the liar?"

"Is it because you don't trust me?" I move closer to him again, drawn by some invisible force I can't resist. "Do you think I'll turn you in to the authorities? I told you I'll never betray you."

"It isn't a matter of betrayal. It's a matter of burden. You don't fucking deserve the burden of knowing what I do and who I truly am. Because make no mistake, Luna, the man I am is the one standing in front of you right now. I'm a man who kills without remorse and then comes to you after and pours all his darkness into you along with his come. I'm not the man you see in the daytime. That man is the true mask I wear."

"It wasn't your decision to make for me, Damien."

"I never wanted my darkness to touch you."

He reaches up, his thumb tracing my cheek, wiping away tears I didn't realize were falling. The touch is so gentle, so familiar, that I almost lean into it before catching myself.

"Your darkness touched me the second you put your hands on me."

I step back, pulling away from his hand, and the separation hurts, like a physical ache that radiates through my ribs and settles heavy in my stomach.

"I save lives, Damien, and somehow, I made peace with loving someone who takes them. I'll never tell anyone. I'll take your secret to my grave. But this... the lies, the deception..."

His eyes widen, panic flickering across his features. "Luna—"

I gesture between us. "This... us... It has to end."

The words tear a hole so deep inside me, I don't know if it will ever heal.

"No."

The word is flat and final, carrying all the authority of a man accustomed to getting his way. He's gotten his way with me too many times.

It stops now.

I move toward the door, needing distance, needing him to leave. "I can't trust you, Damien. How could I ever trust you again? You lied to me for months. Made me question my own feelings, my own sanity. You made me feel crazy."

"I won't let you end this." He blocks my path, and all of a sudden, he's the predator again, all coiled muscle and dangerous intent. I nearly collide with his chest, stopping short at the last second.

"You don't get a choice." I try to push past him, but he's immovable. "Leave. Now."

"No."

The possessiveness in his tone, the casual dismissal of my autonomy, snaps something inside me. The hurt and betrayal and months of confusion crystallize into pure, white-hot rage.

"Get out!" I shove against his chest with both hands, putting every ounce of my strength behind it. He barely rocks back on his heels. "Get out of my house!"

"Luna, calm down—"

"Don't tell me to calm down!" I swing at him, tears streaming down my face despite my determination not to cry. "You lied to me! You manipulated me! You made me fall in love with a wolf in billionaire's clothing!"

He catches my wrists, pinning them between us, his grip firm but not painful. Still, I struggle against him, all my hurt and rage pouring out in a frenzy of movement. I'm not trying to hurt him. We both know I couldn't even if I wanted to, but I need to move, need to fight, need to do something with all this pain threatening to tear me apart from the inside.

"Are you going to zip-tie me now? Fuck me into submission?"

"Do I need to?"

"Let me go." I sob, still struggling against his hold. "Please let me go."

"Never."

His mouth crashes onto mine, urgent and possessive. The lies are still there. The betrayal. The trust ground to dust between us. My mind knows this. But my body, my traitorous body, responds, lips parting, hands fisting in his collar, meeting his desperation with my own.

Because this is real. This heat, this need, this devastating connection that transcends both his identities.

This is the one thing that was never a lie.

Chapter Twenty-Eight

Damien

The moment our lips meet, a dam bursts inside my chest. The rigid control I've spent months constructing—every careful boundary, every practiced separation between the man who courts her and the beast who claims her—explodes into fragments. The pressure that has lived behind my ribs, the constant ache of holding back, releases in a rush that leaves me gasping against her mouth, crumbling under the force of our kiss.

She tastes like tears and rage and love, and I want to drown in her. This is what I've stolen from us. The chance to love without shadows, to touch without deception, to exist in the same moment as one person instead of fragments scattered across two lives.

This connection, honest, unguarded, and real, is what I've been too afraid to give us. What I've been too convinced I didn't deserve to even try for.

"I hate you."

Her growl vibrates against my mouth, but her hands tangle in my shirt, dragging me closer. The contradiction in her words and actions mirrors everything I feel, the self-loathing and desperate love warring inside me.

"I know." I back her toward the couch, my heart hammering a frantic rhythm behind my ribs as our kisses deepen. My hands find her waist, fingers digging in like she might disappear if I don't hold tight enough. "Me too."

I hate what I've done to us. I hate that I was too much of a coward to trust her with all of me from the beginning.

Her fingers shake as she grips my shirt, and I catch her hands, stilling them, pulling back to look down at her pale face. The tremor in her touch and the tears staining her face gut me more than any blade could.

"Luna." I search her face. The storm of emotions there, pain, anger, and love—all of it so raw it squeezes the air from my lungs. My thumbs brush across her knuckles, trying to steady us both. "I'm sorry. Christ, I'm so fucking sorry."

Her tear-filled eyes lift to mine.

"Sorry doesn't fix this."

Her voice is tight and brittle, filled with grief too close to the surface.

"I know." I kiss her again before she can stop me, before I can stop myself, pouring everything I can't say into it. She fights me. Her hands shove at my shoulders, body twisting, but I only kiss her deeper, swallowing her protests. When I pull away, we're both gasping. Her pulse hammers against my palms where I'm still holding her wrists. "But I need you to—"

"Stop." She shoves at my chest, hard enough that I stumble back a step, releasing her hands. "Just stop talking."

I reach for her again, but she pushes me away, harder this time. The rejection catches me off guard, not expecting the force behind it. When she's angry, she's stronger than she looks.

"Don't touch me." Her voice cracks, and she wraps her arms around herself, backing toward the fireplace like she needs something solid behind her. "You lied to me. For months, you lied to me."

"Yes." The word comes out strangled, forced past the tightness in my chest. "But the way I feel about you was never a lie. It's the only real thing in my fucked-up life."

"How am I supposed to believe anything you say? How do I know what's real and what's just another mask you're wearing?"

The accusation hits its mark, and I flinch. I've been wearing masks for so long, I barely know who I am anymore. Except when I'm with her. She's the only person who's ever been able to get past them all.

"You want to know what's real?"

I take a step toward her, but Shadow moves in front of her. He won't let me near her right now. I don't blame him. He knows the time has come to protect her from me.

"This is real. The way I can't breathe when you walk into a room. The way I'd carve out my own heart and hand it to you. The way I'd slaughter anyone, *anyone*, who tried to take you from me."

"Stop." She shakes her head, turning away from me. Tears carve paths down her flushed cheeks, her reflection fractured in the mirror above the fireplace. "You don't get to say things like that. Not after what you've done."

"I love you!" The words rip from my chest like they're taking pieces of me with them.

She flinches as if I've struck her. Her reflection crumples, and she turns away from the fireplace to look at me again.

"I love you, Luna. That's the only truth I know."

"Don't." Her voice is a whisper. "Don't say that now. Not now."

But I can't stop. Now that the words are out, they pour from me like a dam bursting. "I love the way you care for your animals, for everyone around you. I love the way you defy me. Right from the beginning, even when you were terrified of me, you never cowered. I love the sound of your laugh and the way you smile when you see me, both of me. I love the way you feel, the way you smell, the way you taste. I love that you see the good in everyone, even in a monster like me. I love—"

"Stop!" She presses her hands to her ears. "I can't hear this right now. I can't—" Her voice breaks completely, and she doubles over like she's in physical pain.

I move toward her, needing to comfort her, to do something other than stand here watching her fall apart. Shadow's lips pull back from his teeth in a warning snarl. I freeze mid-step, my arms hanging at my sides.

The distance between us feels impossible to cross.

"You hurt me." The words are so quiet I almost miss them. She's still bent over, her hair falling like a curtain around her face. "You made me fall in love with a lie."

The accusation hits me harder than any physical blow ever could. I did hurt her. I took her trust, her love, and her body, all under false pretenses. I'm exactly the monster she thinks I am.

"Luna, please—"

"Get out." She straightens, wiping her tears with her fingers. When she looks at me, her eyes are hollow, empty of everything that used to make them shine. "Please go. I'm begging you."

Panic lodges under my ribs. "Luna—"

"Damien." My name breaks on another sob. "I can't look at you right now. I can't—I need you to leave."

Every instinct I have screams at me to fight, to refuse, to battle for her until she forgives me. This woman is everything to me—the light in my darkness, the peace in my chaos. Without her, I'm nothing but the monster I was before she came into my life.

But the tears streaming down her face stop me. I've hurt her enough. I've taken enough from her without permission.

"This isn't over. I'll give you space, Luna, but I won't give up on you. On us. I won't let you go."

Her shoulders shake with silent sobs, but she doesn't respond. My hand hovers over the mask on the table, the wolf that set all of this in motion, before I draw back. She deserves to toss it into her fireplace and watch it melt.

I reach for my jacket. The movement feels wrong, disconnected. Like I'm watching myself from outside my body, trapped in a nightmare I can't wake from. At the door, I stop and turn back. She stands in the middle of her living room, dwarfed by the space. Surrounded by the ghosts of what we were.

"I love you," I say again, because it's the only truth I have left to give her. "That was never a lie."

She keeps her eyes fixed on the floor, like meeting my gaze would shatter whatever fragile control she's clinging to and destroy what's left of her.

Walking away is the hardest thing I've ever done. Each step feels like I'm leaving pieces of myself behind, my feet like lead, every muscle in my body fighting the movement. By the time I reach my truck, breathing is impossible around the pain in my chest.

I turn back toward the house, and the light from the living room window spills out onto the porch in pale yellow rectangles. Through the glass, I see her sitting on the couch with her face buried in her hands. Shadow presses his massive body against her side, his head resting on her shoulder like he's trying to absorb some of her pain.

She's crying. Not quiet tears but deep, wrenching sobs that shake her entire frame, her shoulders heaving with each one.

My feet move back toward the house before I realize what I'm doing. My hands ball into fists so tight my nails dig crescents into my palms. The need to go back tears through me, to take those steps two at a time, gather her in my arms, and swear I'll never cause her this kind of pain again. But I can't promise her that, no matter how much I want to. She needs space to mourn what we had before I took a hammer to it and smashed it into pieces too small to put back together.

She loves me. The words never crossed her lips tonight, couldn't make it past the hurt and rage choking her, but I know they're there. I felt it in the way her mouth opened under mine and her body melted against me for those few seconds before she shoved me away. She loves me, and I took that gift and destroyed it with my own hands.

But I meant what I said. This isn't over. I'll give her time to process, to heal from what I've done. But I won't give up on us. I can't. She's the only good thing I've ever had, and I'll spend the rest of my life proving I'm worthy of her if that's what it takes.

I get in my truck, a knife twisting in my chest, and press my forehead against the steering wheel.

This is the price of my deception, my cowardice, and my lies. And I'll carry the image and sound of her crying with me for the rest of my life.

Chapter Twenty-Nine

Luna

Three days of silence stretch behind me like an open wound. Three days of ignoring Maren's concerned glances and pushing away the mountain of Chinese food she keeps forcing on me. My stomach churns at the thought of eating.

Three days of replaying that confrontation in my living room. The words echo in my head on an endless loop. His confession, his justifications, his promises that sounded more like threats, and the possessive heat in his eyes when he declared he wouldn't let me go. They tangle together until I can't separate the lies from the revelations and can't tell which hurt more. The deception or the truth underneath it.

I bury myself in work instead, spending extra hours with the fox family that are now permanent residents of the sanctuary. Physical labor helps keep the thoughts at bay. I shovel snow, muck out enclosures, repair fences, and haul feed bags until my muscles scream. By nightfall, I collapse into bed and sink into exhausted sleep, my body drained enough that dreams of him can't find me. The oblivion is deep enough that I don't remember the way his hands felt on my skin or the way he whispered my name in the dark.

But the questions follow me like shadows.

How could I have been so stupid?

What does it say about me that I miss him, both versions of him, with an ache that feels physical?

How can I mourn losing someone who was never real to begin with?

On the fourth morning, Karen's cruiser rolls up my driveway as I finish feeding the resident owls. It's Sunday morning, so I'm alone. I'm the only one here on Sundays, unless Maren stays over Saturday night.

My stomach drops as her SUV comes to a stop in front of the house.

Did Damien kill again?

She climbs out of the driver's seat dressed in civilian clothing. "Morning, Luna."

"Karen." I wipe my hands on my jeans, trying to appear casual while my stomach ties itself in knots. "Coffee?"

"Please."

Inside, I busy myself with the coffeemaker while she settles at my kitchen table, right where my life fell apart less than a week ago. The memories in this room once left me breathless. Now they hollow me out from the inside.

No. I can't go there right now. I can't let the ghost of him haunt me.

But he's everywhere in this house. He took me in every single room, claimed every surface, every corner, it seems. There isn't one place I can go to escape the memory of his touch. And I hate him a little for it, for making my own home feel like a shrine to our destruction.

"How's everything going?"

The question grates on my raw nerves. I'm not in the mood for small talk. Not when my world has fallen apart.

I set a steaming mug in front of her and take the opposite chair, my hands wrapped around my own cup to hide their trembling. The caffeine won't help my anxiety, but I need something to anchor me.

"Karen, I don't want to be rude, but why don't you tell me why you're here? We both know it's not to chit-chat."

The shift in her expression is instant. Off duty or not, she's putting on her cop face.

"Luna, I'm going to ask you something, and I need you to be straight with me. I've known you almost your whole life, and you're an honest person. I need your honesty now."

"Okay."

"How well do you know Damien Wolfe? Really?"

A cold sweat breaks out on the back of my neck.

"We've been over this, Karen. I told you we've been seeing each other casually for a few months."

The word 'casually' almost makes me laugh. Or cry. There was nothing casual about the way he possessed me, the way I gave him my complete surrender. There was nothing casual about the way my heart broke when I discovered his lies.

"Are you really stuck on this idea that Damien is somehow connected to all these murders?"

At one time, I worried Karen was on the wrong track and would try to pin murders on Damien that he didn't commit. But I was wrong. He is guilty. He's my wolf. He's a serial killer. And Karen's suspicions are right. Have been all along.

She sips her coffee, watching me over the rim.

"Something doesn't add up, Luna. Eight people connected to animal abuse cases that came to your sanctuary have turned up dead in the past three months. Another eleven have gone missing without a trace."

My heartbeat quickens, hammering against my ribs.

"And there are all these other unsolved missing persons cases, all accused animal abusers, nationwide. It's like they vanished into thin air."

"Okay." I swallow, hoping she doesn't notice. "So, what does that have to do with Damien? Other than the confrontation with Odell Pearson, the others were people he didn't know or have any contact with?"

"Well, he just happened to show up in town right before all these bodies dropped, and the other missing individuals disappeared after he bought the Morrison Place."

Shit.

Shit, shit, shit.

I force my expression to remain neutral, even as panic claws at my throat.

"Really, Karen? You're a better cop than this. That's circumstantial at best." I'm surprised by how steady my voice is, considering the silent scream trapped in my chest.

"Maybe. But my job is to notice patterns, and this one gnaws at me." She sets her mug down. "Especially since his company specializes in surveillance, which would make covering tracks easier."

The observation strikes a nerve, reminding me how easily he watched and stalked me and how effortlessly he covered his tracks.

A faint sound escapes me, the ghost of a laugh that never quite forms. "You think Damien is what? Some kind of vigilante killer?"

"Not to insult you, Luna, but I think it's a hell of a coincidence that a billionaire tech CEO takes an interest in a small-town wildlife sanctuary and its owner right when dead animal abusers start showing up." The cop in her eyes steps back and lets the woman through. "And I think you're too smart not to have noticed the timing yourself."

The accusation fills the silence. She's right. I figured out my wolf was the killer almost immediately, even before he admitted it to me. And I chose to protect him anyway, first as my wolf and now as Damien. I chose lust, then love, over justice, and now I'm drowning in the consequences.

But how smart am I really when I didn't, or refused to, see what was right in front of me?

"Do you have any evidence?"

"Nope. I can't tie him to any of them. Not one here or anywhere else in the country. I didn't tell you before, but forensics found tire tracks at the site where Odell Pearson's body was discovered. The lab identified them as the model and size tires found on Range Rovers. Damien Wolfe owns four of them."

My heart stutters.

"Now, there are plenty of people who drive Range Rovers, over thirteen hundred registered in Colorado alone, but…" She trails off as she looks at me, almost as if waiting for me to argue.

But I can't speak over the lump in my throat.

"They also found some unidentified DNA near Pearson's body."

Now my heart stops. DNA evidence. Damien wouldn't be that sloppy, would he? But even he's human. Even he can make mistakes.

What if they match it to him?

"And?"

I hope my voice doesn't sound as strangled as I think it does.

"There was a screwup in the lab, and it never got tested. It was sent to Denver on Friday."

I look away, unable to hold her gaze, afraid she'll see the truth written across my face.

"Luna, if you know something, if you're protecting someone, you need to consider what that makes you."

An accessory. An accomplice.

The words hang unspoken between us, but they might as well be carved into the air.

"I don't know anything about those deaths."

It's not a complete lie. I don't know the specifics, the how, or the when.

But I know who.

Karen sighs, and for a moment, she looks less like a cop and more like the woman who used to bring me cookies when I was a grieving ten-year-old and comforted me when Grandpa died.

"You've been through a lot in your life. I know that. Your parents, then your grandfather. You've had more than your share of loss. I'd hate to see you throw your life away for someone who might not have your best interests at heart."

The words sting. Damien deceived me, lied to me, and made me fall in love with two different versions of himself. But even knowing that, even hating him for his betrayal, I can't stop loving him. And I can't stop protecting him, no matter how hurt and angry I am.

"Is that all?" I ask, my tone cool.

She studies me for a long moment, those knowing eyes taking in every mi-cro-expression, every tell. Finally, she nods and stands. "For now. But this isn't over, Luna. Whatever's happening, it's going to come to a head soon. I hope you're on the right side when it does."

I lean against the kitchen counter after she leaves, my hands shaking so hard I have to grip the edge to steady myself. She's right. This can't continue. Sooner or later, someone will put the pieces together. And when that happens, both Damien and I will be exposed.

I'm not so worried about the tire tracks with all the Range Rovers around Estes. But DNA evidence. Unidentified DNA.

Shit!

My mind races through possibilities, each one worse than the last. What if they get a warrant for Damien's DNA? What if they search his properties? What if Karen digs deeper and finds something that connects him to the murders?

Everything between us is shattered. The lies he told, the trust he broke, and the way he ripped my heart apart. It still bleeds from what he did to me. But that doesn't matter. He needs to know that Karen still suspects him. He needs to know about the DNA evidence.

And we need to figure out what the hell we're going to do if she finds something that connects him to those murders.

The thought of losing him to prison or justice or consequences steals my breath. All I can think about is protecting him, keeping him safe.

I can't change what I know. The truth has lodged itself in my chest like a shard of glass, and ignoring it won't make the cutting stop. And no amount of denial will erase what I've learned. All I can do is warn him and hope we can find a way to navigate through this nightmare before it swallows us whole.

I reach for my phone, my fingers trembling as I scroll to his contact. Three days of silence, and now I'm about to break it with a warning that could destroy us both.

But I don't have a choice.

I never really did once I chose to love a killer.

Chapter Thirty

Luna

My hands tremble as I grip the steering wheel, navigating the winding drive to Damien's property. The text I sent him was simple.

> I'm coming over. We need to talk.

The old Victorian house comes into view, and it still seems odd that Damien bought this place. It is so unlike the refined billionaire, but as I park next to his Range Rover and look up at the imposing building, it hits me. My masked serial killer bought a serial killer's property.

Oh, God, is this where he kills?

I press my palms against my thighs to stop them from shaking and concentrate on breathing. In through my nose, out through my mouth, slow and controlled even though my pulse races like I've been running. Though I know deep in my bones that I'm right, I can't afford to think about that right now. There's a more pressing crisis bearing down on us.

Karen has DNA evidence.

The weight of that fact settles on my shoulders like lead. I should be turning him in, not warning him. But love makes us do terrible things, and I've already stepped over lines there's no stepping back across.

He opens his front door before I reach it. He looks like hell. Not at all like Damien or my wolf. He's unshaven, his clothes look slept in, his hair sticks up at odd angles, and dark circles bruise the skin beneath his eyes. Guilt twists through my chest because I know it's because of me.

But I push the emotion away. He made his choices. He built his house of lies.

When our eyes meet, his are a mix of worry, relief, and heat all rolled into one. My body responds the way it always does to him. Arousal floods my veins, and longing tightens in my core. Missing him hurts like a wound that won't close.

"Luna."

He says my name as he stands back to let me enter the foyer. It's still unrenovated, but the space feels larger than it did the first time I was here.

"Come into my office." He rests his hand on my lower back and leads me off to the right of the foyer. I pull away, unable to bear his touch. I'll crumble if I let him touch me.

Athena is lying on the sofa, snoring, and I smile despite the churning in my stomach.

"What's wrong?"

He doesn't bother with pleasantries. He reads me too well.

"Karen came to see me again this morning." The words tumble out in a rush. "She won't let go of the idea that you're connected to the murders. She's even convinced you're responsible for murders all over the country."

"I am. She really is a smart cookie, isn't she?"

"This isn't funny, Damien."

"She's fishing, Luna. She can't tie me to any of them."

"Are you sure?" My voice catches. "Because they found Range Rover tire tracks and DNA at the Pearson scene."

He goes still, that mask of control I'd recognize anywhere now sliding into place. But I see a flash of something in his eyes. Not fear, but calculation? The wheels are already turning.

"What did she say?"

His voice is level, but the tightness in his shoulders gives away his tension.

"That there are too many registered Range Rovers in Colorado to be able to tie it specifically to you. But they're running the DNA. Due to an oversight, it wasn't tested, but it's on its way to Denver. What if it's yours?"

"It isn't." But he doesn't sound convinced. "Besides, they don't have my DNA in any database. Cade made sure of that."

I wrap my arms around myself, chilled despite the fire roaring in the fireplace. He moves to his desk, pressing a button on what looks like a high-tech communication system. The large monitor on the wall flickers to life, showing a video call interface.

"Cade. We have an issue."

The man who appears on screen is familiar. The gala. Champagne and canapés, small talk, and his vetting me. Did Damien put him up to it? To make sure I could be trusted? Every moment of that night is tainted by what I know now.

Damien was my watcher, stalker, serial killer lover.

Say that three times fast.

Cade looks the same as Damien usually does in his business persona. Polished, professional, and controlled. If Damien is calling him, he's part of this. What does he do? Get rid of the evidence? The bodies?

Oh, Jesus. I think I'm going to be sick.

"What kind of issue?" Cade's voice has an edge to it, the relaxed executive from the gala now replaced by someone harder.

"Karen Mills is still sniffing around. They found tire tracks matching a Range Rover and DNA at the Pearson site, and she's determined to make a connection." Damien's tone is all business now, the CEO taking charge. "I need you to find out what she has and how close she is to building a case."

I step back, trying to stay out of view of the camera. This conversation feels dangerous, like something I shouldn't be witnessing.

Cade's expression darkens. "I fucking told you this would happen. Warned you a dozen times. But you've been sloppy, careless, leaving a trail because you're too busy thinking with your dick to use your brain."

The words hit me like a slap. Too busy thinking with your dick. The dismissiveness in his tone, the way he reduces me to some sexual distraction that's made Damien stupid, sets my teeth on edge. How dare he?

"Cade." Damien's voice goes flat and cold, that tone I recognize from when he wears his wolf mask. "Shut the fuck up."

"I'm just saying—"

"I said, shut the fuck up. This is my fault, not hers. Now do your fucking job and find out what Mills knows."

There's a long pause. "Give me thirty minutes and I'll get back to you. But you know I'm right."

"I don't need a fucking lecture, Cade. Just handle it." Damien ends the call with another press of the button.

The office falls silent. I stare at the blank screen, feeling the weight of Cade's words settling over me.

"It's not your—"

"Don't." I turn away, unable to look at him. "Don't tell me it's not my fault when we both know better. If you hadn't been spending every night with me and killing abusers connected to me, you would've been more careful."

"Luna. Look at me."

I don't want to, but something in his commanding tone compels me to turn. He's moved closer, close enough that I can see the flecks of gold in his eyes.

"This is not your fault. I made my choices. I took the risks. The only thing you're guilty of is being brave enough to warn me about what the sheriff has."

"What are you going to do about it?"

"I'll take care of it."

Frustration flares in my chest. "How? What does that mean exactly?"

His jaw tightens, and he retreats behind that wall of control again. "You don't need to know."

"There it is." A harsh laugh forces its way out of my throat, so far removed from actual humor that it sounds like it came from someone else. "There's the real problem between us, Damien. You're doing it again."

"Doing what?"

"Lying to me. Deciding what I can and can't handle. Making choices for me." I take a step back, needing distance. "This is exactly why our relationship will never work. Because you won't be honest with me. You've never been honest with me."

"I'm trying to protect you—"

"By keeping me in the dark? By making me more complicit in your activities?" My voice rises despite my efforts to stay calm. "Don't you see how screwed up that is?"

"I won't put any more of this burden on you. You need to trust me."

"Trust you?" The words taste bitter as I repeat what I said the other night. "I don't know if I'll ever trust you again."

"I hope that's not true, because I can't let you go."

The familiar possessiveness in his voice makes my pulse jump. Even now, even standing here with our entire world crumbling around us, he can still affect me with nothing more than the tone of his voice.

He closes the distance between us in smooth, deliberate strides, moving the way he always does, like he owns every inch of space his body occupies, like the air itself parts to let him through.

"I love you, Luna. I know you're hurt, I know you're angry, and you have every right to be. I'm trying to honor your request for space, but my patience is wearing thin. I can't lose you. I won't."

The declaration sends warmth flooding through my chest. After everything, after all the lies and betrayals, he still has the power to make my heart race with just a few words.

"I don't know how to trust you again." The admission rips open wounds I've been trying to keep closed. My throat constricts and my eyes burn.

He's close enough that I can smell his cologne and see the fine lines around his eyes. "Give me another chance to prove that you can. No more secrets between us, Luna. No more lies."

But even as he says it, his voice carries that familiar note of command, that expectation of obedience that's always been part of our dynamic. He's not really asking. He's demanding because that's who he is.

"There is no us, Damien."

"Yes, there is."

"No, there isn't. It's too much. I need time and space to process everything."

His jaw clenches as he struggles with my answer. Patience has never been one of my wolf's virtues.

"How much time?"

"I don't know."

He studies my face for a long moment, then nods. "Fine. But don't take too long, Luna." He steps closer, and I'm aware of how much bigger he is, how he seems to fill the space around me. It makes my pulse spike with adrenaline. "I'm not a patient man. And I've already given you more space than I can stand."

He leans down, bringing his face close to mine, and his breath caresses my lips. Every nerve in my body fires at once, telling me to step back and maintain the distance I've worked so hard to create. But I can't move, caught in the gravitational pull of his presence.

"Damien—"

His mouth crashes against mine, swallowing whatever protest I was about to make, and it's like a dam breaking between us. A whimper escapes my lips before I can trap it. Every wall I've constructed, brick by painful brick, crumbles in an instant. The anger and hurt that have been burning holes in my chest transform into hunger, raw and desperate and clawing at my insides like a living thing. I should shove him away, should remember all the reasons I'm furious with him, but my hands betray me by fisting in his shirt and pulling him closer, kissing him back with the same fierce intensity, the same reckless abandon that got us here in the first place.

His fingers thread through my hair, gripping tight enough to anchor me to him like he's afraid I'll vanish if he loosens his hold. Desperation pours off him in waves. I can taste it on his tongue and feel it in the way his body molds against mine as if he's trying to merge our bones. His hands drop between our bodies, sliding under my coat, and his fingers tug at the front of my shirt with impatient urgency. This hunger, this wild need that consumes everything in its path and leaves nothing but ashes—this is what I've craved from him since the beginning.

Every cell in my body screams for surrender, but my mind wages war against my flesh, demanding I remember why this can't happen. It takes everything I have, every scrap of willpower I can gather, to wrench my mouth away from his.

"Damien, no!"

Sex, no matter how earth-shattering, won't fix what's broken between us, even if it might burn the edges off the pain for a while. It won't resurrect the trust he shattered or erase the months of manipulation and lies that brought us to this moment.

His hands fall away from me, but I'm too stunned to move away.

I glance down to find two buttons from my shirt scattered on the floor, victims of his desperate hands. I pull the fabric closed over the gap he created before lifting my gaze back to his face.

His eyes have gone black. Pain swims in their depths alongside bitter disappointment. The mask of desire that consumed his features moments ago crumbles and falls away, leaving his face naked and wounded.

Reality settles back over us. I see the moment it hits him too. His expression shifts and hardens as he retreats behind those walls again.

"How long are you going to punish me?"

"I'm not punishing you."

"It fucking feels like it."

He moves closer again, crowding me, but keeps his hands at his sides. My body tenses, uncertain whether I have the strength to push him away a second time if he reaches for me.

"I know I hurt you. But I don't know what else to say other than I'm sorry. I'm not a man who apologizes, Luna. I'm not a man who usually feels remorse."

A bitter, knowing smile tugs at the corner of my mouth. If that isn't the understatement of the century, I don't know what is.

"I'm not sorry for all of it. I'm not sorry about how we came together." That rough timbre slides through his voice, the one that's commanded my surrender in a hundred different ways. "I'm not sorry for having kept my identity hidden at first. But I am sorry for not telling you the truth when I realized I was falling in love with you. When I realized you were falling in love with me."

I open my mouth, then close it, searching for a response that doesn't exist.

"What are you going to do about Karen?" I ask instead, smoothing down my torn shirt and trying to reassemble the pieces of my composure.

His face goes blank, every emotion wiped clean.

"I'll figure it out."

His dismissal sends worry crawling up my spine.

"Are you going to kill her?"

The transformation is immediate and chilling. His eyes turn ice cold, his pupils contracting to pinpricks while his jaw hardens into granite. Every soft line in his face disappears, replaced by angles sharp enough to cut stone. This is the killer. This is what his victims see in their final moments. Not Damien Wolfe, or even my wolf, but death wearing a human mask.

"I don't kill innocents, Luna."

His voice is quiet enough that I have to strain to hear it, but it's loaded with enough menace to make me step backward.

This isn't the man I've fallen in love with, the one who takes me apart with his hands and mouth, the one who makes me forget my own name when he kisses me. This is the predator who's ended hundreds, if not thousands, of lives without losing sleep and will end hundreds more.

But fear doesn't touch me. It should, but it doesn't.

"I'm sorry. I shouldn't have asked that. I know you only kill those who deserve it."

His expression softens, some of the ice melting from his features, but violence still prowls beneath the surface like a caged animal.

"She's doing her job. I can respect that, even if it makes her a problem I need to solve."

I nod, not trusting my voice. Our situation crashes over me again. The impossibility of loving a man who solves problems with violence and death and who lives in shadows I can't comprehend.

"For what it's worth, I believe that you're sorry, Damien. And I appreciate your honesty about what you're not sorry for. But trust..." I swallow hard. "I don't know if I can give you that again."

The agony etched on his face is so intense, a sharp ache pulses in my chest.

"It has to be enough. There is no other option for me, Luna." He pauses, the muscles ticking in his jaw as if he's fighting some internal battle. "But I'll be patient."

"Will you really?" Skepticism colors every syllable.

He nods, but it's obvious what saying those words cost him, by the way his hands flex and his shoulders tense with the effort of restraint.

"But my patience has limits. When it runs out, if you haven't come to me..." His eyes lock on mine, holding me prisoner. "I'm coming for you."

It's both a promise and a warning.

Chapter Thirty-One

Damien

I catch sight of Cade as he leans against my office doorframe, arms crossed. I heard the helicopter land in the clearing behind the house a few minutes ago. I've been trying to concentrate on the reports in front of me for hours, but my attempt is futile because all I can think about is Luna's visit earlier.

It killed me to let her go after that kiss. I was this close to bending her over my desk and reminding her who we are together. But her words gutted me when she said she might never be able to give me her trust again. I refuse to accept that. I refuse to accept anything other than her having the grace to forgive me.

She wants space, but I don't know how long I'll be able to stay away. The last three days without her have been the longest and most torturous of my life.

"I thought you only needed thirty minutes. It's been two hours."

Pushing off the doorframe, Cade walks to the sofa and sits down. "Yeah, well, the county law enforcement databases are surprisingly difficult to hack. When I have some time, I'm going to get back in there and dig around their firewalls to see what they're doing differently. Might be something we can reverse engineer into our systems."

"Cade, I don't give a shit about the county's firewalls or the tire tracks. Tell me what you found out about that DNA."

He slides into business mode. "It isn't yours. I ran it against your profile to be sure. But whoever it is isn't in any public governmental database in the United States. I have the system running against foreign databases now, but that will take six to twelve hours to get back."

Relief floods through me, followed by frustration. "Then who the fuck—"

"Could be anyone." He shrugs, anticipating my question. "Random person who touched something at the scene after the fact. Contamination during processing. Hell, it could be the tech who collected it. But they would be in the system. Point is, Mills doesn't have shit. Coincidences and suspicions. That's all."

I lean back in my chair. "What else does she have?"

"Nothing concrete. She's fishing, hoping you'll make a mistake." Cade pauses. "Speaking of mistakes, I wish you'd told me Luna was in the room earlier. I really put my foot in it, didn't I?"

"Yes, you fucking did. That's your one free pass, Cade. She'll be my wife one day. You better fucking respect her as such."

The words leave my mouth before I've consciously thought them through, and the moment they're out, they slam into my chest and steal my breath. But underneath the shock, certainty settles into my bones. The truth of it resonates through every cell in my body. I'm going to marry her.

Fuck!

I never thought I'd have a wife. I never wanted one. But I fucking want her more than the air I breathe.

Cade arches a skeptical brow, though somehow he is not surprised by my words. "Does she know this?"

"Not yet. But she will."

"You never learn, Damien."

"Actually, I have." I let out a long breath. "She's considering giving me another chance. Thinking about it, at least. And I'm doing what she asked. Giving her the space she asked for. It's fucking killing me."

"That's good news on both fronts, though, right? Her considering and you actually respecting her boundaries for once. That's a big step for you. Don't fuck it up."

"You're an asshole, you know that?"

He shrugs, his mouth twitching into that ghost of a smirk he rarely lets out.

"I might've destroyed everything. But I'm not giving up. I'll do whatever it takes."

"She came to warn you about the sheriff. That's not the action of someone who wants you gone."

"No." I allow myself a thread of hope. "It's not."

"Look, I know I've been reluctant about your relationship. I've made that clear. But she's good for you, Damien. She keeps you grounded. You need that."

That's his way of saying I need someone to keep me from going completely off the rails. No one has ever been able to do that. But if anyone can, it's Luna.

"We'll see."

I glance out the window to my right. She's only half a mile away from me, through those trees, but the distance feels immense.

"So, I have an update on Caleb Hunter."

"Did you find the fucker?" I snarl at the mention of Luna's fuck of an ex. "It's been over almost a month since he threatened her."

"Negative. He knows how to stay off the grid. But we got a hit this morning. The trace I set up running facial rec on all traffic cameras in Colorado caught him for about three seconds heading into the Eisenhower Tunnel."

"East or west?"

"East."

"So he's heading this way?"

"It would seem so, but the camera at the east exit of the tunnel is out of order, so that's where we lost him. But he's not in that fancy car of his. It was a beat-up red pickup. That's probably why we haven't been able to track him. He's not using his own vehicle."

My pulse quickens, and cold fury washes over me, the familiar darkness rising like a tide.

"How this fucker has evaded us for this long is pissing me off, Cade. What good are our systems if we can't track one fucking piece of shit? I want him found. Tonight."

"Already on it. But Damien—" Cade hesitates. "We need to consider that he might try to approach her again."

"Luna's entire property is monitored."

"That didn't stop you from getting to her every night for months," he points out with infuriating logic.

"That's because I could shut off the cameras whenever I wanted to. They're on all the time now that she kicked me out and told me not to come back. And I never intended to hurt her." I slide into protection mode. "Reposition one of the satellites so it monitors her property twenty-four-seven."

Caleb Hunter will get near her again over my dead fucking body.

"Consider it done. I'm going to have to clean up a hell of a mess, aren't I?"

"Yes. He's a threat to her, and you know it."

He exhales, long and slow, the sound heavy with the knowledge of what's coming. "Are you going to tell her about it?"

The word "no" is on my tongue, but if I'm going to earn back her trust, I have to learn to be honest with her, even when it might worry her.

Fuck!

"I will. I'm going to try to see her tonight."

"And about the space she asked for?"

"I agreed to that before Caleb Hunter crawled out of his hole. Her space is going to be encroached on whether she likes it or not until he's found and dealt with."

Cade chuckles as he gets up to leave. "Good luck with that one."

Once he's gone, I try to work, but concentration eludes me. Every few minutes, I find myself checking the sanctuary's camera feeds, watching Luna move through her afternoon routine. She looks tired, dark circles shadowing those beautiful hazel eyes. I saw them when she was here earlier. She hasn't been sleeping either.

I grab my phone and send her a text.

Me

I know you want space, but there's something else we need to talk about. Can I come by later?

It feels like a lifetime passes before my phone buzzes with a reply.

Luna

> Does it have to do with what we spoke about earlier?

Me

> No. But I also have an update on that I can share.

Luna

> Really?? You'll share the info you have willingly?

Me

> I'm trying, Luna. Give me some fucking credit, will you?

I cringe as soon as I hit send. Snapping at her is going to get me permanent banishment from the sanctuary. It's another several minutes of my holding my breath before her reply comes through.

Luna

> Okay, Mr. Cranky Pants. You can come by after dinner. 7 PM.

The relief that floods through me is embarrassing in its intensity, almost as strong as the surprise. She's extending an olive branch. One I don't deserve, but I'll take it. I'll take anything she gives me.

Me

> See you then, little doe.

I wait to see how or if she'll reply. She didn't like the nickname at the beginning, but she doesn't seem to mind it anymore. She hasn't told me not to call her that in a while. When her reply comes, it goes straight to my cock.

Luna

> Until tonight, wolf(e).

Fuck! This woman is going to be the fucking death of me. And I wouldn't have her any other way.

I spend the rest of the day distracted, watching her on the cameras, anticipating seeing her. The way she moves through her sanctuary, checking on each animal with that gentle touch of hers, is hypnotic. Every gesture, every soft word she speaks, feeds my obsession. At six, I step away from the monitors and take Athena for a walk around the property.

"I might not be home tonight, girl, if I can get Luna to let me spread her out on her table. You think I've got a chance?"

Athena gives me a whuff that I swear says "fat chance, buddy" in dog speak. Smart animal. She knows I fucked up with Luna. But I'm willing to be optimistic. Or at least desperate enough to try. I've never been more desperate for anything in my life.

"You be a good girl." I give her one last scratch around her ears. "And maybe I can take you to see her tomorrow."

Yes, that's perfect. Luna said Athena was always welcome. That's my excuse to visit her while technically respecting the boundaries and distance she's asked for. She won't punish Athena for my mistakes. That's not how she operates.

The space she's asked for feels like a chasm between us. I need to bridge it, and I'm not above using Athena. But I need something else too.

Flowers.

That's what you bring when you're trying to apologize, right? If I'm going to grovel, something I've never done for anyone in my forty-six years, I should at least do it right.

The drive to Estes Park takes me through winding mountain roads, the familiar scenery making the drive pass in no time.

The florist shop is a quaint little place tucked between a coffee shop and an art gallery, its window display featuring winter arrangements. White poinsettias, frosted pinecones, and wreaths wrapped in red velvet ribbon. I pull up as an elderly woman flips the sign to "Closed."

I'm out of the car before she can lock the door. She looks up through the glass, takes in my expression and whatever desperation is written there, and her features soften. The lock clicks, and she opens the door.

"We're closed, but you look like a man with an emergency."

"Something like that." I step inside, breathing in the dense floral scent. "I need red dahlias. As many as you have."

She moves behind the counter, already assessing her stock. "Red dahlias specifically? That's particular."

"They're her favorite."

"Ah." Understanding crosses her face. "And you need to apologize."

"That obvious?"

She pulls buckets of flowers from the cooler. "Honey, I've been doing this for forty years. I know an apology arrangement when I see one coming." She selects dahlias first, then adds white lilies and cream roses. "These lilies symbolize regret. The white roses convey a sincere apology. And your red dahlias—those are devotion."

I watch her hands work, building something that looks both elegant and intentional.

"Will it help?" I ask.

She glances up, her brown eyes kind but honest. "Depends on what you did. But it's a good start."

I sign the credit card slip and add five thousand to the tip line. Her eyes widen when she glances at it, but I'm already on my way out the door.

My phone rings as I pass the town limits. Cade's name flashes on the dash display. I tap to answer.

"Yeah?"

"We've got a problem. Caleb Hunter was spotted heading toward the sanctuary twenty minutes ago. Alone, driving erratically."

Ice floods my veins. "Luna?"

"Still in the main house. Cameras show her letting Shadow out the back door for his evening run."

Fuck. That means her protector is outside when she needs him most.

"Patch me into the feed." I press harder on the accelerator. The Range Rover responds, engine roaring as I take the curves faster than I should.

"Check your screen."

The dashboard display splits to show multiple camera angles from inside Luna's house. She's moving around the kitchen, unaware of the danger approaching. The soft flannel shirt she's wearing, one of her grandfather's she loves so much, drowns her slight frame, sleeves rolled to her elbows. Her blonde hair tumbles from a messy knot at her nape, the strands falling across her cheek as she turns.

My hands tighten on the steering wheel. She looks so damn beautiful, so unguarded, with no clue what's coming.

"How far out are you?"

"Fifteen minutes, maybe less if I don't wrap this car around a fucking tree."

I'm going seventy on roads designed for forty, but I don't give a fuck. Nothing matters except getting to Luna.

"There's more. He stopped at Murphy's Gun Shop two hours ago. Picked up a Glock 19 and ammunition. He ordered it online a week ago."

The world goes red around the edges. This piece of shit thinks he can come to Luna's sanctuary armed? Thinks he can threaten the woman I love?

"How does a man with a restraining order against him buy a fucking gun?"

"I don't know. Colorado law prohibits it, but I'll have our people look into it."

It won't matter because I'm going to kill him tonight.

"Alert the sheriff. Anonymous tip about an armed, intoxicated man heading toward the sanctuary."

"Already done, but she's responding to a domestic on the other side of the county. ETA fifty-five minutes minimum."

Fifty-five minutes. Luna could be dead in five.

"Grab the helicopter and get your ass back here. Now."

"On my way. Damien—"

"What?"

"Don't do anything stupid. We can't afford to have the sheriff looking at you any closer than she already is."

Too late for that. If Hunter touches one hair on Luna's head, I'll paint the walls with his blood and deal with the consequences later.

I end the call and focus on the road, but my eyes keep flicking to the screen.

"Call Luna."

The phone rings through the speakers, but Luna doesn't react, and I don't hear her phone ringing.

Where is your fucking phone, Luna?

The call goes to voicemail.

Fuck!

She's moved to the living room now, checking her watch. She's expecting me and has no idea that her psychotic ex-boyfriend is minutes away from her door.

The camera feeds Cade patched through give me eyes everywhere. Interior angles, exterior perimeter, and blind spots I built into the system myself. The bitter irony isn't lost on me that the surveillance system I installed to spy on her is now the only thing allowing me to watch her potential murder in real time.

But right now, I'm grateful for every lens, every angle, every pixel that shows me she's still alive.

Luna pauses, head tilted like she's listening. Then she moves to the window and peers through the glass. Everything about her posture changes. Relaxation drains away, replaced by rigid tension.

"Fuck, fuck, fuck!"

I press the accelerator to the floor. The Range Rover's engine screams as I take a hairpin turn, tires squealing against the asphalt.

The microphone I disabled weeks ago so I wouldn't accidentally trigger it is my enemy now. I can't warn her. But the audio comes through crystal clear as Luna backs away from her front door. Caleb stumbles up her front porch steps, his heavy footsteps and the aggressive pounding on the wood making her flinch.

"Luna! Open this fucking door!" Hunter's voice is slurred. "I know you're in there!"

She approaches the door, calling through it. "Caleb, you need to leave. You're violating the restraining order."

The laugh that escapes his lips is ugly and bitter. "That piece of paper destroyed my life, you bitch! Open the door, or I'll kick it in!"

My hands are white-knuckled on the steering wheel. I'm still eight minutes out, and every second feels like an eternity watching this unfold.

"I'm calling the sheriff."

"Go ahead! By the time she gets here, we'll be long gone. You and I are taking a little trip, baby."

There's a crash as Hunter throws his body into the door. Luna stumbles backward and fumbles around, feeling for her phone in her pocket, and then her face fills with panic when she realizes it's not there.

Go upstairs and get your grandfather's shotgun, Luna!

"Don't make this harder than it has to be!" Hunter's voice booms through the door.

Another crash, and this time the door bursts open. Hunter stumbles inside, his face flushed with alcohol and rage.

"There's my beautiful ex-girlfriend. Miss me, baby?"

"How dare you break into my house!" Luna backs toward the kitchen, her chin up in that stubborn tilt I know so well. "What do you want, Caleb?"

"I want my life back!"

Hunter advances on her. Her eyes whip around the room, like she's calculating distances, looking for escape routes.

That's my girl.

"I want you to call your lawyer and tell him you're revoking the restraining order. I want you to admit you lied about me hitting you."

"It wasn't a lie."

Hunter's face twists with rage, and he lunges at her. Luna tries to dodge, but he's faster than his drunken stumbling suggests. His hand cracks across her face, the sound making my vision go crimson with fury.

"You always were too mouthy for your own good." He grabs her wrist as she tries to back away.

Luna fights back. She's not some helpless victim. Her free hand comes up, nails raking down his face and leaving angry red trails in their wake.

"Let go of me!"

She wrenches her body away, but he outweighs her by sixty pounds. He uses that advantage, slamming her against the counter. The impact drives air from her lungs in a visible gasp. Before she can recover, his hand swings back and connects with her face again—harder this time. Her lip splits, blood welling at the corner of her mouth.

"Stop fighting me, Luna. You brought this on yourself."

A bruise blooms across her cheekbone. Blood trails from the corner of her mouth. The dashboard clock mocks me.

Two minutes and forty seconds away.

Hunter's hand disappears behind his back. When it reappears, black metal glints in his grip. He levels the Glock at her face.

"Now, we're going to have a real conversation about how you're going to fix what you did to my life."

Luna stares down the barrel of the gun. All color drains from her face except for the blood from her split lip, but she holds her ground. Even bleeding, even staring down a gun, her chin lifts in defiance.

"You're drunk, Caleb." Fear roughens the edges of her words, but her voice holds steady despite the tremor underneath threatening to break through. "Put the gun down before you do something you can't take back."

"The only thing I can't take back is letting you destroy me." Hunter waves the gun in the air. "Do you know what it's like, Luna, to lose everything because one vindictive bitch decided to—"

Shadow materializes from the darkness beyond the threshold like a force of nature, 180 pounds of protective fury. Every line of his massive frame screams lethal intent, muscles bunched, and ears pinned flat against his skull. His lips peel back to reveal fangs designed for crushing bone and tearing flesh. The growl that rolls from his chest carries the promise of swift, brutal justice for anyone who dares to threaten Luna.

Hunter spins toward the sound, the weapon swinging wild and dangerous. "What the fuck—"

Shadow explodes into motion. The wolf that Luna has raised with gentle hands and patient love vanishes, replaced by something primal and savage, the instinct to protect her awakening the inherent fierce wolf inside him.

The gun goes off as Hunter staggers backward, the bullet wild and high, lodging in the wall in the hallway, but Shadow's momentum carries him into Hunter's outstretched arm.

They crash to the floor in a chaos of fangs and flesh. Hunter's screams mix with the wet sound of tearing fabric and crunching bone. The gun discharges again, the explosion deafening in the confined space. Shadow jerks and staggers sideways, crimson spreading along his gray ribs where the bullet carved its path. But his paws find purchase on the hardwood, and he positions himself between Hunter and Luna like a living shield.

Luna's voice breaks on his name, anguish and fear bleeding through every syllable.

Hunter scrambles for the gun he dropped, blood streaming from the bite wound on his arm, cursing as Shadow circles him like the predator he is.

Chapter Thirty-Two

Damien

The Range Rover's door slams against its hinges as I launch myself from the driver's seat and sprint toward the house. Luna's scream cuts through the mountain air, the kind of sound that bypasses thought and goes straight to muscle memory.

I move through the doorway like the deadly hunter I am, taking in the scene in a split second. Hunter on the floor, bleeding from a wolf bite, trying to grab the gun just out of reach. Luna, with blood on her face, edges her way around Shadow as she tries to reach the gun before Hunter gets to it, her eyes wide with terror and relief when she sees me. And Shadow himself, magnificent in his fury, standing guard despite his injury.

Hunter's head swivels toward the doorway. Recognition flickers across his face. Recognition and fear. His body lurches toward the gun, his movements sloppy with alcohol and pain and too fucking slow for me. I'm on him before he reaches it, my fist connecting with his jaw with a satisfying crunch of bone.

"You motherfucking piece of shit." I grab him by the throat, hauling him to his feet. "You don't fucking touch her."

I slam him against the wall. Plaster rains down, and a spider web of cracks spreads behind his head. The alcohol-induced bravado leaves his eyes, and terror takes its place.

"Please." Air rattles through his windpipe. His fingernails dig into my knuckles, drawing blood. "I wasn't going to—"

"You hit her." My voice is deadly calm. "You pointed a gun at her. You shot her wolf."

My grip tightens. His face shifts from red to purple, veins bulging at his temples. His mouth opens and closes like a fish gasping on dry land. The fear in his eyes is beautiful. Intoxicating.

"You're going to be begging for death when I'm through with you."

"Damien, stop!" Luna's voice cuts through the red haze of my rage. She's crouched beside Shadow, the gun on the floor beside her leg, as she checks his wound with gentle hands. "You're going to kill him!"

Hunter's windpipe shifts under my palm. Cartilage gives way like wet cardboard. His face deepens from purple to blue.

"That's the general idea, sweetheart."

"Please." Her hand touches my arm now, warm and insistent. "Not like this. Not in my home."

For a moment, the only sounds are Hunter's desperate wheezing and my own harsh breathing. My grip loosens, and Hunter's chest expands. Air rushes into his lungs in a desperate gasp. His legs give way beneath him, and he goes down hard, his body crumpling against the floor.

"If you ever come near her again." My voice carries the promise of unspeakable agony. "I will peel the skin from your body an inch at a time. I'll keep you alive for days while I dismantle you piece by piece. And when I finally let you die, it will be the greatest mercy you've ever known. Nod if you understand."

His head bobs like a dashboard ornament. Tears, snot, and blood stream down his face.

But the rage still burns in my chest. The beast still demands payment. My boot connects with his ribs, and something pops with a wet, muffled sound. I know the exact spots to cause maximum damage. And pain. His body folds and slides across the floor until his skull meets the baseboard with a hollow thunk.

The sound echoes in my bones, making me want to hear it again. I step closer. Another kick. Then another.

"Damien!" Luna's voice is sharper now, cutting through my bloodlust. "Stop!"

But I can't. Not when I can still see the blood on her face and the terror in her eyes when he pointed that gun at her. I grab Hunter by his hair, yanking his head back.

"Look at what you did to her." I force his gaze to Luna's bruised face. "Look at her blood on your hands."

"I'm sorry. I'm sorry, I'm drunk, I didn't mean—"

My fist crashes into his nose, and it flattens under the impact. Blood explodes across his face, and the sound he makes is barely human.

"You meant every fucking second of it." I hit him again. "Just like you meant it every time you hit her in the past."

"Damien, I mean it. He's had enough."

I look up at her, forcing my vision to focus. Fear lives in her expression. Not of Hunter whimpering on the ground. Of me. Of the violence she's witnessing.

"Not like this, Damien. This isn't who you are."

But it is. This violence, this craving for blood—it's woven into me as deeply as my need for her. The man who flies her favorite meals from Denver and the killer who'll slaughter anyone who hurts her exist in the same body.

"Please." Her hand settles on my shoulder, warmth pressing through my shirt, gentle but firm. Her touch calms the beast.

I won't do this here in front of her. I won't taint her with my darkness. Instead, I release Hunter, and he collapses into a pathetic heap again.

"Get out." I step back. "Run. Fast. Because if I see you again, I'll be the last thing you ever see."

Hunter struggles to his feet, slumping against the wall. His face is a ruin of blood and broken bone, and he's holding his ribs like they're on fire. Good. I hope he feels it with every breath.

He won't make it far. The satellite I had redirected to watch Luna will record wherever he goes. Cade and I will find him later once I'm sure Luna is safe.

Then I'll let my monster out, and Caleb Hunter will pay for this.

Chapter Thirty-Three

Damien

Hunter staggers toward the door, leaving a trail of blood on Luna's hardwood floor. As he reaches the threshold, his legs give out. The internal injuries from my kick, combined with the blood loss from Shadow's attack and the alcohol in his system, finally overwhelm him.

He collapses, tumbling down Luna's porch steps in a tangle of limbs. His head strikes the bottom step with a sickening crack, and he goes limp.

Luna rushes past me, her medical training overriding everything else.

"Don't move!"

She hurries down the steps. I follow, watching as she kneels beside him. Even in the dim porch light, I can see it's too late. Hunter's breathing is shallow and wet, blood bubbling at his lips. His eyes are wide with panic, but there's a growing glassiness to them that speaks of severe internal trauma. I've seen enough death to know when a body is shutting down.

"Punctured lung." Luna's hands move over Hunter's chest. "Multiple rib fractures, internal bleeding. Possible brain injury." She presses her fingers to his neck, checking his pulse. She looks up at me, her hazel eyes unreadable. "Pulse is thready."

I feel nothing. No regret. No concern. Just cold satisfaction that the threat to Luna has been eliminated.

She turns back to Hunter. His breathing comes in wet, labored gasps.

"Caleb, can you hear me?" His eyes drift unfocused, staring past her at nothing.

"Call 911." She starts CPR. It's futile, and we both know it. The damage is too extensive. No amount of effort will change that.

"Luna. There's nothing you can do."

She ignores me, continuing compressions with desperate movements. Tears stream down her face as she works, but we both know it's over.

"Luna, stop." I step closer, laying a gentle hand on her shoulder. "Sweetheart, he's dead."

She shoves my hand away, falling back on her heels. Blood from Hunter's injuries stains her hands and clothes.

"Don't touch me."

The words hit like a sledgehammer to the chest. I step back, giving her space as she wipes her bloody hands on her jeans with shaking fingers.

"I need to call Karen."

"She's already on her way. Cade called it in when Hunter first showed up."

"Cade?" Her head snaps up, eyes narrowing. "How did he know to—"

The rhythmic thump of helicopter blades cuts through the night air. We both look up as spotlights sweep across the yard, illuminating the gruesome scene.

"You should go inside and get cleaned up. I'll handle this."

"Handle this?" She chokes out, horrified. "Like you handled him? What's your plan, Damien? Another cover-up? Another body disposal?"

Her accusation cuts deep because it's accurate. My first instinct is damage control, protection, and elimination of evidence. It's who I am.

"If necessary." I won't lie to her. Not anymore. "I won't let anything happen to you."

The helicopter lands in the gravel parking area in front of the wolf enclosure.

"You killed him!" The words explode from her like shrapnel as she stands. "He's dead because of you!"

"He's dead because he threatened you." I take a step toward her despite her obvious revulsion. "I'd do it again without hesitation."

She stares at me, her eyes reflecting the porch light like those of a wild animal caught in headlights.

"Jesus Christ, who are you?"

"You know exactly who I am." I move closer despite her flinch. "I'm the man who hunts and kills the lowest filth. I'm the one who makes you scream night after night. I'm the monster you invited into your bed, Luna."

"I didn't invite you, Damien." Her chin lifts. "You forced your way in."

I won't insult her by arguing, won't add another lie to the mountain I've already built.

Cade leaps out of the helicopter before the rotors stop, carrying a large tactical bag. He takes in the scene with a quick, professional assessment.

"I saw the sheriff's lights as I was on approach. ETA twenty-five minutes at best." He sets down his bag and pulls out a pair of latex gloves. "What happened exactly?"

I give him a quick rundown. He listens without interruption, his expression growing grimmer with each detail.

Cade glances at Luna, noting her blood-streaked appearance, the bruises on her face, and the way she's holding herself apart from me.

"Dr. Foster. Are you injured other than those bruises?"

She swallows, tilting her chin up to meet his gaze.

"I'm fine."

Her voice unravels on the last word.

"I need to check on Shadow." She turns, but Shadow is right there beside her, still on full alert even though he's injured.

"Wait." Cade's voice stops her retreat. "We need to figure out what happens when the sheriff gets here. This scene tells a very specific story."

Luna's gaze darts between us, understanding dawning in her eyes. Her chest rises and falls faster. "You want to cover this up?"

"I want to protect you." I hold her gaze.

"From what? He attacked me. I defended myself—"

"You didn't kill him. Damien did. And the forensics don't support self-defense. Hunter's injuries are too severe and too focused. Any competent investigator will see this as murder."

Luna exhales, stepping back and twisting the edge of her bloody shirt between her fingers. She stares at Hunter's still form, then at me, chest heaving. Finally, she meets Cade's steady gaze.

"So what are you suggesting?"

He reaches into his bag and pulls out several evidence bags containing hair, clothing fibers, and what looks like dried blood. "We redirect the investigation. Make Hunter the perpetrator instead of the victim."

"What are those?" Luna's voice comes out strangled.

"Evidence from the other crime scenes. Daryl Rawlings, the Meyers couple, Raymond Davis, among others."

"Where the fuck did you get those?"

"You don't clean up as well as you think you do."

Cade returns his attention to Luna. "We plant this in Hunter's residence and make it look like he was the one killing them. Frame him as someone cleaning up loose ends by coming after you."

Her eyes widen. "You want to frame a dead man for those murders?"

"It's elegant. He had the motive. Ruined by your accusations, desperate to hurt you. In his twisted mind, killing abusers from your cases, dropping them on your doorstep, and setting it up to look like their deaths were tied to you was the perfect way to hurt you and your reputation before finishing the job personally."

Luna's analytical mind works through the implications. Horror still grips her. It shows in the tension around her mouth and the rigidity of her spine, but she's thinking past it now. She's smart enough to recognize that this could work. It could redirect Sheriff Mills' attention away from me and onto someone who can't mount a defense or claim he was framed.

But I can't let her compromise her morals like that. Not for me.

"No. We're not dragging Luna into this. I'll take responsibility for what happened here tonight."

"Damien, no." Luna's eyes meet mine, torn between horror and pragmatism. "If you confess to this, that will give Karen the excuse to look into you more closely."

"I'm a billionaire with the best legal team money can buy. I can survive the scrutiny."

"I'm not letting you sacrifice yourself for me." Luna's voice gains strength. She crosses her arms over her chest, shoulders squaring.

"You can't be serious about this, Luna."

She meets my eyes, and I see the steel in her gaze. The same determination she shows when she's fighting to save an injured animal.

"I'm a grown woman, Damien. If we're going to fix what's broken between us, you need to trust me to make my own decisions."

"Luna—"

"No." She cuts me off before turning to Cade. "What exactly are you proposing?"

Cade pulls out a tablet and swipes through photos. The basement. Stills from my videos. My justice documented frame by frame. Luna's face drains of color.

"What the fuck, Cade." I angle the tablet away, glaring at him.

Unfazed, he presses on. "Each victim was killed with precise, almost surgical violence. The kind that requires knowledge and planning. But Hunter's attack tonight was sloppy and desperate."

"So, we make it look like he was deteriorating." Luna's mind works through the logic, her breathing evening out. "The earlier murders were calculated, but by the time he got to me, he was unraveling."

"Precisely."

Luna straightens. Her hand moves to her mouth, fingers pressing against her lips like she's testing the lie on her tongue. "What about his body?"

"What body?" Cade looks between us. "There's no body."

I give him a sharp look. "What are you thinking?"

"Simple. Caleb attacked Luna. Luna fought back with Shadow's help. You showed up, punched him, slammed him into the wall, thought he was out cold. While you were tending to Luna and Shadow, he came to and fled. He's not dead; he's on the run."

Cade strides forward, grabbing Hunter's ankle. "Help me get him to his truck." I grab his arms. We hoist the corpse up, and I swing it over my shoulder.

"But the evidence—" Luna steps aside, face still drained of color, watching me carry the body toward Hunter's pickup.

"Goes to his apartment in Boulder." Cade walks to the back of the Range Rover and pulls a tarp out of the back. "I'll plant it there after the sheriff leaves. Make it look like he's been planning this for weeks."

Luna looks at me. "That still puts you at risk. Especially when Caleb's body is never found."

"Let us worry about that, little doe." I cover the body with the tarp.

"Damien, I swear to God, I'm going to kick you in the balls if you don't stop calling me that."

"There's my girl."

"I mean it." Her hand wraps around my wrist. "Isn't it too risky to have you here? Maybe you should go."

"Absolutely not. I'm not letting you deal with this on your own."

"You two can argue about this later. We're pressed for time here. Damien, drive the truck to your place. I'll take the helicopter and meet you there. We'll hide them in the garage until this blows over, then dispose of them. We'll be back in less than five minutes, Luna, and we'll get this scene cleaned and set to match the story."

"How long do we have?"

"Sheriff's probably eighteen minutes out now." Cade looks at Luna. "Are you sure you can do this? Lie to law enforcement about a man's death?"

"You don't have to do this, sweetheart. I'll tell them exactly what I did. Confess everything if you're at all unsure."

I'll rot in prison for the rest of my life if it will protect her.

Luna touches the bruise on her face, uncertainty and determination warring in her eyes as she looks at me.

"He came here to hurt me and my animals. If he'd lived, he would've tried again. If you hadn't gotten here when you did—" Her voice catches in her throat, a soft sigh escaping her lips as her eyes soften. "I can do this."

"Good." Cade turns to head to the chopper.

"Wait." He turns around at Luna's voice. "What about the surveillance footage? The system probably recorded everything."

Cade opens his bag and pulls out his tablet, swiping through a few screens. "Convenient system malfunction during the critical timeframe. Happens all the time with electronic equipment. The system now shows the cameras have been offline since yesterday."

Luna looks back and forth between us. "This is insane. We're really going to do this?"

"That's entirely up to you." I lift my hand to her uninjured cheek, relieved when she doesn't pull away. "I mean it. Say the word and I'll confess everything. Well, not everything."

The rotor blades kick up, slicing through the air. Wind whips around us as Cade lifts off, the helicopter rising into the darkness.

"No." Behind her eyes, uncertainty battles with resolve, but her voice doesn't waver. "You protected me tonight. Let me protect you."

Her words stop my heart. Why would she protect me after everything I've done?

But I don't have time to ponder it now, so I nod, reaching under the tarp and into Caleb's pocket, grabbing his keys.

"You need to change out of your clothes. You can't have Caleb's blood on you. Put them in a tied plastic bag and hide them. I'll incinerate them later."

Horror dawns on her face as she realizes her favorite shirt, her grandfather's flannel, has become another casualty of tonight.

"I'm sorry, sweetheart, but it has to go." She nods as tears well in her eyes.

I cup her face in my hands, and she's too shell-shocked to pull away. I lower my mouth to hers, pressing a soft kiss to her lips. She gasps, but I keep it brief, pulling back, even though all I want is to sink into her and lose myself.

"I'll be back in five minutes. Change and tend to Shadow. Cade and I will take care of everything, I promise."

Luna's phone rings as I get into Caleb's truck. She glances at the display before answering.

"Maren? No, I'm okay... What?" She meets my eyes. "Yes, Caleb was here. He attacked me, but Shadow protected me. He ran when Damien showed up. No, don't come up here tonight. Karen will want to process the scene, and I need to treat Shadow's wound. Caleb shot at him." Maren screeches through the phone. "He's fine. Yeah, okay, I'll call you when things calm down."

She hangs up and looks at me. "Maren listens to the police scanner sometimes. Since the first bodies showed up here."

"Good idea to keep her away. One less complication. I'll be back in five minutes. Now stand back a little. I have to peel out of here to make the tire tracks work."

She nods and wraps her arms around herself. It kills me to drive away and leave her there, but we're running out of time.

Cade and I are back in less than five minutes. He cleans and sets the scene, something he can do with his eyes closed by now, and I go in search of Luna. I find her in the sanctuary treatment room, cleaning Shadow's wound.

"How's he doing?"

Despite the tension in her body and the anguish visible on her face, her hands are steady.

"It's only a graze, thank God. He'll be okay. Won't you, baby?" Her voice trembles as she presses a kiss on his nose. He rubs his head against hers, and then he looks at me.

He's always trusted me with her until that night in the living room. The way he stood between us and then curled himself around her after she kicked me out, he knew I'd hurt her. But as he looks at me now, I feel like we've come to another understanding.

We're both willing to kill for her.

Cade comes into the room. "Everything is set. Sheriff is five minutes out. Do we need to go over the story one more time?"

Luna walks to the sink to wash her hands. "I know what I have to say."

We head back to the house, Shadow sticking close to Luna's side. We climb the front steps. Luna's front door is still hanging off the hinges, but Cade will secure it after the sheriff sees the scene as we've set it. I'll have a new one installed first thing in the morning. A fucking steel one.

"Remember," Cade says. "As far as you know, Caleb Hunter is alive. You have no idea where he went, and you're grateful Damien showed up when he did."

She lifts her chin, breath catching in the night air. "I can do this."

The sirens grow louder, red and blue lights flashing between the trees.

Luna reaches for my hand, her fingers threading through mine, and the simple gesture lands in my chest like a gift I don't deserve.

"No more lies between us after tonight, Damien." Her gaze locks onto mine, unwavering despite the horror of the last hour. "Promise me that."

"No more lies." I let the vow settle between us, knowing it changes everything.

"Then we better make this one count." She squeezes my hand once before releasing it, preparing herself for the performance we're about to give.

The sheriff's cruiser pulls into the driveway, headlights sweeping across the front of the house. As she climbs out of her car, I catch Luna's eye one last time.

She gives me the slightest nod, and I know we're committed now. Partners in this deception, bound together by shared secrets and mutual protection.

Sheriff Mills approaches with her hand resting on her gun, taking in the scene with sharp, intelligent eyes.

"Luna, we got a call about an armed intruder."

And so, the lies begin.

Chapter Thirty-Four

Luna

I can't stop staring at my hands. Caleb's blood is gone, but I can still feel the sticky, viscous sensation of it beneath my fingernails. Karen sits in front of me with her notepad and pen in her hand while Damien and Cade work on making sure the front door can be closed and secured for the night.

The speed with which they cleaned up and staged the scene to match our story is a little disturbing, but I refuse to dwell on that.

"Luna?" Karen's voice pulls my attention back. "I need to go over your statement one more time."

I look up from my hands to meet her keen gray eyes. Her gaze feels like it's stripping away layers of me, searching for the lies beneath the truth. Or is it the truth beneath the lies? I'm not even sure anymore.

"Of course." I sound steadier than I feel. "Whatever you need."

We're sitting in my living room, the same space where hours ago Caleb broke in and threatened me. The same space where Damien...

No. Don't think about that now.

"So, Caleb arrived around seven." She reads from her notepad. "He attacked you, shot Shadow, and then Mr. Wolfe showed up unexpectedly, scuffled with Caleb, and then he fled the scene without either of you realizing he left until after he was gone? Is that correct?"

"Mostly." The lie we've constructed feels wrong as it leaves my lips, like I'm choking on words that don't belong to me. "I was expecting Damien at seven, so his arrival wasn't unexpected, but Caleb showed up a few minutes before."

From his position by the door, Damien watches me with those intense blue-gray eyes that see straight through to my soul.

"And he said he was here to take you with him?"

"Yes. I have no idea why he thought I'd go anywhere with him. I guess that's why he pulled out his gun."

"Was that before or after he struck you?"

I grab the ice pack on the cushion next to me and place it against my bruised cheek. "After."

"She's answered these questions multiple times, Sheriff Mills." Damien's voice comes from behind her, only it's his wolf voice, low and dangerous. "Must you make her keep reliving the events from this evening? Shouldn't you be out trying to find the bastard?"

I look up at him, and he's scowling, and for some reason, it makes me want to smile.

"We're almost done, but let me ask you." Karen stands to look at him. "After you shoved Mr. Hunter's head into that wall and he fled, you immediately called your security consultant—" Karen checks her notes again, "—Cade Crawford?"

"Cade isn't my security consultant. He's the COO of my company, and he oversees our security division. I asked him to pull the security footage. I figured you'd need it. But when he discovered Luna's system was offline, I instructed him to come up here immediately to assess it on-site."

Karen raises a skeptical eyebrow. "In a helicopter?"

"My company maintains a rapid response team on standby at all times. Standard procedure when there's a potential threat to my person or property."

"And Dr. Foster is your property?" Karen doesn't bother to hide the edge in her voice.

Damien's eyes go cold and flat, but I cut in before he can say whatever lethal thing is forming on his tongue.

"Damien and I have been dating for a few weeks, Karen. I told you that. I—"

"Luna's safety is the most important thing to me, Sheriff Mills. I always have a helicopter on standby to get me or my team to her at a moment's notice."

I don't know whether he's lying or not, but something tells me he's telling the truth. A warm shiver ripples through me, and the way his eyes snap to me, I know he saw it.

"And where is this helicopter now?" Karen asks.

"Parked on my helipad next door. I'm more than happy to show it to you if you need to see it."

"Not at this time, but thank you."

Karen makes another note on her pad. "Convenient that Mr. Crawford arrived so quickly. Even faster than I was able to get here."

"Not convenience, Sheriff Mills. Efficiency." Cade steps forward from his position near the door. Unlike Damien's calculated charm, Cade exudes an aura of military discipline and barely restrained power. The perfect attack dog for a man like Damien Wolfe.

Outside, a forensics team photographs the front porch and driveway, their flashlights dancing like fireflies in the darkness. Police radios crackle, voices too low to make out the words.

The clock on the wall reads 10:57 PM. Has it only been four hours since Caleb stumbled into my life for the last time? Since I watched Damien kill him with his bare hands? Since I agreed to lie to protect him, a killer, the same killer who's been in my bed for months and in my heart for almost as long?

My hands shake. I press them flat against my thighs, hoping no one notices.

"Luna!"

Maren bursts through the front door, shaking off the deputy who tries to stop her. Her dark curls are wild around her face, and her eyes are wide with panic. She rushes to me, dropping to her knees in front of my chair.

"Jesus Christ, I know you told me not to come until tomorrow, but there is no fucking way I was waiting. Are you okay? What happened?" She lifts her hands, letting them hover beside my cheeks. "Shit, your face."

"I'm fine." I catch her shaking fingers in mine.

Maren's sharp gaze takes in the room. Karen with her notepad, the deputies hovering near the doors, the forensics team visible through the windows, Cade by the stairs, and finally, Damien standing beside my chair.

"You." Venom drips from that single syllable. "Is this because of you? What the hell did you do?"

"Maren, stop. Damien didn't do anything. He saved me. I told you, it was Caleb."

"I'm going to kill that bastard if I ever see him again."

Don't say things like that right now, Maren. I'm barely holding it together.

"Maren." Karen sighs her name. "This is an active crime scene. Who authorized your presence?"

"No one has to authorize my presence here. I practically live here."

"At this time, I must insist that only family be present until forensics have finished their work."

"Luna and I are family." Red creeps up Maren's cheeks, her temper rising to the surface. I need to intervene before she gets herself arrested.

"Karen, all this activity has stressed many of the animals. I told Maren she didn't need to come, but now that she's here, I need her to help settle them."

Karen closes her eyes for a half second and nods. "Fine. But she stays out of the way."

Maren looks back at me. "Luna, what the hell is going on?"

"Caleb came here tonight. He was drunk and angry." I motion to my face. "He hit me, then tried to shoot Shadow. He's okay." I reassure her again, squeezing her hands when her eyes flash. "He was just grazed. But then Damien showed up, and he and Caleb fought. We thought he'd knocked out Caleb, but while Damien was taking care of me, he took off."

Even though we rehearsed this story, saying the words aloud makes them feel real.

"You let him go?" Maren turns her anger on Damien again.

"Taking care of Luna and Shadow was my priority."

"Where is Shadow now?" She looks around, searching for the protector that rarely leaves my side.

"I put him in my bedroom because he was getting agitated with all the men around. Can you grab him and take him over to the wolf enclosure? Get him away from all these people? And then go check on the other animals to make sure they're all alright?"

Maren nods as she stands. "Yeah. I'll take care of it."

Karen looks toward the door where one of her deputies is motioning for her to come outside. "If you'll excuse me. I need to check in with my team. Don't leave the premises." She gives Damien a pointed look. "Any of you."

As soon as Karen is out of earshot, Maren whirls on Damien, her eyes blazing. "This is all your fault."

Damien raises an eyebrow. "How exactly is Hunter coming after Luna my fault?"

"Everything was fine until you came into her life." Maren looks around and lowers her voice. "First as her creepy masked stalker, then as her lying next-door neighbor. Luna's life has been chaos ever since."

My heart pounds faster. "Maren, please—"

"No, Luna, I won't shut up this time. This asshole manipulated you and lied to you. God knows what else he's hiding." She squares off against Damien despite being almost a foot and a half shorter. "You're a one-man apocalypse. Even your looks aren't enough to make up for it."

Damien's expression doesn't change, but his shoulders tense. He's restraining himself. Because of me.

"Caleb coming here had nothing to do with Damien." I stand and place myself between them. "He came because he thought I ruined his life. Maybe I did."

"That's bullshit!" Maren and Damien say at the same time before they glare at each other.

"I still think it's his fault." Maren turns back to Damien. "You broke my best friend's heart, asshole. No matter what she decides, you and I will never be right. I'm going to be watching you."

I love Maren for how protective she is, but now's not the moment.

Cade steps forward. The air in the room seems to compress around him, molecules bending to make space for a presence that commands attention without asking for it.

"Ms. Rodriguez, I understand your concern for your friend, but this is not the time or the place for this kind of private conversation."

Maren turns her fury on him. "And who the hell are you?"

"Cade Crawford, head of security for Wolfe Technologies."

The energy between them shifts, crackling to life like a live wire touching water. Maren's gaze travels down his frame, studying him, over the network of white scars threading along his throat where his shirt collar gaps open. Then over the hands that rest at his sides, empty but coiled, like sleeping weapons waiting for a command.

Her attention lingers on the silver threading through his dark hair. Not the soft silver of age, but the hard-earned kind that comes from walking through fire.

"Well, Mr. Crawford." The words come out slow, each syllable loaded with challenge. "If you're so good at security, where were you when Luna needed protecting from your boss?"

A ghost of a smile touches Cade's lips. "Ms. Rodriguez, you misunderstand the nature of my employment. I protect Mr. Wolfe's interests. And currently, his primary interest is Dr. Foster and her well-being."

"Maren." I divert her attention before she can continue this dangerous line of questioning. "Shadow really needs tending to. I did a rough clean of his wound and gave him some Gabapentin, but it needs a closer look."

She hesitates, torn between staying to protect me and doing what needs to be done for Shadow and the sanctuary.

"I'll be fine. This will all be over soon."

"Fine." She relents, but it's obvious she doesn't want to. She turns to Damien, jabbing a finger at him. "I'm watching you, Wolfe. If you hurt her again, I will gut you like a fish. Billionaire or not."

Damien doesn't flinch. "I would expect nothing less."

Maren holds his gaze before turning to head upstairs. As she passes Cade, she pauses, looking up at him with narrowed eyes. "That goes double for you, Rambo."

To my surprise, Cade laughs, a low, rumbling sound like distant thunder.

"Noted, Ms. Rodriguez."

Maren storms up the stairs, and Cade watches her go, his gaze lingering on her retreating form with unmistakable interest. I turn to Damien and find him looking at me as Cade slips out the front door, closing it behind him.

The whole fucked-up situation crashes into me. The blood, the lies, the bodies, and now Maren and Cade. A hysterical laugh bubbles up from my chest.

"Did your right-hand man just check out my best friend?"

Damien frowns. "It would appear so."

"She'll eat him alive." I imagine fierce, chaotic, take-no-prisoners Maren against Cade's controlled military demeanor.

"I wouldn't be so sure." He moves closer. "Are you alright?"

The genuine concern in his voice nearly breaks me. How can he ask that? How can he stand there looking worried about my mental state when he's the reason I'm questioning everything I thought I knew about myself?

"No. I don't think I'll ever be alright again."

Pain flickers across his face. "I never wanted this for you."

"Didn't you?" I challenge. "You wanted me to accept all of you. The monster and the man. Well, congratulations. I've seen both now."

"And?"

His hand brushes mine, the touch so light it could be accidental. But nothing Damien does is ever accidental.

"What do you want me to say?" I keep my voice low even though we're alone. "That I'm okay with what happened? That I'm not horrified by what I've become part of?"

"No. I want you to be honest. With me, if not with them."

Honest. What does honesty even mean now? Is it honest to admit that despite the horror and moral revulsion churning in my stomach, there's also a thread of dark satisfaction in knowing Caleb can never hurt me again? Is it honest to acknowledge that when I saw Damien's violence tonight, part of me recognized it as the same intensity he brings to our passion?

"I don't know what I feel anymore." It's the closest thing to the truth I can offer. "I look at you, and I see two different men. The one who spent months deceiving me and the one who will kill to protect me."

"They're the same man. I've never been anything other than what I am, Luna. I just showed you different facets at different times."

"And who are you exactly?"

His eyes hold mine. "Yours. Every part of me is yours. The dark and the light."

The words echo in my chest, finding resonance in places I didn't know existed until he awakened them. Places where the veterinarian, who dedicates her life to healing, meets the woman who welcomed a masked killer into her bed. Places where compassion tangles with desire and where moral absolutes blur into shades of gray.

"I need time, Damien." I repeat what I told him earlier. "To figure out who I am now. I'm not the same woman who almost shot you on her porch three months ago."

He nods. But his face tells a different story.

Maren comes down the stairs with Shadow at her side, her expression still wary but less hostile. "I think the gabapentin is wearing off. I'm going to give him a little more before I take a look at that wound again. He's still a bit agitated."

"Thank you."

He comes to me, and I crouch to hug him, rubbing my hand down his side, careful of his bandage. He rubs his head against my shoulder, his fur warm and soft, and tears well in my eyes. He saved me from Caleb tonight. Both he and Damien, but my wolf threw himself between me and an oncoming bullet, leaving me with an impossible feeling of gratitude.

I lift my eyes to look at Damien, and I know with absolute certainty that my other wolf would have done the same.

My attention shifts to Maren, who's drilling holes in Damien with her stare.

"Thank you for this, Mar."

She runs a hand through her curls. "When we're done here, we're breaking open that bottle of Fireball Ethan gave you at Christmas. We both need a drink, and you look like hell."

"Thanks. You're always so good for my ego."

"That's what friends are for." She squeezes my arm, then turns and makes an "I'm watching you" gesture toward Damien several times, two fingers pointed at him, then at herself, before heading toward the door.

"Come on, Shadow." She calls to him, and I stand up, urging him to go to her. On his way, he stops in front of Damien. He looks up, and when Damien offers his hand, Shadow lowers his head before bumping and licking his palm. A sign of trust between wolves and deference to an alpha.

Damien is no doubt an alpha, and Shadow always deferred to him, trusting him with me. Right from the start.

Maren and Shadow walk out the door, giving Cade a wide berth as they leave, but their eyes lock.

I nod toward them. "It seems I'm not the only one with questionable taste in older men."

Damien follows my gaze, observing the charged interaction. "Cade is only fifty-five. The gray makes him look older. You should see when he lets his beard grow in. But don't let it fool you. He's still quite capable."

"Oh, I've seen what he's capable of."

As Maren walks away, Cade tracks her movement again. She glances back, catching him watching her. Her eyes narrow to dangerous slits, and her lip curls into a snarl, enough to communicate exactly what she thinks of his interest. Cade meets her hostility without blinking, and his lips pull into a subtle but unmistakable smile. An expression that says he's just found something interesting to hunt.

"Cade is going to get himself slapped."

"Or something else entirely."

"Is that a Wolfe Group hiring requirement?" I'm unable to keep the edge out of my voice. "Attraction to stubborn, troublesome women?"

Damien's eyes soften as he looks at me. "Not troublesome. Extraordinary."

The word catches me off guard, warming places inside me that I've been trying to keep cold and rational. I can't afford to melt now, not when I need clarity more than ever.

Karen walks in, and Cade follows.

"Forensics is done for tonight. They may come back in the morning to do one last sweep, but what they found so far matches your version of events." She looks at Damien, then Cade. "I would recommend staying local in case I have any more questions.

"I'm not leaving Luna's side."

I know he means it, but I have to get him out of here. I can't deal with his hovering tonight.

Karen walks out the door, and Damien follows, moving to stand on the porch.

I watch him through the window, taking in the rigid line of his spine and the careful control in every gesture, and my mind drifts to what tomorrow will look like.

Will the light of day make this nightmare clearer, or will it simply illuminate how far I've strayed from the person I thought I was?

One thing I know for sure. There's no going back to who I was before Damien Wolfe climbed into my bed.

That woman died tonight.

Who I am now, standing in the wreckage left behind.

She remains to be seen.

Chapter Thirty-Five

Damien

The night air bites against my skin as I stand on Luna's porch, watching Sheriff Mills and the forensics team's headlights disappear down the gravel drive, taking with them their questions and suspicion. My shoulders drop and my muscles unclench, but the tension that's been knotted inside me all night remains.

"Thank God that's over." Luna steps up beside me, and I turn to look at her. Her voice sounds like sandpaper, worn thin by hours of careful answers and calculated half-truths. In the dim yellow glow of the porch light, she looks like a ghost of herself, all the warmth drained from her face, leaving behind someone pale and brittle.

She was magnificent tonight, revealing nothing that would bring more suspicion down on us. But now, watching her sway on her feet, the cost of that performance sits heavy between my ribs. My eyes drift to the bruises on her face, and the phantom feel of Caleb's bones yielding beneath my hands sends a thrill through me that I have to suppress.

Not now, you sick fuck.

Not with Luna looking like she's one wrong word away from shattering. I wish I could kill that bastard all over again.

"I've got Shadow settled." Maren's voice comes from the door behind us. She must have slipped in through the kitchen while we were distracted by Mills and her team leaving. "He's all drugged up and feeling good now."

Luna nods, running a hand through her hair. "Thanks, Mar. I don't think I could handle this alone tonight."

The words feel like a knife twisting in my gut. I want to be the one she turns to, not Maren. I've protected her. Isn't that worth something? But the truth sits there, unspoken but impossible to ignore. I'm the reason she's shaking beneath her composed exterior. Not Caleb. Not what he did to her. But what I did to him.

What I am.

Maren's gaze finds mine. The hostility in her eyes burns hot enough to incinerate me where I stand. The echo of her words from earlier rings in my ears.

This is all your fault.

She isn't wrong. Everything was fine in Luna's life until I entered it. Now, there's police tape across her property and blood on her hands.

"We should check on the other animals." Luna turns back toward the house. "The commotion likely stressed them all."

I follow her inside, watching how she moves, slightly hunched, as if carrying an invisible weight. She grabs a jacket from the hook beside the door. Even exhausted and traumatized, she's thinking about her animals first. It's one of the things I love most about her.

She and Maren head toward the kitchen to go out the back door. It's the quickest way to the sanctuary's main building.

"I can help." I hate how desperate I sound. Like a kicked dog begging for scraps.

Maren steps outside, but Luna pauses with her hand on the doorknob. For a heartbeat, I think she might say yes, but then she shakes her head.

"Maren and I can handle it."

She turns back, and when our eyes connect, the expression she's wearing drives the air from my lungs.

"Damien, we need to talk about what happened tonight." Her voice catches, and she stops to steady it. "And I need to know the truth. All of it."

My heart pounds. This is the moment I've both craved and dreaded. The chance to reveal myself to her, and the near-certain knowledge that when I do, she'll turn away forever.

"I'll tell you everything." I step closer to her. "Whatever you want to know."

"Not tonight." Her voice is firm. Final. "I need to process what happened. And the animals have to be my priority right now."

Of course they do. The wounded creatures always come first with her. It's equally admirable and infuriating.

Cade is doing a last sweep of the property before he heads to Boulder to plant the evidence in Hunter's apartment. He doesn't need me for that. He's handled worse jobs on his own. And I can't bear to leave her.

"Let me stay." The naked vulnerability in my voice makes me cringe. I've never begged anyone for anything in my life, but with Luna, all my control evaporates. "I don't want to leave you like this."

A softness flickers in her eyes, but resolve replaces it.

"No. I need space, Damien. Maren's here. We'll be fine." She wraps her arms around herself. "I'll call you tomorrow. I'll come to your house, and we can talk then."

The dismissal stings more than I want to admit.

"I don't like the idea of you and Maren outside this late at night."

Her laugh is sharp and humorless. "We'll be fine, Damien. I survived thirty-two years without you."

Ouch.

"Promise me you'll be careful."

"We always are." She pauses. "But I think the biggest danger in my life just asked to spend the night."

I am dangerous. To her safety and to her peace of mind. I've already dragged her into the darkness she never asked for.

"I'll stay until the two of you finish your rounds outside. For my peace of mind, if not yours."

Luna sighs, and the fight leaves her. She's too exhausted to argue, too worn down to push back against my stubborn insistence.

"Fine. But stay out of my way, Damien. I can't do this with you tonight."

"I'll sit in my car. If you need me to help with anything—"

She disappears through the back door before I can finish.

I make my way to the front of the house. Cade is leaning against the passenger side of the Range Rover, checking something on his phone.

"Everything all clear?"

He looks up. "Yes. I need to get out of here if I'm going to beat them to Hunter's place."

"You think you'll make it?"

He arches a brow.

Right. Stupid question. Cade has been handling impossible timelines for me for over two decades. If he says he'll make it, he'll make it.

"Are you staying here tonight?"

"She doesn't want me here. Maren's staying, but I'm not leaving her."

His eyes darken at the mention of Maren's name, but I can't deal with that tonight, any more than Luna can deal with me. For as obsessive as I am about Luna, Cade is ten times worse when something catches his attention.

"I can turn the cameras back on, and you can watch her in your car. Though it might be too suspicious if they start working right after the sheriff leaves."

"I don't need to see inside the house. I just need to be close."

He nods, understanding without explanation. It's one of the things I value most about him. He doesn't waste time with questions when he already knows the answers.

"I'll call you when it's done."

"No, let's keep off the airwaves for the rest of the night. Only call if you run into a problem."

He nods and heads to the truck. After he leaves, I walk to the Range Rover. I slide into the driver's seat, positioning myself so I have clear sight lines to everything that matters. Most importantly, I can see Luna's bedroom window on the second floor.

Luna and Maren work for the next hour, moving from enclosure to enclosure, checking on each animal, offering comfort, and restoring order. Luna focuses on the animals, forgetting her own distress as she tends to theirs.

They finish with the last enclosure, and Luna locks the sanctuary building, double-checking the door before she and Maren cross the yard to her house. She looks my way. Even from here, her expression is clear.

Go home, Damien. You're dismissed.

Fuck! I love this woman. Even when she guts me.

I make a show of starting the Range Rover and driving away. But I return three minutes later, turning off the headlights and the engine as I coast in neutral back up the driveway. I park far enough down that she won't see me if she looks out the window, but close enough that I can still see the house.

The lights come on upstairs. In the warm glow of her bedside lamp, Luna finally breaks. She sits on her bed, and her shoulders begin to shake. Maren sits beside her, wrapping an arm around her as Luna collapses against her friend, her sobs visible even from this distance.

The steering wheel creaks under the pressure of my grip. This is the second time I've made her cry. I want to be the one comforting her. I want to wrap her in my arms and keep her safe from everything. Including myself. But I've lost that right, if I ever had it at all.

Maren strokes Luna's hair as she cries, and Luna's lips move, pouring out words I can't hear. Is she telling Maren everything? About me? About what happened tonight? About what I am?

No. She wouldn't betray me. I'm certain of it.

I stay for another hour, watching as Luna eventually calms. After changing into pajamas, she and Maren climb into bed together. Maren won't leave Luna alone tonight, something I'm grateful for, even as jealousy burns through my veins.

Then Maren gets up and walks to the window. For a moment, she stands there, her silhouette dark against the golden light, and I swear she's looking right at me. Her eyes scan the yard and driveway as if she suspects I'm here, and then she pulls the curtains closed with a sharp jerk, shutting me out.

Chapter Thirty-Six

Damien

Two days later, Luna sits across from me in the armchair by the fireplace. She's on the edge of the seat, back straight, hands gripping her knees, ready to bolt at any moment. An emergency with a yellow-bellied marmot yesterday took up her entire day, preventing this conversation, but ten minutes ago she walked through my door and announced it was time to talk.

Luna's eyes meet mine, unwavering despite the dark circles beneath them. The bruise on her cheek has bloomed into a swirl of purple and yellow, and my blood boils at the sight. If Caleb Hunter were still alive, I'd kill him again. Nice and slow.

"Can I get you something to drink?" I force the words out first, filling the silence before it can become unbearable. My voice sounds steadier than I feel, nothing like the anxiety twisting through my gut. "Coffee? Water? Something stronger?"

"Whiskey. If we're doing this, I need something stronger than coffee."

If she knew what I'm about to tell her, she'd ask for the whole damn bottle.

I nod, moving to the bar in the corner. I pour two fingers into matching glasses, my hands betraying none of the turmoil churning inside me. The amber liquid catches the firelight, reminding me of her eyes when she's angry.

"I didn't tell you the day I was here, but I like how you renovated this office. It feels very you. Dark and mysterious with a touch of modern."

I settle into the chair opposite her, cradling my own drink. Her awkward attempt at normal conversation would be endearing if the circumstances were different.

"You're terrible at small talk, Luna."

She shrugs, and I catch the ghost of that brittle smile I've seen on her face too often recently. "We can get right to it if you prefer."

"This house was not meant to be a home, but rather a place I don't have to hide who I am."

"And who are you?" Luna takes a small sip of whiskey, her eyes never leaving mine. "The billionaire CEO? The masked stalker? The killer?"

Christ. She doesn't pull any punches, does she? No one has ever looked at me like this, seeing all my pieces and demanding I explain how they fit together. It should terrify me, but instead, it makes me want to bare my throat to her.

"All of them. They're not separate people, Luna. Just different facets of the same man."

"Tell me about that man, Damien."

The way she says my name, not with fear or disgust, but with something that sounds almost like tenderness, tightens my chest.

"I killed my first target when I was twenty-one." I choose to start in the middle rather than at the beginning. The beginning is too dark. "He organized dog fights."

Luna's expression doesn't change as she takes another small sip of her whiskey. "Did you plan it?"

"Yes." I hold her gaze, refusing to soften this for her. If she wants the truth, she gets all of it. "Every detail. I'd been tracking him for months, learning his patterns. I wanted him to know exactly why he was dying."

"And did he?"

"Yes." The memory surfaces. His panicked eyes as understanding dawned, the pleading, the promises to change. Like I used to plead. "They all do, in the end."

Luna nods. "How many?"

"Fifteen hundred fifty-eight now." I wait for the horror to register, for her to see the monster sitting across from her. "Including the ones you know about."

Her eyes widen as she absorbs this, her fingers tightening around her glass. But she doesn't jump up and run. She doesn't even flinch.

"Why?"

I can't sit still under her scrutiny. The truth is clawing at my throat, desperate to get out after decades of silence. I need to move. Need to put distance between us before I do something stupid like reach for her and beg her to save me from myself.

I stand and cross to the window, setting my glass on the desk as I pass it. Outside, the forest stretches vast and primeval, the perfect hiding place for predators like me.

"I was nine when my father decided to make a man out of me." The words stick in my throat. I've never said this out loud. Not to anyone. Not even Cade knows the whole truth. "He'd been using his fists since I was five, but that wasn't getting him the results he wanted." I have to pause and force air into my lungs. "We had a German Shepherd named Rex. Beautiful dog. The only thing in that house that ever looked at me with love."

Behind me, Luna inhales a sharp intake of breath, but I can't turn around. Can't see the horror that's dawning in her eyes.

"My father said that caring about animals was for women and weaklings." My hands clench into fists at my sides. "So, he decided to cure me of my softness."

"What did he do?" Luna's voice is almost inaudible.

The memory unfolds like a nightmare I can never escape. "He tied Rex to a post in our basement. Handed me a baseball bat." My voice cracks, betraying the nine-year-old boy still trapped inside me. "He said if I didn't beat the dog to death, he'd do it himself."

Luna's glass hits the floor, the crystal shattering like my childhood did that day.

"I begged him. Pleaded. Told him I'd do anything else." The words are pouring out now, unstoppable. "But he just smiled that cold smile of his and said it was for my own good. That I'd thank him when I was older."

I turn around, and the tears streaming down Luna's face nearly break what's left of my black heart.

"I couldn't do it." I swallow over the lump in my throat. "I dropped the bat and tried to run. But he caught me, tied me to the post next to Rex, and made me hold him while he did it instead. Made me look into the dog's eyes as he died. Made me feel his blood on my hands... my face."

"Oh God, Damien." Luna's voice breaks on my name.

"Rex tried to protect me. He didn't know I was the reason he was being hurt." Another sob escapes her lips. "That's when something died inside me too. Or maybe when something else was born."

I cross back to her, kneeling in front of her chair, desperate to make her understand. Whiskey soaks through my pants while shards of glass I barely feel cut into my knees.

"My father didn't stop there. Every few months, he'd bring home a new animal. Dogs mostly, but also cats. Even a rabbit once. And every time, he'd make me choose—kill it myself, or watch him kill it. He broke my hands more times than I can count because I tried to shield them from the blows. It went on for years. I started breaking their necks before the first blow. It was the only mercy I could give them."

Luna's expression softens, horror giving way to compassion. She reaches for me with trembling hands, cupping my face like I'm something precious instead of the monster I became. "You were just a child."

"I was, until I wasn't." I lean into her touch, starving for gentleness after decades of self-imposed isolation. "My mother stood by and let it happen. When they realized I wasn't going to fall in line, they shipped me off to boarding school. I never saw them again until the night they died."

"I thought you said they died in a home invasion."

"They did."

I wait for her to connect the dots. Confusion furrows her brow, then smooths out as understanding hits. Her hands fall from my face as her eyes snap to mine, wide with shock.

"Damien, what are you saying?" Her voice trembles on the words.

My gaze shifts to the fire, hands gripping my knees to resist touching her, before meeting her eyes again.

"The night of my sixteenth birthday, he showed up at my dorm. They were mostly empty because it was Thanksgiving weekend. There were only three of us there, I think. I was shaken awake after midnight and dragged out of bed. He demanded I come home but wouldn't tell me why. When we got there, he led me down to the basement. There were four dogs and six cats in cages. He'd been starving them for a week."

Luna's face drains of color, and her eyes fill with a horror that tears through me. She doesn't even know my worst sin yet.

"I finally fought back that night. I was bigger than him by then. Stronger. So, I grabbed the bat from his hands, and I—" I swallow. "I broke every bone in his body. One by one. Like he'd done to dozens of innocent animals. Like he'd taught me to do. And I made him beg, like I used to beg."

She reaches for me again, and her thumbs stroke across my cheeks, wiping away tears I didn't realize I was shedding. I haven't cried since the night the last animal died in my arms.

"My mother heard the commotion and came down to the basement. When she saw what I'd done, she started screaming. Calling me a monster. Telling me she wished I'd never been born."

"That fucking bitch." The words explode from Luna, raw with anger I've never heard from her before.

"She grabbed the bat and came at me." I need to purge myself of this hate-filled memory. "Screaming that I should die the way my father did. That it was all my fault all those animals died. If I'd just killed Rex that first time, my father would have stopped."

"No." Luna's fingers tighten on my cheeks as she rests her forehead against mine. I close my eyes. "You are not to blame for those animals, Damien. Do you hear me? Your father was. Only him. And your mother for letting it happen. That little boy you were deserved protection. Those animals deserved protection."

"But they didn't get it. And that's when I understood my father's lesson. I was meant to protect them. But I couldn't." I open my eyes, letting her see the darkness that lives there. "So, I've spent the last twenty-five years making sure no animal suffers the way Rex did. The way all of them did. And if I can't or I'm too late to stop it, I avenge them. I make sure their abusers suffer exponentially worse."

"What happened to your mother?" Her voice is hesitant, and I suspect she knows the answer already.

I pull away from her and close my eyes again, letting my head fall forward as I drown in the memory.

"I wrestled the bat away from her and told her I was calling the police. I was finally going to expose them as the monsters they were. She grabbed a pipe and started toward the cages, and I snapped. It took one swing. The bat connected with the side of her head. She died instantly."

Luna's breath hitches, and it sounds like she's suppressing a choked sob. I can't bring myself to look up and see what her eyes might show.

"I fed the animals and released them behind our house. Then I cleaned up any traces of my having been there and hitchhiked back to school. I was at lunch in the dining hall the next afternoon when the police arrived to tell me my parents had died in a suspected home invasion. They're the first two I killed. I didn't regret it then, and I don't regret it now."

I expect her to push me away and rush out of here. Never look back. But she doesn't. Instead, her soft lips brush against my forehead as she whispers my name and "I'm so sorry."

I stand, needing space to think, to breathe, to figure out why telling her this feels like bleeding out. I move to the window again. The forest spreads before me, swallowed in shadow. The darkness goes on and on, reflecting the void that's taken up residence inside me.

"So, they're why you started hunting animal abusers?"

She's trying to make it simple, but nothing about me is simple.

"No, it's bigger than that. It's about justice where the system fails. It's about consequences for those who think they're above the law. Like my parents."

"Oh, Damien." She chokes on my name, the sound caught in a sob that rises from somewhere deep in her chest.

The window reflects her image back at me, tears cutting paths down her cheeks, her shoulders shaking, and her face twisted with grief. Seeing her cry for me drives the air from my lungs and hollows out my chest.

"Don't cry for me, little doe. I don't deserve your tears."

"The little boy you were does. Those animals do." She swipes at her cheeks. "That's why you said your mother got what she deserved?"

"Yes. They both did." The words are final and unchangeable, just like my past. "They left me a substantial inheritance and my father's real estate development firm. Blood money. That's all it was. The executor of my father's estate oversaw my care until I turned eighteen. First thing I did was liquidate my father's company. Sold every property, every asset. I wanted nothing they'd been a part of. I used the proceeds to start the Wolfe Group."

She crosses the room behind me, her feet quiet on the hardwood floor. Then her scent hits me. That subtle peach fragrance I've grown addicted to, the one that's become as essential as my next breath. It fills the space between us and pulls at something deep in my ribs.

"Wolfe Technologies came first when I patented the surveillance technology I developed while trying to keep bullies out of my bedroom at school. I think I told you I was a scrawny kid until I was sixteen, then I shot up and filled out like a giant." I see the barest hint of a smile on her lips in the glass. "Then came the foundation to support animal rescue efforts. I poured every dime of profit from Wolfe Technologies into it. Finally, my acquisitions firm. It targets those who try to escape accountability by using their wealth. First, I bankrupt them, then I kill them."

I turn to face her. Her dark eyes hold mine without flinching. She takes in each word I've said, storing them somewhere inside that sharp mind of hers. But the revulsion I'm bracing for never appears.

"Wolfe isn't my birth name. When I turned eighteen, I had it legally changed."

"That's why there's nothing about your family history in any of the articles about you."

"Yes. I've spent a fortune keeping that secret buried, creating a fictional background that's rooted in truth. I want no association with the monsters who made me."

"Did your name come first or your tattoo?"

Her hand drifts up, fingers extended but not quite touching me. I close the distance between us until her hand makes the barest contact with my chest.

"The wolf came first. The night Rex died, my parents locked me in the basement with his dead body. It was the middle of winter and freezing down there. There was nothing to use for warmth except some old hunting magazines I found shoved in a cardboard box."

Her palm presses against the center of my chest, right over the wolf beneath my shirt.

"I opened them up and laid them over myself. The cover of one showed a massive gray wolf mid-leap through snow." I place my hand over hers, pressing it firmly against my heartbeat. "Its eyes burned with something I'd never seen before—pure primal fury mixed with intelligence. They weren't like Rex's gentle brown eyes. These eyes held something wild. Something that couldn't be collared or beaten."

"Something that couldn't be broken." Understanding settles into her expression.

"Yes."

The word comes out rough because, of course, she gets it. She knows wolves better than anyone.

"The wolf symbolized something that would never be too weak to protect what mattered. I tore that cover off and hid it. Under my mattress at home. Then later in my dorm room at school. On the day of my parents' funeral, I had it tattooed on my chest. That exact wolf, covering my heart. Every year since, I've added more. Filled it in as my body filled out."

"And the writhing bodies?"

"Each one represents an abuser I've stopped." My jaw tightens. "They writhe in eternal torment beneath the wolf's dominion. Trapped. Suffering. The way their victims suffered."

I study her face, searching for horror or disgust, but I see nothing but tenderness. A recognition of pain she can't fix but refuses to look away from. Her fingers press harder into my flesh, and mine wrap around hers, needing her touch like my next breath.

"Taking the name Wolfe wasn't only about the tattoo, was it?"

"No. It was about claiming my transformation. Honoring what I became that night in the basement. Wolves kill for survival, never for sport or cruelty. They protect their pack. They're loyal and fierce and uncompromising. Everything my parents weren't. Everything I swore I'd become. The name Wolfe is who I was meant to be all along, forged in trauma and fire and the death of everything innocent in me."

"The wolf is your true self." She looks up at me, her hazel eyes shimmering. "The version of you that was born when the boy died."

"Yes." My throat closes around the word.

She takes a step backward, her hand falling away from my chest, and the absence of her touch feels like a wound opening.

"And now, you use all your money to track animal abusers and make them pay for their crimes when the law fails."

"Yes. I memorialize every single one, so I never forget what they took from the world."

I study her face and keep looking for the condemnation I deserve, for the disgust that should be driving her away from me, but I find neither. Just pain and sorrow etched into every beautiful line.

"They all get exactly what they deserve." I move closer, unable to stand the distance between us. "I know reconciling that is hard for someone as good as you. Someone who spends every day saving lives. But I think you understand it on some level. You've experienced that same darkness rising up inside you."

"I'm not like you."

"Aren't you?" I reach out because I can't stop myself from touching her. Her skin is warm beneath my fingertips as I brush a strand of hair away from her face. She trembles under my touch. "I've seen it in your eyes when you're treating an abused animal. That need for retribution."

Luna steps back, creating distance again, and for a moment panic flares in my chest—the certainty that I've finally said too much and lost her. She paces across the room, running her fingers through her hair like she's trying to sort through everything I've laid at her feet.

"Feeling something isn't the same as acting on it."

"No." I follow her with my eyes. "It's not. But you helped cover up Caleb's death. You made a choice."

She spins to face me, eyes flashing with that fire I love so much. "I did it to protect you."

"Is that the only reason?"

"What other reason would I have?"

"Revenge."

Her whole body stills at that one word. She's fighting it. She wants to believe she's incapable of it, that darkness I can see lurking beneath all that light.

"I'm not a vengeful person, Damien."

"No, you're not. You're a light in a world that's mostly shadows. But there are some in you, too, Luna. That doesn't make you a bad person. It makes you human."

"I'm tired of people telling me I'm human. That isn't an excuse for being reckless or oblivious or violent."

My fingers itch to reach for her, to pull her against my chest and prove with touch what words can't capture. The urge to show her what human really means. Messy and perfect and worth protecting at any cost.

"So, why did you help us cover up Caleb's death and go along with framing him for my murders?"

"I told you—"

"Yes, you wanted to protect me. And I appreciate that, sweetheart." Her eyes find mine, and for a heartbeat, the wall between us crumbles. "I didn't expect it. And I fully intended to take responsibility for what happened because he hurt you. But I feel no remorse for killing him. I'll kill anyone who hurts you."

"Damien, you have to stop saying things like that."

"Why? It's the truth." I'm crossing the distance between us before the thought forms. "You want honesty from me? Here it is, Luna. No more secrets. No more walls." My voice drops lower. "You want to see who I really am? The parts I show the world and the parts I keep hidden? I'm stripping myself bare in front of you. As bare as I strip you every night."

Heat flashes in her eyes, and I take another step closer.

"So, I'll ask you again. Why did you agree to frame Caleb for my murders?"

"Because I can't bear to think about you going to prison." The admission tears from her throat. "And because he tried to kill me. He shot Shadow. He threatened my sanctuary, all my animals!"

There it is.

"And if he'd succeeded? What would you have done then, Luna?"

"I don't know."

Her face betrays everything. The way her eyebrows draw together, the slight downward pull of her mouth, and the rapid pulse visible at her throat. She's staring into an abyss that stares back. The same abyss I've been walking the edge of for years.

"Yes, you do." I close what's left of the distance between us, cupping her face in my hands, careful of her bruises. She's trembling, but she doesn't pull away. Her eyes stay locked on mine. She doesn't flee from the darkness she sees there or the matching darkness she's discovering in herself. "That's what terrifies you. Not me or what I've done, but recognizing pieces of me in yourself."

Her lips part as if she wants to deny it, but no sound comes. The truth sits between us like a living thing, breathing and growing and demanding acknowledgment.

"Show me."

My brow furrows. "Show you what?"

"The rest." Her chin lifts. A gesture that is so brave it carries more courage than most people possess in their entire bodies. "You said you're giving me all of you. I want to see it."

Understanding dawns, and with it, a mixture of terror and anticipation.

"You want to see my trophies?"

She doesn't flinch. Doesn't hesitate. Just nods with the certainty of someone who's already made peace with whatever comes next.

I cross to the far wall, where leather-bound volumes create a perfect facade. My fingers find the hidden panel, the keypad glowing to life under my touch. Eight digits. The date everything changed. The bookshelf whispers open on silent hinges, revealing blackness beyond.

"Are you sure?" My voice catches on the question. What lies beyond this threshold has never been seen by anyone but me. "This room doesn't just show you who I am, Luna. It shows you who I've always been."

She closes the distance instead of retreating. Her eyes lock on mine, unflinching and fierce. The same fierceness that allowed a nine-year-old boy to survive his father's lessons.

"I'm sure."

My palm finds the curve of her lower back, guiding her into the darkness. Motion sensors detect our presence, and lights come on in sequence, illuminating my private museum of justice, my shrine to all the innocent lives I've avenged.

Every muscle in my body goes rigid as I wait for her reaction. This room will either bind us together or tear us apart. Either way, after tonight, there will be no more secrets between us.

She'll know who she's fallen for. And maybe, if I'm lucky, she'll love the monster too.

Chapter Thirty-Seven

Luna

The room steals my breath, but not for the reasons I expected. My stomach had been twisted in knots, braced for something horrific. Blood-stained trophies. Gruesome mementos.

Instead, I'm surrounded by life.

Thousands of photographs line the walls, each showing an animal in various stages of healing. Dogs with missing limbs learning to run again. Cats with burned fur growing back glossy and thick. Livestock, once emaciated, now healthy and well-nourished. The images blur together as my eyes fill with tears I didn't know I had left in me.

"What is this?" The words escape as a whisper. I move closer to examine a photograph of a pit bull, scars crisscrossing its muzzle like a roadmap of pain, but its eyes... *God*, its eyes are so trusting as it gazes at the camera.

"She was my first Athena." Damien's voice comes from the doorway, quiet and careful. "And why I do what I do. Every animal that hadn't already died was rescued after I dealt with its abusive owner."

I move around the room on unsteady legs. Some of these faces are familiar. Not only from my own cases, more than I knew about, but I've seen many of their recovery stories shared online and in veterinary circles, celebrating their transformations.

"You fund their rehabilitation?" My ribcage feels too tight. Air moves in and out but doesn't seem to reach my lungs.

"Yes, through the foundation." He steps into the room but keeps his distance, as if I'm a wounded animal he might spook. "I follow their progress and make sure they get whatever they need. Medical care, behavioral therapy, special equipment."

My fingers find a small silver tag beneath one photo. The engraving reads "Jasper—March 16, 2022." The metal is cold against my skin.

"And these dates?"

"The dates I delivered justice." No euphemisms, no softening of what he's done. Just brutal honesty that makes my pulse skip.

A chill races down my spine, and I wrap my arms around myself. The methodical nature of it all—the planning, the execution, the documentation—should terrify me.

Instead, heat builds in my chest. Not horror, but something far more dangerous. The warm satisfaction of seeing monsters finally face consequences. The fierce pleasure of knowing someone fought back for those who couldn't fight for themselves. Someone willing to become the monster so others don't have to.

"How do you find them?"

"Various ways. I've developed algorithms that monitor social media and police reports for animal abuse cases. Sometimes the foundation receives tips from rescue organizations."

I pause at a photo of a gray wolf, its intelligent eyes reminding me of Shadow. "This is why he trusted you." I remember how my wolf had sat before Damien's masked figure. "He sensed what you do for them."

"He also knew I'd never hurt you."

The words wrap around me, loaded with meaning, like a promise written in blood.

But he did hurt me, even if it wasn't intentional.

I continue my journey around the room, each photograph a testament to lives saved through violence.

In the far corner, a small table holds a collection of masks. Earlier versions of the silver wolf mask I've come to know so well. They trace an evolution, becoming more refined and distinctive with each iteration.

"Why the mask?" I pick one up, running my fingers over the rough edges.

"Practical reasons, at first." He moves to stand beside me, close enough that his warmth seeps through my clothes to my skin. "Concealment, intimidation. Later, it became something more. A separation between the man who runs the Wolfe Group and the one who hunts in the night."

"A separation that became complete when you met me." Understanding dawns, bitter and sharp. "Two personas for two relationships."

He nods, those dark eyes never leaving my face. "I didn't plan that. It just happened. As I fell in love with you, I needed a way to spend more time with you. Accepting your masked stalker as a killer was one thing, but accepting him as your new neighbor was another completely."

"So, you lied." The words taste like ash. "For months."

"Yes."

At least he doesn't try to deny it.

"You stalked me, manipulated me. Made me think I was losing my mind."

My voice splinters despite my efforts to keep it steady. We already had this conversation the other night, with no resolution, but I can't let it go. Hot and angry tears threaten behind my eyes. I'm so fucking tired of crying.

"Yes." Still no excuses. No justifications. "I did. But I never meant to hurt you."

I want to scream at him. Want to throw something. Want to make him feel even a fraction of the betrayal tearing through my chest. But I also want to touch him, press my face against his neck, and breathe him in until this ache in my soul subsides.

"It wasn't about trust, Luna. Yes, there was concern at first that if you knew my true identity, you'd be tempted to turn me in. But what I feared most was your rejection. The thought of losing you caused me to make some bad decisions."

"Bad decisions? Is that what we're calling psychological manipulation now?"

His jaw tightens, but he doesn't flinch from my sarcasm. "What would you call it?"

"Fucked up." I replace the mask, and my fingers brush against his as I withdraw my hand. The contact moves up my arm and into my chest. "So fucked up I don't have words for it."

"And now?" The question emerges wrapped in false calm, but tension threads through his frame like a spring wound too tight.

"Now that I know everything? I do know everything, right?"

"Yes. I have no more secrets from you. And now you have a choice. Stay and accept all of me, or leave and forget you ever knew either version."

"As if I could forget." The words slip out bitter and raw. "Do you think I haven't tried? Do you think I haven't spent sleepless nights wishing I could scrub you from my memory?"

Pain he's unable to hide without his mask flickers across his face.

I turn away from him, surveying the room once more. All these animals were given second chances because of Damien's brutal actions. Lives saved through the taking of other lives. The contradiction should be impossible to reconcile, but looking at these photographs, feeling the weight of all that suffering transformed into healing...

But haven't I already accepted it? That morning I found the first body on my porch and felt that flicker of savage satisfaction once the terror had faded. The way I responded when I confronted him on my porch, when he entered my bedroom, mask and all. My decision to help cover up what happened with Caleb.

"I've never felt this way before, Luna. I didn't know I was capable of it. Of wanting someone so completely. Of needing them. Needing you."

I spin to face him. "But you always told me I was yours. How is that not needing me?"

"I thought all I needed was your body and your surrender, but you gave that so willingly." His voice grows rougher. "It was such a beautiful gift. I wanted more, and before I knew it, the heart I didn't think I had was beating only for you."

I can't breathe. He's standing here undefended, has stripped away the armor he wears like a second skin, and it's everything I've ached for and everything that terrifies me.

"What are you saying, Damien?"

He moves toward me. "I thought my parents killed that part of me a long time ago, the part that could feel something real for another person. The part that could love." He takes my hand, placing it over his heart. The rapid beat pounds against my palm. "But this is real, Luna. You changed everything."

The warmth of his chest seeps through my fingers, and I hate how right this feels. How safe his touch makes me feel. It always has.

"How can I trust anything about you now?"

"You can't. Not yet. But I'm standing here without masks, giving you all of me. Showing you all of me. The good and the monstrous. Giving you the knowledge to destroy me. That's something I've never offered anyone."

"You broke my heart, Damien." The words shred my throat on the way up.

"I know, sweetheart. I'm so sorry." His free hand comes up to cup my cheek. His thumb moves across my skin in slow strokes. "But if you give me another chance, I'll spend the rest of my life showing you that your heart is the most sacred thing in my life. Even more than your body."

His mouth quirks. That damn smirk trying to break through. Heat unfurls in my core.

Unbidden. Unwanted. Undeniable.

"Your priorities are showing, Mr. Wolfe."

"Can you blame me? Have you seen yourself?"

The ease between us returns, as natural as breathing. My heart still aches, but the edges of the pain soften.

I study his face for a long moment, then step back. Distance. I need distance to think. My chest feels too tight, my thoughts too loud. I need room to breathe.

"I can't walk away from you." My throat tightens. "I love you, Damien, despite everything. I think I have from the first moment you touched me."

Relief floods his features, so powerful I can see it in the way his entire body seems to exhale.

"But I don't know if I can be what you want. If I can accept all of this."

He takes my face in both hands. "You don't have to decide everything right now. But I need you to understand one thing, Luna." His eyes sweep across my face before finally locking with mine. "I love you. And I won't let you go. Not now, not ever. I've claimed you, and you've claimed me in return. Whether you realize it or not."

I hate that my body responds to the possessiveness in his voice, even as my mind rebels. "That's not your decision to make, Damien. Love isn't possession."

"Isn't it?" His thumb traces over my lower lip, and I can't stop the tremor that runs through me. "Tell me you don't feel this connection between us. Tell me you don't wake in the night, reaching for me, wishing I was there with you. Tell me you haven't thought about me every minute since that first moment I touched you."

Damn him!

His arms encircle me, pulling me against him, and my breath hitches at the feel of his body against me. I bury my face in his chest and let out an exhale.

"I want to trust you, Damien. I want to believe that you love me." I pull back far enough to see his face, searching for truth in his eyes. "But I need to understand something."

"Anything."

"If you love me the way you claim, how could you lie to me for so long?"

He goes quiet. His gaze drops, lifts, and drops again. "Because I'm selfish. I wanted more time with you before you had to make this choice. I was terrified that knowing the truth meant losing you, and that was unbearable."

"So you took my choice away."

"Yes. And I was wrong."

I search his face for any hint of deception. All I find is honesty bleeding through his features, regret carved into the lines around his eyes.

"Then no more lies. No more masks. If we do this, if we try to make whatever this is between us work, I need the truth, Damien. Always. Whether you think I can handle it or not."

"I will never lie to you again."

The ferocity in his voice, the way his gaze locks onto mine like an oath—I believe him.

Maybe I'm a fool. Maybe I'm signing up for more heartbreak. But as he lifts me into his arms and carries me from his room of rescued souls, I know I'm crossing another line I can't uncross.

The darkness I've kept contained for so long has found its mirror in him. And God help me, I'm done fighting it. I'm choosing him, choosing us, with everything I am.

Chapter Thirty-Eight

Luna

I slide down his body when we enter his office again.

When his hands lift to unbutton my shirt, when his mouth brushes my throat and he bites down hard enough to make me gasp, all rational thought abandons me.

His touch is everywhere at once—one hand gripping my waist, another cupping my breast, then moving up to thread his fingers into my hair.

It's desperate, almost violent in its intensity, like he's trying to memorize every inch of me in case I disappear again.

His tongue sweeps across my neck, heat and moisture leaving me dizzy, as he makes his way to my mouth. I tilt my head back, opening to him. His kiss is fierce, a collision of tongues and lips and ragged breaths that quicken until my heart threatens to burst out of my chest. I taste mint and whiskey and something uniquely him, and my knees go weak.

My pulse hammers in my throat as warmth floods between my legs. Desire, lust, and love claw through me, lacing with longing, with the ache of nights spent apart. I need him inside me, claiming every inch until I'm his again.

"The desk."

My voice trembles as the massive piece of furniture looms behind me, papers and expensive electronics scattered across its surface.

He doesn't pause. He grips my hips and hefts me onto the desk's slick surface, scattering documents and pushing aside several very expensive computer screens like they're nothing.

"Damien." I breathe into his mouth as they crash to the floor.

"I'll fucking buy new ones."

I moan at the desperation in his voice, heat skittering across my skin.

"Do you know how often I've thought about this?" He breathes against my neck, his voice rough and broken. "How many times I thought about having you here on this fucking desk?"

His hands find my jeans, his fingers tugging at the waistband. I lift my hips, and he peels the fabric down my legs as I shrug out of my shirt and bra. The denim pools at his feet. The desk's cool wood shocks my bare ass and thighs. Then his hands return, trailing fire across my skin. The space between us crackles with tension, loaded at the edges and building.

"Turn around."

Heat spirals through my core at those two words.

He yanks me off the desk, and I spin, my body responding before my brain registers the command. This is our dynamic, the push and pull of dominance and submission that always leaves me breathless and wanting more.

I brace my hands on the desk, and he moves behind me. His body covers mine, pinning me in place, his chest flush with my spine, and the thunder of his heartbeat drums against my back.

I bring my arms behind me, crossing my wrists in automatic surrender. I wait for the bite of the zip ties, the familiar binding that transforms me into someone both helpless and cherished, trapped and treasured.

His palms stay planted on my hips. Nothing circles my wrists. His breathing changes, becomes uneven and ragged, and we both go statue-still. The question sits on the tip of my tongue.

"Aren't you going to—"

His body shudders against my back. "No. I want you to be able to touch me, Luna."

My palms find the desk's surface, fingers spreading wide for support. His zipper cuts through the silence, then he drives into me, fast, hard, and desperate, exactly what we both need. A cry scrapes past my lips as I arch my back, the desk's cold edge biting into my hips. The gnawing emptiness from our time apart dissolves as he fills every starved inch of me.

"Christ." He groans, his voice strained. "You feel—fuck, Luna."

He sets a relentless pace, unleashing all the need we've both carried. His hands clamp on my waist with bruising force while I thrust back against him, matching his hunger with my own.

My hands scramble for purchase on the smooth surface of the desk, but then I remember I don't need both hands to brace myself. I can touch him. My hand finds his thigh, wrapping around solid muscle that flexes beneath my grip. The connection unravels his control. His rhythm falters and breaks.

"Luna." He breathes my name like a prayer, an apology, and a promise all rolled into one.

The frantic edge that drove us together dissolves, replaced by tenderness so profound it threatens to shatter me. He curves his body over mine, a shelter of flesh and bone, while his mouth trails a path along my spine. His lips find the curve where my neck meets my shoulder, and my breath catches. Tears threaten, hot behind my closed lids.

My fingers find his on my hip, sliding between his until we're tangled together. A broken and beautiful sound rips from his throat, and I squeeze our joined hands.

"I love you." Three words, stripped bare of everything but truth, every barrier he's ever built. "I love you so fucking much."

My throat seizes, and words die before they reach my lips, crushed by the pressure in my chest. My pulse hammers against my ribs as I press back into him, my body saying what my voice can't.

When he reaches around to touch me, his fingers finding my clit, I shatter. The orgasm hits like a collision. Sudden, violent, and devastating. My spine arches as I cry out his name for the first time since knowing who he is.

He follows seconds later, his body going rigid against mine, his muscles locking as my name spills from his lips. The sound travels through me in waves that leave my limbs weak and shaking.

My forehead presses against the cool wood of his desk. Neither of us moves, our chests heaving in unison, his ribs expanding against my spine with each breath, and tremors run through his fingers where they hold me.

When he withdraws, the emptiness he leaves behind swallows me whole. I press my lips together to trap the sound trying to escape. His palms steady me as I turn to face him. His eyes are wide and unguarded, like every wall he's built has crumbled at once.

He's still fully dressed, his pants still at his thighs, the evidence of our orgasms glistening on his length. The sight sends another hot pulse sliding between my legs.

He leans down to press his lips to mine again. "I love kissing you."

This kiss is different, soft and gentle. His fingers caress my cheeks while his lips part mine with patient pressure. No rush, no desperation, just his mouth learning mine like he has forever to get it right. My knees buckle, and I melt into him, gripping his shirt to keep upright.

The kiss feeds a hunger deep inside me, an ache for closeness beyond the physical.

"I'm sorry I ever denied us this," he whispers against my lips.

"Please never do it again."

"Never."

The need to touch him, to reassure myself that he's letting me in, overwhelms me. I reach between us, wrapping my hand around his length. The way he arches into my fingers, groaning softly, sends a fresh pulse of triumph and tenderness through me.

He threads his fingers through mine, stilling my hand, as he releases my lips. He lifts his head and meets my eyes, and I see the worry in his.

I lift my hand to his face, my thumb tracing his cheek, loving that I can touch him now. "What's the matter?"

"You're not going to change your mind, are you?"

"Are you?"

"Never." The word tears from him again.

He brings my hand to his mouth and presses his lips to my palm. The ache I've been carrying in my ribcage loosens, my breath flowing easier than it has in days.

"Good." A real smile pulls at my mouth for the first time since this nightmare started. "Now, why don't you take me upstairs and fuck me properly?"

His grin turns wickedly familiar, the same curve of his lips I know from all those nights beneath his mask. It's the first genuine smile I've seen from him since everything went to hell, and it's like watching the sun come out after a storm.

He steps closer, tilting my chin up so our lips meet in a soft, lingering kiss.

"I'm sorry, did I not just do that, little doe? I know it's been a couple of days, but your memory is surely better than that."

The sarcasm is so him, so perfectly my wolf. I laugh, breathy and light, and stand on tiptoes to brush my lips against his.

"I want you to make love to me, Damien."

His eyes darken, and his fingers press into my flesh. He whispers my name as if it's the most sacred thing he knows.

"Come on," he murmurs with a half-smile that crinkles the corners of his eyes. "I'm taking you to bed, little doe."

Chapter Thirty-Nine

Luna

Damien grips under my thighs, his powerful hands lifting me with ease. My limbs wrap around him, a breathless laugh escaping my lips as he holds me against his solid chest, our bodies touching everywhere. My heart hammers against my ribs—not from fear, but from anticipation. From the knowledge that everything has changed between us.

"If you come upstairs with me, I'm not letting you out of that bed until morning." His breath warms my ear. "I've never made love to a woman, Luna. All I've ever done is fuck. Will you be my first?"

I nod, skimming my nose along his cheek, and whisper my consent. He carries me upstairs to his bedroom, his hands gripping the bare flesh of my ass. I study his profile in the low hallway light. He's so beautiful, with his chiseled jaw covered in the lightest stubble, the lines around his eyes, and his gray temples. And I know in this moment that I want to look at this man for the rest of my life.

Late afternoon sunlight filters through the thick leaded glass windows as we step into his bedroom. A fire crackles in a stone hearth, its surrounding tile work restored, showcasing the mansion's Victorian heritage. In stark contrast to his sleek Denver penthouse, the room is filled with dark walls, glowing sconces, and heavy wooden furniture, making it feel intimate despite its generous size. The room breathes history while embracing the contemporary, its original architectural details marrying with modern luxury, creating something both timeless and lived-in. And it matches the man carrying me. Solid, uncompromising, and touched with barely contained wildness.

By the time he reaches the massive four-poster bed that dominates the space, his pants have slipped to his ankles. We barely make it without him tripping, and I laugh against his skin where my tongue traces the pulse point at his throat.

His grip loosens as he sets me on the floor, and for a suspended moment we stand there, looking at each other. Candlelight flickers from every surface, flames dancing on the bedside tables and dresser, illuminating his face in gold and shadow. I quirk an eyebrow at him.

"That seems like a fire hazard. Pretty sure of the outcome today, huh?"

"Call it confidence in my powers of persuasion." His smirk tugs at one corner of his mouth as he nudges the fabric pooled around his ankles, stepping free.

His unwavering faith in us, in me coming back to him, makes my throat tighten. He lit these candles knowing—not hoping, but knowing—that I'd be here with him tonight. The arrogance of it should rankle and trigger my instinct to rebel against anyone who thinks they know my choices before I make them. Instead, warmth spreads through me, dissolving the last walls I'd built around my heart.

My fingers tremble as I reach up to trace the line of his jaw. "I've wanted to touch your face so bad. When you wore that mask, I could never—"

"I know." His voice rasps with emotion as his hand covers mine, holding it to his cheek. "Now you can. Anytime you want."

His lips meet mine in a gentle kiss, nothing like the claiming ones before, and it steals my ability to think. His hands cradle my face, his fingers tracing my cheekbones, careful of my bruises, until tremors roll through my limbs. My body surrenders without thought, muscles melting into his warmth while my mind reels from this contradiction, my heart struggling to reconcile this gentleness with the brutality I've known.

"I need you." The plea breathes out between kisses. "All of you."

He pulls back, and the tension melts from the corners of his eyes while hunger deepens in their depths. He reaches for his shirt, fingers working at the first button, but I catch his wrists in my hands.

"Let me."

He drops his arms to his sides. My hands take their time as I release each button, savoring the gradual revelation of his skin, the heat radiating from him as I push the fabric aside, exposing the intricate wolf inked on his chest. The shirt slides from his shoulders, dropping forgotten at our feet.

His hands find my hips, caressing me wherever they can reach, leaving trails of goosebumps in their wake. Being naked in front of this man is as natural as breathing now. The firelight reflects in his dark eyes as he studies me without metal between us.

"You're beautiful." Wonder softens his tone. My cheeks warm at the raw devotion I hear. "So fucking beautiful it hurts to look at you sometimes."

"So are you."

My eyes drink him in, memorizing every inch of his exposed skin. My fingers trace the detailed tattoos, the wolf standing defiant in the midst of hell, so fitting and profoundly meaningful now that I know the secrets of his past.

He holds his arms out to his sides. "Every inch of my body is yours, Luna. See me. Touch me. Claim me."

My eyes begin their true exploration in the light. The scattered scars tell stories he hasn't shared. The tension across his shoulders speaks of burdens carried alone. And the slight tremor in his hands when he touches me, as if he still can't believe I'm here, choosing this.

Choosing him.

He pulls me against him, skin against skin, and his shudder vibrates through my bones.

"I've dreamed of this." His lips brush against my collarbone, leaving a trail of warmth. "Of holding you like this. Of you still wanting me even after knowing everything I've done."

"I do want you." My fingers thread through his dark hair. "I want Damien, and I want my wolf. I want all the parts you've kept hidden."

He lays me back on cool sheets that quickly warm beneath us, his touch reverent where it once was possessive. His hands glide along my skin, rediscovering every curve. When he settles over me, I gasp as the weight of him presses me into the mattress, solid and real.

"I can't promise to be gentle." His thumbs trace circles on my hipbones, contradicting every word with their tender touch.

"Your gentleness and your brutality both live in these hands." My palms cover his, pressing them deeper into my skin. "Give me the man who treasures me and the one who devours me. They're both mine now."

His mouth begins a slow journey across my skin, and my pulse jumps beneath his lips.

He takes his time exploring me, his mouth leaving a trail of heat along my throat, shoulders, and the valley between my breasts. Each touch ignites tiny flames beneath my skin. My nipples pucker, aching for his mouth, and when his lips wrap around one sensitive peak, I arch against him, a soft moan escaping me.

"That's it, sweetheart," he murmurs around the hard bud. "I live for the sound of your pleasure."

I pull his lips to mine and kiss him like I'm drowning, like he's the only air I'll ever need. My mouth opens against his, desperate and hungry, while his fingers trace the curve of my sides, dancing across my stomach. Everywhere except where the ache pulses the strongest. The anticipation builds until I'm trembling beneath him, my skin hypersensitive to every whisper of contact.

I beg him to end my sweet torture. "Please."

When he enters me, reality shrinks to just our joined bodies, and the rest of existence falls away. The press of his chest against my breasts, his stomach flush with mine—it feels like coming home after years of being lost. His eyes never leave mine as he moves inside me, our bodies finding a rhythm that belongs only to us. This isn't our usual desperate, clawing need. This is love, worship through touch. He overwhelms every sense. The weight of him pressing me into the mattress, the thick stretch of him inside me, filling places that ached without knowing why.

He's spent hundreds of hours inside me, but somehow this feels brand new, as if we're touching for the first time.

"Luna." He groans my name. "You feel like heaven."

I wrap my arms and legs around him, urging him deeper. He responds with a low growl that reverberates through both our bodies. We move as one, savoring each sensation, sharing breath between parted lips.

His hands tangle in my hair, and for the first time, he kisses me while we move together, deep, claiming kisses that taste of forever.

His hips shift, finding that perfect spot inside me, and I cry out into the space between our lips. He repeats the motion, and I gasp and arch, my nails digging into the small of his back.

"Don't stop. Please don't stop."

But instead of continuing, he slows, his movements becoming deliberate torture that keeps release just beyond reach. Each stroke builds toward something that never quite arrives, drawing out the pleasure until I'm on the edge of madness.

"Let me." My fingers dig into his hips, attempting to still his maddening pace. "Let me love you."

Understanding lights his eyes. He rolls us over, letting me straddle him. He's never allowed me control before, not even that night on the porch. His struggle plays across his face, jaw clenching and muscles tensing. The instinct to dominate wars with his desire to give me what I want.

"Trust me." I place my hands flat on his chest, feeling his heart thundering beneath my palms.

I move my hips in slow circles, learning this new position with him, this new dynamic. The power of being above him, of controlling our pace and depth, is intoxicating.

The skin of my inner thighs burns where it meets the coarse hair on his legs. The angle sends sparks shooting into my core, each shift forward bringing pressure where I need it, a friction against my clit that makes my breath catch. His face changes beneath me, his eyes rolling back when my muscles clench around him.

I lean down to taste the salt-slick hollow of his throat. His sharp inhale and full-body shudder tell me everything I need to know about what he needs from me.

"You're so beautiful." I echo his words from before.

My hips roll forward, and a sound tears from his throat, deep, broken, and hungry. Candlelight flickers across his face as his mouth falls open, eyes squeezing shut. His jaw goes slack, his features softening as I unravel him piece by piece.

His hands settle on my hips, pressing into the soft flesh but following my movements rather than dictating them. He's letting me lead, letting me love him the way I've longed to. I rock against him in slow waves, each motion pulling another groan from his chest. His fingers tremble against my skin, his hold going slack as I claim him. He lies beneath me, unguarded, open, and surrendering everything, and my breath stutters in my throat.

I lower my body down, resting my weight on him as I kiss him, my hair spilling around us like a silk curtain, blocking out everything but his mouth and mine. Our tongues dance together, following the rhythm of our bodies below. When I sit up again, riding him with increasing confidence, his hands find my breasts, his thumbs circling my nipples until I'm gasping his name, ragged and breathless.

Heat coils tighter in my core with each roll of my hips. Pressure builds behind my ribs and in my belly, threatening to tear me apart.

He sits up and pulls me against him until no space exists between us. We move together, our foreheads touching, sharing the same air, breathing each other's exhales. His chest presses against mine with each breath, our hearts hammering in matched tempo. My fingers dig into his shoulders as his palms slide down my spine, steadying my movements.

This level of connection—I've never had this with another man. It terrifies and thrills me.

"I love you." This time, it doesn't sound like a confession torn from his throat. It sounds like the truth. "I love you, Luna."

"I love you too." The whisper carries everything I feel, every cell inside me alive with it. "All of you."

The words seem to crack through his final barrier. His grip tightens on my hips, fingers digging in. Our rhythm turns frantic, chasing release together. When he throbs inside me, my climax rips through me with devastating force. I cling to him as my body contracts around him, muscles clenching in waves that steal my breath. He shudders beneath me, his mouth finding my neck between gasps. His lips move against my skin like he's memorizing the taste, the texture, and the way my pulse races under his tongue.

Tremors continue to shudder through us both as he pulls me down with him, our bodies slick with cooling sweat. His fingers comb through my hair as our heartbeats resume their normal pace. He's still buried inside me, our connection unbroken, and my heart fills with the certainty that this is only the beginning.

He shifts, rolling us carefully onto our sides without separating. His arms tighten around me. I can feel his heart still pounding, gradually slowing to match mine.

"I don't deserve you." His breath warms my forehead.

"That's not your decision to make." I tilt my face up to look at him. "I choose you. Both of you. All of you."

His eyes shine in the firelight. He kisses me, slow and thorough, saying everything words can't capture. When he pulls back, he rests his forehead against mine.

"No more secrets." His voice is rough. "I promise. No more masks."

I seal the promise with another kiss, softer this time.

We lie there as the fire burns low, tangled together, neither willing to break contact.

His lips caress my temple. "Stay with me."

"Forever."

Chapter Forty

Luna

Morning light filters through unfamiliar curtains, and for a heartbeat, I don't recognize where I am. The sheets smell different, expensive, with that crisp hotel-like scent that screams money. But beneath the fresh linen is his cologne. Vanilla and amber mixed with musk, woodsy, and masculine. The scent winds through the fabric, through my hair, and across my skin.

Damien.

My pulse speeds up even as I hover between dreams and wakefulness, responding to the dangerous edge woven into his smell.

My nipples tighten against the expensive cotton. Blood pounds in my ears, between my legs, everywhere his scent reaches, which is everywhere.

The memories crash over me like a tidal wave. Of the way Damien made love to me for hours, his hands and lips on my body, gentle at first, then demanding as my wolf rose to the surface. The way he let me make love to him, using every part of my body to vow ultimate devotion.

But now, as I shift and the lingering aches in my body protest the movement, I wonder how long I'll be able to survive him.

I prop myself up on my elbow and look down at him, letting my eyes trace over his body.

In sleep, the hardness leaves his face, making him look younger and almost vulnerable. His dark lashes cast shadows on his cheeks. His full lips are parted, and one powerful arm flings over his head while the other still grips me close, even in unconsciousness.

Sunlight creeps across the floor through the gap in his curtains, the beam stretching longer as the sun climbs. Minutes blur together, and time loses meaning in the quiet as I watch him sleep. Then, as if my gaze alone triggers something in him, Damien stirs. His eyes open and lock on my face in the same breath, going from asleep to fully alert in an instant, another reminder of his predatory nature.

"Morning, beautiful." His voice is rough with sleep, and his hand finds mine where it rests on his chest. "How long have you been watching me?"

"Not long," I admit, unable to suppress a smile. "You look almost harmless when you're asleep."

A slow grin spreads across his face, and he cups the back of my neck, pulling me down for a kiss. He brushes his lips against mine. Now that he's let himself kiss me, it's like he can't get enough.

"You're still here."

"Did you think I'd run?" I trace patterns on his chest to have an excuse to keep touching him.

"The thought occurred to me." His free hand trails lazy circles on my bare shoulder, then down my back to the curve of my ass, raising goosebumps and making my breath hitch. "People tend to see things differently in the light of day."

I catch his wandering hand and bring it to my lips, pressing a soft kiss to his palm. His fingers smell like me, like sex, like claim and ownership.

"I meant what I said last night."

His eyes darken. Heat floods those blue-gray irises, turning them stormy. "Which part? The 'fuck me harder' part or the 'I'm yours forever' part?"

A warm laugh escapes me. "Both."

His hips shift beneath me, his body stirring to life.

"Keep talking like that, and you won't be getting breakfast anytime soon."

I run my fingers along the sculpted line of his jaw, marveling at the fact that I can touch him now. "I wanted to ask you something."

"What?"

"Did you pay off my mortgage and student loans?"

He doesn't even hesitate. "Yes."

The casual admission makes me want to both smack him and kiss him.

"What about the donation for Titus' enclosure?"

He doesn't bother with words this time, just raises an eyebrow.

"Why?"

"Because you're mine to take care of now. And don't fucking look at me like that. This is how it's going to be. Get used to it."

"I'm annoyed at the presumption." I brush my lips against his. "But thank you."

When I start to pull away, his hand fists in my hair, holding me in place. "More."

I laugh, the sound trapped between our mouths, but I give in. The kiss goes on until my chest burns and my head swims. When we finally surface, both pulling in ragged breaths, he's wearing this look—satisfaction bordering on smug, like he's just conquered the world. My heart kicks hard against my ribs, expanding until it feels too large for the space it occupies.

Then his smile fades, and he brushes a lock of hair behind my ear, his fingers lingering against my cheek. "I'm not an easy man, Luna, and that's not going to change, no matter how much I love you."

"I know." I sit up, clutching the sheet to my chest. "I'm not asking you to change. But I need to make sure you understand, Damien. No matter how much I love you, I won't tolerate any more manipulation or secrets."

He shifts beside me, sitting up and settling back against the headboard. His hand finds the edge of the sheet. With one tug, the fabric slides down, pooling at my waist. Cool air hits my skin. His gaze travels over my exposed breasts, my stomach, lingering on every inch. I suspect I'm going to spend most of my time naked now that I'm in a relationship with my wolf.

"What about my work?"

The euphemism almost makes me laugh. His work. Like he's an accountant instead of a vigilante who leaves bodies in his wake.

I take a deep breath, having thought about this while I was watching him sleep.

"I won't ask you to stop. I don't have the right to ask that, and I'm not sure I would even if I did."

Surprise flickers across his features. "Most women would demand I give it up."

"I'm not most women." I reach out, tracing one of the warped human figures climbing up his arm. The ink is beautiful and terrible, like the man wearing it. "But I need to understand. What I saw the other night, that cold rage, that capacity for violence. Is that always there? Beneath the surface? Is that what allows you to do what you do without remorse?"

He's quiet for a long moment, his blue-gray eyes never leaving mine. "Yes."

I appreciate that he doesn't try to soften it.

"It's part of who I am. Has been since that night. The only difference now is that I've learned to channel it, to control it rather than letting it control me."

I lean forward, pressing my lips gently to his. "Thank you." The words brush against his mouth. "For telling me the truth."

He pulls back to study my face. "And does the truth change how you feel? Now that you've seen what I'm capable of up close?"

I witnessed his violence firsthand, the cold, calculated way he incapacitated Caleb, causing the injuries that led to his death. I should have been terrified and repulsed. Instead, I felt protected. Even God help me, aroused, though not until later, by the raw power he commanded with little effort.

"No. But I can't be a part of what you do, Damien. I can look the other way because I know for some of these animals, the only justice they'll ever receive is the one you mete out for them. And while part of me says it's wrong, that no one has the right to take another life, no matter the justification, the other part..."

"Understands the necessity," he finishes for me. "Recognizes that sometimes the system fails, and someone has to step into that gap."

"Yes."

The admission unlocks something inside me, like opening a door I'd kept bolted shut.

"Having dark thoughts doesn't make you a bad person, Luna."

"Maybe. But there's a difference between having dark thoughts and acting on them."

"A smaller difference than most people realize." His thumb traces the curve of my cheek. "We all have the potential for violence, Luna. The only question is what catalyst will bring it to the surface."

Damien reaches for me then, pulling me onto his lap with ease. I straddle his thighs, his hands settling on my waist.

"I'm not going to stop, Luna." There's no room for debate in his voice. "But I won't be reckless about it either. No more gifts. When someone disappears without a trace, that's how you'll know. And you can choose to acknowledge it or look the other way."

It's a compromise. More than I expected him to offer. Less than the world would say I should accept. But we left the world behind somewhere between the mask and the blood.

Now we're just two broken people finding completion and safety in each other's darkness.

"Okay."

The word barely makes it out before I'm kissing him. Sealing it. Making it real.

The gentleness lasts seconds before heat takes over. His palms move over my skin, and my body responds with a shudder that starts deep in my core.

"I need you." I breathe the words into his mouth, the aches in my body forgotten, morphing into another kind of ache entirely. "I need you inside me."

He lifts me like I weigh nothing and settles me onto the bed. Sunlight streams across the mattress, across us. He moves over me, blocking out everything but his face. For the first time, I can study him in full light. See everything he's feeling written in his expression.

"I love you."

I pull him down to me.

"Show me."

He starts with soft kisses along my jaw and down my throat, taking his time to worship every inch of exposed skin. His stubble scratches against my sensitive flesh, a perfect contrast to the gentleness of his lips. When he finds that spot where my neck meets my shoulder, the one that makes me gasp and arch beneath him, he lavishes attention there until I'm purring.

His hands trace my body like he's memorizing it all over again, but this time without the urgency of our previous encounters. Every touch is deliberate and meaningful. When he takes my breast in his mouth, I arch into him and hold him closer.

"Damien."

His name escapes my lips on a gasp, and he moves to the other breast and devotes himself to it with the same hunger.

"Love hearing my name on your lips." His words vibrate against my nipple. "Say it again."

"Damien."

He smiles against my skin.

When at last he slips inside me, it's with a slow stroke that makes my spine curve, my thighs tighten around his hips, and my walls clench around him, drawing him in. We both groan.

"God, you feel incredible." His forehead drops to mine, his breath hot against my lips.

"Look at me," I whisper as his eyes drift closed, and when his lashes lift and his gaze meets mine, I see everything there. His love, his vulnerability, and his complete surrender to this moment between us.

The pace that builds is gradual, our bodies slick with sweat, every nerve ending alive and singing.

"Come with me." I dig my nails into his ass. "I want to feel you lose control."

He begins thrusting deeper, and the world shatters. My body seizes around him as his name rips from my throat. My thighs shake against his hips as waves crash through my core, my orgasm tearing through me. He groans, pulsing inside me.

My muscles clench and release, and his hips jerk, his cock twitching as he empties himself. His mouth finds mine, tender in the aftermath of our frenzy, and his hands glide over my skin, his touch gentle where it was bruising moments before.

Every kiss, every caress, every whispered endearment is a promise between two damaged souls who found salvation in each other.

As I drift in the aftermath, I can't bring myself to regret a single choice that brought me to this moment.

Chapter Forty-One

Luna

I steady myself against the tiled wall as steam swirls around us, the hot water finally running cool. Damien's hands linger on my hips, his thumbs tracing lazy circles, promises I won't let him deliver. Not now. Not when my stomach is literally eating itself from the inside out.

"Luna. We're already in here. It's the perfect place to get dirty."

I press my palm flat against his chest. "No."

"No?"

His lower lip juts out in an exaggerated pout that I never imagined I'd see on the man in front of me.

"I'm so weak from hunger, I'm going to pass out if you don't get me some food." I duck under his arm and reach for my towel. The cool air hits my wet skin, sending a shiver rippling through me. "I'm serious, Damien."

He crowds into my space as I wrap the towel around my body, his mouth ghosting over the pulse in my neck, and my heartbeat stutters and jumps against his lips.

"How about I take you to lunch at Nancy's?"

The offer tempts me more than it should. But reality crashes back in. The one that exists beyond this bathroom, beyond his bed, beyond the bubble we've constructed around ourselves for the last twenty hours. Where the outside world and all its complications don't exist.

"I can't." I turn to face him, water droplets racing down his chest in paths I want to follow with my tongue. The sculpted planes of his stomach, the sharp cut of muscle at his hips—everything about him is designed to make me forget my responsibilities.

Focus, Luna.

"I need to get to the sanctuary. Maren's there alone. None of the volunteers are coming in today."

His jaw tightens, the muscle jumping in a way I've learned is a sign he's trying not to argue.

"You have to eat."

"I know." I step past him into his bedroom, his gaze tracking my movements. The weight of his attention is almost physical, sliding over my skin in heated waves. "Come with me. I'll make grilled cheese sandwiches and tomato soup for all of us."

"What are you, twelve?"

I turn a sharp gaze on him, ready to defend my food choices, but his teasing smirk melts my irritation.

"You can stay here and find something to eat on your own, if you prefer."

"Fine." The word comes out clipped, edged with frustration. His fingers find the edge of my towel, tugging. "But first—"

I slap his hand away. "Stop it."

He grins, shameless, and tries again. I catch his wrist this time, laughing because this playful back-and-forth is new.

"You're impossible."

He dips his head to kiss my shoulder, and my traitorous body leans into the touch before my brain catches up and reminds me we have places to be.

"Damien." I step away, putting distance between us before I give in. "I need clothes."

I came over yesterday afternoon for a conversation I was sure would end in tears and recriminations. Some final, terrible closure that would let me move on with my life. I hadn't anticipated the revelation that shattered and rebuilt everything I thought I knew about him. Staying the night wasn't even on my radar. Or staying the morning. Or agreeing to forever with the serial killer who broke my heart and then somehow pieced it back together with blood-stained hands.

My clothes sit folded on top of his dresser, neat in a way that screams Damien's particular brand of control. He must have gone downstairs at some point when I was sleeping and grabbed them from where we'd abandoned them in his office. I pick up my jeans, shaking them out.

"What about the rest?" His voice carries amusement.

I eye my underwear with distaste, the lace looking sad and crumpled. The shirt's no better—wrinkled and reeking of yesterday's anxious sweat. "I'm not re-wearing those."

"I like where this is going." He crosses his arms, leaning against the bedpost with water still beading on his skin like some kind of pornographic statue come to life.

"You would." I pull on my jeans, the denim rough against my bare skin. "Do you have a shirt I can borrow?"

His expression darkens. My pulse spikes and my mouth goes dry. Hunger flashes across his face, primal and obvious, but beneath it lurks a devotion that makes my stomach flip. The way he looks at me, like I'm both salvation and ruin, a treasure he'd burn the world to keep. I'm only beginning to understand the weight of being so thoroughly wanted.

He moves to his closet, pulling out a light blue button-down.

"This one."

I slip my arms through the sleeves, and it engulfs me, the hem falling to mid-thigh and the shoulders drooping well past mine. I start buttoning it, moving from bottom to top, but his hands cover mine, stopping me halfway up.

"I want to do it."

His fingers work the buttons with a gentleness that seems at odds with what I know he's capable of. But his breathing's gone rough, each exhale a little too deliberate, a little too controlled. When he reaches the top button, his knuckles brush against my throat, and his eyes have gone molten.

"It's just a shirt, Damien."

"It's my shirt." His thumb traces my collarbone where the fabric gapes, dipping into the hollow of my throat. "On your body. Marking you as mine in a way everyone can see."

"Okay, caveman."

He pulls me flush against him, and the hard length of him presses against my stomach. "You're going to smell like me all day."

I push at his chest, fighting a smile that wants to break free. "Get dressed before I change my mind about lunch."

He releases me with obvious reluctance, pulling on boxer briefs and jeans. I watch him button his own shirt, black this time, rolling the sleeves to his elbows. The morning light catches the tattoos on his forearms, those warped human figures that no longer seem quite so monstrous now that I understand what they represent. Each one a life he ended, a victim he avenged, a monster he put down. They're a memorial and a confession inked into his skin for anyone who knows how to read them.

"We're insane, aren't we?" The words slip out before I can stop them.

He pauses. For a moment, he looks at me, and I can't read his expression.

"Probably."

I sink onto the edge of his bed, suddenly needing to sit. "We're building a relationship on the foundation of your deception, my forgiveness, and a shared conspiracy to frame a dead man for murder."

"Murders. Plural." He sits beside me, close enough that our thighs touch. "Don't shortchange my body count."

A laugh bubbles up, edged with hysteria, because what else can I do?

"God, that shouldn't be funny."

"But it is." His hand finds mine, lacing our fingers together. "Dark humor for a dark situation."

I stare at our joined hands. My fingers look small wrapped in his. The shape of his hand catches my attention. The way his fingers sit slightly crooked, bones that were broken, over and over, and never properly healed. Evidence of his father's brutality. I lift them to my lips as I blink back tears.

"Our foundation is built on more than just those things, Luna. It's built on love." I open my mouth, but my words die on my tongue. "Yes, I know it started with secrets and lies and my obsession, but I think I fell in love with you the second I laid eyes on you, even though I had no idea what it was."

My eyes soften at the sincere expression on his face, at the vulnerability there that he only shows me. Even though we talked all of this out last night and this morning, I'm still wrapping my mind around our new reality.

"You're a serial killer, Damien."

"Yes."

"And I'm a veterinarian. I save lives."

"You do." His thumb strokes across my knuckles.

"I helped you cover up Caleb's death." My voice comes out steady despite the magnitude of the admission.

"You did." There's no shame in his voice, no regret. "And that secret binds us tighter than any wedding vow could."

My heart rate spikes at the words "wedding vow."

I turn to face him. "That's what I mean. Our relationship, the future of it, isn't built on normal things. It's forged in blood and lies and choosing each other over everything else."

"Is that a problem?" His eyes search mine.

I examine the question, turning it over in my mind. Twenty-four hours ago, I would have said yes. I would have run screaming from this reality. But that was before I understood what we really are to each other.

"No. It's the opposite. Because you've shown me the absolute worst of yourself, and I've chosen to stay. I've become complicit in your crimes. There's nothing left to hide."

"No more secrets." His free hand cups my face, his thumb brushing my cheekbone. "I promised you that."

"And I trust you." The words feel like jumping off a cliff, but the fall is exhilarating. "Which is insane, because you lied to me for months. But I trust you more now, after seeing everything, than I would if you'd been honest from the start."

His eyebrows rise. "How's that logic work?"

"Because now I know what you're capable of." I lean into his touch. "The manipulation, the violence, the cold calculation. And I know you've chosen not to use any of it against me anymore. You've given me power over you by telling me the truth. I could destroy you with what I know."

"You could." There's no fear in his admission.

I brush my lips against his. "But I won't. Like you won't betray me again. Because the cost is too high for both of us."

"Mutually assured destruction as the foundation of a relationship." His mouth quirks. "That's healthy."

"It's honest." I stand, pulling him up with me. "We're not a normal couple, Damien. We're never going to be normal. But we're real."

He draws me close, his forehead pressing against mine. "Real enough that it scares the shit out of me."

"Good." I slide my hands up his chest, feeling his heart race beneath my palms. "You should be scared. I've seen the monster under your mask, and I'm not running. That makes me dangerous."

"You're the most dangerous thing in my life. Luna." His voice drops to a whisper. "Because you're the only person who could actually hurt me."

This man, this killer, this damaged soul who looks at me like I'm the only light in his universe, is terrified I'll break him.

"I won't." I cup his face in both palms now, holding his gaze so he can see the truth in mine. "I won't hurt you. I won't leave. I won't—"

His lips capture mine, stealing my breath and my words. His kiss tastes like promise and possession, like every dark thing we've confessed and every twisted truth we've accepted.

When we break apart, his eyes have gone dark with emotion. I'm not going to be able to hold out against that look for long. I step back, smoothing down his borrowed shirt.

"If I don't get some food in me soon, I'm going to eat you instead."

"Now that sounds like a meal I'd enjoy." His hands reach for my hips.

I dance out of range, heading for the bedroom door. "Grilled cheese. Soup. Sanctuary. Maren. Remember?"

He follows me down the stairs, grumbling under his breath, as I go in search of my purse and phone.

We enter his office. Athena snoozes in her bed in the corner. Her head pops up when we walk in, tail thumping once against the cushion in lazy greeting. I grab my purse from the back of the armchair where I'd abandoned it yesterday.

"You know what the crazy part is?"

"What?"

"I feel safer with you than I ever have with anyone." I pause, meeting his gaze.

He holds up my coat, and I slip my arms into it. "Maybe safety isn't about being with someone who'd never hurt you. Maybe it's about being with someone who could destroy you but chooses not to."

The truth of it resonates in my bones. I'm as complicit as he is now. Damien could ruin my life with a single decision. And I could ruin his just as easily. We hold each other's fate in our hands, and that mutual vulnerability creates a foundation stronger than any built on comfortable lies or convenient half-truths.

Outside his windows, the early afternoon light paints the world in shades of gold and possibility. Somewhere out there, my former life continues without me. But the Luna who believed in black and white morality, who never would have understood how love and violence could coexist in the same breath, is gone now.

In her place stands someone new. Someone who looks at the man across from her and sees both monster and savior. A woman who's made peace with the blood on her hands and the choices that put it there, who's chosen darkness with open eyes and called it love.

I turn to him and press the front of my body against his, needing the contact. "Thank you."

"For what?"

"For trusting me enough to show me the truth. For giving me the choice instead of making it for me."

He wraps his arms around me, leaning down to bury his face in my neck, his breath warm against my skin. His chest expands against mine as he inhales, like he's trying to capture my scent and lock it somewhere deep inside him.

"I love you, little doe."

The nickname that once irritated me now feels like an endearment, a reminder of what we've survived to get here.

"I love you too." I press a kiss over his heart. "Every stalking, spying, murderous, obsessive, possessive, controlling piece of you."

Chapter Forty-Two

Damien

A chirp comes from inside Luna's purse, and she steps out of my arms to retrieve it. Athena rises from her bed and waddles over to me. I crouch to scratch behind her ear. I'd risen before sunrise and fed her, then let her out, but she's restless and ready for some attention.

"Shit."

"What?"

I walk up behind Luna and peek over her shoulder. She has eleven text messages and five missed calls.

"I don't know, but I have to get home now."

She dials Maren's number as we get in the car, cringing when her friend's voice comes through after only one ring.

"Well, well, well. Look who finally remembered she has a phone. That dick better have fucked you until your head popped off your shoulders because that's the only acceptable excuse for ghosting me all morning."

Even though she's not on speakerphone, every word echoes in the car because Maren only has one level. Loud.

"I'm sorry, Mar. We lost track of time."

"Is that what the kids are calling it these days?" Maren snorts. "You're lucky I stayed here last night. I rolled on over to check the critters around six this morning because I couldn't sleep anymore, and Ricky has learned how to open his cage door."

"I was afraid of that. What did he do?"

"He got into the fridge, ate my stash of blueberries, all the bananas, the turkey sandwich I left here yesterday, which had avocado on it, and now he's got the shits."

"Oh, Rick." Luna's head falls back against the seat.

I have to bite my lip to keep from laughing. It's not funny. But it is.

"Oh, and he figured out how to turn on the TV in the lobby, and it was blasting Game of Thrones. All the inside critters were awake and in a ruckus. I've finally got everyone settled, but we're going to need to order more Gabapentin because I went through a lot of that shit calming everybody down today."

"Mar, I'm so sorry."

"Whatever. I'm over it. But you better have gotten your world rocked last night to ignore me like that."

"Is that why you called me five times?"

"Oh, no, it's not, actually. I may be over having to wrangle this three-ring circus, but the Wolfe's asshole sidekick has been here since ten, waiting for the two of you. He's getting on my last fucking nerve so bad, I'm plotting ways to murder him."

"Why is Cade there? Why didn't he come to Damien's?"

Luna looks at me with confusion, and I shake my head. I have no idea.

Maren snorts again. "Apparently, he did. But he turned right back around and left when he heard you screaming upstairs. I told him he should have at least checked to make sure you weren't being tortured or murdered, but he said it wasn't those kinds of screams."

Luna glares at me, but what the fuck did I do wrong? I didn't show up unannounced at somebody's house.

I pull into the sanctuary's long driveway and park next to Cade's Tahoe. Why the fuck did he drive up rather than take the helicopter?

"We just pulled up. I'll be right in." She disconnects the call and glares at me. "This is your fault."

I grab her hand and bring her fingers to my lips. "And I don't feel the least bit of remorse."

"Of course you don't." She tries for stern, but her lips betray her, curving up at the edges.

We exit the car, and Athena scampers over to greet Ghost, who's relaxing on the main house's front porch. I follow Luna into the sanctuary's front door. The moment we step inside, Maren's voice carries from the back treatment area.

"I swear to God, Rambo, if you don't back the fuck off, I'm going to punch you in the nuts."

"Twenty-three minutes." The smirk in his voice is audible from here. "That's how long you've been cursing at that equipment. I could have solved your issue in five."

"Did I ask?" The sound of something clattering against a countertop punctuates her frustration. "Go mansplain somewhere else."

"You know, most women appreciate my expertise."

"I don't need your help. Has anyone ever told you, you're an arrogant pain in the ass?"

"Yes, frequently. But judging by how flushed you get when you're yelling at me, I think you might actually enjoy a little pain in the ass now and then."

"That's it!" Maren screeches.

Luna pushes through the swinging doors. The scene that greets us is both hilarious and terrifying, with Maren brandishing a tranquilizer injection pole at Cade, the long aluminum rod extended to its full six-foot length. He stands with arms crossed over his broad chest, one eyebrow raised, unfazed by the needle-tipped weapon hovering inches from his throat.

"Come on, old man, give me a reason."

"Maren."

Luna's voice breaks the standoff. Maren wheels around, dropping the pole to her side.

"Oh, thank God. Get this walking red flag out of my sight."

I bite back a laugh. She's not wrong. Cade is an absolute red flag for most women.

"Where's Ricky?"

"He's on the sofa in your office, playing with his monkey. Don't worry, he has a diaper on."

"Come on, let's go see him. How bad was it?"

They head toward Luna's office, and I turn to Cade. "What are you doing here? Why didn't you call? Or better yet, why didn't you bring the helicopter back?"

"I did. It's on the helipad in your backyard."

"How did I not hear you arrive? And isn't that your car outside?"

"No, that's your Tahoe." His expression is carefully neutral, but I catch the hint of amusement in his eyes. "And you were a little busy when I arrived."

"That doesn't answer my question. Why are you here? At the sanctuary?"

"Wanted to make sure there were no loose ends to tie up."

His presence today has nothing to do with the loose ends related to Caleb Hunter's death. He's here for Maren.

"Any word?" I keep my voice low, mindful that she might still be close enough to hear.

"Yes. Boulder police discovered evidence linking Hunter to several unsolved murders. Sheriff Mills got the call at nine twenty-one this morning. Since Boulder's outside her jurisdiction, their locals are taking point."

"And the neighbor situation?"

Cade gives me a withering look. Hunter's eighty-five-year-old neighbor had exited his apartment to walk his dog just as Cade was finishing the staging of Caleb's place, minutes before sunrise. The job had taken longer than planned. The building's security cameras and what Cade found inside the apartment had complicated things.

"Handled. According to the old man's statement, he saw Caleb exit his apartment carrying a duffle bag. Limping. Hoodie on."

I hold his stare, searching for any hint of doubt, then nod once. "You're the master, Cade. But you're absolutely sure this never comes back to Luna? I don't give a fuck what happens to me. Just not her."

"You're both safe."

Luna emerges from her office, carrying a diaper-clad raccoon waving a stuffed monkey in front of him. His other paw rests on her right breast. I sigh. He and I are going to have to have a talk.

Maren trails after them, and when she spots Cade, she scowls. "Why is he still here?"

The air between them crackles with an electricity neither of them will acknowledge.

"I'm going to give Ricky a quick bath, and then I'll head into the house to fix us some lunch."

"I'd be happy to make lunch." Cade's offer lands in the space between them like a grenade.

Luna and Maren stare at him like he's announced he's taking up interpretive dance. I don't. I've tasted his cooking. The man can turn basic ingredients into something that belongs in a restaurant.

"You obviously have your hands full, and I'm more than happy to whip something up for all of us."

He moves toward the door without waiting for permission or protest. Luna's gaze finds mine again, questions written across her face. Maren's eyes burn holes in Cade's back as he disappears through the doorway.

"He'll probably poison us." Maren holds her hands out to Luna. "Here, let me give Ricky his bath. Go make sure he doesn't put arsenic in whatever he's going to 'whip up.'"

She takes Ricky and stomps through the doors leading to the bathing area, her footsteps heavy enough to echo on the tile.

Luna turns to me. "There goes my grilled cheese and soup. Can I trust him in my kitchen?"

"Cade is a certified master chef. He trained at Le Cordon Bleu in Paris."

Her eyebrows shoot up. "You're really going to have to give me his story sometime."

"No can do. Cade's story is his own to tell."

The front door chime rings. Fuck! What now? I follow Luna to the lobby. Sheriff Mills stands inside the entrance, her expression serious.

"Hi, Karen." Luna keeps her voice light. But her body tells a different story, the way she angles herself toward me, closing the gap between us. "What brings you by?"

Karen removes her hat, running a hand through her hair. "Came to update you on the Caleb Hunter situation. Got some news from Boulder PD this morning."

Luna tenses beside me, and I wrap my arm around her waist. I love being able to touch her in the daylight.

"They found some pretty disturbing stuff, Luna. Place was a mess. Looks like your ex was deeper into drugs than anyone realized. Cocaine, mainly. They also found evidence linking him to the bodies dumped here and in the park."

Luna's breath catches, the sound sharp in the small room. It's not an act. The color drains from her cheeks, and her fingers grip my waist. Discomfort radiates from every line of her body.

Guilt.

Despite everything she said this morning about accepting what we did, words are easier than living with the weight of it. The reality of framing a dead man, of manufacturing evidence, of becoming complicit in a crime—that's going to take time to settle into her bones. If it ever does.

"Looks like he was trying to set you up." Karen's gaze moves between us, measuring our reactions. "Best they can figure, he was killing them to frame you for the murders." She pauses. "And it gets worse. Found journals, plans... looks like he was planning something real nasty as his grand finale. We think your showing up when you did, Damien, saved Luna's life."

"Jesus." Luna's hands tremble as her eyes snap to mine.

Cade planted only some of what they found. But the rest? That was already there. Real evidence detailing his plans for Luna. Pages of revenge fantasies. The specific, methodical ways he intended to make her suffer before he killed her.

I told her about it as we lay tangled together in bed last night, her body warm against mine. Not the graphic details. I gave her the choice, and she declined, but I'm a man who heeds the lessons he's learned, who understands the cost of deception. I will not keep secrets from her ever again.

Rage tastes like blood in my mouth. Killing Hunter once wasn't enough. It was a mercy he didn't deserve. I should have taken him back to my basement and drawn it out. Should have made him beg. Should have shown him exactly what happens to men who threaten what's mine.

"So he's..." Luna's voice wavers.

"In the wind. Boulder PD has a BOLO out for him. He's considered armed and dangerous." Karen's gaze shifts between us. "Keep your eyes open. If he shows his face around here again, you call me immediately. Don't try to handle it yourselves."

Her gaze lingers on me, but there's less suspicion there now. The evidence against Caleb is solid enough to shift her focus.

Chaos erupts from the back room, splashing sounds, followed by Maren's colorful cursing.

"Ricky, you little shit! Get back here!"

The doors burst open, and Ricky comes tearing through, dripping wet, making a break for freedom, with Maren hot on his heels. Ricky chitters as he scampers between Karen's legs, leaving wet paw prints on her uniform pants.

"Sorry! Slippery little bastard jumped out of the tub!" Maren lunges for him, but he dodges her.

The muscles in my jaw twitch. Leave it to that pervy raccoon to provide the perfect distraction. Maybe I'll let him feel up Luna once in a while.

Karen steps aside, chuckling. "Well, I can see you've got your hands full here. I'll let you get back to it."

The door closes behind her, and I finally allow myself to breathe. Maren manages to corner Ricky near the reception desk, scooping him up with a triumphant "Got you, you little escape artist!"

The raccoon chitters at her but settles into her arms, head on her breasts, looking quite pleased with himself.

"Well, that was fun." Maren wrings water from her hair as she looks at Luna. "You are so buying me Wicked tickets. They're coming to Denver in February. And you—" She turns to me, one finger extended like a weapon. "You're going to stop fucking her for five minutes so she can come with me to the show. Actually, you're the one who should pay for it, Mr. Billionaire. And dinner. And a limo. And I'm sure I'll think of something else, so get out that fat wallet of yours."

I raise both hands, palms out. My mind's already calculating. Orchestra seats, backstage passes, maybe dinner with the leads.

Luna laughs and holds out her hands for Ricky. "Want me to finish with him?"

Maren waves her away and heads toward the swinging doors again. "Nah. I'm already wet. And not in the way I like to be."

"Come over to the house for lunch when you're done," Luna calls after her.

"So GI Joe can poison me? No thanks."

Luna exhales a small laugh, but a concerned look crosses her face. "The attraction between them worries me."

I draw her to me, savoring the way she curves into my embrace without hesitation. Fuck, it feels good to be able to do this. She leans against me with a soft sigh and wraps her arms around my waist.

"Yeah. That's probably not a good idea."

"Why? Is he a serial killer?"

"Haha, wise ass. No, but if you think I'm obsessive and possessive, Cade makes me look sane."

The line between her brows deepens, but I don't elaborate. Maren getting involved with Cade is asking for all sorts of trouble none of us needs.

"I love your arms around me." She presses her lips over my heart, and the simple gesture nearly undoes me.

I guide her toward the door, keeping her wrapped against me until the last possible second. Only when we have to step outside do I let her go.

"Come on. Cade's probably got lunch ready by now, and you need to eat, Dr. Foster. You're going to need your strength tonight."

When we reach her front door, I turn her to face me, my voice rough.

"I love you, Luna. And I'm going to spend the rest of my life making up for all the ways I've hurt you."

Her eyes soften, and she reaches up to cup my face. "I'll hold you to that. And you better be prepared to fuck me into oblivion as the wolf for the rest of your life too, because I want both of you. I want Damien and my wolf."

The heat in her voice and the hunger in her eyes set my blood ablaze. Her lips curve in a smile that promises pure temptation wrapped in sin.

"Maybe you should consider stocking up on Viagra, old man."

Desire roars through me even though she called me an old man. I move before thought catches up, grabbing her and pressing her back against the door. My mouth crashes onto hers, the kiss all heat and hunger and desperate need. She melts into me, soft and pliant, as I claim every inch of her mouth.

I pull back and press my forehead against hers, both of us breathing hard. "I'm going to fuck you against this door one night, right after I make you come on my fingers again."

Her breath catches, and her body trembles against mine. When she looks up at me, her eyes have gone dark. "Then I'll return the favor on my knees until you forget everything but my name."

My hand finds the doorframe and grips it hard enough to make my fingers ache. Anything to stop myself from taking her right here.

"Jesus, fuck, Luna."

She laughs and rises on her toes to brush her lips against mine before reaching behind her for the doorknob. Ghost and Athena push past me to enter behind her as Shadow and her three cats come running from inside, a collision of fur and enthusiasm.

She drops to her knees and greets them all with hugs and kisses. The fat one hisses, and Shadow knocks Luna onto her ass with the force of his greeting. This is a sight I want to spend the rest of my life coming home to.

I have a home for the first time in my life. And it's all because of this woman.

Epilogue

"**R**icky, where are you?"

I stand on the porch of the sanctuary's main building, my eyes sweeping the yard. Ten minutes of searching, and still nothing. The familiar weight of worry settles in my chest as I scan every shadow and every corner where my troublemaker might be hiding. The early evening air carries the scent of pine and the distant sound of nocturnal animals stirring, but no chittering from my missing raccoon.

I've been looking for him since I realized he wasn't in his cage with Zorro. Although we call it a cage, the combination indoor/outdoor enclosure they share is a raccoon's paradise. But Ricky figured out how to open the door about eight months ago, and no matter what Maren and I do, no matter how many new double locks we install or alarms Damien sets up, he manages to break out.

Maren.

The worry that's been gnawing at me for three days surfaces again. She's been gone without a word since Tuesday afternoon. I came back from running errands in Estes, and Cindy, our newest intern, said a man had stopped by to see her. They argued. She could hear raised voices from inside my office before he tossed Maren over his shoulder and carried her, kicking and screaming, out the front door, driving off in a large SUV that looked like a tank.

Even if the security cameras hadn't been disabled in what Damien called a "suspicious malfunction," I'd know he took her. Maren and Cade have been dancing around each other for months. Well, she's been dancing around him while threatening to have him murdered if he doesn't leave her alone. Most of it is an act. I've known Maren since college, and I know when she's interested in a man.

But why did she leave with him? She doesn't bail on me or the sanctuary. Or on her grandmother. I called Estella yesterday to check on her, but I didn't ask if she knew where Maren was. There's no point in worrying an eighty-year-old woman.

If Maren is with Cade, and I'm almost sure she is, he wouldn't hurt her. At least, I hope he wouldn't. But where the hell did they go?

Her purse is still here. Her phone too. I found that out when it started chirping in the desk drawer from the dozens of texts I sent asking where she was. Maren doesn't go anywhere without her phone.

But she just vanished. Poof. Gone. Kidnapped by Damien's COO.

I'm trying not to panic, but it's hard, especially with how out of whack my hormones are. I didn't even get a chance to tell her.

"Ricky!" I call out again, louder this time. "If you don't come here right now, no banana peanut butter pop for you tomorrow."

Nothing. Silence and the distant hoot of an owl.

My frustration builds as I turn and walk back through the door. I move through the building, checking all of his usual hiding places one final time. Most of the animals have settled for the night—the soft sounds of sleeping creatures, the rustle of bedding, and the occasional contented sigh from one of our permanent residents.

Ricky couldn't have gotten out unless one of the interns made a mistake when I was in the barn feeding Cotton and Patches. He has to be around here somewhere. Trouble is his middle name, though if you asked Maren, she'd say it was "boob-obsessed furry sexual harasser."

Shit.

I can't even manage not to lose one of our animals when Maren isn't here. Some veterinarian I am.

When I reach his enclosure, Zorro sits alone on his favorite perch near the viewing window, washing his face with black paws. The indoor portion of their habitat sits empty except for him. My heart sinks.

"Rick! Come on, buddy, where are you?"

I unlock the enclosure door and step inside, searching every nook and cranny. The outdoor section, accessible through a large pet door, is equally vacant. My pulse picks up as I check the door mechanism. It's still functioning, which means he didn't break out through there.

"Ricky!" My voice echoes through the building, higher now with the first threads of real panic.

I pull out my phone and dial Damien's number, pacing toward the front of the building. He should be heading over from the estate, where he still works remotely most days.

Six months of living with him has settled into a rhythm I never could have imagined with my wolf. His presence in my bed every night and morning, coffee brewing before I wake, the way he watches me tend to the animals with that soft expression he reserves only for me. The one that morphs into heat and desire in an instant.

"Hello, beautiful."

His warm voice carries that dark edge that makes me wet from just a few syllables. Even more so now that my hormones are insane. Heat pools between my legs, and I press my thighs together.

"I'm pulling up."

I look out the front window and see the golf cart he uses to travel between our properties. The Bureau of Land Management gave him permission for a driveway easement through the federal preserve that sits between our property lines. How he talked the federal government into letting him pave a path through protected land is beyond me. Advantages of being a billionaire, I guess.

"Have you seen Ricky anywhere? He's not in his enclosure with Zorro."

The main door opens with its familiar squeak, and Damien walks through, phone pressed to his ear. He ends our call and slips the device into his pocket, his eyes assessing my expression. My breath catches at the sight of him, windblown hair from his golf cart ride, and the silver strands at his temples askew.

"The little troublemaker's missing?"

He approaches, and my body reacts to his proximity like it always does—pulse quickening, skin warming, and that pull low in my belly that makes me want to press against him. I give in to the urge to touch him, reaching up and pulling his head down to mine for a kiss.

His arms wrap around me as he deepens it, groaning into my mouth. My breath hitches as he hardens against my stomach, and every nerve ending in my body lights up. The taste of him, the scent of him, the way his hands span my waist—it's overwhelming.

Jesus. My libido is in overdrive. I pull away before I drag him to the lobby floor and let him violate me seven different ways.

"Fuck, Luna." Damien shakes his head as if clearing it, a sexy smirk curving his lips. "I missed you too, little doe."

The endearment sends heat straight to my core. He doesn't call me that often anymore, except when we're intimate. His eyes have gone midnight black, the gray-blue of his irises swallowed up, leaving only the kind of dark that means restraints and surrender and losing myself to his control.

My breath hitches as my mind conjures the image of zip ties cutting into my wrists, the cold bite of concrete against my knees, and his voice commanding me to take whatever he gives. The fantasy draws a whisper of sound from my chest, small and needy, barely more than air.

His eyes sharpen. He heard it.

No. We have to find Ricky.

I step back, giving myself space from the heat emanating from his body, and focus on finding my troublemaker. The worry crashes back over me.

"I can't find Ricky. I finished the evening check, and he wasn't there." I cross my arms, trying to look calmer than I feel, but my voice betrays me.

His mouth quirks up in that half-smile I love. "Luna, he's probably somewhere causing maximum chaos while looking completely innocent."

"That's not helping." But despite my worry, Damien's presence steadies me. He has this way of making everything seem manageable, even when I'm spiraling.

"When's the last time you saw him?"

I think back through the day. "This afternoon, when I gave him his snack of apple slices. Tate was on the porch with him when I left to run to the post office. I didn't see him when I got back. I assumed he was around somewhere. Tate didn't say he was missing. Maybe I should call Tate. He left around four."

I reach for my phone on the counter, babbling to myself, but Damien snatches it from my hands before I can dial.

"Don't bother Tate. He would've told you if Ricky was missing. We'll find him."

I run a hand through my hair, tugging at the messy knot that's been annoying me all day. The elastic band snaps as I pull, releasing the strands from their confinement. The summer heat is getting to me, and I swipe a small bead of sweat from the back of my neck.

"What if he got out somehow? There are coyotes out there, and mountain lions, and—"

I'm starting to spiral, and I hate it. This isn't me. I'm steady and calm under pressure. But not lately. Not with my best friend missing, the news I still have to give Damien, and the changes happening in my body.

"Hey."

His voice snaps me back—dark and calm and reasonable. That tone of absolute authority makes my pulse stutter and more warmth spread between my thighs despite the knot of worry in my chest.

"Let's think about this. Where would a bored raccoon go if he wanted to cause trouble?"

My mind races through possibilities. "I've checked all his usual spots..." I trail off, realizing I haven't checked every single space in the building.

"Or?" Damien follows me, unhurried and not as concerned as I wish he'd be. Ricky's obsession with my breasts tests his patience, but right now I need him to care more. "Maybe he figured out how to get into the house. You know how food-motivated he is."

I stop and stare at him. "The house? But how would he—"

"Luna, that raccoon has the problem-solving skills of a toddler with an engineering degree. If he wanted to get to your kitchen, he'd find a way."

The logic makes sense, but worry has sunk its claws in deep. "But what if he's hurt? What if something happened, and he crawled off somewhere to die—"

"What if he's currently raiding the refrigerator and getting fat on leftover Chinese food?"

I want to smile at that image, but my chest is tight with anxiety. "You don't understand. He's not just another animal, Damien. If something happened to him…"

My voice falls apart on the last word, and tears threaten. The hormones are making everything amplified, every emotion more overwhelming and less manageable than it should be.

"Luna."

Damien's tone shifts, deeper now, with that edge of command that goes straight to the primitive part of my brain.

"Look at me."

My eyes snap to his because that voice demands obedience. His gaze has sharpened, and the civilized mask slips away, revealing the apex predator beneath. I know this version of him.

My wolf.

"We're going to walk to the house right now and check. If he's not there, we'll come back and search every inch of this place until we find him."

The authoritative tone steadies the chaos spinning through me. My breathing slows, and the panic that was building ebbs back to manageable worry. At the same time, it makes my nipples ache and my core clench with want. The things this man can do to me with just his voice. It alone can remake me.

"Okay."

He extends his hand.

"Come on."

I take it without hesitation, letting him lead me toward the door. His fingers interlace with mine, and some of the tension leaves my body.

We walk the short distance between the sanctuary and the main house, our feet crunching on the gravel path. My attention catches on Maren's SUV parked in the driveway, and the worry that's become constant background noise surfaces again.

"Have you heard from Cade?"

Damien's pace slows, but his grip on my hand stays firm and warm, anchoring me to his side. "No. I told you I haven't."

"How can you not hear from your COO for days and not worry? Isn't he supposed to be working?"

"Cade is always working. And he doesn't need to be micromanaged. Things are getting done. That's all I care about. Where he does it and with whom is none of my business."

His evasiveness pisses me off. "He kidnapped my best friend, Damien. That is damn well your business, because it's mine. Tell him to bring her back."

"Sweetheart, I don't know if he has her. Maren is a grown woman. Maybe she decided to take a couple of personal days."

"Maren wouldn't blow off work. That's not her style."

He's quiet for a long moment, and I can almost hear him weighing what to tell me.

"If they are together, it's their business, Luna. Getting in between Maren and Cade isn't wise."

"You don't think Cade would—"

"No." His voice cuts through the evening air.

But the certainty in his tone doesn't match the tension in his shoulders. We both know what Cade is capable of. Things that would terrify most people. The question is whether Damien is right about Maren's safety.

I want to ask more questions, but we've reached the front door.

"Whatever happens when we go in there..." Damien pauses with his hand on the doorknob, and something in his voice makes my pulse skip. "Remember that I love you."

I frown at the odd comment. "Why would you—"

The door swings open, and every thought in my head evaporates.

Shadow bounds toward us, almost knocking me backward in his enthusiasm, but it's what's tied around his neck that makes me freeze. A red silk ribbon resting against his gray fur, elegant and out of place on my wolf.

Behind him, perched on the back of the sofa like he's holding court, sits Ricky. In his black hands, he grips an enormous bouquet of deep red dahlias—my favorite flowers, the ones Damien surprises me with regularly now.

"Oh, thank God." Relief crashes over me so hard I feel dizzy. I drop to my knees to hug Shadow, burying my face in his soft fur, before glaring at my raccoon.

"Ricky, how did you get in here?"

He chitters at me, then plucks a fistful of petals from the stems and hurls them in my direction like he's the offended party.

But even as I'm scolding him, something feels off. The ribbon around Shadow's neck. The flowers clutched in Ricky's paws. And the way all three cats are arranged on various pieces of furniture like they're posing for a photograph. My heart beats faster, but for different reasons now.

Ricky chitters at me again, then proceeds to pluck more dahlia petals and fling them in my direction with impressive accuracy. Each crimson petal hits my hair, my shoulders, and my arms, like he's showering me with confetti. He looks pleased with himself, proud of his handiwork.

I push to my feet and turn toward Damien, a question forming on my lips, but the words die in my throat.

He's down on one knee.

My heart stops. Actually stops, then starts again with a thud that echoes in my ears. The room tilts, and I have to press my hand against the wall to stay upright.

"Come here, Shadow."

My wolf trots over as if they've practiced this. Damien's fingers work at the ribbon, sliding it free from Shadow's neck, and something small and brilliant tumbles into his palm. He looks up at me, and the expression on his face steals what little breath I have left.

"Luna."

His voice is rough with emotion, and tears blur my vision. I can't look away from him, can't breathe, and can't think past the way my heart is trying to beat right out of my chest.

"I love you." He drags his tongue across his bottom lip, and his eyes soften in that way they do now when he looks at me. "I don't deserve it. We both know that. But you love me anyway. Love for me is more than what we have in the dark. It's watching you save a baby deer at three in the morning. It's the way you sing to injured animals while you work. And it's the way you look at me and see someone better than I am."

He holds up the ring, and even through my tears, I can see it's perfect. A cluster of diamonds sits atop a simple band, catching the lamplight like captured fire. It's beautiful, elegant, and timeless. But it's the expression on Damien's face that steals the strength from my legs. The love in his eyes runs so deep and honest it strips me down to nothing, leaving me vulnerable and aching and wholly his.

"Will you marry me?"

The sob that escapes me is part joy, part hormonal overload, and part disbelief that this incredible man wants to spend his life with me.

"No. I can't."

The words leave my mouth before I can stop them, and hurt sweeps over his features. His face closes off, the emotion in his eyes slamming shut as the dark side of my wolf comes to the surface.

He stands, stepping closer to me, his large frame towering over me the way he does when he wants to intimidate me. But I don't let him anymore, and he knows it.

Still, he doesn't understand why I'm saying no, and I'm sobbing too hard to explain.

"I can't." My breath hitches as I grasp the front of his shirt, needing the anchor of his warmth. "Not until..."

His eyes lose their edge, but the line between his brows deepens as another sob wrenches from my chest, then another. Heaving sobs I can't seem to control. The hormones have rewired something in me, turning every small thing into a tidal wave that drags me under.

"Luna." He pulls me against his chest, and some of the tension leaves his body. "Fuck. Why are you crying like this? If you don't want to marry me—"

He stops, the words paining him, and I cry harder because I'm hurting him and I don't know how to make him understand.

I bury my face in his chest, shaking my head against his shirt, breathing in his scent—vanilla and amber and the clean, masculine scent that always makes me feel safe. His arms tighten around me, protective and warm.

"I... I... want to," I manage between sobs, my voice muffled against his chest. "But..."

"What is it, sweetheart?"

The words spill out before I can stop them.

"I'm pregnant."

His entire body goes still against mine. Not just tense, but motionless, like he's stopped breathing.

"My hormones are insane, and I sobbed for twenty minutes because we ran out of strawberry jam, and I know we haven't talked about this, and it's terrible timing, and I don't even know how it happened because we're usually so careful, but apparently not careful enough, and—"

His mouth covers mine, cutting off my babbling. I melt against him, my breath hitching against his lips. The kiss tastes like relief and joy and promises I want to spend the rest of my life collecting.

When he pulls back, I search his face for any sign of anger or disappointment. "Are you mad?"

I miscarried our baby last fall, when I didn't know he and my wolf were the same man. That pregnancy was unplanned too, but it's different now. We're together, there are no more secrets between us, and he wants to marry me. But that doesn't mean he wants children. He told me once he had no desire to father anything.

He cups my face in his hands, thumbs brushing away my tears, his intense eyes holding mine captive. "Luna, considering how often I come inside you, I'm surprised it took this long."

I hiccup, lifting my fingers to wipe away more tears. Relief makes me dizzy. "I know we haven't talked about this, but we can't get married until we decide what to—"

He kisses me again to shut me up, and I lose myself in the taste of him. When he releases my lips, he presses his forehead against mine.

"Listen to me, Luna. If you want this baby, I want this baby. But you know the kind of man I am. I'll be a shitty father."

"No!" I shake my head and grip his face in my hands, needing him to understand. He'll be amazing.

"Yes." He grasps my wrists, his touch gentle but firm. "My capacity for emotion and love is exclusive to you. But I'll do my best with any children we have."

Another sob escapes my lips. One day, he'll know that his capacity for love is infinite.

"Now, I asked you to marry me, but we both know it wasn't a question."

A choked laugh replaces my sob. He's right. He'd drag me in front of a justice of the peace, kicking and screaming. But I want to marry him. This man I love with everything I have, and with a depth that rewrote the meaning of the word itself.

This man who loves me in a way I used to think only existed in books.

This man, who will be the father of my children.

But I still can't let him always have the upper hand.

"So, you're going to force me to marry you?"

"If I have to, yes. Especially now. Our kids won't be bastards."

His response is so him, and my heart trips over itself in my chest. Possessive and demanding and always certain of getting what he wants.

"Then it's a good thing I want to." I blink away the last remnants of my tears. He slips the ring on my finger, and of course it's a perfect fit. "Are you sure about the baby?"

He presses another soft kiss to my lips. "If you're happy, then I'm happy."

I rise on my toes to deepen the kiss, pouring all my love and gratitude and overwhelming joy into the connection between us.

A sharp thunk against the back of Damien's head makes us jolt apart. The entire bouquet of dahlias bounces off his skull and tumbles to the floor, petals scattering everywhere. Ricky sits on the back of the sofa, arms crossed, chittering at us with what can only be described as raccoon profanity.

I burst out laughing at the offended expression on his masked face.

"I think someone's jealous."

Damien rubs the back of his head, glaring at the unrepentant raccoon. "Well, he better get used to sharing. There's a hierarchy in this house, and you're looking at the alpha." His arms tighten around me. "And if he doesn't stop copping feels, I'm turning him into a winter hat."

I laugh harder, the sound bubbling up from a place of absolute happiness. Everything is perfect. Damien, our baby, and our future together.

"I love you."

"You're the love of my life, little doe."

My breath catches. He tells me he loves me constantly—whispers it, growls it, says it like a prayer. But that phrase, those specific words, he's kept locked away until now. I can feel the truth of them in my bones, matching the intensity burning in his eyes.

His mouth finds mine again, the kiss soft and reverent, like he's sealing a promise.

Ricky throws another handful of loose petals at us, not satisfied with his first protest, and I grin against Damien's lips.

Forever with this man and our growing family, furry and otherwise, sounds like complete perfection to me.

Thank you for Reading

Thank you so much for reading Luna and Damien's story. I genuinely hope you enjoyed the ride and emerged from the emotional chaos relatively unscathed. If you're feeling a little wrecked, that's normal.

But here's the silver lining: this isn't the last time you'll see them! They'll be making appearances because, let's be honest, I'm not ready to let them go either.

Coming in 2027—Watch Me Bleed

Cade and Maren's story.

A standalone dark romance packed with age gap tension, opposites attract chemistry, and enemies-to-lovers heat. These two have been living rent-free in my head since the moment they decided to hijack scenes in Luna and Damien's books, demanding their own story with zero regard for my sanity or writing schedule.

Read a Sneak Peek Here: https://dl.bookfunnel.com/f19q9bvmjr

Please Review

Here's the thing about reviews—they're kind of a big deal for indie authors like me.

Reviews help our books get noticed, build momentum, and reach readers who might love them. They're one of the most powerful ways you can support an author, and trust me, we notice and appreciate every single one.

So if you enjoyed WATCH ME BURN, I'd be incredibly grateful if you'd leave a review on Amazon, Goodreads, and/or wherever you share your reading recommendations. Even a few sentences go a long way.

Thank you so much for your support—it truly means the world!

Below are easy links for you.

https://www.Amazon.com/review/create-review?&asin=B0FM16P23X

https://www.goodreads.com/book/show/240038283-watch-me-burn

https://www.bookbub.com/books/watch-me-burn-a-dark-stalker-romance-watched-in-darkness-book-2-by-v-e-huntley

The BloodStone Legacy Series

Damnation

Atonement

Redemption

Watched in Darkness Series

Watch Me Break

Watch Me Burn

Watch Over Me Prequel Novella

Watch Me Bleed—Coming 2027

Sacred Sins—Coming 2027

Shadow Ice Brotherhood Series

Frozen Fury—Coming 2027

Frozen Wrath—Coming 2028

Frozen Savage—TBD

Frozen Sins—TBD

Frozen Vengeance—TBD

Frozen Menace—TBD

Strike & Surrender Series

Strike Hard, Surrender Softly—Coming 2027

Strike High, Surrender Deep—Coming 2028

Strike First, Surrender Last—TBD

Strike Fast, Surrender Slow—TBD

Strike Once, Surrender Forever—TBD

Strike Strong, Surrender Sweet—TBD

Follow Me

For more previews, deleted scenes and goodies, sign up for my newsletter:
Sign Up Here
https://vehuntley.com/

Connect with V.E:
https://www.facebook.com/v.e.huntley.author
https://www.instagram.com/vehuntley/
https://x.com/vehuntleywriter
https://www.tiktok.com/@vehuntley
https://bsky.app/profile/vehuntleyauthor.bsky.social
https://www.pinterest.com/vehuntleywriter/
https://www.goodreads.com/author/show/50245965.V_E_Huntley
Join my Whispers After Dark Facebook Group – it's a place we can talk about all
things books, especially naughty things
https://www.facebook.com/groups/v.e.huntleys.whispers.after.dark

Acknowledgements

With every book I release, I'm hit with this overwhelming wave of gratitude for all the people who make this wild journey possible. Writing is inherently solitary. It's mostly me alone with my characters, questionable life choices, and an alarming amount of sugar, but I absolutely couldn't do this without the people who believe in me and my slightly unhinged stories.

First and always: Hubby Chris. Thank you for believing in me and these increasingly dark and twisted stories I keep dreaming up. Thank you for never questioning why I spend so much time thinking about morally gray anti-heroes and the chaos they create. Your faith in me makes all the difference.

Elle, I learn something invaluable from you with every single book we work on together, and honestly, none of my stories would be what they are without your insight, expertise, and patience. Thank you for making me a better writer.

To my incredible ARC team, street team, readers, and all my amazing fans and followers. You are the heartbeat of this journey. My beautiful, book-loving collective, I truly can't thank you enough. You read my books, champion them, and share them so generously with the world. I'm endlessly grateful for each and every one of you!

About the author

I'm a retired producer who's spent most of my life telling stories in one form or another. Just ask my cats—they've endured years of me reciting entire dialogue scenes to them when all they desperately wanted was a nap.

My childhood fear of Dracula was so intense I couldn't sleep without the lights on and my mother standing guard at my bedroom door. Fast forward a few decades, and that terror has morphed into a full-blown obsession with all things dark and twisted.

After more than twenty years in film and television, I decided to follow my true calling—writing dark, steamy romance about anti-heroes who swear too much and have serious anger management issues, and the strong, spirited heroines who refuse to put up with their nonsense (but love them anyway).

When I'm not writing, I'm watching movies, reading, traveling, or adding to my husband's never-ending honey-do list (it's basically a part-time job at this point). You can find out more about me on my website, www.vehuntley.com.

www.ingramcontent.com/pod-product-compliance
Lightning Source LLC
Chambersburg PA
CBHW020542120726
47903CB00001B/82